"Stunning, original, beautiful, intriguing, and mesmerizing."
—Errant Dreams Reviews

"[Ms. Singh] has a knack for writing characters that are truly believable, and admirably strong and resilient."
—Dark Faerie Tales

"One of the most immersive and consistently creative works in urban fantasy."
—Grave Tells

"[A] fabulous addition to the paranormal world."
—Fresh Fiction

"[A] powerful, riveting novel. I found myself wholly absorbed."
—Dear Author

"Dark, lush urban fantasy, steeped in violence and power."
—Heroes and Heartbreakers

Archangel's War

Nalini Singh

JOVE
New York

A JOVE BOOK
Published by Berkley
An imprint of Penguin Random House LLC
penguinrandomhouse.com

Copyright © 2019 by Nalini Singh
Penguin Random House supports copyright. Copyright fuels creativity, encourages
diverse voices, promotes free speech, and creates a vibrant culture. Thank you for buying
an authorized edition of this book and for complying with copyright laws by not
reproducing, scanning, or distributing any part of it in any form without permission.
You are supporting writers and allowing Penguin Random House to continue to
publish books for every reader.

A JOVE BOOK, BERKLEY, and the BERKLEY & B colophon
are registered trademarks of Penguin Random House LLC.

ISBN: 9780451491664

First Edition: September 2019

Printed in the United States of America
1 3 5 7 9 10 8 6 4 2

Cover art by Tony Mauro

1

The Blade

Dmitri stood on a high Tower balcony, the wind whipping at his hair with a bite that said fall was coming as it pasted the back of his T-shirt to his body. Winter had ended, and spring as well as most of summer had passed while Raphael and Elena slept; fall hovered on the horizon. "I walked with Raphael through the colors of fall more than once," he told the woman who stood at his side. "Leaves of orange and crimson and yellow raining down on our heads."

Honor tugged out the hand he'd fisted in the pocket of his pants. He opened it, allowed her to weave her fingers through his own. "Is there more trouble?"

"Yes, I can feel it building." He and the rest of the Seven had held off all challengers to date, thanks to the help of those in the Cadre who refused to allow the scavengers to swoop. Even now, huge birds of prey circled the sky and cougars napped in Central Park, while Caliane's most experienced squadron patrolled the borders of the city.

"Why the quick challenges?" Honor ran her free hand down the bare skin of his arm. "It's not even been a year."

"The army that came with Favashi might've turned back, but it wasn't by choice. They're Lijuan's people through and through, and they've been whispering in the ears of parasites like Charisemnon that this territory is his for the taking." Lesser angels, too, had attempted to mount a challenge.

Dmitri had decapitated the first.

Illium had burned the second down to the ground with his power.

Venom had used two razor-sharp knives to shred the third to pieces.

No one else had dared in the interim, but they would. "I just got Jason's latest report—his operatives have confirmed that Lijuan's people are spreading the rumor that Raphael's disappearance is connected to Favashi's—that she infected him with the poison she carried inside her. Bastards are saying he's either dead or dying and stronger powers must take over his territory before the vampires begin to rise in bloodlust." Dmitri was also being accused of acting "above his station" in continuing to hold the territory. As if he had intentions to take it over. *Fools.*

Leaning her head against his shoulder, Honor watched a condor fly to land right beside them. "You're not letting all the whispers about you being a traitor get to you, are you?" A stern tone. "Because I'll have to get tough if you are."

He would've smiled if his heart wasn't so dark with fury at the threats that hung in the air; his wife knew him far too well. "I've dealt with it before." No one outside of Raphael's inner circle seemed to accept or understand that he was right where he wanted to be. He and Raphael had a relationship of loyalty and trust melded with old pain that the Cadre couldn't hope to comprehend.

Before being archangel and second, they were friends. That friendship had only deepened after the sire fell in love with Elena. Prior to that, Raphael had been falling into the cold of immortality, becoming distant in a way that had begun to erase the friend who'd fought beside Dmitri in many a battle. "I'm more worried about the vampires."

"At least bloodlust hasn't been a problem yet."

"No." Dmitri had sent Andreas to deal with the first vampire kiss that had tried to flex its muscle. The warrior angel had put those vampiric heads on pikes and stabbed the bloody pikes in a city square. Dmitri liked Andreas—he knew how to make a point and he was as relentlessly loyal to Raphael as Dmitri.

No other kiss had dared make so much as a peep.

"It won't last," he told Honor. "I'll have to be more and more brutal." Vampires were driven by bloodlust—that was a fact of life. Dmitri had long ago disciplined his own urges and he'd have helped Honor do the same if her mortal calm and thoughtfulness hadn't carried over seamlessly during her transition.

It was possible that her constant proximity to him helped, but regardless, his wife was one of the most stable young vampires he knew. Yet she still practiced honing her control with the dedication of a woman who had been a guild hunter before she became a vampire.

Many other vampires, however, were arrogant of the danger and didn't bother.

Without archangelic control, those vampires would soon begin to forget fear and cause carnage. His only choice then would be a cold and fast wave of death that carved terror into the hearts of mortals and vampires both.

The condor that had been sitting beside them took off in a jagged sweep of wings that hit Honor's right leg. Circling the air in front of them, it opened its beak and released a grating shriek. Birds flew up from every roof in the city at the same instant. The wind rose, slamming at them like an angry opponent.

Planting her feet wide to maintain her position, the soft ebony of her hair streaming behind her, Honor said, "What's happening?"

Dmitri didn't know, but his eyes turned toward the Enclave, where the sire lay as motionless as the dead—and Elena was lost inside a chrysalis that didn't pulse or show any other indication of life.

2

The Sleeper

Archangel Cassandra turned restlessly in her Sleep. Peace would not come, her mind flashing with images of a future she did not want to see. But it had never been a choice for her. Eyes open or closed, clawed out or whole, she *saw*.

The threads of time.

Shining and bright.

Dark and broken.

Tangled and silky.

She *saw*.

Yeah, well, I'm not convinced on the whole predestination thing.

That voice, so young, so rash, so determined. The child had altered time, torn apart the future glimpsed.

"Prophecy of mine," Cassandra mumbled in her broken Sleep, her vast mind sensing the energies rising, the future morphing yet again.

An archangel in Sleep gave out no energy, could not affect the world. This was known, had never been questioned. It protected both the Sleeper and the world. For who could predict the dreams or nightmares of an ancient immortal being? What terrible changes might be wrought in the world without intent or thought?

But Cassandra hung on the twilight verge between wakefulness and Sleep, with a gray awareness of the external world. She stretched out her arms and wrapped them around an energy that would burn down the world.

3

The Legion

The Legion sat watch, their patience endless. Time was a thing that had no meaning to them. The mourning Bluebell spoke to them at times. He told them that six months had passed, then seven. The Legion asked him what this meant.

He said. "A monarch butterfly emerges from its chrysalis in ten days. A child grows in the womb for nine months. The earth completes a revolution around the sun in twelve months. It takes decades for a seed to grow into a mighty oak. An angelic child is not considered an adult until they have lived one hundred years. Seven months is . . . a drop in the well of time."

The Bluebell said this, but the Legion saw new lines of pain score his face with each day that passed in silence in the room where the Legion kept watch. Their archangel slept unmoving under a spidery blanket of white that came from the chrysalis that had enclosed Elena.

Elena, who was one half of the *aeclari*. Elena, who grew things. Elena, who had a house of glass that was always green and warm. Elena, who was a warrior. Elena, who spoke to the Legion in ways no one else had ever spoken to them.

Elena, who lay silent inside a chrysalis.

The filaments from that chrysalis had spread rapidly across

the room in the past hour, as if feeding on an energy the Legion could not see, could not sense. The midnight of Raphael's hair was barely visible, the huge width of his wings obscured. The chrysalis that had been too small was no longer visible.

Does the chrysalis grow?

We cannot see.

We cannot know.

It cannot grow in an hour.

The filaments grow.

And grow.

Snow silk covers the walls.

We cannot taste energy.

But the filaments whisper over the room.

The chrysalis must grow.

We cannot see.

It was too small.

Where will her wings fit?

The Bluebell made us remember butterflies.

We forgot butterflies.

He showed us a too-small chrysalis.

But Elena is not a butterfly. An angel does not emerge from a chrysalis.

Why do the filaments spread?

Does the chrysalis grow?

We cannot see.

The voices were him and he was the voices. They were Legion.

"We watch," the Primary said. "We protect."

But things were altering in front of them, a faint glow emanating from where the *aeclari* had been before the filaments obscured both Raphael's body and Elena's chrysalis.

Beyond the balcony doors now partially covered with the snow silk of the filaments, the Bluebell turned. His eyes widened at seeing the ocean of filaments, the glow. But before he could open the closed doors, a familiar voice entered all their minds.

Leave now. It was an order from an archangel. *Clear the skies above. Empty the land around. GO.*

The Legion were moving even as the last word echoed in their minds. They were Raphael's Legion, Elena's Legion, and they had been given an order. The Bluebell wasn't Legion. He was one of the Seven. Unique. With his own mind.

Torment wrenched his features, but he inclined his head, and the Primary saw him form the word "Sire."

All of them moved.

The Bluebell dropped to the grass, then ran inside the house.

The Legion broke into four parts and swept the area. Winged beings were already flying toward the river at high speed, their faces stark and their jaws determined. The Legion dropped down in front of cars moving on the nearest road. The cars were not so close to the *aeclari*'s home, but the archangel hadn't said how far to clear.

When the first two cars halted with a screech that caused a burning scent to rise to their nostrils, the Legion wrenched the doors open and hauled the startled vampires out. A group of the Legion rose into the air, two to a vampire. Another group found four humans in a third car, a vampire's cattle heading home. The scared cattle whimpered at being taken by the Legion but didn't struggle. Neither did the vampires after they saw the angels racing from the Enclave to the water.

Golden light poured from the windows of the *aeclari*'s home.

Many of the angels streaming over the water held vampires or humans in their arms, getting their households out of danger. The Bluebell was one of the last to fly out of the Enclave, and though the Legion did not speak to many outside of the *aeclari*, they spoke to him: *Are the aeclari's people safe?* This was important. The Legion knew. The *aeclari* had bonds to those who lived in the house.

Yes, I got them out. The Bluebell, who could fly faster than the Primary and sometimes raced with the cars of the Blade and the Viper, fell off the cliff with his wings licked by a golden light so bright that it was difficult to face. In one hand, he held a large rectangular thing, in his other, items they recognized.

Several of the Legion flew to him, and took the things. They did not understand things, but these were linked to the *aeclari* in their mind. *We will fly them to the Tower.*

Most of the angels kept on flying toward Manhattan, and

those of the Legion that carried vampires or mortals kept going, too. But the Primary turned once he was over the center of the river, as did those of his brethren who flew only their own bodies.

The Bluebell halted in front of them, the silvery blue of his wings spread and his face awash in the scorching light that had turned the river to gold.

And the light, it grew, and grew, and *grew*.

Until at last, the light was so bright that it became fire and even the Primary couldn't bear it and threw up his arm in front of his eyes. The last thing he saw was an intense white brilliance.

The punch of the explosion blew them all back.

4

Raphael came awake with the side of his face on dirt so hot it glowed, his rest prematurely ended, and his new heart not yet ready. It had, he realized, broken under the weight of the violent energy release and exposed the small mortal heart within. That small heart had exploded from the pressure.

Fragments swam in his blood, weaving their way through his entire system. A system devoid of wildfire. Devoid, too, of the golden lightning. Uncaring of the loss and of the agony in his chest, he opened his eyes . . . and looked into those of liquid silver.

He held that molten gaze for an eternity.

She didn't respond, the silver cloudy and hazy before she lowered her lashes again.

Dazed, he told himself, she was simply dazed and emerging from a long sleep. She had been wrenched too early out of the chrysalis that would consume her even as it remade her. It'd take her time to awaken fully.

The world glowed around them, golden fire crackling, a cocoon formed of pure energy.

He'd last seen her in a shared dream, as they fought the vicious strength of the Cascade to save her mind, her memories, *her*. In the end, this had been their only choice—for Raphael to release the raw violence of his power and hope it fatally disrupted the chrysalis process, tearing Elena from the grip of the Cascade's machinations.

But though he'd punched his power into the earth, it swirled in the air around them, as if there'd been so much that even the earth couldn't contain it.

Raphael cared nothing for that. His only focus was Elena.

The closed fan of her lashes threw shadows onto her skin, her lips soft, and he could almost believe she was simply resting beside him in their bed. But even in sleep, his Elena was never so motionless, never so serene.

A nightmare gnawed at him: that the worst had happened, that the chrysalis had succeeded in its purpose and created a being with Elena's face, but without her soul, without her memories, without her laughter and her spirit.

His nails dug into the dirt, the grit hard and hot.

He forced himself to take in the rest of her. The chrysalis had been too small. He'd seen that for himself. It could not hold his hunter's strong, lithe body, didn't have space for the wings of the warrior who was his consort.

Cracked pieces of the chrysalis lay all around her. The inner surface of the broken pieces swirled with wildfire: white-gold with violent swirls of blue . . . and now, an opalescent shade that morphed from midnight to dawn then back again. Elena's skin glowed brighter than the wildfire, as if she had a light within. The Cascade had tried to turn her into a repository of power, so that he would have a source of extra fuel when he went into the war on the horizon. It had tried to turn his Elena into nothing but a reservoir.

As if he would trade her for power.

As if he would be alive without her.

As if he wouldn't give up eternity for her.

Raphael had stopped the horrific unwanted process. But to save his Elena's soul, her memories, he'd had to do it while the chrysalis was too small. Her body hadn't had time to grow. It was small, misshapen. She was badly hurt and *he* was responsible.

His hand fisted on the dirt, his eyes stinging.

He squeezed them shut and when he next opened them, his

pupils had adjusted to the piercing golden light that drenched them. He saw his Elena again. Why were her knees . . .

Raphael sucked in a breath.

She was not misshapen, was not wounded in a way that would mean centuries of constant pain. She was whole. At some point, she'd managed to tuck her knees to her chest, curling her body around it. Like a child in the womb . . . but Elena was no child.

As he watched, she sighed and began to uncurl, a butterfly emerging from a too-small chrysalis. It seemed impossible even though he was watching it happen. And then he understood. Her body had made a trade.

Elena was whole—but at a price.

Her legs were long, the legs of his tall hunter who could haul him down for a kiss with a hand on his nape. Her arms were the right size to throw knives and shoot a crossbow and spar with him with skill and humor. Her face had begun to fill out, though her cheekbones still cut like glass against her skin.

Then came the price: she was *far* too thin from her shoulders down, her rib cage prominent and her collarbones jutting out. Thin didn't do enough to describe it. She was emaciated, her bones held together by tendons and covered by a translucent layer of skin. That skin continued to glow softly from the inside out, making his tough-as-nails hunter seem to be some ethereal otherworldly creature dropped into the world before she was ready.

It'd infuriate her, but such a terribly fragile body—nothing but bone and tendon and a luminous inward light—could bend and curve and fit inside a too-small chrysalis without losing pieces of itself.

She had made the right trade because flesh could be nourished. Missing limbs might take an eon to regenerate for an immortal so very young . . . because the Elena in front of him was not mortal. Not with eyes of liquid silver.

Raphael didn't care if she was mortal or immortal—whatever happened, they would go into it together. That was their promise. He worried about her physical body only to the extent that he couldn't bear for her to be in pain. All he truly cared about was if *she* had come back to him; his Elena's heart, his Elena's soul, his Elena's courage.

He'd given her a piece of his heart, but only so she could make it hers.

Never had Raphael been afraid except when it came to his warrior lover. He was an archangel. Beyond fear. But in that moment fear closed its cold hands around his throat. Breath tight in his lungs, he made himself take in the rest of her face. Short strands of near-white hair lying across her cheek. Fine bones under her translucent skin—but that skin was Elena's dark gold. The glow hadn't faded.

As if her blood was liquid gold and the light of it shone through.

She blinked, shook her head a tiny fraction. Around her fell the last pieces of the chrysalis as her legs unfurled to their full length. Her eyes opened again and when they met his, they were clear, a pure silver without the gray of humanity. That, however, could mean the worst had happened. That his Elena was immortal but lost to him forever, a container of energy without soul or self.

I would rather die as Elena than live as a shadow.

His hand flexed painfully then fisted again, dirt and grit crushing into his skin. He would do what he had promised. He would end her if she was no longer his Elena. He would not allow an empty shell, a corruption of life, to walk around with his consort's face. He would not allow the Cascade to degrade his Elena. But first, he would know.

Every muscle in his body locked, he reached out with his mind. *Elena-mine.*

No response, no sense of a presence inside his head.

He clenched his jaw. It wasn't over yet. Her ability to speak to him mind-to-mind had been stolen long before the chrysalis. What they'd done together, wrenching her out of the chrysalis, shattering it before it was done consuming her, that might've compounded the harm. The piece of his heart that he'd given her held incredible power, but her body might not have known how to utilize it to protect her mind against the forces tearing at it.

She'd been his Elena in the dream where they'd met before he released his power, but he had no idea how much time had passed in the dream. Had it taken him seconds to expend his power? Days? Months? What had happened to his consort's mind and self during that time?

"Hbeebti." His voice was raw. And his heart, it was in pieces inside him. A new heart would grow in its place, was already beginning—though it faltered and stuttered, slowed by his lack of power. *"Elena."*

Nothing, no response.

He had no weapon, no energy to form angelfire, but he was an archangel. His base strength was enough to break her neck, tear her limb from limb.

Mouth opening in a yawn, she blinked again and gave a harder shake of her head, strands of her hair floating up into the golden energy, and her forehead lined in a frown. His pulse pounded, his regenerating heart sucking energy from his limbs—because arms and legs weren't a priority when you had a heart to grow.

There wasn't much that could kill an archangel. Burned to a cinder by an ordinary fire, they would wake—perhaps after years, but wake they would. Blown to pieces by anything but the powers of another archangel, they would eventually regenerate from a single piece and rise again. Only another archangel could kill an archangel.

Some laws of nature were fundamental. Even the Cascade could not alter them.

His growing heart continued to draw energy from other nonessential parts of his body.

Raphael might lose some flesh during the process, might even lose an arm or a leg, but it would not be anything in the scheme of his immortal life. Nothing akin to Elena's fragility. His hunter, who had never been fragile, would swear a blue streak at becoming conscious of her current state.

He couldn't wait to feel her ire, fight with her over her stubborn need to quickly regain her strength. She'd probably want to begin lifting weights before she could walk. He'd hand her the damn weights himself if she'd just talk to him, tell him they'd made it, that the Cascade hadn't won this battle.

Around them the golden energy continued to glow and form small eddies in the air, tiny lightning flashes hidden within it.

He reached once again for her mind. *Elena, do you hear me?* His chest ached.

If she was gone, this was it for him. He had lived over a

thousand five hundred years. It was enough. If Lijuan had risen monstrous while he and Elena slept, he'd do what he could to burn out that scourge because Elena would want him to do that, but he would not live thousands of years without her. He could not live another day without her. *Warrior mine*, he said with his mind, repeating the words aloud.

His body felt heavy, lethargic, but he lifted his hand to cradle her cheek. Gently, so gently. Her skin felt like the fine rice paper his mother had used to wrap homemade sweets for him when he was a child. It had torn so easily. He would not tear his Elena.

Warm, she was warm. But her eyes, they were closed again. Silver glowed against the diaphanous shell of her lids. Had the chrysalis consumed her from the outside in? Had he stopped the process in time? Or had he taken too long and she'd been consumed down to the merest speck, only to begin again, this time as an empty husk meant to hold energy?

If it was the latter, the woman he loved beyond life, beyond eternity was gone, their love story ended and his immortal existence with it. So be it. But he would know first. He would be *certain*. "Until you speak, I will wait." He would know the instant she opened her mouth whether he held a creature of the Cascade or his Elena.

And if she never spoke? That would be an answer in itself. His hunter was not a woman to hold her silence.

"In the end," he said, "before I released the power in my body, I spoke to Cassandra. You and I, *hbeebti*, we changed the prophecy." He wanted Elena to open her eyes and ask him if Her Evilness was *finally* going to die, wanted to hear her groan when he told her what Cassandra had said:

The future aligns. Paths are chosen. Death comes. Such death, child of flames.
Goddess of Nightmare.
Wraith without a shadow.
Rising into her Reign of Death.
Wings of silver. Wings of blue.
Mortal heart. Broken dreams.
Shatter. Shatter. Shatter.
A sundering. A grave.
I see the end. I see . . .

"Not exactly an improvement over the last one, Archangel."
That's what Elena would say were she awake. "Lots of dark
portents and shattering, and now there's a grave, too? Great,
just great."

Had it been his and Elena's grave that Cassandra had seen?
For if death came, they would lie together in the earth. He
would not permit a sundering—not in life and not in death.
Whatever their future, they would walk into it together. Never
divided. But if this wasn't his hunter, she had already left him.
He would have to follow. "Elena, wake for me," he whispered
on the stuttering beat of his broken heart.

A whisper of warm steel in his mind. *Umm?* A sleepy
sound.

His tiny regenerating heart began to pound as loudly as if
it was fully formed. Because that sleepy murmur, it had
sounded like *his* Elena. The warm steel? That was her strength
tempered with heart. "Guild Hunter?"

She yawned and shifted closer, until her breath kissed his
skin. He ran his thumb over her cheek with immeasurable
care, afraid to snag it and break the fragile surface. "Elena,
wake up." *Please.*

Raising a hand that was far too slender, her bones defined
against her luminous skin, she rubbed at her face without dis-
lodging his hand from her cheek. When she dropped her hand,
she gave him a quizzical look. "Archangel, is your hair on fire?"

5

Raphael stopped breathing. The pounding in his chest turned into a roar in his ears. "Is it?" He didn't care.

But Elena did. Before he could stop her, she reached out an arm so thin it was barely there, and patted at his hair, as if putting out the flames. "There." When she drew back her hand, he saw no scorch marks.

She frowned and stared at her palm, then at his hair again. "They're back." Leaving the strange fire alone, she put her hand over the one he had on her cheek. "I think I'm glowing." Her voice was husky, of a woman coming awake after a deep sleep. "Am I glowing?"

Raphael nodded, clenching at the grit and dirt with his free hand. The dirt was real. The tiny stones within that jabbed into his palm were real. His consort was real. Speaking to him.

"Damn it." She shifted even closer, and her breath turned shallow. It took her minutes to speak again, her lungs and heart struggling to keep up with her need to move. "I don't want to be a glow-in-the-dark hunter." A sudden smile that reached eyes that were hers even if they were all silver with no gray. "At least we'll match. You on fire. Me glowing." But her smile of delight faded almost before it was complete. "I have legs. Arms. Eyes."

She turned her hand in front of her, examining the brittle structure. "My bones are like matchsticks." A scrunched-up nose. "Do you think I'm as breakable as I appear?"

Raphael nodded again, his soul stretching from its tiny curled-up ball. Elena was herself. The rest they could figure out.

"Ugh." Dropping her hand, she blew a strand of hair off her face, then reached up to tug at that hair. "Am I going loopy, or do I have tiny feathers at the ends of my hair?"

Raphael hadn't noticed, his focus on knowing who or what existed in his consort's body, but he saw that she was right. Her hair had reached the middle of her back before the chrysalis. Now, it barely brushed her jaw and at the end of each strand was a tiny, tiny, *tiny* feather of the same shade as her hair. "Your Bluebell will be jealous he no longer has the most unusual hair in angelkind." Black tipped with blue.

"No one will notice. You have to look real close." She dropped her hand onto his where it lay on her cheek. "I think the feathers got confused and ended up in the wrong place on my body." A bleakly haunted look. "I feel the urge to stretch my wing muscles . . . but there's no weight at my back. The chrysalis was too small."

Raphael saw no sign of the extraordinary wings of midnight and dawn that were his consort's. He didn't even know if his own wings had survived the cataclysmic release of power. He moved the muscles that would lift one.

Elena's gasp was soft. *"Archangel."*

His head too heavy to lift, he brought the wing over her . . . and saw that it was pure white fire. A cauldron of white fire. An inferno without end.

"That explains why you set your hair on fire—you're going to be hell on the furniture." She raised a hand without fear, this warrior consort of his. The fire clung to her when she retracted her hand, but it didn't burn.

No part of him would ever harm her.

She laughed, playing the fire over her palm like a small pet. For a moment, she'd forgotten her own loss. "Those wings are seriously badass." After returning the flame to his wing, as if returning a feather, she pushed against the arch of it. "I can feel muscle and tendon and bone. Do you think you'll be able to turn the understructure to fire, too, when you want to? So there's nothing physical to attack?"

"We will find out." He brushed her hair off her face. "Do you remember the dream?"

"Yes. I remember everything." She pressed a hand over her heart. "That was a weird-ass thing to do, Archangel."

Pressing his forehead to her own, he smiled. "What other woman can say her lover actually gave her his heart?"

Her lips twitched, but the bleakness remained. "Do it," she whispered. "Rip off the Band-Aid fast."

He lifted himself up slightly, then moved his hand off her cheek to run it down her spine. And froze. "I can feel something." Shifting so he could look at her back, he was aware of her holding her breath. So was he.

What he saw was unlike anything he knew. "It's a slightly raised tattoo of wings." Perfect in every intricate detail, down to the filaments on each feather. "With all your colors." Rich black shading outward to indigo, deepest blue, and dawn, with primaries of a shimmering white gold.

Elena's breath hit his skin in a hot, jagged exhale. "Baby wings?" Hope was a song in her voice. "Like with Aodhan's nephew?"

Angelic babies were born more with an impression of where wings would grow than actual wings. "This isn't the same," he told her. "Those wings are transparent and clearly show folds where the wing will eventually spread out over the back as the baby develops. On a baby, you can't see the full wing shape."

"I remember now. Like an origami puzzle, with multiple folded layers."

"Yes." Elena's by contrast . . . "The tattoo is of your full wings, just in a size proportional to the canvas of your back."

A small silence before Elena said, "Was it like this the first time? When I was Made?"

And he realized that in all their time together, that was the one question she'd never asked him. Because her wings were a wonder she accepted with no need of further knowledge. "No," he answered. "Your wings grew as an adult angel's would after an amputation. Naked wings covered only by a fluff of baby feathers emerged slowly out of your back. Once the whole wing was there, the adult feathers began to grow outward from your back." He ran his fingers over the graceful arch of one wing.

A shudder rolled through her. "I can feel your touch and it's almost like you're stroking that sensitive part of my wing. Why, if my entire wing structure is gone?" It was a rough, angry whisper. "Why do I want to open and close them if they're forever static? Tattooed wings can't fly, can't open, can't shiver under your touch."

Lowering himself back down so he was facing her, he put his hand on her cheek again. "Wings with no substance can fit inside a chrysalis that is too small." His fierce hunter had fought to regain all of herself. "You made the only choice you could."

She put her hand over his wrist, her grip unexpectedly strong. "Well, it sucks and I want to kick something, but right now, I'd probably break my foot trying." The next sound from her throat was one of wordless rage.

He couldn't fix this for her, couldn't explain a tattoo disparate from any he'd ever seen. Instead, he enfolded her taut-with-anger form in his arms, his warrior consort who had come back to him from the edge of the abyss—and who didn't know the meaning of surrender. "We survived the Cascade's attempts to part us," he reminded her. "We'll survive this, too."

Elena held on to her archangel as he held her, her hold ferocious in its possessiveness. *No tears*, she vowed on a wave of red-hot fury. The Cascade would get no more pain out of her. She might've lost the glorious wings of midnight and dawn that had been her own, but she'd come back to her archangel as herself—and he was whole, too, with no physical damage from the massive power release.

Though, with an archangel, it wasn't that simple.

She tightened her grip.

How long they held one another, she didn't know. His wing was heavy on her despite its fiery appearance, and his chest warm, his smell *him*. Just Raphael. She inhaled it in like it was air and it settled into her cells. When she finally straightened out her body again, anchored by him, by who they were together, her eye fell on the Legion mark on his temple.

The sight made her glance down, below her left breast, for the dark mirror. It was gone, her skin unmarked. She pushed at the glowing translucence of it and thin "cracks" of light spread out under her skin. It was oddly lovely. "Yep, not normal."

Raphael's laugh was deep, a sound she felt in her bones. And his eyes . . . the color was a blue so pure it hurt—and in that blue was a love that marked her. "I believe that is an understatement, *hbeebti.*"

At last, they shifted to their backs, with Elena lying on Raphael's wing as she'd done so many times since they'd found one another. Flickers of white fire danced over her skin like fireflies and it made her smile. Her archangel had come out with his wings intact. Her own, she could bear losing—it hurt like a bitch, but she'd deal. For Raphael to lose his? No, it was an impossibility she refused to countenance.

Above them swirled golden light shot with lightning. "That looks like your new Cascade-born power. It feels like it, too." Portentous and cold and violent in a way that was without motive. Just power so strong it sought to take total control, reshape the holder in its image.

"Why is it just hanging around?"

Her archangel didn't seem very interested in that particular oddness. He'd turned onto his side again and was playing with her hair; as she watched, he examined the tiny feathers on the ends of the strands with intense fascination. Her lips curved. She didn't rush him and time moved slowly in their cocoon of energy.

When Raphael did look up at last, he said, "I sent it into the earth. It must've been too—"

"Raphael." She slammed her palm against the dirt wall next to her. A wall that glowed with golden power, complete with hidden bolts of lightning. "Our people." Her heart thundered—that huge heart that had somehow managed to fit inside her and felt fairly normal . . . except for the odd beat that was too big, too loud.

Eyes of crushed sapphires met hers and she could almost see time unfolding as he returned to that pivotal moment. "I got out a warning right before I earthed the power. I sent the warning out to the limit of my range."

Jaw hard, he said, "But the time between the warning and the earthing may not have been enough—I have no way to judge the passage of time between where we were and here." Lines marked his forehead. "I heard the faded echo of Illium's voice acknowledging the order, but whether that was real or my mind filling in the gaps, we will not know until we emerge."

Elena swallowed. No angel, vampire, mortal could've survived the kind of power in Raphael's veins. The power he'd released. The power that enclosed them in an eerily lovely lightning fire.

Gripping her fear for their friends, their family, in a tight fist, she focused on the strangeness around them and, lifting her hand, brushed her fingers through the power.

Flickers of golden lightning dropped from above to cling to her skin, as it had before everything went to hell. There was nothing inherently wrong with the power—it had scared her because of how strong it was and how distantly immortal it made Raphael, but the power itself wasn't malevolent. It could be shaped and remade to be what he needed. In its raw form, however, it was a violent storm.

"In our shared dream I told you to release it." Guilt gnawed at her. "If people die—"

Raphael shifted onto his elbow and placed his other wing over her again, cocooning her in himself. "We made the decision together." His gaze refused to allow her to look away. "We'll deal with the consequences together."

Elena lay a hand over his wing and nodded. That was their promise: Together. Always. "How weak are you?" His lack of power could be a death sentence. The Cadre respected only the most brutal strength—because an archangel without power couldn't control the vampires in his territory. And now, with the Cascade in play, power had become an even more visceral weapon.

"Your heart exploded during the power release," he said. "It's in my bloodstream now." He sounded not the least worried about having bits of a mortal heart floating around in his body.

She still couldn't believe he'd *done* that: given her a piece of his archangelic heart, then put her dying one in the cavity created when he'd torn out his own.

"My new heart is regenerating slower than it should and my limbs feel heavy," he added, "but I have felt this way before, a long time ago after a battle where I fought to the last drop of strength in my body. A little time for my energies to recover, and I will be in flight."

He frowned. "That my wings are afire . . . I cannot explain it except to theorize the white fire is now part of my flesh and bone. Integral to me—like an arm or a leg. Even now, I feel my body drawing on that strength to build my heart."

Elena saw the white fire begin to flicker and splutter as he spoke. Shifting her gaze, she held those eyes of Prussian blue that seared her soul. "It won't be enough." She couldn't allow him to shield her from the truth. "Not with all the craziness going on with the Cascade. All the other archangels have new powers." He'd be vulnerable, considered weak. Easy prey.

Raphael went to reply when Elena felt a sudden bright jolt hit her bloodstream. She gasped. Both of them stared at the part of her hand where a tendril of golden energy had been dancing. "Did that just . . ."

"The energy went into you." Raphael raised an eyebrow. "Elena-mine, it appears you are to inherit my Cascade abilities."

6

"If I am to be consort to the first archangel-Made," Raphael continued, while she was still gaping at the idea of all that deadly power in her body, "I will undertake my duties with utmost solemnity. I'll throw great balls and invite—"

She poked her highly amused archangel in the shoulder. "Don't you dare even joke about that." No matter if a fine tendril had sunk into her, this power wasn't hers. It tasted of Raphael, a piece of him that had become detached from his body.

The jolt from the single tendril shivered through her bloodstream, seemed to make her blood glow at a higher intensity. Her skin felt electrified. "Is my hair standing up like Einstein's?"

"It is my eternal regret that I could not talk that mortal into becoming a vampire."

"You knew Einstein? Wait, no, stop distracting me." She gasped again.

A second tendril of power had just dropped from the storm above to punch into her bloodstream.

Raphael's eyebrows drew together. "Your eyes were liquid silver when you first opened them. They've now faded to a more mortal shade near the pupil, but there's a deep glow to them."

"A glow-in-the-dark hunter with equally high-viz eyes and probably radioactive blood. Just what I always dreamed of being."

Ignoring her muttered diatribe, Raphael angled his head closer. "You also appear to have gained a hint of a particular blue around the pupils. It's extremely faint, like a stain on the edge of the black."

"Well, you had to go give me a *piece of your heart*." Her mouth dried up at the renewed memory of how he'd literally torn out his heart for her. She slapped her hands on his chest. "You ever do anything like that again and I'll use you for target practice."

His smile creased his cheeks, lit up those extraordinary eyes with an inner light that outshone the golden lightning that swirled ever faster above them, a hurricane in the making. "I will buy the knives for you."

Lips twitching, she attempted a scowl, failed. "I guess being a glowing toothpick isn't so bad," she said with a grin of her own. "I bet I can make good money on the talk show circuit."

His smile deepened. "You are very certainly my Elena."

Yes, she was. "Lemme look at your eyes, see the damage." She'd seen nothing concerning so far, but she worried what else he'd lost. The world was a lethal place for an archangel without power. But she saw what she'd always seen: a blue so deep it was eternity.

Her breath came easier. "Your eyes are as unearthly as ever."

"I am an archangel." It wasn't a boast, just a statement of fact.

The donation of a piece of his heart had fundamentally changed her then barely immortal body. His own body, she realized, was too powerful to be impacted by a small human heart. "Why did you keep it?"

He didn't ask her what she meant. "To stay a little mortal for you."

Her eyes burned. Moving even closer under the warm heaviness of his wings, she brushed strands of hair off his face, the color darker than the night. The Legion mark on his right temple was dull, flat. Even as her stomach twisted at this further indication of all he'd lost to save her, a third tendril of Cascade-born power dropped onto the back of her hand . . . punched inside.

"Does it hurt?" Raphael was no longer smiling. "You're gritting your teeth."

"I get pins and needles all over my body when it goes in." Flexing the hand that had taken the latest hit, she lifted it deliberately to the power that was an increasingly turbulent storm over them. It slipped into her in fiery droplets. "Ten," she said at the end, having counted each tendril as it sank into her.

Then it stopped.

The power danced over her skin, twined around her wrist, wove itself into her hair, but didn't penetrate her skin. She watched the storm, felt understanding whisper on the edge of her mind, just out of earshot. "I feel 'full'—there's nowhere for the power to go now."

Raphael's voice was granite when he said, "Before we interrupted the process, the Cascade was attempting to turn you into a power reservoir."

"So I'm a partial reservoir?" Thinking about that, she shrugged. "I always held a drop or two of wildfire for you." She placed one hand beside her shoulder, palm-up in a silent invitation; Raphael closed his own over it. "I don't mind holding a little more power in reserve." It'd give Raphael a small advantage in battle—though ten droplets wasn't exactly a game changer when he'd given up all his power.

Although . . . Her throat dried up, her pulse a booming bass. *"Raphael."*

Golden lightning was suddenly electric over Raphael's skin, his hair, his wings. Prussian blue turned to gold as the energy played across his irises. Without warning, the power *slammed* into him with a force so violent that his body went rigid, his spine an iron rod. She went to try to fight it—with what she didn't know—but he squeezed her hand and held it to the earth.

Panic a trapped butterfly in her skull, she closed her free hand over his and held on to her archangel while the power howled around him, into him. His hair blew back in the gale-force winds that existed inside the storm. His skin cracked with veins of gold that healed in a heartbeat, only for it to happen again and again. His hair turned gold with the sheer amount of energy pouring into him. His eyes were molten gold shattered with lightning.

When she tried to connect her mind with his, all she heard in return was roaring static, as if he stood in the middle of a wind tunnel, his words stolen before they ever reached her. Her own hair blowing back from her face and lightning strikes hitting her skin only to bounce off, she came as close as she could with their clasped hands between them. Never would she let him go.

A blinding blaze that forced her eyes to shut, a final roar of sound in her ears, followed by a "pop" as the pressure equalized . . . and it was over. She blinked open her eyes to utter calm. The earth around them continued to glow—but it was pulsing red now. As if so much heat had been released into it that things that shouldn't burn had begun to burn. The golden Cascade-born energy no longer swirled above and around them.

It was inside Raphael.

Motionless, she stared.

The crashing sea in her mind, salt-laced and familiar . . . but infinitely colder. Until her veins were ice and her breath was particles of frost.

So? asked her archangel.

She gave a slightly hysterical giggle. "Talk about glow-in-the-dark." His skin was lit from within, his eyes a vivid *living* gold, his hair tipped with flames. When she batted at it, the damn energy just hopped over to her hand and danced over her skin. "I guess the Cascade isn't keen for you to be without power." Her stomach was one big knot.

"It seeks only chaos. There is no chaos in one power." Raphael shaped the Primary's words with intricate concentration, as if doing something as mundane as forming words was far beneath him now. As if he'd ascended beyond being an archangel.

Fuck that.

Elena smashed a fist through the ice, kicked the stomach-knotting fear to the curb. She hadn't survived being consumed by a goddamn chrysalis, then come back to life with an archangelic heart inside her chest, and a torturously sensitive tattoo instead of wings, to lose Raphael to a power that wanted to shape him into a being monstrous enough to fight Lijuan.

Fucking Cascade could go take a fucking hike.

Breaking their handclasp, she grabbed his face in her hands and slammed her mouth over his. Her entire body keened at the deep sense of homecoming, of being exactly where she needed to be. *I missed you, Archangel.* Wrapping her arms around his neck, she held him tight and deepened the kiss.

Raphael's mind cleared in a single passionate second, the taste of Elena slicing through the grasping cold of enormous power. He'd never been *this* powerful, not even prior to the chrysalis. Until he felt that his mind could reach all corners of his territory. Until he could be a god.

Elena licked her tongue across his.

Carnal need and searing love collided, and he was once more very much a man, earthy and of this world. Not an archangel with delusions of godhood. Not Lijuan's mirror. He was Raphael and he was with his strong, stubborn, dangerous consort. There was no distance with his hunter, and never would be.

Thrusting one hand into her hair, he gripped the strands in a powerful fist, and drank her in. He was furious with her for being so hurt, for making him slice off her wings. Knowing she'd had no control over it didn't matter. Not in this moment.

He couldn't hold the fury inside.

She felt it—and kissed him back even harder, the steel and warmth of her in his mind and sharp tugs on his scalp from the hands she'd locked in his hair. Running his palm down her side, he flinched at the barely sheathed bone of her rib cage. "You need food." His breath was harsh pants; inside him, the power continued to rage, a hurricane without end.

Elena stared at him for a long second . . . before throwing back her head and laughing from deep within her belly. If her kiss had grounded him, her laughter *owned* him. He just watched her, drinking in a sight he'd feared he'd never again witness.

When she finally managed to bring herself down to snorting giggles that kept on setting her off again and caused his cheeks to crease, he said, "What is so amusing?"

A loud snort.

Raising her hand to her mouth, she tried to stifle her giggles and failed. His own smile cut deeper into his cheeks. Both wings spread over her now, he shifted his hand to her hip. The bone was sharp and hard, her skin beyond thin, but Elena put her hand on his and said, "Hold on as you always have."

Raphael went to argue—and saw the implacable determination in her laughing gaze. *We are us.* Warm steel in his mind. *Damn Cascade doesn't get to mess us up. And if my bones are hollow, I'd rather know now.*

7

Raphael was the one who gritted his teeth this time. "Your bones are not hollow. Or I would've crushed your hand earlier." Shoulders easing at the reminder that she'd come out unscathed from his brutal hold, he curved his hand more firmly over her hip. "I reserve the right to change my mind at any moment."

"You're sounding very Archangel of New York. It's hella sexy." She kissed him again, the edges of laughter on the corners of her mouth, crumbs of mortality that she'd carried through an impossible transition.

He fell into the kiss. Lightning-infused power arced around them, going from him to wrap around her, only to return back to him. The power felt . . . warmer on each return, as if it was being kissed by her as he was being kissed.

He didn't know how long they kissed, but glittering angel dust coated her lips when they drew apart. Her taste coated his.

Branding one another all over again.

"I was laughing because food's like a persistent and highly annoying ghost haunting me." She traced the lines of the Legion mark, which Raphael could feel burning with a cold immortal power. "I've been eating for an eternity and still lost all this weight."

She snapped her fingers. "I'm gonna write a lifestyle book to go with my reality show. It'll include what I call the Cascade Diet. Eat everything—including the kitchen itself if you like—and come out with a negative weight."

"I am not amused."

Her lips kicked up, her eyes dancing. "But you are gorgeous." Another kiss, her arms wrapped loosely around his neck like they were lying lazily in their bed. "How's the power?"

"Becoming mine." His consort's kiss had cut through its initial attempt to shape him while he was overwhelmed by the sudden violent boost. "The Cascade is foolish to believe it can mold me in the image it desires."

"You're speaking of it like the Cascade is a living thing." She chewed on her lower lip. "Though, yeah, it did keep throwing obstacles in my path when I was chasing Archer. Definitely seemed like a mind behind it."

"If it is an agent of chaos, then it doesn't have to be sentient. It simply has to stop that which would stop chaos—and buttress that which encourages it."

"A single-minded and relentless force." She blew out a breath that caused a tiny feather to dance in the air. "I wish it was real so I could kill it."

"Yes." His vision was shattered lightning, his heart an organ that beat strong and true—it had healed fully the instant the golden lightning thrust into him. "Right now, however, we have a more pressing problem." Turning over onto his back, he looked up and up and up and *up.* "Do you see blue skies?"

Elena squinted up. But she got distracted before she found the skies Raphael had seen. "Is it my imagination or is that half a chair sticking out of the top of the . . ." She looked around, *really* seeing their environment for the first time. Yes, she'd noticed the dirt, but her neurons had just processed it as, "Dirt, okay." Apparently, said neurons thought it was usual to wake up on hot dirt.

In her defense, she *had* just escaped a chrysalis that wanted to eat her brains. And the hovering Cascade power had blocked out the dizzying sides of the small cavern in which they lay—a cavern lit only by her glow and his, with the dirt adding in some ember red for ambience.

"Are we at the bottom of a hole in the earth?" She poked at the wall closest to her, came away with hot dirt on her fingers. It didn't burn—maybe because she was glowing brighter than the dirt. "Where's our bed?"

"Burned to cinders by now."

Worry, hot and sharp, spiked again—not for the bed or their home, but for their friends and family. "Do you think Deacon will put me at the top of his list again?" she said, because it was easier to think about innocuous things than to give in to the frantic voice of fear that their survival had meant death for those they loved. "I mean, I *am* best friends with his wife."

"We lose our home and you mourn the loss of your weapons. Truly, I know you are my Elena."

"I mourn my amber earrings, too, and your ring's gone." She scowled. "I will rectify that at once."

"Here." As she watched dumbfounded, he reached into the overheated dirt and pulled out a particular glowing piece. "I believe this is amber."

Her mouth dropped open. Actually dropped open. Forcing it shut before it froze in that position, she said, "Did you *make* amber?"

"We had many trees on our land. Amber is fossilized tree resin."

Her wonder took a nauseating dive. "So either the surge of supercharged archangelic power speeded up the process . . . or we've been asleep a gazillion years?" Everyone they knew might be gone, the world changed in ways they couldn't comprehend.

"I can't get through to anyone, so it's possible, but I do not think the latter can be true." He put the cooled hunk of clear amber into her palm. "We stopped the chrysalis process early, and the entire aim of it was so you could be a power reservoir when Lijuan rose. I do not think your favorite archangel plans to Sleep an eternity."

Exhaling, she nodded. "Smart man." She lifted the amber in front of her face. "This is beautiful." Not pristine in its clarity as she'd first thought, but with bubbles inside that looked like miniature explosions caught forever in motion. It seemed appropriate for how the piece had been formed. "No house, no weapons, no . . ." She moaned. "My *greenhouse*."

Raphael put his arm out so she could lie on it. "I'll gift you an even bigger one."

"All your things, Raphael. That gorgeous painting by Aodhan." Her heart hurt at the idea of all that beauty destroyed.

"He will paint us a better one."

Her shoulders began to shake. "Is that going to be your answer for everything? We'll make a better version?"

"Yes," said the archangel who'd once had no sense of humor—but who was now joking with her with deadpan seriousness despite the cold, heady power that filled him to the brim—it spilled from his eyes, danced in his hair.

"Montgomery's not going to be pleased with the new décor." Because this was their home around them. That half-buried chair high above, the random piece of stained glass welded to the dirt, an astonishingly well-preserved little statuette sitting at the end, near Raphael's feet.

"I shall tell him to steal us treasures for refurnishing."

Elena snorted out a laugh . . . but the darker, bleaker possibility she didn't want to face clawed at her mind. The one where Raphael's warning hadn't been heard. The one where Montgomery and Sivya had been in the house when it was destroyed. The one where the explosion wiped out Manhattan.

She couldn't think that and survive. She needed one fucking win over the Cascade, a big finger raised up to the force that would destroy their lives in its quest for whatever the hell it was questing for.

"Your anger is sparks in my mind. I have missed your fury, Guild Hunter."

Elena hadn't realized she'd maintained the mental connection between them. It had been so effortless. "Huh, looks like your insane heart transplant's boosted my mind-to-mind strength." A good bonus when she wasn't too sure about the rest of her. Because what if she literally couldn't put on weight? What if the interrupted process meant she'd be a slightly gussied-up skeleton forever?

No need to panic just yet. Save it for later. Plenty of things to stress over before we get to that.

With that cheery pep talk to herself, she looked up again,

squinted. "That *might* be the sky, though don't quote me on that." If so, it was a miracle they weren't swimming in lava because they were down *deep*. "Were you trying to melt us a tunnel to China so we could attack Her Evilness by stealth?"

"It is a thought." He dug something else out of the soil next to them. "Look, Elena."

It was another chunk of amber, but this one held a perfectly preserved flower. Her heart flowered just like it. Rising, she put both chunks next to the statuette, then lay back down against her archangel. The tattoo brushed against something and sensation rippled through her as if she'd snagged a feather on a protuberance.

Clenching her jaw, she forced herself to breathe. And decided to ignore that whole situation for now. Because, on the list of panic-inducing items, there was currently one clear champion. "Why is no one poking their head over that hole?" she said, and it came out a rasp. "Why isn't Bluebell yelling down at us already?" Her throat grew thick, her eyes hot. "Why isn't Sara ripping a strip off me for doing this to her again? *Where is everyone?*"

8

The Legion

The blinding blast had sent the Legion spiraling into the waters of the river, their wings unable to deal with the massive crush of energy. The Bluebell had gone in beside them. But they all came up through the churned-up water, having been far enough from the explosion that the impact had been painful but not catastrophic. No vessels had been close enough to suffer damage, all weaker angels already far distant.

It did take time for them to regain their ability to fly; the concussive shock of the blast was yet ringing in their heads when they began to rise up out of the water. And though the Bluebell had feathers, his wings far heavier in the water than the Legion's sleeker shape, he reacted the fastest. Water streamed off his wings in a shimmer of droplets that reflected the sunlight.

Rising up beside the Bluebell's hovering form, the Primary followed his gaze.

Where the *aeclari*'s house had once stood was now a bubble of what appeared to be molten lava.

Lava does not form huge bubbles above the earth.

Lava does not hold its shape.

Lava is of the earth, a luminous secret.

Lava should not be here.

As his brethren spoke inside his mind, he and the Bluebell rose higher in silence, high enough that they dared fly across the impossible construct. The lava was alive, sliding and moving with languid grace in hues of red and orange and yellow and everything in between. Yet it held its shape. In the very center was a small clear circle but it was overrun with molten heat before they could get close enough to view what lay within.

Any closer and the Bluebell's feathers would singe, the Primary's skin begin to ulcerate and slough off.

"Remind you of anything?" the Bluebell murmured, as sweat rolled down his face, steam a halo around him. His wet wings no longer dripped, the heat evaporating the water before it left his feathers.

The Primary considered the furnace below, sent the question to his brethren. They all said one word and so did he: "Cassandra."

"Yeah." The Bluebell drew back from the heat, an unreadable emotion on his face. "The last time she created a lava sinkhole, it swallowed a vampire. This time . . ." Darkness in eyes the color of aged coins the Primary had seen in the deep. "We wait. We watch."

"We wait. We watch."

9

"Err, Archangel? That doesn't look like blue sky anymore." She hoped it wasn't sky at all—because a world with a sky molten and deadly wasn't a world in any kind of good shape.

Raphael's response was unexpected. "Cassandra may still be falling into Sleep." Gold lightning lived in his eyes, eerie and unfamiliar. "I lost her right at the end, before I earthed the power, but the descent into Sleep is a long process. If some vestige of her remains awake, she could be protecting us."

Elena stared up at the dot far above, saw in it echoes of the sinkhole that had begun all this. "As long as she isn't whispering creepy prophecies in my head, I have no problem with Cassandra." The Ancient was just a messenger.

She sat up on a wave of effort. And belatedly realized a pertinent fact. "I'm buck naked." All glowing skin, electrified hair, and breathless lungs. "Assuming that *is* Cassandra and she'll allow us through, can you use your glamour, hide us?" She had no wish to flash New York with her bony ass.

"Glamour is child's play with the amount of power currently in my system." Hair yet afire at the ends and lightning cracking his skin, Raphael sat up beside her, looked up. He was beautiful beyond compare. He was also dangerous and deadly and a *power.*

His jaw muscles tightened. "Part of me does not wish to surface."

Chest constricting to the edge of pain, she followed his gaze. "We have to have hope." She was speaking as much to herself as to her archangel. "Without hope, the Cascade wins."

"Hope." Raphael brushed his wing over her back and the tattoo whispered sensation through her—as if she had feathers, too, over a wing understructure of bone and tendon and muscle and nerves.

Her ghost wings were torturous in many ways, but this? Elena gloried in it.

They rose to their feet together . . . and that was where she hit the first snag. Her spindly toothpick legs couldn't support her body. She would've crumpled if Raphael hadn't caught her, held her close. "Hope," she said again when cold fury seared his features.

"Hope," he gritted out, and it wasn't the most heartfelt pledge—yeah, her archangel was pissed—but she'd take it given the circumstances . . . and try not to let her own anger take root. Elena P. Deveraux, Guild Hunter and consort to an archangel, was not about to let the Cascade twist her personality to bitterness and despair. She was going to fucking *own* this new chance at life.

Raphael spread his wings.

"Wait!" Elena nodded to the area behind the glory of his wings. "The amber and the statuette."

Raphael lowered himself on one knee, his arm locked tight around her hips to stop her from falling. He used his free hand to grab the precious items and pass them up to her. Clutching them to her naked chest, she said, "Let's do this."

A last glance from eyes that were the wrong color and alive with deadly power before Raphael scooped her up in his arms. Elena pressed a kiss to his left pectoral muscle and *hoped.*

Flaring out his wings, he rose in an effortless vertical takeoff.

Elena whooped at the sensation—flight was beautiful and she'd never be jaded about it. And this, it might be their final moment of happiness if what lay beyond was a devastated wasteland.

Dipping his head, Raphael kissed her and she tasted power, love, *Raphael*, before they broke apart and turned their faces upward. "Together," she said, her voice firm.

His response was immediate and absolute. "Always."

The red-orange "sky" began to disappear as they got closer to the top, falling away on either side like molten doors sinking back into the earth. The two of them shot up and out. The temperature was just on the edge of cold, the sun bright.

Gold met silver . . . and they turned as one to look down.

Their home was gone. So was the greenhouse. Blast damage was evidenced by broken trees and what looked like a car flung upside down in a tangle of shattered wood, but their nearest neighbor was some distance away and that house appeared undamaged except for shards of glass that glinted in the grass around it. Its windows had blown out.

Nothing moved in that direction. No birds, no people, no cars.

The skies were empty.

"We must look toward the Tower."

Elena clenched her abdominal muscles. "Do it."

All the air rushed out of her a heartbeat later. Directly in their line of sight and not ten meters away hovered two familiar faces. "Bluebell." A whisper. "And the Primary." Both looked a touch worse for wear, but otherwise fine. At that instant, they appeared to be arguing—as much as the Primary argued with anyone.

Beyond them hovered countless more wings of Legion-gray . . . silhouetted against the skyscrapers of Manhattan. "Can you ask about Montgomery and Sivya?" Their butler and cook were the most likely to have been in the house when it exploded.

Raphael spoke mentally to Elena's Bluebell on the heels of Elena's request. *Illium.* He, too, needed to know this answer.

The blue-winged angel's head swung toward them. His eyes scanned the skies in a futile search—Raphael and Elena were invisible inside the glamour.

Sire?

Raphael saw the angel swallow hard even from this distance, his body held with a rigid stiffness.

Elena and I have returned, Raphael said, for he would not draw out his people's pain. *Montgomery and Sivya?*

Safe. Illium shuddered, every muscle in his body seeming to unlock. *We cleared everyone within a large radius and your home was already a no-fly zone with heavily patrolled borders. There should be no casualties.*

Raphael passed on Illium's words to Elena. A shimmer of wet on her irises. Squeezing her eyes shut, she spoke in a voice thick with unspoken emotion. "I'll take that as a win."

"As will I." They had not risen on the cold bodies of others, had not stolen life by sending others into the abyss.

Sire, what should I do now?

Raphael had never heard Illium sound so uncertain, so shaken. *Watch over this chasm until I can return to refill it.* The sides looked to have been forcefully compacted by his power. The hole should fill if he could collapse those walls.

Jason is in the city. Illium's eyes still searched for them, though he was well aware of Raphael's ability to create glamour. *Together, we can take care of it.*

"Your Bluebell needs to see us," Raphael murmured to Elena. "I will ask him to come to the Tower."

"I'd need to see us, too, if we got eaten by a chrysalis then exploded our house." The strands of her hair waved around her face in the gentle but crisp wind, the tiny feathers glittering a touch in the sunlight.

Illium's face was stark with need when Raphael spoke the invitation, but he was one of Raphael's Seven for a reason. Squaring his shoulders, he said, *I will wait for Jason and collapse the hole first. Should I do a run inside to retrieve anything salvageable?*

This was why the blue-winged angel was one of Raphael's most trusted people. He had courage and intelligence both. *No, Illium, on second thought, you and Jason should stay away from the chasm. I do not know if any remnants of Cascadeborn power linger within and how those remnants will react to anyone but Elena and me.*

Raphael could survive even if buried under tons of rock and dirt infused with wild Cascade energies, but Illium was too young. *Keep watch until I return. Then we will go to the Tower together.*

Sire. Ellie . . .

She is the Ellie you know. Her physical state would matter as little to Illium as it did to Raphael.

Raphael spoke next to the Primary. He had no need to announce his and Elena's return—it had taken about thirty seconds after they'd exited the hole, but the Legion were once again a murmur at the back of his mind. He knew his consort heard them, too, for they were as much hers as his.

Raphael. Aeclari. *Elena.* Aeclari. *We waited! You have come!*

"Whoa." Elena winced. "I think they're trying to whisper, but seven-hundred-and-seventy-seven whispers pack a punch." But despite the barrage of noise, her lips curved. "It's good to be home."

Elena. Aeclari. Raphael. Aeclari.

What do you need?

We are your Legion.

Help Illium maintain a watch over the chasm, Raphael ordered.

He directed his next words to the Primary and Illium both. *Contact me at once should the chasm change in any way. Do not go any closer than you are now.*

Sire. Two minds, two very distinct mental voices, the rest of the Legion fading away to a background murmur.

Raphael flew toward Manhattan, angling his flight so that the wind of his passage blew Illium's hair off his face. The angel's startled laughter held a sharp edge. The kind of edge that came from relief so visceral it was painful.

Cupping his hands to his mouth a second later, the blue-winged angel yelled out, "Ellie, I saved your crossbow!"

In Raphael's arms, Elena's face cracked into a grin so broad that it lit up the cold places inside him. As long as she existed, he would always be a little bit mortal, but he would have to be careful with this Cascade-born power. It continued to fight to manipulate him, continued to attempt to push him into a coldness that would make the most cruel, heartless decisions seem tenable.

"That is true love if ever I heard it," he said to his delighted consort.

"I'm going to kiss him when I see him next," she vowed.

"I suppose as he is so loyal I shall resist the urge to smite him."

Elena's laughter wrapped around him as the two of them flew across the choppy waters of the Hudson. As they did so, he spoke to the others of his Seven who were within his mental reach: *Dmitri, Jason, Venom.*

A dark-haired form appeared on a high Tower balcony moments later. Though he was but a pinprick from this distance, Raphael had no doubt at all that it was the vampire who had walked by his side for a millennium: Dmitri. His friend and his blade.

Your suite is ready. Dmitri's voice was as hard as stone. *Keir is in the city, as is Nisia.*

Send both to meet us. He understood the hardness in his second—Raphael had been the same when he'd found Dmitri again after his friend had been abducted and tortured and broken in a way that had forever changed him. Some emotions were too big to show. They had to be contained in a tight fist lest they crush you.

Raphael—how bad is it?

When Raphael repeated Dmitri's question to Elena, she snorted. "Tell the Dark Overlord that we're breathing but also glowing. And if he tries any scent games, I'll sharpen my toothpick arms and stab him with them."

Lips curving, Raphael passed on the message.

I see the white-haired bad influence is still with you. Despite the cutting words, Dmitri's tone had begun to unbend, as he permitted himself to believe in their return.

Jason's voice was the next in Raphael's head. *Sire. Do you wish a report?*

And that was Jason, loyal to the bone but unable to speak of emotions to anyone but the woman he loved. *Soon. For now, handle the borders. I'm guessing the explosion was spectacular. It may attract attention.*

The explosion lit up the sky across the entire city, Jason confirmed. *Lady Caliane sent her best squadron to New York to help protect our borders. I will join them with a Tower squadron.*

Venom's voice slipped into his mind in a sinuous flow. *Sire. It has been too long a wait.*

The vampire with the eyes of a viper was often considered sophisticated and urbane—but Venom's voice held no sophistication then, was open in a way Raphael knew the vampire was to only a rare few. He responded without words, with the kind of mental contact only an archangel could make.

Even as he did so, huge winged birds took off from the roof of a skyscraper below them.

"Raphael, are those condors?" Arching her head over to the side, Elena blinked. "I swear I just saw a jaguar sunning himself on a roof." She rubbed at her eyes.

Raphael had caught the same fleeting impression of a pelt of spotted black and gold; halting in the air, he turned to check.

He and Elena stared at the splendid beast together. As if sensing them, it raised its head and yawned, exposing a set of gleaming canines.

"This land will soon be far too cold for such creatures," Raphael murmured.

"No, see—someone's set up heat lamps for it to sit under." As the beast lazily shifted its tail back and forth, Elena whispered, "Don't look now but there are a bunch of pumas over on that other roof."

"Elijah." An archangel who had once been a general in Caliane's army, and who could call birds of prey as well as large cats.

"He must've sent them to help protect your territory while we were lost in weird-ville."

"Not the first thought that would come to the mind of another archangel," Raphael murmured. "Yet I find I agree with you." Perhaps it was the droplet of humanity in him, or maybe it was the relationship he had built with the Archangel of South America, but he didn't believe Eli would attempt to annex his territory.

He resumed his journey to the Tower.

10

Venom stood waiting beside Dmitri now, his body held in
that languid way that was natural to him—but there was nothing languid about the youngest member of Raphael's Seven.
He was coiled as tight as Dmitri. That no one else waited on
the balconies told Raphael that—excepting the healers—his
men hadn't informed anyone else of their return.

He swept by deliberately close to the balcony, much as he
had with Illium. They held their feet under the buffeting, their
heads angling up as if following his flight path onto the balcony that led to his and Elena's Tower suite.

The doors stood open, Keir and Nisia on the other side.

"Can I reach out and poke Nisia?" Elena whispered, even
though her voice would not escape the power of the glamour.
"Will she feel it?"

Lips curving, Raphael said, "You remain sore about what
Nisia said to you?" She had never actually finished telling him
about that conversation, but it wasn't difficult to imagine Nisia
making Elena an unwary victim of her somewhat sharp sense
of humor.

"Maybe. Just a little." Teeth biting down on her lower lip as they passed the healers, she stretched out a hand to tap the exposed part of Nisia's collarbone.

The healer jumped, her hand rising to her chest and her simple gown of midnight blue swirling. "Ringworms," she said very precisely in the aftermath, sending Elena into a paroxysm of laughter.

Raphael had to make himself let her go. Laying her down on their bed, he forced himself not to help as Elena pushed herself up into a seated position and began to tug the sheet up over her body. Wounded or not, his consort remained a warrior and that was how he'd treat her.

"Psst." Elena pointed at the wardrobe. "Pants, Archangel. Only I get to admire that delicious view."

Raphael raised an eyebrow, his lips tugging up slightly at the corners; in truth, he'd forgotten his own state of undress in his concern over her. "I live to obey, *hbeebti*," he said, and found a pair of dark brown pants he often wore while sparring with Elena or his Seven.

"Ask me some day about a time more than a thousand years past when I was in a company of warriors who wore only paint on their skin when they went into battle," he said afterward.

"Pictures or it didn't happen," she said, a little breathless as she finished tucking the sheet under her armpits.

He laughed, and he'd have thought that an impossibility only moments earlier.

Behind them, Keir and Nisia had shut the balcony doors, now pulled blackout curtains across them. Elena and Raphael rarely made use of those. Most often, the doors were shielded only by curtains of gauzy white. No one in the city was suicidal enough to land on this balcony and attempt to stare inside, but Raphael appreciated the healers' care. Elena would choose when she wished to show herself—no one would steal that choice from her.

Nisia turned on the lights.

The bright light threw Elena's emaciated form into sharp relief, too many shadows and hollows in her. Gut clenching and shoulders knotted, Raphael had to fight to keep his voice steady. "Ready?"

"They've both already seen all there is to see, so yeah, let's do it." The pragmatic words of a warrior, but her gaze was soft when it met his—vulnerable in a way she showed no one else in the world. "Come here first."

Her hand was warm on his cheek, her kiss fierce. "I know I look like a bag of bones, but I'm *me* and we're together." Words that dared him to do anything but believe. In her. In them. "We'll write our next chapter the way we want it—and we'll keep on kicking destiny's ass."

He took another kiss, his hand fisted in her hair and his tongue aggressive. But when they parted, he was the one who felt owned. Branded.

Rising, his hair falling over his forehead, he said, "Not one chapter. Many."

A quick grin. "A freaking tome," she vowed. "Oh, and can you find me a phone? If I don't call Sara, she'll scalp me. Beth, Eve, my grandparents . . . Raphael, I have so many people in my family now."

"Not one of whom will begrudge you the time it takes to have this consultation." With that, he stepped back and dropped the glamour.

Keir and Nisia were seasoned healers who had seen much over the millennia of their existence, but both sucked in an audible breath at first sight of Elena and Raphael. Keir, his dusky face ageless, pressed his lush lips together and bent to kiss Elena gently on the forehead. The golden brown of his wings shimmered under the overhead lights.

Nisia, meanwhile, raised an eyebrow. "You haven't been drinking my potion, I see."

"I dunno." Elena shrugged. "Maybe it's internal parasites."

Snorting, the healer shook her head. "It is good to see that being encased in a chrysalis hasn't done anything to dent your winning personality."

"Well, Elena." Keir sat down on the bed on one side, the black silk of his hair cut in layers that brushed his jaw. "You are always my most interesting patient."

"Hey, Raphael's glowing like a lightbulb and his eyes are gold lightning."

"In archangels, such strange things are expected."

A gentle knock came on the door then, and Raphael realized Dmitri *had* told another person of their return. Opening that door without exposing Elena, he took in the tray in Montgomery's hands. The vampire wore a black suit over a crisp white shirt, was as cool and collected as always . . . and the tray, it trembled.

"Thank you, Montgomery." Raphael accepted the tray piled with food and drink. "My apologies for blowing up the house you kept so beautifully." Neither Elena nor Raphael were of the kind to infuse a house with small domestic touches that turned it into a home—that was Montgomery's domain.

A shaky smile. "I have three warehouses full of treasures. Now I will have room to display them."

Setting the tray aside on a table inside the door, Raphael stepped out and then—for the first time in an eon—wrapped his arms around Montgomery. The vampire who was his butler had been a contained man from the first, not one to give in to displays of emotion. But today, he wrapped his arms around Raphael in return and held on with strength that would've surprised those who saw only his elegant surface.

Neither one of them said anything, and when they drew apart, Montgomery's features were set in their usual composed lines and his hands no longer trembled. "I didn't know if food was needed, but you always eat after *anshara* and that is the closest thing to this I could imagine."

"It is needed. Tell Sivya to prepare Elena's favorites."

"She has already begun."

Stepping back into the bedroom, Raphael nodded at his butler before shutting the door. When he turned, it was to see that Elena had a healer on either side of her, the two frowning as they checked her over using both their healing abilities and medical instruments pulled out of large open cases on the floor.

"Oh man that smells good!"

Placing the tray on his consort's lap, Raphael went to step outside to speak to Dmitri and Venom before he flew to Illium, but Elena glared at him. "You need to eat, too."

To his shock, he realized he did. As long as an archangel ate now and then, he didn't really feel hunger except in exigent circumstances; today, it gnawed at him. He sat down on the bed, and suddenly the huge span was full of wings. Keir and Nisia were being scrupulous about holding theirs close to their bodies, but there was only so much they could do.

"There is no need to waste your energy on proper etiquette," he told them. "Neither Elena or I will consider it a trespass should you brush our bodies."

Nisia gave a small nod of acknowledgment, while Keir allowed his wings to ease a fraction.

Leaving them to their work, Elena and Raphael ate with a determined focus that had the tray cleared within ten minutes. Raphael looked to Elena. "More?"

She patted the sheet over her dangerously concave stomach. "Don't know where it's going, but yeah."

He wasn't the least surprised to open the bedroom door and find a fresh tray waiting. After the two of them had demolished the food on that, Raphael ran his eyes over his consort. "You're not glowing as much."

She examined the skin on the back of her hand. "I think you're right." Then it was his turn to be scrutinized. "Your eyes are beginning to show hints of blue." She held out her arm when Nisia requested it. "Go, find out if Lijuan got dead while we were dozing."

"You are an eternal optimist." He rose off the bed, but didn't leave. *Hbeebti.*

It's all right, Raphael. Eyes that had settled into a luminous silver at the edges bleeding into gray, with the faintest hint of blue nearest the pupil, held his. *Now that the first shock is past, I can handle the examination of my back, the tattoo.*

No. Raphael would not budge on this. *It happens now, while I am here.*

His hunter gave him a lopsided smile. *Yeah, fine, I'm freaked.* "I need you to examine my back now," she said to the healers. "I have a very strange tattoo."

Neither Keir nor Nisia argued.

"Shift forward," Keir said. "Just enough so we can see the entire mark."

Having walked around to the back of the bed, Raphael stood watch as Elena did as instructed. Her tattoo was even more detailed than he'd realized. Each filament was defined with care, down to the small feather on her left wingtip that always liked to grow its filaments in the opposite direction to all other feathers.

"It is as if your wings have been made small and burned

to your back." Nisia ran an experimental finger over one feather.

A lightning flicker of power had the healer jerking her hand back with a jolt. "My apologies." She shook out her hand. "That was unexpected."

"Did it hurt?" Elena's forehead scrunched up. "I felt the energy zap you."

"Not so much pain as . . . I believe your body is telling me the area is private and to stop poking around."

Keir was more careful when he chanced a touch, but got a jolt, too.

Despite the hazard, the two healers did a thorough examination. When they were satisfied they'd seen the entirety of it, Elena shifted back to lean against the headboard. "Bad news?"

"No news is the better descriptor." Lines marked the corners of Keir's eyes, unfamiliar etchings on a face that had always been flawless in its delicate beauty. "It is tempting to compare your wings to an angelic infant's, but that feels wrong. Nisia?"

"I agree. She has far more sensory capacity than a babe." Nisia frowned at a reading on the device in her hand. "Infants do not sense their wings until they gain an understanding of what they are."

"Guess it'd be confusing for them if they can't see what's there." Elena tapped a finger on the sheet. "Makes sense it'd be different for an adult."

"It's as if certain elements of your body have been scrambled." Nisia touched a strand of Elena's hair. "You have tiny feathers in your hair, while we have found no indication of wing understructure on your back."

"We *have* discovered evidence that this marking you call a tattoo extends deep, through all the layers of your flesh."

"Give it to me straight—is this it?" Firm voice, unflinching gaze, Elena's question demanded utter honesty. "Am I stuck with a tattoo or is there a chance my wings might grow back?"

Keir's timeless eyes held Elena's. "I can give you no definite answers. This is a thing that has never happened." A smile as gentle as his voice. "You keep being new, Elena."

Nisia, still staring down at her device, murmured, "Are you hungry?"

"Yes, it's weird." Elena made a face. "Those immortal ringworms are hard at it."

Nisia's lips twitched. "Tapeworms, my dear, tapeworms." She showed the screen of the device to Keir. "If I'm reading this correctly, her skin depth has increased by point two millimeters in the minutes since I took the first reading."

Elena stilled. *Archangel, did Nisia just say what I think she said?*

Yes, I believe so. Your body is rapidly burning fuel to make you stronger. His hands clenched to bone whiteness on the headboard. *It is why an archangel eats with vigor after the deep, healing rest of* anshara. *The food replaces the energy used during the healing process. It also helps complete final repairs.*

She lifted a hand to touch his. *And I've got a chunk of your heart booming away in my chest.*

"IV nutrition," Nisia said after she and Keir finished consulting with each other. "It's a much faster way to get calories into you."

The healers sprang into action on those words, and Elena was soon hooked up to a drip in either arm. As Keir was explaining that the IVs were set up to release their contents over the course of an hour, golden lightning zapped up the lines and sucked the bags dry.

"Whoa."

11

Eight bags later and Elena could see the change: she was now extremely thin rather than skeletal. People might comment on her being all skin and bone, but they wouldn't call the undertaker on her.

Her wing tattoo, however, remained unchanged. Keir and Nisia couldn't find any sign that she'd begun to develop the understructure needed for flight. It was a blow, but she wasn't giving up; angelic bodies healed by priority. Critical organs first, then skin and limbs. Wings fell in the latter category.

"Stop," Elena said when Nisia went to grab bags nine and ten. "I think I've reached maximum capacity for processing calories in one go." Her yawn cracked her face. "My body's going to conk out soon"—sudden lethargy weighed down her shoulders, made her eyelids droop—"but first I need to make some calls."

Archangel, she said mind-to-mind, her heart aching, *when you have time, will you bring me the quilt my mom made for me?* She'd left it in the storage locker all this time, the sweet loving memory of it too entwined with pain, but today, she wanted her mother's embrace in whatever way she could have it.

I will do it as soon as I finish talking to Dmitri—he is waiting outside. Pressing a kiss to her lips, Raphael passed over a phone he'd asked Montgomery to bring up, then he and the healers walked out.

Keir and Nisia had their heads together. The two needed to process the readings and samples they'd taken, while Raphael had to meet with his second. She knew what it had taken for him to leave her, blew him a mental kiss. He turned at the doorway, his gaze shot with lightning. "Rest, *hheehti*. You can play with your crossbow tomorrow."

"Hah." Sliding down the bed as he shut the door behind him, she brought up the phone. It took her two tries to input Sara's number.

"Hello." A noncommittal answer from the director of the Guild; she was no doubt wondering how the hell a stranger had gotten through to her private line.

"No, you didn't accidentally eat LSD-laced fish," Elena said to her best friend, referring back to their conversation when she'd first woken as an angel.

Silence from the other end, before Sara said, "Ellie, I'm going to strangle you this time."

Elena grinned despite her heavy lids. Because this was her and Sara. Real. Normal. Friends. "I look so pathetic and spindly right now that I bet you'd feel guilty doing it." Though that wouldn't last long if she kept processing fuel at this rate. Already, she could feel her muscles strengthening, her bones gaining heft.

"Ellie." Sara's voice was thick. "I'm coming over."

"No, give me a few days. I'm probably going to be asleep for most of them." She yawned so hugely she was sure her face would crack. "How's Eve?"

"Acting out. She stole Ransom's motorcycle from the Academy lot and took it for a joyride."

Eve had always been scarily well-behaved. "Hey, we turned out fine and we once stole a Cadillac."

"Borrowed," Sara said pointedly. "The director of the Guild can't be a felon."

Another giant yawn broke Elena's laughter in two.

"Ellie, you sure I can't run over there and give you a hug?"

"No, not yet. I need recovery time." Seeing her this way would undo any good her call had achieved. "I've got to touch base with a few other people before I fall asleep. But I'm back and I'm not going anywhere."

Ending the call with Sara soon afterward, her limbs so heavy by now that they felt like lead, she tapped in the number for her younger sister. It was a miracle she remembered any numbers at all with the sleep-fogginess in her brain.

Beth turned out to be with Majda and Jean-Baptiste Etienne—two people who'd already suffered unimaginable torture and loss. Her grandmother broke down in tears at the sound of her voice, while her grandfather was stolid but shaken.

Beth was mute.

Elena would deal with this, find some way to make emotional recompense for the pain she'd inflicted, but she'd do it face-to-face not over a telephone line. Promising to call again soon, she hung up and, eyes too heavy to keep open, dialed Eve.

Her youngest half sister didn't pick up.

So Elena called five times in a row—until Eve finally answered with a snarled, "What?!"

"I hope you didn't scratch Ransom's bike. He's in love with that—"

"Ellie!" It was a scream.

The rest of the conversation was rapid and excited and Elena had to talk her sister down from stealing another ride and zooming over to the Tower then and there.

After reluctantly agreeing to wait to visit, Eve said, "Shall I tell Father?"

Elena's body stiffened, nervous tension acting as adrenaline in her veins. "Are you home?"

"Yeah. Grounded." The teenage eye-roll was almost audible. "I stayed out past curfew, then came home and decided to drink Father's expensive brandy. Stuff is gross. I poured most of it in the garden, but he's convinced I'm an alcoholic."

Beth, Majda, and Jean-Baptiste weren't the only ones to whom she owed an apology. This girl wasn't the tough but stable little sweetheart who'd held Elena's hand the last time they'd seen one another. Anger lived in her now. But it would have to wait until she could put her arms around Eve and hold on tight.

"Take him the phone." Jeffrey and Elena might never heal the fractures between them, but she wouldn't add to his torment.

Jeffrey Deveraux had already lost a beloved wife and two cherished daughters. The man who had married Eve and Amy's mother, Gwendolyn, wasn't the same Jeffrey who'd blown bubbles with Elena in a sunny backyard or the one who'd fought for her right to see her dead sisters' bodies. She'd needed to know the monster hadn't made Ari and Belle like him, so Jeffrey had taken her to them. He'd held her hand. And he'd cried.

He hadn't been the best father, but he didn't deserve the horrific pain of thinking he'd lost a third daughter.

"Father," she heard Eve say, "someone wants to talk to you."

Elena could imagine her father's raised eyebrow at anyone calling him on his daughter's phone, knew he was most likely removing his wire-rimmed spectacles as he considered whether to take the call without asking for further information. CEO of a mega-empire with fingers in every pie in the city, Jeffrey was not a man who liked a lack of control.

Today, however, whatever he saw on Eve's face had him coming on the line. "Jeffrey Deveraux."

"It's Ellie."

The silence this time was piercing.

"We'll talk more later. Tell Eve I'll call back to let her know when she can visit." Elena hung up with that—she felt cowardly for it, but a girl had her limits. She'd just emerged from a chrysalis that wanted to consume her like a tasty snack and her body was falling asleep around her; she wasn't ready to deal with Jeffrey and the complicated history that tied them together.

An echo of memory, the scent of his aftershave suddenly bright and clear. He'd given her his scarf so she wouldn't be cold. She'd accepted it because it wasn't only pain that lay between them but a thousand childhood moments of happiness and family. Her and Jeffrey, they'd never be easy with one another, but at times, they managed to meet halfway, the recriminations and the hurt held at bay.

The brush of a slender hand on her brow. *Sleep,* azeeztee. Maman *is here to watch over you. Don't worry about your papa—I will make it right.*

Even mostly asleep, Elena knew her mother was dead, that this was the phantom of a memory . . . but she decided to believe. Just for this fragment of a moment when she was hurt and tired and beginning again. "*Maman* . . ." The phone slipped unheeded from her fingers, her body crashing into sleep.

Lightning danced over her skin, her veins a glowing network hidden by the sheet.

12

Raphael knew why it was only Dmitri who'd come up to the balcony outside his and Elena's living area. He and his second, they had a unique relationship. Raphael might've been several hundred years old when he first met Dmitri, but Dmitri had been a married man by then, a farmer confident in his skin and open in his love for his wife.

The two of them, they'd always met as equals.

As he stepped out onto the balcony, his second turned and looked at him with dark eyes that gave nothing away . . . but he strode across the space to meet Raphael halfway. They raised their right hands, clasped each other's forearms, leaned in for the embrace of warriors. "It is good to have you back." Dmitri's voice was potent with emotions unspoken but understood. "I'm putting in for ten years' vacation leave starting today."

"That bad?" Raphael asked as they drew back.

"Charisemnon keeps trying his luck, Neha watches in enigmatic silence, Michaela's disappeared into her mountains, and China's lost so many people without explanation that large swathes of it are silent."

"Michaela?" he said, picking out the most intriguing detail among all that Dmitri had recited.

His second folded his arms, biceps taut and skin a bronzed hue that would hold its color even in the heart of winter. "Jason's confirmed she's in her stronghold near Budapest, but she hasn't been seen in flight for at least five months." A shrug. "No one's dared misbehave in her territory yet. Her generals have orders to kill at any sign of insurrection. That's it. No other punishment. Straight up beheading. It's efficient."

Raphael couldn't disagree with the admiration in Dmitri's voice. It was a simple and effective way to keep a territory in control while the archangel in charge went dark. "It's not unknown for archangels to go under for months at a time." Even members of the Cadre occasionally needed time to simply exist.

Raphael was too young to feel the urge, but he knew his mother had taken such time during his years as a child. "Michaela's not much older than I am." A matter of five hundred years, give or take. "But she has recently had to deal with a meat 'infant' and possession by Uram. Perhaps it has put her in a bad mood."

Dmitri barked out a laugh. "I can see her sitting in a funk in her stronghold. At least she's not creating more problems. Charisemnon, on the other hand, is being an asshole—it's only having Titus at his border that's keeping him in check."

"The birds and cats are Eli's?"

A short nod. "I found a damn lynx on the hood of my Ferrari the other day. Thing snarled at me." Scowling, he continued on. "In other interesting news, Suyin asked to relocate to New York and go into combat training. I authorized it, put her under Honor's tutelage."

Raphael raised an eyebrow. With skin of cool white and hair of ice white, her cheekbones sharp as blades, Lijuan's niece could've been her aunt's twin if not for her dark eyes and the beauty spot under the corner of her left eye—and her lack of a killing instinct. Suyin had been Lijuan's prisoner for thousands upon thousands of years, a fragile artistic being so traumatized that she was fading from life when rescued.

Dmitri nodded. "I wasn't expecting that, either, but Honor says she's a quick study and determined to be ready to fight Lijuan when her aunt rises again."

"A motive to be respected. Especially after the torture she suffered under Lijuan."

His second's expression was dark, but his tone pragmatic as he continued his update. "Haven't heard much from Astaad and Alexander—they've both been busy coping with massive ice storms."

Parts of Alexander's desert territory were susceptible to ice, but Astaad's territory was nearly all tropical. "The islands?"

Dmitri nodded. "Residents barely own cardigans, much less snow gear. I've sent supplies and so have Michaela and Lady Caliane." He shoved a hand through the black of his hair. "That's not all of it—Alexander's also been hit with flash floods, while the monsoon season in Neha's territory is threatening to become monsoon year."

"Elijah?"

"Plagues of wasps. Swarms have killed at least ten people so far." He braced his hands on his hips. "Titus and Charisemnon have the opposite problem to Neha: drought. Wildfires are running rampant across the savannah."

"It's gotten worse."

A nod from his second. "We've been lucky in the scheme of things. A couple of torrential lightning storms, a few more minor geothermal issues in the area you already evacuated, and, bizarrely, an infestation of ladybug beetles in a small town. No damage from the bugs, but they creeped out a bunch of people."

Dmitri cocked an eyebrow. "Did you know fear of ladybugs has a name? Coccinellidaephobia."

It was an amusing thing he'd have to tell Elena. The rest however . . . "Favashi?"

"No sign of her since she disappeared into the lava with Cassandra. As for her territory—Lady Caliane keeps me updated when she isn't threatening to boil me alive for not letting her see you, and she says that while Neha's had to cope with some refugees from China, it's nowhere near the number she expected. Not even after accounting for the vanished villages."

"Lijuan's people are loyal." Many would say to the edge of madness. "Aodhan, Naasir, and Galen remain at the Refuge?"

"Yes. Galen wanted to send the others back to New York, but I told them to stay. I didn't want to leave him without powerful backup."

Raphael locked eyes with Dmitri. "What has happened?" Galen was Raphael's weapons-master and well able to deal with any threat excepting attack by one of the Cadre.

"Things are moving under the Refuge."

The Refuge *never* shook. Legend said it had been anchored by the cataclysmic power of Sleepers who wished never to wake. "Do not tell me you believe in the legend of the Ancestors, Dmitri?" Said to slumber below the Refuge, the Ancestors were whispered to be the first of Raphael's kind, angels so old they were another species.

"Sire, at this point, I'm ready to believe in the fucking tooth fairy."

Raphael clasped his second on the shoulder. "Thank you for holding my Tower safe."

"Next time, I'd appreciate you warning your mother that you're about to take a nap." A black scowl. "Lady Caliane's last threat included having me drawn and quartered."

"You survived." That he had was a measure of his mettle; Raphael's mother, after all, was an Ancient.

Dmitri's next question was quiet. "Elena?" A worry in his dark eyes that would astonish Raphael's consort, the two were such determined adversaries.

"The Cascade has underestimated my hunter's will." He opened out his wings to check their status. They remained aflame but the odd feather was beginning to show through, so the white fire was apt to settle in the coming hours. "I must go and close the chasm from which Elena and I arose."

"Raphael." Arms folded again and feet set apart, Dmitri got in his way. "Contact your mother before you go or I swear I'll tie your wings together and drag you inside to make the call."

The cold power in him whispered for him to take offense at such insubordination, but Raphael had no intention of becoming its puppet. "I will do it as soon as I fulfil a promise to Elena." Dmitri was right—Caliane might've once been mad, might've left him bleeding and broken in a forgotten field, but she'd risen sane and she'd been firmly on his side since.

Nodding, Dmitri left to return to his duties, while Raphael swept off the balcony to head to the storage unit where Elena kept her childhood. She visited the space regularly, made sure her things were free of dust, told him stories about pieces when he was with her, but while she'd given her sister Beth anything she wanted from within, she'd never brought a single item home herself. Today, however, when he returned with the quilt and opened it over her, she tugged it closer and snuggled down.

He brushed his hand over the near-white silk of her hair, what he felt for her such a huge violence inside him that it had no name. "To the end and beyond, hunter-mine."

Forcing himself out of the room, he shut the door quietly behind himself, then went to the screen mounted on one wall of the suite's library. He could've used a phone to call Amanat, but Caliane didn't trust in such things. She was barely comfortable with the system that allowed them to see each other as they spoke.

The face that answered on the other end was a familiar one: uptilted eyes of dramatic green, hair of a deep, deep red, skin that was close to translucent and wings of copper silk.

Tasha would never pass unnoticed through a crowd.

Her eyes widened at seeing him, a gasp exiting her throat. But the woman—and warrior—who'd been his lover when they were young angels first spreading their wings was already moving out of shot, and he knew she was getting his mother.

Tasha was as loyal to Caliane as Dmitri was to Raphael.

When Caliane appeared on the other side, it was with a frown marring her forehead. "What—" She cut herself off, her face softening in a way it only ever did for Raphael. Placing her hand on the screen on her side, she whispered, "My son. You are home."

Raphael echoed her gesture on this side, placing his palm over hers. "We will speak further soon, Mother. I must take care of my territory now."

Caliane had been an archangel longer than Raphael could imagine; she didn't argue against his priorities. "That upstart vampire you call second needs to learn how to speak to his elders, but he has done you proud." Regal and a touch haughty, Caliane's words nonetheless held the approbation of an archangel who had never been afraid to have strong people around her. She had taught him how to rule by example.

Until the madness. Until the death.

"I never doubted he would." He inclined his head. "I will go now."

"Before you do—your consort?"

Once, that might've been a barbed question, but Caliane and Elena had made their peace. It would always be an odd peace with jagged edges, but that was what happened when two strong women collided and one of them was used to being obeyed in all things—while the other obeyed only the dictates of her conscience.

"She is resting," was all Raphael said; he and Elena would have to speak when she woke, decide their next course of action. Until then, he'd share nothing of her physical state.

After ending the call, he looked into the bedroom. A glint of hair of near-white . . . and the muted glow of her skin beneath the quilt. His hunter was curled up on her side in a tight ball, her knees tucked to her chest and her spine curved, her head curled over her knees. The tattoo on her back pulsed with light in time with her heartbeat.

Jaw clenched, he fought the urge to shake her awake from that torturously constricted position that had permitted her to emerge from the chrysalis with all her limbs. He lost the battle. *Elena.*

A sleepy mumble from her mind, the warm steel of her presence a kiss.

Muscle memory, he told himself. That was all. But he touched the back of his hand to her cheek to reassure himself of the life of her.

Sighing, she snuggled deeper into the bed . . . just as droplets of fire fell from his wings to dance over the exposed side of her face. She shivered as first one small flame sank into her flesh, then another, but didn't wake.

The power spread under her skin in a soft burst that made her veins pulse a luminous gold for a startling second before the effect faded into a softer radiance. Soft or not, his hunter remained very much "glow-in-the-dark."

He could imagine her displeased scowl when she woke.

Leaning down, he pressed his lips to her cheek. "If it is any consolation hunter-mine, my wings continue to burn and my eyes are alive with lightning."

Archangel. A soft, sleepy murmur from a mind caught in deepest sleep but aware of him and what he meant to her.

The hand clenched around his heart stopped squeezing. *Sleep,* hbeebti. *I will be home soon.*

He stopped long enough to pull on a sleeveless tunic, and put into his pocket a set of small sample bags Keir had left behind. "Your scientists," the healer had said, "will no doubt appreciate any samples you are able to retrieve from the chasm."

As he took flight from the balcony off their bedroom, he paid attention to the performance of his wings, checked his speed. Everything felt as it ever had, as if he had flesh and blood, feathers and bone and tendon under his command.

Satisfied with his ability to control his body in the air, he swept across the glittering sunlit skyscrapers of his city, past the showy forms of trees ablaze with one last burst of color before their winter slumber, and over the chilly waters of the Hudson. Calmer now, it glimmered under the early afternoon sunshine, sparkles dancing off its surface.

He could see Illium's wings from here, the wild blue vibrant even against the crystalline blue of the sky, the silver filaments bright shards. The angel held a hover near the edge of the cliffs. He'd also ordered members of his squadron and of the Legion to create a wide barrier around the dangerous hole in the ground.

No unauthorized wings moved in the air above, and no one walked anywhere in sight. *Illium, have there been any reports of casualties in the Enclave?*

No. I had members of the squadron fly over the area—they reported no fallen or wounded individuals.

Angling his body to wing high above Illium and the others, Raphael took in the wound in the earth. From so far above, it was a dark blot in the landscape, a scar that should not exist.

No power swirled in or around it. No lava glowed.

Dropping down, he landed on the very edge of the hole. Illium and the Primary soon came to land on either side of him. When he glanced at the Primary, he saw a strange thing: the Primary was now almost completely colorless. The transition had begun before Raphael went to sleep in the bed beside Elena.

The second becoming, that's what the Legion had told Elena when she asked why they were losing the colors that had begun to appear in some of them. As Elena had regressed back into humanity, the Legion had regressed into the grayness that was the color palette with which they'd risen from the lightless deep.

But Elena was no longer mortal, and yet the Primary remained colorless. "Has the second becoming ended?"

The Primary tilted his head to the side. "No," he said after a pause to consider the question. "We are deciding."

Putting the matter aside for now, Raphael looked into the chasm created by the power that was ice in his veins. Such a cold, *cold* power. A power that whispered in his ear that Lijuan was an imposter and he was the true god.

The one who should be worshipped.

13

A kiss of heat inside him, a pulse of defiant life. A piece of Elena's heart, refusing to surrender him to the immortal cold.

Raphael fisted his hand. "I'm going to fly down and ensure there are no hidden dangers." As he would not become a mindless tool for the Cascade, he would not build his and Elena's home on poisoned soil.

Illium stirred. "Sire, you just emerged. I'd rather you didn't disappear back into the black hole."

The angel with eyes of aged gold and a face of pure beauty—gaunt now in a way angels rarely became—was too young to give Raphael orders. Their relationship was far different from the one Raphael had with Dmitri. Raphael had held Illium as a newborn, known him as an unwieldy child angel with wings he could barely control.

He'd watched the youth Illium had become fall so madly in love that his heart had broken forever with the loss of his mortal lover. And he had known Illium as a young warrior who mourned the loss of a friend who had been trapped inside his own torment for two hundred years.

All these things and more made up the ties between Raphael and Illium. "I have nothing to fear down there," he said, for the greatest risk was in his blood, in the power that sought constantly to shape him into a weapon of chaos.

Lijuan believed herself a goddess, so he must be a god.

The Cascade was nothing if not a blunt hammer.

"If I cannot contact you"—Illium set his jaw—"I'll fly in to search for you."

"Let us hope it doesn't come to that." Raphael stepped into the chasm, his wings spread to control his descent.

His primaries didn't come close to touching the edges.

In places, the walls around him were glassy. Either the energy he'd released had solidified natural minerals into a glassy surface, or pieces of their home had become bonded to the earth. Here and there, he saw the odd item he recognized—a spoon, part of a stair railing—but the majority had been pulverized.

Sorrow sang an unexpected song in his heart. The Enclave home was where he'd first made love to Elena. It was a place all of his Seven had called home many times over their lifetimes. It was where he'd begun a friendship with Elijah. And it was the house in which his mother had come to stay after waking from madness.

But . . . he'd built this home as a lone archangel. He would rebuild it as one half of an unbreakable pair.

Most of the earth is simply compacted, he told Illium. *I should be able to churn up the dirt so that the walls collapse inward, eliminating most of the hole. What space remains, we will fill using soil excavated from other areas.*

That new skyscraper being built in Soho, Illium said. *Tons of earth just sitting around. I'll put a squadron on standby to bring across as much as we need.*

Raphael continued his descent. There were no scorch marks, nothing that indicated a raging fire. Just crushed and broken things that spoke to the violence of the power inside him. Halfway down, he halted and placed his hand against the soil, felt a faint warmth—it was an echo, an imprint left behind by the energy that crawled across his wings and lived in his bloodstream.

He kept on dropping.

A glint caught his eye. After tracing his way back to the spot, he laughed at what he saw. Carefully digging out the leather-bound book with gold lettering on the spine, he dusted it off and put it in a side pocket of his pants. Elena would be aghast that of all their books, it was Imani's tome on angelic etiquette that had survived unscathed.

He picked up nothing else on the way down and was soon standing with his feet on the earth where he had awoken with Elena. Pieces of the chrysalis lay broken around the imprint of his consort's body. Crouching down, he reached out to touch one.

It crumbled into dust so fine it was mist in the air.

Nothing but a discarded shell. Devoid of Elena's energy, it could not exist. He took a sample of the dust for the scientists in any case, stored it away with Imani's worthy tome.

As he rose back to his feet, he found himself searching for a mind so old it made his bones ache. *Cassandra?*

Silence. Not even the distant murmur of a presence. Yet he had no doubts the lava shield had been hers. Perhaps she hadn't even been aware of it, the act done by the last vestiges of her conscious mind. He would have to speak to Elena, confirm whether she sensed any remnants of the Ancient's consciousness. The archangel with the terrible gift of foresight had always spoken to his hunter the most.

For Elena was Cassandra's prophecy.

After taking another look around to ensure he'd missed nothing, Raphael spread out his wings and began the flight upward. He scanned the walls as he flew, but the only other thing he recovered was a spoon that had been bent and twisted into such a strange and complicated shape that he thought Elena would find it intriguing.

As he slipped it into a pocket, he considered whether she would want to decorate their new home herself . . . and laughed at the sudden impression of utter horrified negation that came through loud and clear. *Guild Hunter?* He hadn't realized he'd reached for her until her response.

Go away. Am sleeping. A grumble of words. *Woke up at nightmare image of having to choose paint colors and carpets for formal dining and living areas. I can make a nest of our suite, but then you're on your own.* Her mind was already fading as she spoke the last words, her body too exhausted to do anything but rest.

But she'd left him with a smile on his face. The two of them would put their stamp on the house in ways that mattered, with items that held meaning to them, but otherwise, they would rely on Montgomery. As Raphael had done once before. A relatively new archangel at the time, he'd been content to live in the first iteration of his Tower—his household staff had consisted only of his cook, Sivya, and her assistant. It was Neha on whose advice he'd built the Enclave home.

"This land is young as you are young," she'd said on her visit. "It suits you—but your Tower is a rough construct. Some in the Cadre will look down their nose at your lack of a formal court and consider you weaker because of it. You must build a residence fit for an archangel."

During the build—to which Raphael had lent his strength—he'd begun to notice that nothing was ever out of place at certain times of day. Tools were clean and sharpened; water, mead, food, and blood supplies provided like clockwork; broken items replaced and the detritus taken away.

When he'd asked Dmitri who was responsible, he'd been introduced to a dark-haired vampire who met his eyes only in flashes, the physical scars of his human life as a low servant yet apparent on his face and upper body. But even then, Montgomery had not flinched at being in the presence of an archangel.

By the end of the build, Raphael had such faith in the quiet and hardworking vampire that he'd put Montgomery in charge of furnishing the entire house. *That* was when Montgomery had flinched. "But, sire, I am only a servant!"

"You are a man who notices the smallest detail. I have faith in your ability to create a home suitable for an archangel."

It had taken Montgomery a year. He'd asked if he could go to Neha's court, to Titus's, to Uram's, to Lijuan's, so he could see examples of an archangelic home, and Raphael had sent him off with suave and sophisticated Trace as a guide.

Montgomery had come back with painstakingly knotted silk carpets from India, wall hangings from Africa, a hand-carved settee from the hinterland of Uram's territory, artisan-painted screens from China.

He'd also returned with a statuette he'd found "abandoned" in Neha's court.

It had taken Raphael two decades to realize that Montgomery had "rescued" the item because it wasn't being appreciated. By then, the vampire was running his home with elegant efficiency and his tendency to rescue items now and then was a small peccadillo. Raphael quietly returned what needed to be returned, and Montgomery continued to ensure his house was a stunning showpiece in the formal areas—and a welcoming haven elsewhere.

Emerging into the sunshine on that thought, he told both Illium and the Primary to clear the skies and to ensure no one had returned to nearby homes since their earlier evacuation. "I do not foresee a second explosion but let us not take any chances."

Only once the two confirmed the area remained devoid of unauthorized life did Raphael drop back down into the chasm. Halting a quarter of the way up from the bottom, he began to surgically target the walls with his power. What emerged from his hands was a melding of vivid blue and lightning-shot gold.

The archangel he had been and the archangel he was becoming.

He had to recalculate after the first hit did more damage than good; his power was violently strong, more so than prior to the chrysalis. It took him three strikes to gain an accurate gauge of what was needed. The chasm began to crumple inward with slow grace below him as he flew up, continuing to weaken the walls as he went.

This time when he shot out into the fall sunshine, it was to turn and see the scar in the earth collapsing behind him. The rumble of sound was huge and dull, and it seemed that the soil moved in slow motion. But dust soon puffed into the air, the rumble ceasing as the earth settled. Loosened by his strikes, much of the compacted soil had released itself back into the chasm, but a significant dent remained.

Wings of blue edged in silver in his peripheral vision. *I will take care of it, sire.*

Raphael nodded. With Elena resting, her Bluebell would miss nothing while he completed this task. Raphael, meanwhile, needed to fly over his territory, take stock of what had happened in his absence—and remind the world that the Archangel of New York was back. Complete with wings of white fire and a cold power that had torn a hole in the fabric of the earth.

Elena opened her eyes in a familiar kitchen, the warm smell of baking in the air. Smiling, she ran her fingers along

the counter and called out her sisters' names as she walked
toward the back door. The grass outside shimmered emerald
under a soft sun, Marguerite's flowers bobbing prettily in the
garden she'd planted a month earlier.

Elena had helped. She'd dug her hands into the soil and
carefully placed each small seedling. "Will they flower soon,
Maman?" she'd asked.

"Yes, these ones will." Marguerite's fine-boned face was
shaded by the large white hat she always wore in the garden,
but Elena had heard her smile. "They are pretty things that
grow quickly and only last one season, but ah, such joy they
give us for that season, *non?*"

Elena, her own hat on, snug and dirty "gardening" sneakers
on her feet, had nodded. "Yes, this garden is pretty."

"A fleeting, bright beauty."

Beyond the garden, at the back of the yard, Elena saw a
woman sitting in the swing Elena's papa had created using a
plank strung with ropes to the branches of a big tree. The
woman's legs were long, the dress that covered her body a
gown of frothing pale green that licked around her ankles.

Elena had never seen such hair: waves of purest lilac that
fell down her back like water, arresting against the woman's
pearl white skin. Her wings were lovely arcs of violet so deep
it was blue, and her eyes . . .

"Why can I see your eyes?" Elena crossed the grass to sit
on the swing that had appeared beside Cassandra. Though
they had met only in thought, she had no doubts that this was
the Ancient cursed with the gift of foresight. And she felt no
surprise that Cassandra was here, in this place that was Elena's pocket of memory.

Those eyes of an extraordinary and unexpected seafoam
green that bled into indigo with edges of clear-sky blue turned
incandescent with the light of Cassandra's smile. Twin auroras
of breathtaking beauty.

"This is your dream, child, and it appears you do not wish
to see blood." A deepening of Cassandra's smile. "I have not
seen the serene and the peaceful through my eyes for an eternity. I had forgotten such hues existed."

Elena kicked off the ground to swing gently beside Cassandra. The skirts of the Ancient's dress rippled in the wind

as they swung. Her own legs, Elena saw, were clad in black hunting boots and black pants. "I thought you went to Sleep?"

"I did, but still I dream." A sigh. "I wish I did not, but the dreams are so vivid they disturb my rest."

"Your voice is different." Young, without the weight of incredible age.

"This is a young place." Hands clasped around the ropes of the swing and bare feet held off the ground, Cassandra looked around. "Happiness lives here."

"Yes." Elena nudged aside the nagging feeling that the happiness wouldn't last, that the sunshine would soon be clouded. "Did you just come to visit?"

Cassandra stopped swinging and gave her a strange, thoughtful look with those eyes so lovely and haunting, strands of her hair flirting with her cheek. "I have not just visited anyone for . . ." Her hands tightened on the ropes.

"You don't have to remember," Elena reassured her. "Sometimes, I don't like to remember." Shadows danced in the kitchen windows, and Elena told herself that was her *maman*, moving about as she made Elena's favorite cookies. Or maybe it was Belle grabbing a soda after her dance lesson. It might even be Ari, come to find a snack. That was all. Nothing else. Nothing dark.

"It has never been the remembering that is the problem. It is the seeing." Despite the lonely darkness of her words, Cassandra began to swing again. "I came to give you a gift, prophecy of mine, but I find it difficult to form the thought. Most of me is Sleeping."

"I'm resting, too," Elena shared, suddenly certain of that. "My wings are nothing but color and hope." Her back felt empty, a needed weight missing. "Do you think I'll fly again?" In the dreamscape, the potent emotion of the question was a distant cloud on the horizon.

Lilac hair streamed behind Cassandra as she pushed herself higher and higher on the swing. She didn't answer for a long time, but that was all right, because Elena was swinging, too. It was on a whoosh back that she heard Cassandra call out, "We are flying now!"

Elena laughed and kicked her feet even harder.

And she forgot that Cassandra was in her dream for a reason.

14

Coming awake on a yawn, Elena rubbed knuckled fists over her eyes. "As far as my dreams go," she muttered to no one in particular, "that one wasn't too weird at all."

A rustle that sounded like wings settling. But not angelic wings. The sound was too small. She lifted her lashes and found the room draped in the deep orange-gold light of late afternoon or very early evening. Someone had pulled back the blackout curtains but left the gauzy curtains as they were.

Those curtains were moving in the wind, the balcony doors having been cracked open. The latter couldn't have been for long because the room was nice and warm . . . but it had been long enough for a snow-white owl to wander inside. It stretched its wings again before looking at her with eyes of shining gold.

It looked so real, not an illusion at all. When it walked back out through the doors, the curtain draped over its body. She saw it sweep away into the sunset light, silent and lovely. A second owl joined it moments later. Beautiful, unearthly creatures who'd never done her harm, but who'd been harbingers of so much pain to come.

I came to give you a gift.

Elena gasped in a breath; she'd inadvertently held her breath since her first glimpse of the owl. "Thank you," she whispered; she knew how much Cassandra loved her owls.

No ancient mind in her head, not even a faint sign that Cassandra had heard.

Oddly disappointed, she sat up properly . . . and saw the crutches leaning up against the bedside table. "Nisia, I love you." It had to be the Tower healer who'd thought of that; she'd been around Elena enough not to expect good behavior. Sans crutches, Elena would've probably settled on crawling to the facilities.

She did *not* need an audience while she did her business.

Too much the hunter not to understand her body, however, she spent several minutes stretching in bed before she slid her arms into the crutches, took a firm grip on the handles, and got herself up. "Woohoo!"

Unfortunately, her celebrations proved premature; her knees began to crumple the instant she tested putting weight on her legs rather than the crutches. "Okay, then, no miracle cure." She hadn't expected one, but a girl had to try.

At least her arms and shoulders were working well enough to utilize the crutches. She managed to close the balcony doors and reinstate the thicker curtains, then get herself to the bathroom and do what needed to be done. The lure of the shower was too much to resist so, after a moment's thought, she turned on the water, then sat down in the huge shower cubicle designed for wings.

She shampooed her hair half expecting the teeny feathers to fall off, but nope, they stayed happily attached to the strands on her head. Truth be told, she was kind of fond of those feathers. They were a marker of survival as far as she was concerned. It felt luxuriant to put conditioner in her hair, then run a loofah over her skin after she lathered it with a special macadamia oil-infused soap that she'd bought from a stall in Times Square before everything turned to custard.

"I've been in a chrysalis for months," she muttered. "I deserve fancy soap." The scent of the soap, the heat of the water on her skin, it was pure heaven, but her muscles were quivering by the end.

Not in the mood to be hauled out naked even by Keir and Nisia, she congratulated herself on having had the foresight to put several towels right outside the shower. After switching off the water, she grabbed the top towel from the pile and dried off her hair and most of her body while still seated.

She then spread the used towel on the floor of the cubicle so she wouldn't slip as she got to her knees, grabbed the crutches from outside the door, and hauled herself to her feet. The maneuver left her breathless, her huge heart pumping double-time, but she wasn't sorry in the least.

Her next achievement was to get her skinny ass to the glass shelf on which she kept her pampering supplies. Managing to grab a thick tube of body lotion using her teeth, she carried it back to the bed. Not elegant but it got the job done.

Collapsing onto her back on the bed, she gave herself a good few minutes to recover before she sat up and, switching on a bedside lamp, began to work the body lotion into her skin. She examined her body with a critical eye at the same time. Her skin continued to glow, but it had quieted down to a significant extent. Looked like the glow-in-the-dark phase of her life was on its way out.

Eerie inner luminescence aside, her skin was its natural hue—a dark gold that came to her via her grandmother's Moroccan heritage—but it appeared fragile, her veins dangerously visible. In better news, her bones did appear to have a normal heft and strength to them. She'd ask Nisia to check for tunnels or hollow patches but right now, her bones looked to be the strongest part of her body.

After finishing with the body lotion, she touched her face, found sharp cheekbones, and jawbones defined enough for the runway, but it felt like her skin was stronger there. "Let's hope that means good things for the rest of me." Recovered enough to attempt a bit more bad behavior, she made her way to the closet and snagged the summer pajamas Sara had given her for her last birthday.

At least not all her clothes had been destroyed.

The bottoms of the pjs were pink and white striped shorts with white lace trim, the top a silky-soft pink T-shirt with a scooped neck and a white print—the silhouette of two angels kissing in the moonlight. Elena loved it, not just for the design but for the softness of the fabric. It'd also work to give the healers access to her body while keeping her from flashing the world.

She wasn't even going to try for a bra. Neither Keir nor Nisia would even notice she had breasts unless those breasts started sprouting tendrils or spontaneously grew two nipples each. Grinning, she took the clothes back to the bed, and got dressed sitting up.

Next, she sent a message to Nisia alerting the healer she was up: no sense wasting time. The more calories they could get into her, the faster she'd be back to full strength. Then, phone gripped in her teeth, she hobbled her way to the living area. *Archangel?* She reached out with her mind as her ass hit the sofa cushions, the compulsion to ensure Raphael was okay not one she could fight. Not this close to their return.

The salt-laced sea crashed into her mind, the feel of Raphael a touch distant. *Elena-mine.*

A movement outside the uncurtained balcony doors caught her attention before she could reply. Her eyes widened. *Birds in the sky, but non-creepy.* An important fact. *Condors. Three of them sweeping and dipping just off the balcony.*

Even though she was still breathless from the trip to the living area, she got up and hobbled over. She knew the temperature outside was liable to have dropped, but she opened the doors nonetheless so she could watch the birds without the barrier of glass. Not that she was stupid about it. She stayed firmly in the doorway, a good distance from the open edge of the railingless balcony.

Are the birds doing anything of note?

Raphael's voice was stronger and more resonant now; he had to be heading back toward Manhattan.

I think they're leaving. The three birds she'd seen had just joined a much larger group. *A massive vee of them, heading south.* The sight of so many birds of prey together was beyond majestic.

I have spoken to Dmitri, Raphael said after a short pause. *He tells me the pumas and other large cats are also departing the city.*

Elena shivered as the wind blew her hair off her face, but she stayed in place, her gaze on the departing wave of birds.

Elijah must've gotten word of Raphael's return, was retreating from his fellow archangel's territory before Raphael had to ask. A friendship between two archangels would always be a finely balanced thing—there was too much power involved for it to be otherwise.

The condors a distant blur now, she turned and got the doors closed with creative use of her crutches. Right as Nisia walked through the door. "Of course you are not resting like a sensible being who just emerged from a chrysalis," the diminutive healer muttered, her ankle-length gown a dark blue that Elena hadn't properly noticed before. As always with Nisia's work clothes, it was simple but beautifully stitched.

"In my defense," Elena said, "I appear to be the first non-insect to emerge out of a chrysalis, so I figure I get to make my own rules." She got her butt on the sofa cushions again—not exactly gracefully, but hey, she hadn't done a face-plant. That counted as a win in her book.

A thought struck her. "Unless . . . do creatures other than insects make chrysalis-like things? Chance I'm going to grow a chitinous shell or the wings of a butterfly?"

Nisia listened to her heart using a prosaic stethoscope. "Butterfly wings are a ridiculous idea. Do you know what size they'd have to be to have any hope of holding up the weight of an adult angel?"

Scowling at whatever Elena's mega-heart was doing, she picked up Elena's wrist to check her pulse. "A hard shell, on the other hand, might be an excellent safety measure for a consort who keeps breaking herself. Also, why do you believe I know anything about what makes a chrysalis and what doesn't?"

"Because you are a font of endless knowledge, my dear Nisia." Keir walked in with a smile, his body clad in flowing pants of chocolate brown and a tunic in a similar shade. It sounded so dull, but nothing was ever dull on Keir. He was a beautiful man, and one with an inner peace that made it seem as if he'd been born hundreds of millennia ago rather than only three.

"See," she said to Nisia, "even Keir expects you to know everything."

Harrumphing in a way only Nisia could, the healer continued her examination while Keir set up the IVs. As they worked, Elena admired Nisia's wings—dark gray with white spots, she'd never seen them up so close. "Your feathers are so pretty." Far more delicately beautiful than she'd ever realized.

Glaring at her as if she'd offered a mortal insult, Nisia stuck silvery things to Elena's temples that led to a machine Keir had pulled out of another room. Then she pressed the stethoscope to Elena's chest again. "Your heart is behaving oddly." The healer sounded irritated. "It's beating in a rhythm that's not yours."

"Huh?" Elena scratched her head, the damp strands of her hair cool against her skin. "How can you tell?"

"You're a hunter. Surely you know mortal and immortal hearts beat in unique rhythms."

"I mean, yeah, vampiric hearts can slow down to the point of almost not beating, but Raphael's heart feels pretty normal to me." She'd fallen asleep more times than she could count with her head on his chest, the steady beat of his heart lulling her into a deep rest.

"It may seem similar," Keir murmured, "but there are minor but telling variations. The older the angel, the less power the heart needs to exert to keep the body functional. Prior to being encased, your heartbeat was close to a mortal's."

"Is my heart beating like an archangel's now?" She couldn't see a downside to that.

"No, not quite." Nisia scowled at another device in her hand. "It's beating as if you're a three-hundred-year-old immortal rather than one barely born."

"Her own cells must be merging with Raphael's donated heart," Keir murmured to Nisia. "The innate structure of her, her DNA, is yet morphing."

The two switched into another language, the back and forth rapid.

"That's another thing," Elena interrupted when the discussion showed no signs of ending. "Why did my body accept the heart? What about donor rejection, all that stuff?"

Both healers stared at her. It was Nisia who said, "You were encased in a chrysalis like a giant insect and you're worried about tissue rejection?"

"I'm just saying."

"It was ambrosia that made you an angel," Keir reminded her. "Ambrosia that came from Raphael."

The pieces clicked. She and her archangel, they'd always been two parts of a whole. Settling back with a deep sense of rightness inside her, she stopped interrupting the healers and concentrated on zapping the IVs dry.

"I spot no signs of a chitinous shell," Nisia said at one point. "It appears only your head is hard."

Elena grinned. "Takes one to know one."

Keir snorted a laugh—the first time Elena had ever heard him make such an inelegant sound.

Nisia was still glaring at him when the two left a half hour later. Elena wanted to go visit Tower friends, drop by the Legion's green skyscraper, but even she wasn't insane enough to attempt any of that in her current state. So there she sat with a blanket over her legs, mentally cursing the Cascade using blue words in multiple languages.

A knock on the door.

15

Come in before I die of boredom!"

The face that peeked around the door was thinner than when she'd last seen it, but as ridiculously pretty. She held out her arms. Illium came inside in a rush, his eyes brilliant with emotion, but halted a foot in front of her. "Will I break you?"

"I'm going to hit you in a second."

A wicked grin before he put his arms around her . . . with conscious care. Elena told herself to be patient; she'd be careful, too, if a friend came back looking sixty-eight percent dead.

Good thing he hadn't seen her at ninety-three percent dead.

"I brought you a present," he said when he drew back. Stepping out, he returned with her special lightweight crossbow.

"Eeee!" Elena made grabbing gestures.

Laughing, he placed it in her hands. Then he proceeded to crash onto the sofa beside her and raid the fresh tray of food Montgomery had left for her. His wing brushed her side, warm and heavy. An intense happiness uncurled deep within her. This was normal, her friendship with Illium an easy thing that didn't stand on ceremony.

As he ate, she petted and stroked her beloved crossbow.

It didn't surprise her that Illium didn't mention her lack of wings—he probably assumed they'd grow back, as was usual with angels who lost their wings in accidents or otherwise. Stomach tensing, she decided to let that subject lie for now.

It didn't strike her till five minutes later that a person who couldn't fly didn't need a specialized crossbow. The blow hurt. *Fuck that,* she thought furiously. *Deacon handmade this crossbow for me and I love it.* No goddamn Cascade was going to steal that joy from her.

Another thought blindsided her a second later. "Hey, hold on! Did you go inside the house to get this?" Her heart was ice.

"Uh-huh," Illium said from around a mouthful of tart.

Putting the crossbow aside with slow deliberation, she turned and grabbed the front of his sleeveless leather tunic. "Let me get this straight. You went back into a house that *was about to blow up* just to retrieve my crossbow?"

"I saved Aodhan's painting, too," said the blue-winged demon she was going to kill the instant she was strong enough. "Oh, and the jeweled blade the sire gave you."

"He's going to murder you, too."

Illium shrugged muscled shoulders. "Worth it."

"Nothing is worth your life!" Releasing his unrepentant form, she picked up the crossbow again. "I should shoot you with this."

Instead of another infuriating riposte, he leaned in close. "Ellie, will you be all right?"

She heard the tremor in his voice, saw the pinched look in his eyes, her Bluebell who had grieved so long for his mortal lover. He didn't forget the people he claimed—and he hurt for an eon if they were lost.

Raising one hand to cradle the side of his face, she said, "I came back from the dead, didn't I? *Twice.*" The first time, she'd fallen in Raphael's arms, her back broken and her consciousness fading. "My track record's pretty good."

Illium bowed his head, let her run her fingers through the blue-dipped black silk of his hair in soothing strokes. Outsiders might see them interact and believe it an omen of betrayal but those outsiders knew neither her heart nor Bluebell's.

Illium chose to serve Raphael, his fidelity to his liege beyond question. He coveted nothing of Raphael's and had been devastated when it appeared he might ascend early and have to leave the Seven. Elena still worried about that. He was becoming more and more powerful, but he wasn't ready for the Cadre, wasn't tough enough to withstand their brutal politics.

Today, he smiled at last and returned to the food.

"You want to know who asked after you?"

"I can guess."

"Not all of them you can't." A gleam in his eye. "The man who sells bagels on the roof and has a little sister who he brings to work sometimes."

"Piero?" She thought back to the last bagel she'd shared with the former petty criminal, the one where she'd lost three feathers: shimmering indigo and dawn, midnight black, charcoal gray with indigo at the edges.

Her heart had broken a little more with each one.

Ridiculously touched by the idea that Piero had worried about her, she said, "How is he?"

"Doing a roaring business, but he asks every angel who drops by his stand for news of you. Go say hello to him when you can."

"I will."

"Your father came, too."

Her spine turned into an iron rod. "Jeffrey in the Tower?" She'd expect frogs to fall from the sky first.

"Wasn't a doppelganger, I promise. I even asked Dmitri if he was breathing and looked human."

Elena couldn't find the words to reply. She was just glad she'd called Jeffrey.

"He cares about you, Ellie." An odd tone to Illium's voice. "My father . . ." A rough exhale. "Never mind."

The comment broke through her paralysis. "What is it?" Illium never talked about his father.

He just shook his head today, too. "Jeffrey's here and he cares enough to keep track of you."

At least he stuck around.

Elena had spoken those same words or similar enough plenty of times. She'd loved her sparkling, effervescent mother so much. So had Jeffrey. Marguerite had always been the laughing, loving heart of their family, sunshine bottled up in a delicate frame, her love for her husband and daughters worn on her sleeve. But, when the worst had happened, that love hadn't been enough to convince her to fight to hold on to life.

She'd forgotten Jeffrey and Elena and Beth in her grief over Belle and Ari. Elena's final memory of her mother would always be a swinging shadow on the wall, a high-heeled shoe abandoned on tile. Marguerite had chosen to leave them. Jeffrey had chosen to stay. At times, it was that painfully simple.

16

The skies above Manhattan were night-dark by the time Raphael landed on the balcony outside his and Elena's living area. Warm light poured out through the glass, welcoming him home. His consort was ensconced on the sofa, lovingly polishing what looked to be a well-used set of throwing knives.

Looking up from her task, she raised an eyebrow. *Why are you standing there staring through the glass like a creepy stalker?*

He felt his lips twitch. *I was simply admiring my consort.* Entering, he walked across to press a kiss to her nape. "Where did those come from?"

"Deacon used my old throwing blades to get the weighting right for my new ones. He kept the old ones in storage for reference. Sent them over today to keep me company while he forges new ones." She played a blade through her fingers with a dexterity he wouldn't have expected so soon after waking. "I told him to send the bill to you."

"Excellent. Even the greatest weapons-maker alive is not permitted to give my consort blades." It was a promise between them now, his insistence on being the only man who ever gave her a blade. "Do I see a blue feather lying over there?"

"Illium visited." She scowled as he came around the sofa to take a seat on the coffee table in front of her, his wings spread out behind him. "That idiot flew back into the house to grab my crossbow, the jeweled blade you gave me, and Aodhan's painting."

Of course Illium would've saved that precious piece of art. "He's an incredibly fast flyer."

"Don't tell me you're not furious with him for taking the risk."

"It would do no good. Your Bluebell will never be sorry for what he did." Lighthearted and joyous, Illium rarely turned intractable—that didn't mean he wasn't stubborn. "I've known him from the day he was born. When he decides a course of action is the right one, no one can make him repent—as a child, he'd take punishment for such things but would not say sorry."

"Ugh." She dropped her head back on the sofa, the fine strands of her hair spreading out across the velvet gray. "So, how was it? Your flight. Smite anyone while being Scary Raphael?"

He'd known she'd guess why he'd been absent so many hours. "I came close with one senior angel who allowed matters to slide while I was gone. No excuse except ennui—I've demoted him and that area of the territory will now be handled by a vampire of Dmitri's age who normally works under Nazarach."

Elena shivered at the name of the Atlantan angel. She'd never taken to Nazarach, considering him cruel beyond anything which could be justified. As an archangel who needed strong angels he could trust to do their jobs controlling vampires, Raphael had a different point of view, and the two of them had agreed to disagree on the issue.

"Did you fly as far as Atlanta?"

Raphael nodded. "It took far less effort and time than I expected. These wings are fast even now they're no longer aflame." Then he told her the most intriguing thing. "I was nearly in Atlanta when we spoke of Elijah's condors."

Elena's mouth fell open. Shutting it on a snap of sound, she shook her head hard. "You're telling me I made contact with you across multiple states?"

"Your voice was crystalline."

"I wonder how far we could stretch it." He could see her hunter's mind working furiously. "Big advantage in a hostile situation." But though her words were practical, positive, and her body looked more substantial than when he'd left, he felt her inside him, tasted her sorrow.

Elena had cherished her wings, the gift of the sky one she'd never taken for granted. They'd often gone for long flights for no reason but that she wanted to fly. She'd told him her ten-year flight plan was to learn all of Illium's tricks so she could play them back on the blue-winged angel.

He went down on one knee in front of her. With her knives in her lap between them, he took his consort's lips in a kiss that was a kick to his heart, a wrench to his soul. *My Elena.* The only woman who would ever live inside him in this way.

Her neck was painfully slender under his palm as he slid his hand around to her nape, her skin yet holding a faint glow. But the arms that came around his neck were fierce and tight and he found himself shifting his embrace to hold her harder, closer . . . until a deadly sharp point jabbed him in the gut.

Breaking the kiss, he looked down at the weapons in her lap. "Some men would consider this a very bad sign."

"Good thing you know better, Archangel." Kisses along the side of his face as he emptied her lap of the knives, then pushed the blanket aside to lift her up into his arms.

As he carried her into their bedroom, he said, "Keir will scalp me for this and I will let him."

Elena's eyes glowed silver as she brushed her mouth over his. "I need this more than I need medicine or food or air."

Placing her on the bed, Raphael stripped off his clothes with warrior efficiency. The faded and well worn-in items fell to the floor in a careless pile as his consort watched him; her gaze held a hunger that went far deeper than the flesh. Its twin gripped him by the throat. Between them pulsed the clawing need to reclaim the bond the Cascade had attempted to break.

When he came over her, his wings spread out on either side above them, she sighed and pressed her palms to his chest. "Sometimes, I convince myself I've imagined exactly how magnificent you are, then you walk into a room and boom, there I fall all over again."

Raphael couldn't speak, his need a voracious storm that threatened to crack his skin, spill out into the world. He kissed her instead, pouring all his love, all his terror into it. Her hold possessive and without boundaries, she took every ounce, demanded more. When power began to crackle under his skin, the golden lightning fighting the reins, he wrenched those reins with brute force.

"Whoa." A single word whispered against the dampness of his lips, Elena's hands stroking down his shoulders to his biceps.

Glancing down, Raphael saw his chest fissured by golden energy. "I have it leashed." It came out cold, deadly.

"There you go, being all sexy Scary Raphael again." Elena traced a line down his cheekbone and her finger came away painted by lightning that twined around the digit before sinking into her skin. Shivering, she wrapped both arms around him and tugged his head back down.

Carnal heat burned out the cold, engorged his blood vessels, made his skin gleam with sweat. *If you were not yet healing, I would be a brute.* Claim her so deep and hard that he'd leave an imprint inside her nothing could erase.

Raphael. Elena arched under the raw sexual words from her archangel, surrounded by the crackling violence of his power. It was in the burn of his kiss, the rough heat of his skin, the electric blue of eyes once more shot with lightning.

Does it hurt? Those eyes were icy, almost cruel.

No.

They fell into each other, no more thoughts of power and chaos or anything else outside them. She didn't know when her clothes came off, only that Raphael's skin brushed hers, his hands stroking down her body. She felt no heavy pressure however, knew he had to be worried about crushing her. It wasn't an issue she'd ever before encountered—in bed, there were no boundaries between them.

Clarity came, with it an acute sense of anger, because this was an *actual* problem. She stood on her anger hard before it could rise to the surface, but when they broke the kiss this time, Raphael's eyes blazed the blue at the heart of a flame and his chest heaved. "Come up with a solution," he said instead of just breaking things off—that would've *hurt.*

As it was, she kissed him hard before saying, "I have to be on top."

He flipped their positions . . . and she saw that her body was covered with tendrils of golden lightning that had fallen from him. His entire body, in turn, was riddled with cracks of gold.

Fisting one hand in her hair, he hauled her down for a kiss.

Breathtaking power in his every heartbeat, in his every touch. White fire licked over his wings once more, fell on her body when he curved his wings around her. His unhidden possessiveness undid a knot inside her she hadn't even known had formed: the icy fear that without wings, she was no longer the woman with whom Raphael had fallen in love.

Stupid. Her archangel had chosen her when she'd been a breakable mortal. Theirs wasn't a love that was brittle and conditional. It was forever and it was brutal in its need. No matter their physical state.

He thrust his tongue inside her mouth, molding her breast with one hand. She moaned and gripped at his hair, rubbing her body against the sleek muscle of his. She was covered in so much of his power at this point that she could no longer tell when it sank into her. It was electricity over her skin, living electricity that tasted so deeply of Raphael that she had no compunction in laying herself bare to it.

A moment to gasp in a breath, Raphael's voice harsh as he said, "Does it disconcert you? The lightning?"

And she realized the same stupid fear gnawed at the deadly archangel who held her. "If you're into a mildly glowing skeleton," she said against his kiss-wet lips, "I'm into a sexy archangel painted in lightning."

Their next kiss was a slow and erotic thing infused with piercing love. When Raphael nudged her into the right position, she held her breath and sank down on him. Her inner flesh was slick with need and swollen with arousal, her hands braced on his chest, his holding her hips. It was a tight slide but she didn't take it slow—she couldn't, not the first time. Her pelvis met his, his cock held possessively inside her.

She shuddered in a relief so deep that it brought tears to her eyes.

Raphael sat up, cradling her against him as she straddled his body. They pressed their foreheads together, Elena's fingers brushing his jaw and his hand stroking up her spine. "I love you until I can't breathe."

"It will only ever be you for me, Elena. I am yours." His wings came around her, enclosing them in a cocoon of white-gold energy so brilliant that the only other thing she could see was the violent blue of his eyes.

They began to move together. Far slower and with more care than they'd ever before done, but this wasn't about wild sex. Their need was far more visceral. When tears rolled down her face, Raphael kissed them away. And when he buried his face against the side of her neck and squeezed her painfully tight, she stroked his hair and kissed his temple and whispered that they'd make it, that nothing would tear them apart.

When the wave broke, it did so in a blaze of white-gold that caused dazzling afterimages behind her eyes. Holding on to her archangel, Elena allowed his power to burst into every cell in her body. Fear had no claim on her anymore.

Not here. Not with her archangel.

Cold Cascade power or not, no part of Raphael would ever hurt her.

Lightning cracked her skin and exploded from her pores.

17

The Legion

The Legion saw searing light pour out of every window of the Tower suite that was the *aeclari*'s and they saw angels all over the city land on any available surface. High on the Tower, the Blade ran inside from where he'd been standing on the balcony, and the Viper ran in with him.

In the streets, mortals looked up, and froze.

But the Legion didn't rise, didn't head to the Tower. Instead, the Primary stretched his mind and spoke to the Blade. *Stop.*

No response, but thirty seconds later, the Blade returned to his balcony. Hard, dark eyes landed on the Primary—who had flown on silent wings to crouch on the edge of that space.

"Why?" the Blade asked, a device in his hand that the Primary had learned was used for communication. Others in the world did not speak to their brethren as the Legion did. Others were not always together even while alone. It was a difficult thing for the Legion to grasp and had been since their inception.

The Primary considered his words. "Elena and Raphael are not afraid." That which tied the Legion to the *aeclari* had become stronger in the aftermath of their return. The Primary could not hear their thoughts and did not know what they were doing, but he felt a visceral peace at this moment, a sense of acceptance without boundaries.

He understood joy in its purest form.

He struggled to put this knowledge into words for the Blade, who was as loyal to the *aeclari* as the Legion. Then he understood. "They are home."

The Blade's jaw worked, but he gave a curt nod and began to bark orders into the phone. "No one approaches the suite. Cordon off that level until we hear from Raphael or Elena."

The Primary swept off the balcony and back to his perch on the building which was the Legion's. *We must make many seedlings,* he said to his brethren.

The voices that returned to him were his and theirs both.

For her. For Elena.

Her growing things are gone.

We will make more.

Aeclari. *We hear their song.*

18

Raphael's mind emerged from the wild storm of pleasure wrapped in incandescent love to find his hunter limp against him, her arms lazy around his neck. Always, she would hold him. Even when he harbored a power colder than winter's icy kiss. "Elena?"

"Mmm." A yawn against his neck. "I didn't think you could get any better at this, studmuffin, but you've proved me wrong. Pretty sure my bones have melted. Also sure I don't care."

Cheeks creasing, Raphael ran his hand down her spine. And frowned. "*Hbeebti,* sit up."

Elena kissed his throat before obeying. Her hair was tumbled around her face, her hands on his shoulders, her lips swollen from his demands as well as her own. "What's the matter?" She lifted her arm, stared at it. "Am I imagining it or do I look more normal?"

Raphael realized he'd missed the most obvious change: she remained far thinner than her usual muscled sleekness, but was no longer of a weight that would draw concerned attention. "Your entire body has gained a layer of flesh, and the alien glow is gone from your skin."

"Eyes?"

"No change excepting the lack of a glow." A liquid silver with a hint of blue and a touch of gray. A blending of mortal and immortal. All good . . . but for one critical thing. "I can't feel your tattoo." He ran his hand over the area. "No ridges, nothing but your spine and skin."

Going motionless, she said, "That's extremely weird because *I* still feel as if you're stroking my feathers. Sensation's actually grown more intense than before we had crazypants sex flavored with white fire."

"Turn so I can see your back."

She began to untangle herself from him. "Don't look until we can look together."

Raphael nodded, then got out of bed and held out a hand.

Elena took care joining him, her hand locked to his. But she grinned the instant her feet hit the carpet. "I don't think I need the crutches anymore." Two seconds later, she proved that supposition correct: the two of them walked into the bathroom together.

"No breathlessness, no jelly legs," she said once they were inside. "Crazypants glowing sex is now my favorite kind."

Shifting on her heel so her back faced the full-length mirror, she took a deep breath and looked over her shoulder at the same time that Raphael moved so he could see her back. The tattoo was gone.

Elena's eyes narrowed. "Touch that area."

A shiver ran through her when he did . . . and the outline of the tattoo reappeared . . . edged in white fire.

The coolly fiery silhouette held for a long moment after he removed his hand, before fading slowly into her skin.

Elena faced him. "Any ideas?"

Her entire body began to glow lightning gold before he could respond, the brilliance so vicious that it was a burn on his eyes.

She blazed like a star before the light disappeared without a trace.

Blinking past the shards of shadow and brightness in front of his eyes, Raphael saw his hunter had acquired a new tattoo. It was on her left temple and it was an exact mirror of the Legion mark on his right temple, except that hers wasn't a glittering blue touched with wildfire white. It was a verdant forest green that shimmered.

"Did I grow a third nose?" Elena winced. "I have, haven't I? Or is it an extra ear?"

Taking her by the shoulders, he turned her to face the mirror. Lips forming into an "Oh" Elena brushed her fingers over the mark. "*Aeclari* are mirrors," she whispered, repeating words the Legion had first spoken.

Then it happened again. Golden lightning erupted along the side of Elena's face. When it disappeared, so did the mark. Elena brushed her fingers over her once-more pristine skin. "I'm glitching as my body tries to find equilibrium. I woke too early, before everything was in place—but, on the flip side, I have an archangelic heart and access to power that's yours by right."

"Perhaps." He ran his hand down her spine again.

No fiery outline of wings on her back this time, her skin a smooth dark gold.

"Looks like that glitch has corrected itself." Elena's gaze was on the mirror, her voice soft. "I didn't feel you caress my feathers."

"*Hbeebti.*"

Fingers brushing his jaw. "It's okay, Raphael. Truly." A determined smile over a foundation of grit and loss. "I had an experience no mortal could ever hope for—I flew in the skies on my own wings. Now I'm a weird-ass hybrid who glows randomly. It's going to be a new adventure."

He wrapped her up in his arms, his mind ice-cold.

Were the Cascade a living being, he'd shred it to pieces.

He made contact with Elijah that night, using the large screen in his and Elena's living area. "Eli," he said, "I would do this in person, but I cannot leave my territory yet."

"I would not expect such, my friend," Elijah replied, his golden brown eyes warm. "It is good to see you."

"I thank you for the assistance you offered by sending your birds and cats. It is a debt between us."

Elijah shook his head, the golden strands of his hair bright even in the artificial light of the room where he stood. "Such things are not a matter of debt. I know you would do the same were the situations reversed."

A few years past, Raphael wouldn't have known whether he would or not. Now, he was a little bit mortal and he'd built a relationship of trust with another archangel. The cold power born in the Cascade might battle him when he made such choices, but he had too many pieces of Elena in his blood for it to succeed.

He had not forgotten his earlier thoughts of godhood. Had he fallen for the sinuous whispers of the Cascade, would he have become a parasite akin to Lijuan? Would he have gone so far as to feed from Elena's soulless facsimile? His gorge rose, rage a scalding burn through his blood.

"Yes," he said past the ugliness of it. "Should you ever need my help, I will be there." Such generosity and empathy did not come as easily to him as it seemed to come to Elijah, but he was well over three thousand years younger than the South American archangel so perhaps that was a kind of maturity that grew with age—*if* the seeds were present.

"Have you heard the news about China?" Elijah's expression turned grim.

"The empty villages? Yes. My spymaster will be giving me a full briefing tonight—he returned from China only hours prior to my own return."

"Mine flew homeward a week ago, and he reports signs of increasing vampiric unrest. They skitter in fear at the archangels who fly overhead but they know they are not under constant watch—and sanity falls when bloodlust rises."

"I see Neha is currently on watch." Prior to calling Elijah, Raphael had glanced at the updated oversight schedule sent through to Dmitri. "I do not think we have to fear rampant blood madness." The Queen of Poisons, of Snakes had very little patience for such anarchy.

It was one of the regrets of Raphael's life that his friendship with Neha had broken so badly in the aftermath of her daughter's execution. Yet she hadn't tried to take advantage of his absence, so perhaps all was not lost between them.

"No." Elijah resettled his wings. "But when you speak to

your spymaster, ask if he saw signs of unusual activity among villagers in the most remote areas. My spymaster is convinced the villagers are not acting 'human' but he was unable to find any evidence that they are reborn."

Zombies two-point-o, a pajama-clad Elena muttered into Raphael's mind from where she sat on the sofa wrapped up in a soft blanket, out of sight of the screen; the Guild director had sent over a few more weapons for her from the Guild's stores, and she was examining them to see if they'd suit, while buffing off any marks with a soft cloth and adding oil where it was needed. *Of course our favorite batshit crazy archangel is creating creepy things even in her Sleep. Because the creepy, it never rests.*

Raphael had to fight not to let his lips twitch. "I will pass on any information we have. Please give my consort's regards to yours. She plans to write Hannah a letter soon."

"Hannah will be most pleased to hear from her. Be well, Raphael." Elijah signed off.

Raphael turned to his consort just as a black-winged shape landed on the balcony outside. They'd left the doors open to the glittering spectacle of Manhattan, for Elena drew strength from the sight of her city and the cool night air was a thing easily remedied. "Jason," he said to his spymaster.

"Sire," replied the member of his Seven who was the most difficult to read. "It is good to have you home." Then, to Raphael's surprise, he came close enough for them to clasp forearms and embrace in the way Raphael had done with Dmitri.

Jason was not an angel who embraced easily.

After they parted, Jason turned to Elena and the light caught on the lines and dots of the tribal tattoo that marked the left side of his face. "I am glad you are safe, Elena." Reaching into a pocket, he pulled out a small object. "I saw this in a market in China and bought it for when you woke."

A startled blink before Elena took the oval-shaped article made of metal that had gone slightly green from age. It was a carved box, Raphael saw, the design raised and intricate. But this was a gift from a spymaster. "It contains a secret," Raphael murmured, certain of his conclusion.

"Hmm." Setting her jaw, Elena bent over the puzzle box.

First, she pushed various parts of the box in one direction, then the other, one by one. When it remained locked, apparently nothing more than a pretty ornament, she began to push in two directions at once.

Nothing.

A narrow-eyed glance up at the angel who'd given her the gift, an angel with wings of a soft black as inky as the night, an angel who lived in the world of secrets and shadows. "Is there really a secret or are you and your archangel messing with me?"

"There is a secret." Solemn words from a man who smiled rarely and most often with the princess who held his heart. "The trick is—"

"No, don't tell me." Lines on her forehead, her attention already back on the puzzle box. "You and Raphael talk while I figure it out."

"Will you have a drink, Jason?" Angels of Jason's level of power could no more become intoxicated than Raphael, but the taste was pleasing.

Jason inclined his head. "It has been a long day."

But he would go home, flying longer still, of this Raphael had no doubt. "Mahiya did not come with you on this journey?" Jason had been training his princess in the techniques of a spy so she could accompany him on some missions at least—gentle Mahiya had put her foot down and stated that she intended to be his partner in every way . . . and that she missed him when he was gone.

Jason was not proof against such unhidden love, not after a lifetime of loneliness. "China is too dangerous," he said to Raphael. "Mahiya agreed with me—she knows I would worry about her in such a place and has no wish to divide my attention." He took the tumbler of amber liquid Raphael held out. "She grows in skill day after day. In the future, you will have a pair of spymasters, not only one."

"Such an advantage will be welcome." Raphael poured himself a drink, too. "I've just been speaking to Elijah." He summarized Eli's words about the villagers. "Did you notice any strange behavior?"

19

Nodding, Jason took a sip of his drink. "For the most part, they act as is normal, expected, but every so often, their bodies jerk—as if being pulled by invisible strings."

"Told you—better, more improved zombies," Elena muttered, her head bent over the puzzle box.

"An apt description," Jason said. "These are not the dead turned reborn, but their eyes are not . . . what they should be. The irises appeared an intense black to me rather than even a very dark shade of brown. It is not a natural mortal hue."

"Are they a threat?"

"At present, they appear to be going about their ordinary lives—farming for the most part. There is a chance it's the same infection that took Favashi, but that it impacts mortals in a different way." Jason's wings rustled as he flared them out before folding them back in. "It could also be connected more immediately to Lijuan."

Raphael sipped at his cognac as he considered Jason's words. "If so, she has not gone into Sleep," he said at last. "A Sleeping archangel cannot impact the world around her."

"I have sent operatives to all of her strongholds. There is no sign of her or her most trusted people."

"China is a vast land."

"Yes, and she has held it for millennia—it's possible she built a hiding place long before we were born. To be used only once, so it could never be known."

"Ah-ha!" Elena's triumphant cry caught both their attention.

Part of the puzzle box had come away from the center. As they watched, she pushed two specific spots using the edges of her nails and multiple other pieces snapped out from the box to reveal a set of tiny metal darts. The box itself had turned into a blower from which the darts could be shot.

Elena's face was a study in wonder. "This is *amazing*, Jason! Raphael, check it out."

Raphael examined the object with interest. "A great artisan put months of work into this." It was a piece of art as well as a weapon.

Accepting it back, Elena picked up a dart using two fingernails. "I wonder if it still works. Can you throw me a disinfectant wipe from the stuff Nisia left behind?"

After Raphael did so, she sanitized the blower, then very delicately inserted a dart into the device.

Aiming it at the opposing wall, she blew.

The dart flew straight and true to come to a sudden stop in the wall. Small as it was, it was barely visible. Jason retrieved it. "I believe you need to poison the tips for full effectiveness as a weapon," he said upon presenting it back to Elena.

"I'm totally going to do that. Never know when a secret poison dart might come in handy." A brilliant smile. "Thank you, Jason. Though . . . it is a little terrifying that you picked up exactly the thing I would've coveted had I seen it."

"I'm a spymaster," Jason said. "It is my calling to notice such things."

"Venom's poison is potent."

"Hah!" Elena laughed at Raphael's suggestion. "I'm going to ask him." Tipping out the darts onto a side table with extreme care, she began to clean and oil the moving parts of the device.

Jason, meanwhile, turned to give Raphael the rest of his report. His people had discovered more ghost villages devoid of life. "We haven't yet found any bodies." The spymaster also confirmed that the vampires were getting restless. "The smart ones have started to notice that the archangels never land in China—it's made them bold."

Jason's words bathed Elijah's earlier concern in a new light. Blood would flow like water should the massive number of the Made in China realize its soil was poisonous to the Cadre. "We have kept you long enough, Jason." His spymaster's task was to unearth the problems; Raphael and the Cadre were charged with discovering the answers. "It is time you turned your wings homeward to your princess."

Inclining his head at Raphael, then Elena, Jason left as silently as he'd arrived. It wasn't until after he was gone that Elena put down the puzzle box and said, "I didn't know Jason liked me that much."

"He is a hard angel to read, even for me, and I have known him nearly all his life." All but the formative first years that had woven aloneness into Jason's bones. "But never take Jason's quietness for disinterest, Guild Hunter." He ran his hand through the silk of her hair, the tiny feathers at the ends delicate yet strong.

Leaning her head against his thigh, she said, "You'll have to do a rotation in China, won't you?"

"Yes." His gaze might've been on the glitter and lights of Manhattan, but it was a land of death and vanishings that he saw in his mind. "Mother stepped in during my absence and will continue to cover for me for the time being, but it cannot be for too long, or it will raise questions about my ability to do all that is required of an archangel." Once that happened, war was inevitable.

Ice wove through his veins, the cold Cascade power eager for violence.

The next day, Elena learned that, despite her lack of wings, her DNA was "mostly" angelic, though that was only an interim result; her DNA was fluctuating and transforming from hour to hour.

"Frankly, Elena, you're weird." Lucius, calm and gentle, threw up his hands.

She laughed; it was either laugh or cry and she'd cried all

the tears she was going to—now it was time to kick the future's ass. "Is that your official diagnosis?"

"My official diagnosis is that you're definitely immortal. The rest is subject to change." The soft yellow of his wings rippled in unfamiliar agitation. "Also, you have strange glowing cells inside you. Come look through the microscope."

Striding over to the device, she put her eye to the viewer. A happily glowing cell floated by, followed by one that looked normal to her non-scientist eyes. Drawing back, she checked the skin of her hands. "I'm not glowing. I stopped sometime last night."

"If that changes, come straight here so I can take a sample. I need to see if your cells morph when you glow."

"Uh-huh." Elena couldn't help thinking how she'd gone glow-in-the-dark in Raphael's arms. "Give me a syringe."

Lucius sighed, his handsome face set in lines that shouted, "Grant me patience." "Do you know how to use one to draw blood?"

"Well . . . no."

"Just prick yourself and put a couple of drops in here, then close the stopper." He passed over a small glass vial, then added two more. "Get me samples from the archangel, too. He's also got glowing cells."

"What we did, it changed both of us." His heart in her chest. Her heart in fragments in his system. Their minds locked together in the dream.

Leaving the infirmary, the vials tucked safely into a zippered pocket of the hip-length black leather jacket that Beth had sent over, she found herself drawn to the balcony at the end of the hall. Phantom wings tugged suddenly at her back, a maddening muscle echo her body couldn't forget.

Gritting her teeth, she continued on. The balcony had no railing—and Elena not only didn't have wings, her bone structure wasn't strong enough to withstand any kind of a real impact, far less one from so high. She'd splatter herself into pieces.

Regardless, she stepped into the doorway . . . and lifted an eyebrow. "Did you summon me?"

"You were speaking of blood." Under the haze of a misty rain, the Primary was a crouched gargoyle, gray and motionless but for his mouth.

Oddly, Elena wasn't disturbed by his knowledge. The Legion were a hum at the back of her mind now, there without intruding. "You listened in?"

"No. We just feel it."

That made no sense but this was the Legion. Making sense wasn't their strong suit. "So, any input on the glowing cells situation?"

"The sire's blood traveled across the bed and was absorbed by the chrysalis. We watched it. We did not interfere."

And that was *after* the damn insane archangel had given her a piece of her heart. All that archangelic blood inside her when Raphael released violent energy meant for an archangel. Powered by his blood, her body had obviously stolen some . . . but what was it *doing* with it? "Anything else happen while we were napping?"

"Right before you woke, the filaments that formed the chrysalis grew and grew, spreading like spidersilk across Raphael and the room." His bat-like wings stayed motionless even as the wind riffled his hair. "Before then, a long time before, we had a thought that the earth would help you, so we brought the soil from your garden and it was dark and rich, and we placed it over the chrysalis and the sire's sleeping body."

Elena thought back—they'd woken on such dark soil. A remnant of the Legion's offering? "I remember bringing that soil into my greenhouse." She smiled at the memory of Illium's complaints about how hauling bags of soil was beneath his dignity—but he'd done it anyway, on the condition she plant some bluebells in the soil.

Her hands itched. "How is your garden? Can I come play?"

Welcome. Welcome. Welcome. Elena. Come. Come. We wait.

So much excitement that her head hurt but she didn't censure them. They'd missed her, these strange beings unlike any others in the world. She'd missed them, too. "Give me a few minutes."

The journey to the ground floor was the easy part—all she had to do was get in the elevator. Even crossing the grass to the Legion building didn't take much out of her—she was definitely stronger after the psychedelic sex mojo with Raphael. Fine droplets of water beaded on her jacket, clung to her lashes, the cool, damp day beautiful to her. Then she reached the bottom of the wall of vines that led up to the entrance to the Legion's home . . . and reality hit with a backhanded slap.

Visit'll have to wait. Things ached inside her, the need for the earth curling her fingers into her palms. *I'll fall and break my butt right now*

Elena. Elena. Elena. One of the Legion landed beside her. *Come.*

She went to repeat that she couldn't when she realized he was waving for her to move to the right of the climbing wall. Keeping her questions to herself, she followed him around the corner and, after he lifted it up, under a heavy weight of vines. There, hidden behind those thick ropes was a door that had been opened from the inside.

"Hot damn." Soul flowering at the humid warmth that whispered outward from the doorway, she slipped in. The Legion fighter came after her. As she watched, he locked the door securely behind him—it involved two iron bars and a third crossbar.

The first thing she did was take off her boots and socks and curl her toes into the grass underfoot. The second was to shrug off her jacket. Fall was locked out, summer in full bloom within. She stood in a grove of orange trees plump with unseasonal fruit. Plucking a ripe one, she used one of her knives to cut it into pieces and held out a slice to the Legion fighter.

The Legion didn't need to eat, but anytime she gave them food, they accepted.

The fighter took the slice, looked at it with intense interest, then ate it. Peel and all.

Grinning, she disposed of her own peels at the foot of a tree, where it would become part of the earth once again, then just walked around, breathing in the smell of the earth, and of green growing things.

Elena. Come.

Heading toward the two members of the Legion who'd spoken to her, she saw an empty garden lush with dark soil. A row of potted seedlings sat beside it. "Is that for me?"

For you. We make. For you.

Her throat closed up. "Thank you." Going down to her

knees, she sank her fingers into the soil and sighed. "I needed this so much."

Humming quietly under her breath, she began to plant. She was aware of the Legion around her, above her. One was a helpful presence that passed her the potted seedlings, while another flew down with a tray on which sat a large bottle of Nisia's new concoction, meant to complement the IV calories. Elena drank it without complaint.

Once she'd planted her small garden to her satisfaction, she helped weed the other gardens on this floor, and checked the orange trees for any indication of damaging insect activity. The Legion brought her berries to eat, flowers to look at, acting like small children excited to show her their favorite things. This was the paradox of the Legion—they were infinite in age, yet at times, innocent as children.

Deeply content and less tired than she'd expected by the time she finished gardening, she said good-bye to the Legion before exiting via the secret entrance to return to the Tower. Suhani, the receptionist, had been away from her desk when Elena left the Tower, but now beamed and waved at her, so Elena walked over.

The vampire's smile deepened, but there was sadness in the brown of her gaze. Suhani had seen Elena come through these doors the very first time, when the Archangel of New York had summoned Guild Hunter Elena Deveraux to his tower. Later, she'd seen Elena reappear with wings, and now the wings were gone.

Yeah, it was going to be an adjustment for all of them.

About to say hello, Elena got distracted by the utterly lovely bonsai on the polished black marble counter behind which Suhani held sway. "This is glorious work." The Japanese red maple had been painstakingly shaped into its miniature form with intricate delicacy, the color of the leaves an astonishing and flawless scarlet.

"Oh, thank you." Suhani blushed under the burnished brown of her skin, her hair a deep brown-black that she always wore in a sleek knot. "I used to do it a hundred years ago, then fell out of practice, but I have a few that have survived my benign neglect."

Elena had never asked Suhani's exact age, but felt the cool

and deadly weight of that age in her bones. Suhani might work reception, but she was no less than lethal. She was also a dedicated member of the "Bring back *Hunter's Prey*" lobby, and had a scrapbook about the show that she'd pull out at any opportunity.

"You have a true talent. Can I . . . ?" Elena lifted a hand.

"Of course!" Bright, happy eyes. "If you really like it, I would be honored to gift you one from my collection. I have a *sakura* that—" Her smile faded as the maple shot up two inches. Right under Elena's hand.

Elena jerked back. But the maple, it grew . . . and grew.

20

Suhani stumbled out of her leather executive chair and back as roots burst out of the glazed ceramic pot in which the bonsai had been contained. Those roots fell over the side of the counter and seemed to be searching for soil, of which there was none in the marble and gloss of the lobby.

That didn't stop the tree. Branches grew longer and stronger. The trunk thickened and rose toward the ceiling. Leaves expanded in size.

When it did finally stop, it was with a shake that sent a perfect scarlet leaf to land on Elena's boot. The maple now stood eight feet above the counter. Which hadn't cracked despite the massive new weight.

Suhani made a wordless noise.

Elena hunched up her shoulders. "I am *so* sorry."

Coming around the counter, her steps neat and clipped due to the constriction of her tailored designer dress of deep pink, the receptionist bent back her head to take in the tree. "It's real?" A whisper. "I'm not hallucinating?"

Not certain herself, Elena reached out to touch a tree root. It was hard and solid under her palm. Alive. "Real."

Suhani stretched out her hand, hesitated. But she was

obviously freaked out enough that she needed confirmation. "Real." A breath as she jerked back her hand, huge eyes on Elena. "What do I *do*?"

Elena examined the tree again. "It's healthy. Shame to let it die. I'll ask the Legion to see if they can move it." She winced. "Sorry about the mess in your workspace, and damn, your computer's on the floor with a cracked screen." She crossed mental fingers that Suhani had backed up her files. "I'll make sure it's all replaced."

Suhani didn't appear to have heard; her eyes were fixated on the maple. "No one will believe me. *I* don't believe me."

Elena wasn't sure she believed her own eyes, either. *Er, Archangel? Are you in the Tower?*

The rain in her mind, the crashing sea. *Yes. I'm on my way to speak to your Bluebell.*

Um, mind coming down to the lobby first?

I am intrigued.

Elena stared at the tree again, trying to wrap her mind around the fact that she'd somehow put it on steroids. Then her nape prickled. Of course Raphael hadn't taken the elevator. He'd simply flown to the ground and entered from the outside. "So," she said without turning, "I did a thing."

A sudden squeak . . . before Suhani keeled over in a dead faint. The vampire's head would've hit the floor if Elena hadn't caught her—with arms that quivered. "Shit, I forgot to warn her you were coming down." For having worked so long in the Tower, Suhani remained starstruck by angels.

"I will take her." Raphael carried Suhani around to settle her in her leather chair. "You have decided the Tower needs more greenery?" he asked afterward.

"I was just in the Legion building! None of the plants there did *that*." Elena bit down hard on her lower lip. "It was a really *old* bonsai, too. How do I make that up to her?"

Raphael raised an eyebrow. "Only you would worry about such a thing. You are consort to an archangel, Elena."

"Doesn't change the fact I wrecked her freaking ancient bonsai!"

"Tell her she was carried in the arms of an archangel." Pure chrome blue arrogance. "She will give you every one of her bonsai in return." He pulled out a feather that was showing signs of naturally falling out, dropped it on the counter. "There, debt not only paid, but interest on top of it."

"Stop, stop, your modesty is too much." Elena glared at him. "Will you *please* take this seriously? I grew a fricking tree out of a miniature."

"I cannot see how you can use it in battle." Raphael rubbed his jaw. "Perhaps you can grow sudden trees in the path of enemy angels. Boom, smack. Truly, it is a power most terrible."

"I swear, I'm this close to decking you." But he'd made her relax, want to laugh at herself. "Yeah, fine, growing trees isn't awful in the scheme of things." In point of fact, it was pretty neat.

"Would you like to see if you can repeat it?"

Elena grinned. "Yes, let's go." She glanced at Suhani, who was starting to come around. "Can you mind-talk one of the healers to come check on her?"

A shake of his head at her softness, but he summoned the healer. The doors opened on the experienced vampire medic just before Suhani rose to full consciousness. "I'm so sorry, Suhani," Elena said again. "I'll find you another hundred-year-old bonsai."

The other woman frowned, blinked, her pupils huge.

"You fainted," Elena explained. "Raphael put you in the chair so you'd be comfortable."

Raphael shifted into Suhani's line of sight. "It pleases me that you are not hurt."

Huge eyes before they rolled back in her head and she passed out again. Elena groaned. "That was not funny. The poor woman is in total awe of you."

"As she should be." A squeeze of her nape. "Suhani is a mid-level vampire who cannot afford to feel anything but fear and awe for angelkind. Bloodlust lies just beneath her skin."

Elena found it difficult to see prim and proper Suhani as consumed by bloodlust, but she knew the compulsion existed in all vampires. The old and disciplined ones like Dmitri had long ago gotten it under control, but even Dmitri wouldn't deny its existence. "What's going to happen to Honor? Ashwini?" Former hunters and young vampires both. "Are they at risk?"

"Honor has a near-preternatural calm within her. Keir has commented on it—as if she is much older than her years."

"I know what he means." Elena always felt calmer and more centered around Honor, her presence a deep, content pool.

"As for Ashwini, she walks to her own beat, and none of us can predict her development—but she is a hunter, with the attendant discipline." The two of them stepped out into the misty rain. Putting one arm around her, Raphael flew them up onto the upper entrance of the Legion building.

Elena! Aeclari! Raphael! Aeclari!

The voices were a storm that rapidly contained itself into a rumbling murmur. Despite her recent visit, she sighed anew at the beauty inside the humid warmth of the Legion's home. Flowers bloomed out of season, vines crawled up the walls, grass grew underfoot. And when they asked for the seedling of a tree, the Primary urged them to follow him to the ground floor.

Elena couldn't resist burying her nose in the crook of Raphael's neck as he took them down, her lips tasting his skin. His eyes flamed blue fire at her when their feet hit the ground.

Tree children. The Primary waved to an entire row of potted plants. *For you. We made for your new house of glass. Two are trees.*

Elena's throat got thick. "The mandarin orange," she said, her voice husky. "Archangel, can you place it in a clear area?"

Raphael soon had the pot positioned, while the Primary looked on silently. Up above, hundreds more faces were turned their way. It should've been eerie to glance up and see all those gray faces looking down, bat wings held in silence, but she couldn't be frightened of the Legion, especially when they whispered excitedly in her head.

Show us, Ellie. What is this? Show us.

"Not sure there'll be anything to see," she muttered. "I have no idea how I did this the first time."

"Consider your thoughts then, and try to repeat them."

Elena frowned. "I was just admiring the bonsai, thinking how wonderful it was." As wonderful as this gift to help her repopulate her greenhouse. She stroked the glossy leaves, admiration and joy in the contact.

Nothing happened.

Disappointment gnawed at her, the wound surprisingly brutal. *I feel like a child throwing a tantrum, but I needed this more than I knew. Just* one *thing to balance out having lost my wings.* A stone in her gut, she petted the tree's leaves. "Not your fault."

The roots of the plant erupted out of the sides of the pot, spraying her with dirt. She scrambled back and out of the way before getting to her feet. The tree grew. Tiny white flowers bloomed on the branches, formed into mandarin oranges, turned plump and ripe.

Chosen to fit inside her greenhouse, the final tree wasn't huge, but it was taller than Raphael, its branches heavy with fruit.

Elena began to smile, then grin, her cheeks aching.

On the other side of the tree, the Primary stood motionless. When he did finally speak, it was with a chorus of hundreds of other voices, an unearthly choir. *This, we have not seen. Not in all our eons of life.*

21

Still on a high from the whole tree thing, Elena had showered and was pulling on fresh clothes—clothes that actually fit, because Montgomery was a magician—when her phone buzzed. Earlier that day, she'd given the phone to Vivek and he'd loaded it up with the numbers of friends, family, associates, but this one came up as unknown.

She answered it anyway. Every so often, she liked to startle a hapless telemarketer by informing them whom they'd inadvertently cold-called. Her favorite one was the vampire who'd thanked her for hauling him back to his angel eight years ago. "Met the love of my life six months later. She's fine as fine can be and she don't take no shit, and now we have a little man of our own. His name's Eldev after you."

Later, he'd sent her photos of his ebony-skinned and chubby-cheeked "little man," the kid's smile a weapon, it was so adorable.

"Ellie?"

"Beth." Elena sat down on the edge of the bed, dressed only in her panties and a strappy tank. "This isn't your number."

"Oh, this is Grandma's phone. She finally let Grandpa get her one, though she mostly leaves it lying around gathering dust." Her younger sister's voice wobbled. "I wanted to talk to you."

"Are you at Majda and Jean-Baptiste's?" Unlike Beth, Elena found it difficult to call them Grandma and Grandpa—despite all the torture and pain they'd suffered, the two were eternally young and would stay that way forever. "I'll come over." No point hiding now that she no longer looked like an escapee from the local boneyard. The world would make of her wingless state what it would.

"No, we're at our place." Beth's response sparkled. "You're coming? For real?"

"Yes, for real," she said on a wave of affection for this sweet, pretty woman who'd once been Marguerite's baby girl. "I'll drop by to say hi to Sara on the way, so give me an hour or so."

"I'm going to bake your favorite cake."

"Bethie." Elena took a deep breath. "I don't have my wings anymore."

"Are you sad?" Soft words. "You loved your wings."

"I was." But she'd done her mourning—and she'd said fuck you to the Cascade by coming out of hell with the ability to bring things to lush, green life. If Lijuan burned down the world, Elena would bring it back to life. The Cascade could go suck on that. "Now I'm just glad to be home."

"I missed you so much." A quickly muffled sob.

Elena swallowed. "I'll be there soon." No matter what, Beth would always be Elena's baby sister, the bewildered little girl who'd clutched her hand with a soft and pudgy one as they laid their sisters then their mother to rest.

After hanging up, Elena called Ashwini. "You free to give me a ride? I don't think I should be driving just yet—bit out of practice."

"I'm already in a car out front of the Tower. Wait till you see the ride I requisitioned."

Elena's eyes narrowed; Ash *definitely* got a kick out of messing with her friends using her ability to glimpse snatches of the future. "Be right down."

It didn't take long to pull on black jeans, a metallic blue sweatshirt printed with the Tower logo, socks, and boots. She still wasn't sure about the shorter hair, but a few brushstrokes and it was done.

Grabbing her leather jacket, she headed out.

She found Ash sitting behind the wheel of a topless baby pink Cadillac. Her fellow hunter's sunglasses were a reflective gold, her dark hair streaked with the same color, and the hoops that dangled from her ears an Indian design that featured a waterfall of bells. A brown leather jacket worn over a scoop-necked black tee and dark blue jeans completed the outfit.

"I feel underdressed now," Elena said, opening the passenger-side door.

"Would I do that to you, Ellie?" Ashwini passed over a box wrapped in silver paper.

"Smartass."

"Hey, why have the third eye if I can't use it to wink now and then?"

Grinning, Elena settled into the seat before she set to ripping open the package. Inside, she found a pair of mirrored sunglasses tinted a deep graduated purple that looked fantastic against the near-white of her hair. Also in the box were a pair of hoop earrings similar to Ash's, except that hers were a stunning beaten steel.

She touched one earlobe. Yep, as she'd suspected, the chrysalis had "fixed" the piercing hole. Then she saw the hoops were designed to clip on. "Seriously, you're getting worse in your old age." Scowling mutter or not, she put on the earrings.

A sharp grin from her friend. "Now we're ready."

They roared off.

The car attracted plenty of attention—and so did Elena. When they stopped at a light, the neighboring motorist did a double take, looked behind her, then bit down on his lower lip before leaning out his window and shouting, "Welcome back, Guild Hunter! Anyone who survives the fucking house explosion from hell is a legend in my book!"

Elena gave him a playful salute. She knew the whispers would've already begun; speculation about how she'd lost her wings would soon become everyone's favorite activity. The worst would be among the immortals. Some outside the Tower would cackle in glee at her loss, while others would look on her in suspicion for being neither vampire nor human nor angel.

Did she care? Only if it impacted Raphael.

As they zipped along, the wind playing through their hair, Ashwini updated her on Guild news and other random bits of information. "Ransom's probably going to be waiting inside Sara's office," she said at one point. "Man's done so many slow drives past the Tower since you woke that Dmitri asked him if he wanted to join Tower security."

"He and Nyree found a house yet?"

"He won't talk to me for a month if I blab all his news."

"Tell me about the Slayer situation then." Hunters policed their own; the Slayer was their big bad, the hunter tasked with executing those who'd crossed a final line.

"Sara went with the team." Ashwini took a corner with smooth speed. "All senior active duty hunters take the assignment on rotation, with three of us on call at any one time. I've been through the training already, so have Ransom and Demarco, Hilda, Rose, and Kenji. Sara dusted off her active duty skills and put her name on the list."

"This is my not-surprised face." Sara was director of the Guild partially because she cared so much for her people—everyone knew that if it all went to shit, Sara would shield them from angry angels or pissed-off vampires until things calmed down. "Any of us going to allow that to happen?"

Ashwini snorted. "As if. She's too important to risk on a Slayer hunt. Demarco's in charge of the roster and he keeps 'forgetting' to add her name. I think she might be starting to get suspicious."

Shoulders shaking at the thought of Sara's toe-tapping irritation pitted against Demarco's "oh shucks" charm, Elena leaned back farther in her seat. "I'll do the training, too, once I'm back at full strength." She might no longer have wings, but she hadn't lost her hunter-born ability to scent vampires—as if that was so deep a part of her, nothing could erase it.

"Told Sara to save you a spot in the training schedule down the track."

"Keep going and pretty soon you'll be whispering portents like Cassandra."

"Hah!" A huge grin. "I got some other juicy news. Demarco has a girlfriend."

"What?! And you didn't lead with that?" Demarco was good-looking, no doubt about it, but he seemed to put out some pheromone that made women see him only as a great guy to have as a buddy. "Is she a good one?"

"Ransom's Nyree introduced them. You'll never guess what she does for a living."

"Another librarian?"

"Nah." Ashwini took the turn into the Guild HQ parking lot. "Girl's a hard-ass tattoo artist. Ink all over. Piercing through her upper lip and eyebrow. Boobs straight out of some fantasy comic strip, sleek muscle everywhere else. Taller than Demarco by a couple of inches and you know he's no shortie, and here's the kicker—she hauls him to her for a kiss every time she sees him."

Slipping into a free spot, Ash pulled the parking brake and turned off the engine. "Woman thinks he's the hottest thing since sliced bread. He looks dumbfounded every single time, like he can't believe his luck."

"I like her already." Elena was still grinning at the idea of meeting Demarco's girl when she walked into the HQ.

"WELCOME BACK!" boomed the gathered crowd, as golden balloons fell on her head and streamers went off everywhere.

She was engulfed in friendly arms a second later, hugged again and again by her friends and colleagues. Ransom crushed her close and, beard stubble rasping against the side of her face, whispered, "Nyree's pregnant. Five months."

"Eee!" Elena squeezed him back. "I'm going to get the baby a miniature leather jacket. Don't you dare let anyone else do it."

Then there she was: her best friend. Sara held her for a long time before they drew apart. Champagne corks popped and music thundered, but all she saw were her friend's deep brown eyes. Sara had grown out her bangs and wore her hair swept back in a neat but soft bun, her fitted dress a knee-length orange sheath that flattered her sleek body, her dark skin glowing with life.

Her voice was rough when she said, "Welcome back, Ellie."

Nothing more needed to be said, not here, not now.

"Ellie." A tumble-haired Demarco thrust a glass of champagne in her hand, then did the same for Sara. "Come on you two, it's party time!"

When Elena mentioned she had to call Beth first, Sara

shook her head. "I already told her you'd be late. She loved the idea of the party, said it gave her more time to bake. You'd better be ready to eat."

As it was, Elena turned up to her sister's home with Sara, Ransom, Ashwini, and Demarco in tow. Her hunter friends hung back near the cars, while Elena went ahead.

Beth, small and curvy, cried and ran into her arms. Holding her sobbing little sister, Elena wished she could turn back the clock, erase Beth's pain. "I'm sorry, Bethie," she said when Beth's tears came to a hiccupping halt.

"You came back." Beth wiped at her face with hands that had flecks of flour on them. "And you didn't choose to go away."

Unlike Marguerite.

"I'll never choose it." Never make her sister believe she didn't matter enough for Elena to fight to live. "Now, where's my favorite niece?"

Wiping away the last remnants of her tears, Beth smiled and ran her hand down her full-skirted white dress patterned with red hearts. "Tell Sara and the others to come in. Maggie's out back. She'll be so excited."

Once inside the house, Elena's fellow hunters headed straight for the table piled high with baked goods. Beth beamed before taking Elena's hand and leading her to the kitchen. "There she is." Beth pointed through the kitchen window into the backyard, her smile softer, her heart right out in the open.

It wasn't only Maggie playing on the back lawn. Jean-Baptiste was all hair of gilt and sun-kissed skin, while Majda's skin was a darker gold, her hair holding a little more color than Elena's. Elena's grandfather was a warrior, tall and muscled, her grandmother petite, with hearth and home her core.

The love between them shone.

Today, the two were blowing bubbles with their energetic and laughing great-granddaughter. Marguerite's baby's baby. Elena went motionless at seeing the translucent and rainbow-hued bubbles float up into the air, against the dark green of the trees. "How was Majda after I . . . after what happened?" Their grandmother had survived a nightmare, only to return to a world in which her cherished daughter was dead.

Jean-Baptiste had warned Elena that Majda's heart couldn't bear another such loss.

"Not good, but I kept her busy with Maggie." Beth, so frivolous to those who couldn't see beneath her pretty dresses and feminine makeup, and so loving to her people, patted Elena's arm. "She's saved all of us. And she hasn't forgotten her Auntie Ellie—asks all the time about you."

Elena made herself smile through the pain in her heart. Maggie would have the childhood she and Beth hadn't—she would get to enjoy the bubbles and the backyard, secure in the love of a mom who'd never *ever* choose to leave her.

Her niece shrieked when Elena appeared in the doorway. Abandoning her bubble-making apparatus, she made a beeline for Elena, yelling, "Auntie Ellie! Auntie Ellie!" Her arms came up partway and Elena strode over the grass to pick her up and twirl her around.

Her arms were strong enough for this, for love.

"Auntie Ellie!" Maggie kissed her cheeks when she stopped the swirl. "Where did your wings go?"

"I don't know," Elena said through a rough throat. "I'm going to be an auntie without wings now. Do you mind?"

A hard shake of Maggie's head. "You're my favorite!" Her dark eyes sparkled, her silky black hair sticking to her cheeks, one small barrette already halfway falling off, the other precarious but holding. "Wanna blow bubbles?"

"Yeah." It was time to make new memories of backyards and bubbles in the sun.

Elena carried her niece to where her grandparents stood waiting. Majda watched her come in poignant silence, her beauty worn and tired in a way that had nothing to do with food or rest. "Elena." A soft whisper of welcome as she cupped Elena's cheeks and kissed her on the forehead; her fingers trembled, the clear turquoise of her eyes shimmering oceans.

Jean-Baptiste stroked his hand over Elena's hair at the same time, his features locked with a control that was brutal.

Maggie reached out to pat her great-grandmother's cheeks dry. "Is okay Gamma. Auntie Ellie's home now."

22

Maggie's words rang in Elena's head that night as she got ready for bed. No one but her niece had asked about her wings. Not her hunter friends. Not her family. She'd noticed the soft pats on the back and the gentle smiles, so they weren't ignoring it. Rather, they'd chosen to focus on the joy of her return rather than what she'd lost.

Muscled arms wrapping around her from behind, Raphael's naked chest pressing to her back, her camisole and panties a thin barrier between them. He was still wearing his pants, but it did nothing to hide the power and hard strength of him. "I feel so weak against you now." Her fingers clenched on the edge of the bathroom counter.

The dangerous blue of his gaze met hers in the mirror. "You've never been weak, Guild Hunter, not even at your most wounded."

Elena wanted to kick the cabinet. "I don't know what's wrong with me. Everyone was so wonderful to me today. I should be happy." But she wasn't, she was angry and that anger was threatening to turn toward the man who had torn out his heart for her.

"The Cascade stole your wings." Raphael's voice held that

edge of cold power that was slowly becoming familiar. "You are determined to push that to the past and move on, but you have a right to your anger." White fire licked over the arch of his wings, the dancing energy seeming to taunt her.

Turning in his arms, she shoved at his chest. "I can't even be properly angry at you!" And *that* made her angry. "I love you too much!"

"I am here, Elena, for your anger and your love both." He closed his hands over her wrists. "Together. Always."

"But we *can't* now!" The hot ball of lead in her stomach exploded into a conflagration. "I can't fly with you! I can't dance with you in the sky, not like before!" Everything had changed and they couldn't ignore that, not between the two of them. *She* couldn't ignore it, couldn't keep on pretending she was over it.

"When I fed you ambrosia, I didn't know you would wake as an angel." His hands tightened on her wrists. "I didn't even know what it was I tasted in my mouth. I expected to have to face your wrath when you woke as a vampire. Wings do not make you my lover. That has always been your heart, your spirit, your courage—and your fury."

"But we built a life together in which I could fly beside you. It's gone now!" No more midnight flights where they played together in the sky. No more tangled wings while they slept.

"Then we build a new life together."

"What if it's not like before? What if it's worse?"

"What if it's better?"

"Argh! I need you to get angry and fight with me!"

A startled smile on Raphael's face. It made him look incredibly young. She could've never imagined him this way when they'd first met on the Tower roof what felt like a lifetime ago. He'd been so inhuman then, a being of power and cruelty who'd made her close her hand over a blade to prove a point.

Her blood had dropped to crash against the rooftop on which they stood, small brutal paintings.

Now he was her lover and her eternity . . . and he wouldn't be this man if he hadn't been so foolish as to fall in love with a mortal.

Hauling down his head, she kissed him hard. Maybe she couldn't play with him in the skies—and yeah, that would piss her off forever—but she'd fly with him in this way. Their bodies entwined, their hearts beating as one. Because he was hers and *she* was the only one who could break them. So screw the anger and the self-pity.

Breaking the kiss just as she was really getting going, Raphael gathered her up in his arms and strode out the bathroom door. She slapped his gorgeous shoulders when she realized he was heading toward the balcony doors. "Don't you dare!" It was freezing out there.

He didn't stop.

"Raphael! I'm only wearing a camisole and panties." A new set that fit her thin frame and that she'd had delivered herself because she and Montgomery had an unspoken agreement—he could do what he liked with her wardrobe, but her underwear drawer was off-limits. "I'll turn into an icicle."

"Such a lack of faith in my abilities, Elena-mine." He shook his head, a look of mock sadness on his face; there was no cold in him now, no distance. "Has my glamour ever before let you down?"

She fought not to laugh. "Your glamour is fantastic," she said in her most adoring tone, fluttering her lashes at the same time. "It's the best glamour in the world. I still don't want to be bare-ass naked above New York. Part of me keeps expecting the Cascade to come back for another go."

Raphael kissed her, and it tasted of angel dust. The special blend created for Elena alone, erotic and luscious and toe-curling. Her nipples tightened to hard little points. "That's not playing fair," she breathed against his lips.

"Your taste addicts me," was the rough-voiced response.

Another slow kiss. "I know you love me," she said in the aftermath. "I know it was never about wings." She struggled to explain the feelings tearing at her. "But before, I felt like a partner. Now . . . I've never been so weak." Even as a mortal, she'd been stronger than most—a consequence of being hunter-born. "I've never been fragile, not even as a child."

Unwavering eye contact, the chrome blue alive with lightning. "I could've killed you at any point during that time. Ripped you limb from limb without breaking a sweat."

She sat up in his arms, scowling. "Really, that's your idea of a pep talk?"

"You have stood your ground against me from the first time we met, when I saw no value in humanity and could've crushed you with no thought to what I was destroying. Power and strength have never been what makes us equal, *hbeebti*."

The words hit hard.

Her lover was an archangel, one of the Cadre of Ten. The only being that could kill an archangel was another archangel. Elena stood no chance and never had. Yet they'd fought together, flown together, battled the reborn together, sent Lijuan to hell together.

"I feel dumb now." And light inside, as if the bubbles she'd blown with Maggie were in her veins. "Can we forget this ever happened?"

His smile was dawn on the horizon . . . dawn edged with frost. The sheer violence of his new power cracked his skin with gold when he kissed her. She locked her arms around him and took the ice, took the lightning, took him. And when they hit the night skies above Manhattan, she felt not even a touch of cold, Raphael using his power to both shield them from the world and cocoon her in warmth.

They flew above a city of steel and light and color, and out to the ocean beyond. "I barely have any well-fitting underwear as it is," she murmured against his mouth when he incinerated her camisole and panties before they could fall into the ocean. "Don't let this go to your head but you're so sexy that, right now, I don't even care."

The archangel who held her was lethal beyond compare . . . and his smile, it closed its fingers around her heart and made her breath catch. His kiss was raw heat and furious demand, the hand he ran over her body rough with possessiveness and hot with need. One muscled arm kept her locked to him as he squeezed her breast with the other.

Elena's entire body clenched. She felt no fear, even high above the Atlantic; Raphael would never let her fall. They kissed, touched, tasted, their skin heating from the friction. Breath coming in hard pulses, Raphael said, "Dive?"

"Go."

He angled them down . . . and folded back his wings, turning himself into an arrow headed toward the water. Elena screamed and laughed . . . then gasped in wonder as they crashed into the ocean encased in a protective shield alive with lightning. Legs wrapped around Raphael as they floated down and down into the fathomless dark, she felt wild and alive and *real*.

Raphael ran his nails down her back.

She shuddered hard. "The sensations are back." Of an intimate caress on her wings, of contact she'd permit only one being in this world.

One hand going to her nape, the other repeating the touch. Groaning, she closed her hands over the arches of his wings, and massaged down at *just* the right pressure to make him insane. The kiss was all teeth and sex this time, their bodies hot and sweaty as they slid against one another.

She rubbed against him before reaching down between their bodies to close her hand around the thickness of his cock. Rigid steel covered in silk, he thrust into her hand. Already wet for him, she kissed her way desperately down his neck while continuing to torment him.

His wings began to glow. Her core pulsed.

When he put his hands on her hips and hauled her into exactly the right position to take him, she laughed the husky laugh of a woman who knew she was irresistible to her lover. Moaning as he thrust into her, she dug her nails into his flesh, coming around him on the first stroke.

He wasn't holding back.

It was an aphrodisiac beyond compare.

Had anyone been able to see through the glamour, they would've witnessed the ocean explode with a hidden sun.

The next day, Elena took her knives and walked into a small practice ring low down in the Tower—she didn't need the massive space of the main ring. Not today. It was time she got back to strength training—and figured out her current body. She could compensate for weak muscles and shaky arms, but she had to see if her hand-eye coordination had survived the chrysalis.

She was only ten minutes into it when Dmitri walked in dressed in black cargo pants and a black T-shirt decorated with the faded logo of a metal band. "Space is taken," she said with a scowl. "I booked it last night."

"Came to see if you needed any help." A smirk. "I'm feeling sorry for you since you're so skinny and pathetic right now."

Elena gave him her most fake smile. "Want to act as my target? I'm sure it'll improve my accuracy one hundred percent."

Dmitri raised both eyebrows, then smiled, slow and sensual. "Why not?"

And so began the craziest throwing session of Elena's life. Dmitri was a deadly fast vampire and her muscles remained wobbly, but it turned out that her hand-eye coordination was just fine. So was her ability to think on her feet. Ten minutes. Twenty. Thirty.

She threw a second blade on the heels of the first, after he'd already committed to his avoidance strategy.

It slammed home in Dmitri's shoulder. The hilt quivered from the impact.

They both froze for a taut, silent second. Until the wet patch on his T-shirt began to spread. "Fuck! Get that out right now! Honor will goddamn murder me." She'd never expected to score such a solid hit—Dmitri was too fast, too experienced. "I'm getting you some blood."

Elena ran to the fridge just outside the training ring, grabbed a bottle. Powerful as he was, the infusion of blood should cause the wound to heal in a matter of minutes. *Well* before Honor laid eyes on it. Because it was one thing to threaten her friend's bastard of a husband, quite another to wound him badly.

Hilts didn't quiver that way unless the blade had hit bone.

Dmitri had finished pulling out the knife by then. Flipping it around, he lobbed it back to her. "It's just a scratch. Like being bitten by a mosquito."

"Shut up and drink this." She thrust the bottle into his hand.

"Such solicitude. I'm touched."

Tendrils of fur and champagne wrapped around her, decadent chocolate sinking into her taste buds at the same time. Gritting her teeth, she backed off. "Scent games? You want me to stab you again?"

Having finished half the bottle, he lowered it and shrugged. "I'm the one bleeding." He touched the wet patch—which had stopped its terrifying spread at last. "No more mollycoddling you, sweet Elieanora."

"You're an asshole," she said past the avalanche of drugging scent, though her lips wanted to kick up. The asshole happened to be the most powerful vampire in Raphael's territory, brutal and deadly—and he'd just told her that he was taking off the kid gloves.

As a compliment, it was a damn fine one.

Shit, she *owed* him now. He'd been *nice* to her. It was an utterly horrifying thought. But not enough to stifle her grin. Her hands closed on the hilts of her blades. "Ready for round two, or does bubby-wubby need another bottle?"

Dark eyes gleamed, champagne spun in her head, and Dmitri *moved*.

Her blades flew like silver fire, streaking through the air with lethal accuracy.

23

One month after the ridiculously fun session with Dmitri—
not that either one of them would admit that even on pain of
hideous torture—and Elena wasn't yet as muscled as she
would've liked. Her weight was only up to eighty-five percent
of her normal, so she still felt a bit too insubstantial, but she
no longer had any appearance of illness.

The sex mojo had returned twice more in the week after
the knife session. Her body had stopped glitching after the
second boost. After that, anything she'd achieved, she'd done
so through teeth-clenched hard work.

When she applied to the Guild to return to active duty, Sara
said, "You have to pass the post-injury physical."

Elena would've been insulted at any other response. Guild
medics gave her a clean bill of health, though lightning fissures did still break out over her body at times—as if a bite of
Raphael's power had woven itself into her bones, the heart in
her chest strong enough to manage archangelic energies.

Her status on the taxonomic tree however, continued to
give everyone fits. She was immortal, of that there was no
doubt. Not an almost-immortal like a vampire, not a baby

immortal as she'd been before the chrysalis, but equivalent to an adult angel of around three hundred.

Except she wasn't an angel. Her DNA was distinctly odd and the only wings she had were phantom ones that tormented her with how real they felt. At times, she had to check in a mirror, confirm there was nothing on her back, no graceful arches, no feathers of midnight and dawn.

Elena struggled with that until Naasir, of all people, decided to pay her a visit. "I am the only one of my kind," he said to her as they sat on the edge of a balcony, their feet hanging over it and the metallic silver of his hair choppy and striking against the rich dark of his skin, the undertone of gold reminiscent of a leopard's coat.

Elena pinned him with a narrow-eyed gaze. "Do tell me more about your unique kind. I'm all ears."

Naasir threw back his head and laughed, a beautiful wild creature who delighted in playing this game with her. She'd forbidden Raphael from answering the question, from telling her of Naasir's origins or where he fit in a world of angels and vampires and mortals; this was a mystery she'd solve herself.

Naasir leaned in close, the metallic silver of his eyes in no way human, and whispered, "I have the pelt of a tiger sometimes." He held out his arm and, as she watched, his skin turned striped.

Gasping, she grabbed his arm without thinking. She and Naasir weren't close as she was with Illium, but he didn't reject her touch. Rather, he sat with the patience—and smirk—of a smug feline.

"I came here because Jessamy told me that you are now a one-being, too." A penetrating glance, his head cocked in a way that wasn't human, wasn't angel, wasn't vampire. "Before, I was lonely. Then I found my family."

She knew he was talking about Dmitri and Raphael and all the others of the Seven.

"Then I found Andi." Pure delight at the thought of his mate. "I am a one-being, but I am not alone. You are not alone."

No, she wasn't alone. And she was deeply, fiercely loved. "Thank you," she said to the wild creature who'd come such a long way because he'd known she needed him. "Will you stay?"

"Only today." A smile that was all teeth. "I will go home via the India-China border. The current quiet makes my fur stand up the wrong way—I smell the darkness building. I'll spy for Jason."

"Yeah, I have that itchy feeling, too." As if a volcano was getting ready to blow—but none of the archangels or their spymasters had found anything of note. Even the unexplained disappearances in China had stopped. So had the ice storms, geothermal disturbances, flooding, and swarms of wasps.

The world was at peace.

But as Caliane had pointed out: "The eye of the storm is always dead calm."

Everyone was waiting for storm winds to hit again.

She waved Naasir off only hours later, then turned to her archangel. "Any news?"

A grim shake of his head before he took a hard kiss, then rejoined a squadron training exercise. He was putting all his spare time into helping their people become stronger, more prepared for whatever was about to hit. Elena, for her part, was sparring against strong vampires and angels every day—Raphael included—as well as picking up local hunts. It was good to get out, test her body in the real world, add another layer of strength. She needed to be ready to stand beside her archangel when the eye passed.

A week after Naasir's visit, and she'd just completed her third successful retrieval.

Having delivered the runaway vamp to his angel, Urizen, she now stood on top of the seven-story building owned by the angel and smiled. Around her was a garden starting to hunker down for winter, but with enough color in it still that she'd spotted the vines and tree branches from the sidewalk.

Urizen had been delighted at her interest, had shared that he personally took care of the space. "Please go up. I'll join you after I've dealt with Ox."

"Is that really his name?"

"Worse. He chose it." The short and stocky angel with wings of off-white brushed with streaks of sunset orange had thrown up his hands. "Now he tries to run only ten years into his Contract, as if he did not walk into vampirism with his eyes open." Exasperation altered into cool resolve, the cream of his complexion suddenly without warmth. "I do not enjoy punishing my vampires. The garden will be a welcome balm in the aftermath."

Before walking into the immortal world, Elena hadn't understood that not all angels were cruel and heartless. Many were like Urizen, forced into cruelty to rein in vampires who would otherwise splatter the world in scarlet. Because while Ox was no genius, he *was* viciously strong, had come at Elena with teeth bared and hands clawed.

Vamp was on the edge of bloodlust.

Jaw tight because there was a chance Urizen wouldn't be able to haul him back, leading to an automatic execution order, she turned her attention to the garden. A few hardy plants hung on to their fall foliage, the yellows, reds, and oranges brilliant against the azure of the cloudless sky.

No angels flew in that sky. Anyone not on sentry duty was probably watching the winged game of baseball Illium's squadron had put together, with Illium as referee. He only ever played if Aodhan was also playing.

She was about to run her fingers along the trunk of a five-foot-tall tree with leaves of dark red fading into deep brown when she remembered she had to think "don't grow" thoughts while doing so. It had been three weeks since she'd last accidentally supercharged a tree, but since this was on a roof, she decided not to risk it. Instead, she admired it from afar, picked a couple of weeds out of a patch of hardy winter-greens, and tried to narrow down a fresh gingery scent that lingered in the air.

She'd just worked out that the source was a small ground-cover plant when a movement from the taller building to the right caught her eye. It proved to be a flutter of color situated a couple of stories higher than her current position; her first thought was that someone was about to lose a towel they'd hung over the railing to dry.

Then her brain put all the pieces together.

Elena began to run, her heart pulsating in her mouth. She knew her voice couldn't travel that far, but she yelled out a desperate warning to whoever was looking after the toddler who'd managed to climb over the balcony railing and was now clinging to it by his fingertips while his legs kicked helplessly in the air. He had to be screaming, but no one ran out of the apartment to rescue him.

No angels in the sky. Urizen deep inside his home. No one on a nearby balcony who could scramble to get to the child. Raphael was fast, but she had no idea of his current location and the kid had a matter of seconds at best.

Shh. Shh. Shh.

She touched her mind to Raphael's anyway, because if this all went how she thought it would, both she and the little boy would need healing. *Serious* healing.

Raphael! Urizen's place!

No more time.

She couldn't fly. But her bones had been pronounced immortal-strong. And seven stories was survivable for an immortal of three hundred if she fell correctly and made sure her head didn't get separated from her neck. Decapitation would be a serious bummer to her desire to spend eternity with Raphael.

All these thoughts and more passed through her mind in the second it took her to cross half the length of the roof. The rest of the time, she spent calculating her odds. The distance between the two buildings wasn't huge. If she jumped at the right moment and aimed her body weight perfectly, she could put herself in the correct position to catch the little guy before he fell. Curl her body over and around him and her stronger bones would take the impact of the fall.

One of the toddler's hands slipped off the railing.

He was going to fall at any second.

Elena's foot hit the edge of the roof and she launched herself into the air, her eyes never leaving the child.

He lost his final grip just as a frantic female face appeared at the balcony. Her terror shattered the quiet, but Elena barely heard it, her body flying through the air. Angles, weight, position, her hunter's mind worked it all out with ruthless efficiency . . . and a small, screaming weight fell into her arms, the momentum of the catch sending her tumbling.

Fuck, this was going to hurt. Bad.

She tucked herself around the little boy's petrified body as the air rushed past them at terminal speed.

24

Raphael! Urizen's place!

Raphael switched direction without hesitation, pulling such a tight turn that his wing muscles protested before they blazed into white fire and he was moving at speeds that turned the world into a barely visible blur.

That hadn't been terror in Elena's voice. It had been determination coupled with a sense of desperation. He wasn't far from her but the journey there felt like an eternity. He arrived over Urizen's building . . . just in time to see Elena catch a falling child in her arms and begin to spiral down to the ground.

Raphael flew toward her at lightning speed, but he knew he wasn't going to make it. The child's weight and momentum were causing her to drop at a catastrophic rate and she hadn't begun very far from the ground. She was going to smash herself into pieces. But, tightly curled as she was around the child, she might save that small life. Raphael knew the choice she'd tell him to make if he had to choose between saving her and saving the child.

The child. Always the child.

He went to try and cut under her, catch her and the child both, though he knew the attempt was futile. Even wings of white fire couldn't eliminate the space between two objects. His heart screamed. *Elena!*

A sudden explosion of light above him . . . and no bloody bodies on the street. Low as he'd flown, he had to land or smash into a wall. When he looked up, what he saw had him launching into the air once more. Elena stared at him in silence. Even the screaming child had gone silent, shocked by the sudden halt.

"Raphael." It was a whisper. "Am I levitating? Just to clarify, I'm fine with levitating rather than being hunter-flavored mincemeat." She looked down. "Phew. Even if I stop levitating now, this baby will be fine and worst I'll get is a turned ankle."

"Land." His voice came out hoarse. "Land, Elena."

"Land?" A furrowed brow, a taut voice. "Archangel, I haven't exactly figured out the levitating thing yet."

Breathing with icy calm even though his newly regenerated heart was a massive drum, he put his hand on Elena's shoulder and pushed her down until her feet touched the asphalt. The screaming woman from the balcony had disappeared, was probably frantically running down the stairs to get to her son.

Who was now beaming at Raphael through a tear-streaked face, all dark eyes and hair, his skin a pale brown. He held out two chubby arms right then, and Raphael plucked him out of Elena's hold. The child laughed and tried to reach for his wings.

In front of him, Elena folded her trembling arms. "There's gratitude for you. I saved his life and he goes gaga over you. Typical." Her voice shook, no bite in her tone and her pupils huge.

"Elena, look over your shoulder."

"Did I magically grow wings?" she said with a wry smile before glancing back. She froze. Her throat moved in a hard swallow. She turned back to him very, very slowly. "I wasn't levitating."

"Seth!" A woman's desperate cry. "Seth!"

"Mama!" The toddler leaned out toward his sobbing mother; he was grinning, having managed to grab hold of Raphael's feathers before his mother arrived.

The distraught woman hugged her son close, her entire body shaking hard enough to fracture. "Thank you, thank you, thank you," she said through her tears. "We were dancing in the lounge with the music up, and I had to go into the kitchen to check on the stew. I was away for two minutes. I don't know how he—"

"Climb chair mama!" her son informed her with delighted pride.

They all looked up to the outdoor seating on the balcony. The woman's face went bone white. "I'm going to go throw that in the Dumpster right now." Wiping off her tears with the back of one hand, she looked from Elena to Raphael, finally seemed to realize who it was that had caught her boy. "T-t-thank you."

"I'm glad I could help." Elena's voice was stronger, but Raphael saw the rigid tension in her neck, the dark blot of her dilated pupils.

"Go, be with your son," Raphael said, giving the child's mother permission to run—he could see the need in her eyes. No ordinary adult mortal liked coming face-to-face with an archangel.

Children were another story.

Young Seth, unaware he'd used up one of his lives as well as his mother's, waved at them over his mother's shoulder.

Elena waited until the twosome had disappeared into the building before she stepped close to Raphael. "Are the you-know-whats on my back still there?" she whispered, scared that talking about the impossible would poof it out of existence.

Her archangel nodded.

Breath shallow and fast, she dared look over her shoulder . . . to see unearthly wings of white fire electric with a storm of golden lightning. That lightning moved, dazzling and alive, but the shape of her wings remained unbroken. They were big, the same size wings she'd had before the chrysalis. "Touch it," she rasped, not ready to believe she wasn't hallucinating.

Maybe she'd hit her head hard when she landed, was now in la-la land.

Raphael made contact. Elena shivered, sensation arcing through her nerve endings.

"I feel no solid surface." Raphael touched her again; when he withdrew his hand, it came out coated with tiny lightning strikes that sank into his skin. "Do you want to attempt flight?"

"Yes, I have to know." A light flashed not far in the distance at the same instant. "I think we're being paparazzied." Regardless, she drew in, then spread out her lightning storm wings. "Wish me luck. Vertical takeoffs were never my forte."

She was four feet off the ground before she realized what had happened. The pulse in her neck skittered, her skin hot. *Home, Archangel.*

I'll fly under you.

Neither one of them had to articulate the reason why— Elena had no idea where these wings had come from or how long they'd last. But as she took to the sky, she felt no fear, only a bone-deep joy. The events of the past few minutes— *such a short time*—ran through her mind in a repeating loop.

"I can't believe I asked you if I was levitating!" she called out to Raphael once they were high enough up that no one else was going to hear them.

I will be magnanimous and blame it on shock. It will be a hushed secret between an archangel and his consort.

Laughing, she swept to the left, then back around to the right to test her maneuverability. *They function just like flesh and blood wings.* Eyes hot, she had to blink to clear her vision. *You gave me your heart, a heart that can process violent Cascade energies—you gave me back my wings, Raphael.*

The salt-laced sea in her mind, huge and cold and of Raphael. *I may have provided the raw material, Guild Hunter, but you made the choice. Wings of fire and lightning can fit in a chrysalis that is too small.*

Despite her desperate desire to fly and fly, she went straight to their Tower balcony. After landing beside her, Raphael cupped her face and pressed his forehead to hers. There they stood, no words needing to be spoken.

When they did walk inside and down to the infirmary level, it was to run into Dmitri. He took one look at her and shook his head. "Don't scorch the walls."

Striding over, Elena hauled down his head and kissed him hard on the lips. "Today, even you can't annoy me," she said into his stunned face before releasing him.

A laugh sounded from not far down the corridor, where Dmitri's wife had just emerged from Lucius's office. Honor's eyes were dancing. Dmitri, meanwhile, was looking at Elena in utter horror. "We will never speak of this again," he said. *"Ever."*

"I think he could use a hug," Elena said to Honor.

"You two are awful together and I love you both. And your wings are a showstopper." With that, Honor walked over to console her scowling husband.

Raphael meanwhile, was wearing a suspiciously bland expression.

Elena jerked up her head as they continued on down the corridor. "What?"

"I have never seen that look on Dmitri's face in all my life. I also cannot wait to see the look on your face when it sinks in that you kissed Dmitri."

"All worth it." Full of sunshine and sparkles and freaking puppy dogs, Elena all but skipped into Nisia's office.

The Tower healer and Keir were seated on a small dark blue settee, their heads bent over a pile of charts and notes. A single glimpse of Elena and they were over her like a rash, muttering and examining and talking in a fluid language Raphael told her was a variant of Aramaic. It was as Keir was about to take a reading that her wings disappeared in a silent whoosh.

Elena tried not to panic. "Raphael, what's my back look like?"

"Your leather jacket boasts two wing slits with the edges sealed shut as if by heat." He helped her get the jacket off. After which, she pulled off the long-sleeved T-shirt she'd been wearing underneath. Turning her body toward the mirror Nisia held up, she sucked in a breath.

A familiar tattoo covered her back: a fiery outline of wings that blazed before settling into a glittering light under her skin.

"Your wings have always been present," Raphael murmured, running his finger along the edges and making her toes curl. "At least since the day we first saw the fire tattoo."

"I don't know how to bring them back." It was hard to breathe.

Eyes as blue as a mountain sky met hers. "Remember how you learned to fly?"

"You pushed me off a cliff."

Nisia held out a palm. "Wait, just wait."

"I am not sure that's the greatest idea," Keir began, but Elena was already putting her clothes back on.

Dire alarm marking their faces, the healers hurried after Elena and Raphael as she and her archangel strode out onto the balcony. When she saw the Legion's gray wings filling the air, she knew Raphael had called them. Her personal catching team. She walked to the very edge. "I'm ready."

No hesitation, no questions; the love of her life pushed her into a deadly fall before sweeping down and below her with his arms open, ready to break her fall. Elena didn't panic, just thought of her wings. Her body kept accelerating. And accelerating. *Shit.* She was about to slam straight into her archangel. *I need wings now!*

A wrench at her back. A jerking halt.

"Yee-fucking-hah!" She dived straight at Raphael, laughing, and they played like wild winged children. The Legion swept and flew around them, their voices in Elena's head.

We have not seen this.
We did not know.
The chrysalis was not too small for this.
You are new, Elena.
We are new.
We are . . . happy.

25

Caliane's tone was frosty when she called Raphael that night. "You did not have to keep your consort's lightning wings secret from me." Her eyes were the same shade as his and at that instant, they were Arctic ice. "I am not the enemy."

"No, Mother, you are not." She had fought for him since her return. At the same time, she had once been an insane archangel who'd left him to die on a forgotten field, his blood rubies on the green, green grass.

Raphael couldn't forget, saw both sides of her. And so, he chose his words with care. "We did not wish to speak of it until we knew all there was to know about Elena's new physical state. Unfortunately, an accident with a child altered the timeline."

"I see." The slightest thaw. "I will accept that as a warrior's decision not to expose her strength to all the world while it is nascent." A raised eyebrow. "Where *is* your consort?"

"Right here, Lady Caliane." Stepping into frame, Elena inclined her head just enough that it was polite without calling her own status as Raphael's consort into question. "Would you care to see my wings more closely?"

Appearing mollified by the offer, his mother nodded.

Elena's wings erupted out of her back in a flash of electric lightning, a storm surge barely contained. She shifted so that Caliane could get the full effect.

Raphael had rarely seen his mother lost for words, but today, Caliane was silent until she said, "You, my child, are a being of change." It wasn't an indictment. "My son will certainly never suffer ennui with you as his love."

His mother signed off soon afterward.

Of course they flew that night.

Elena's wings dazzled against the ebony of the sky. *I look like a giant lightbulb, don't I? One of those ones they have at the science center with all the arcs of electricity inside.*

Raphael felt his cheeks crease. *You are extraordinary.* So preternaturally beautiful that he knew anyone looking up at the sky would be spellbound. *A career as a spy, however, might be beyond your reach.*

She burst out laughing, and they flew on. They danced. An archangel and his consort tangling limbs and bodies in a carnal union that made them both whole.

It was as they were returning home, their clothes lost over the ocean and Elena held in Raphael's arms so that his glamour would cover her, that her wings spluttered out. Frowning, she bit down on her lower lip. "I can't make them come back."

"You may have overexerted yourself."

"Yeah, you're probably right." But her face was tight, her body tense.

Being unable to give her solid answers, being unable to *fix* this, it had his power calcifying into granite edges inside him, hard and cutting.

After arriving home, he wrapped her up in his arms and wings and kissed her until nothing existed but the two of them.

Breathless in the aftermath, Elena tugged Raphael into the bedroom. "I think we need round two today."

They fell into bed together, with Elena lying on Raphael's chest, his wing over her body. She stroked his hair back from his face. "I've complicated your life, haven't I, Archangel?" He was one of the Cadre, a being used to control—but he could do nothing to control what was happening to her and it was savaging him.

She'd tasted the cold fury of it in his kiss.

"It rages through me, the anger," he told her, the lines of his face flawless in their masculine beauty and his voice a thing of frigid death. "I want to break the world."

"That's the Cascade pushing you. It wants violence, death, anger." Fisting a hand in his hair, she said, "Fight it. Stay my Raphael."

Cold immortal eyes. "No matter who or what I become, I will always be yours." As he gripped the back of her head and drew her down into a kiss, she realized he'd never made the promise she'd demanded.

While Raphael fought the rage that wanted to take root inside him, his consort spent the coming days testing her wings, figuring out their endurance.

"I must go to China," he told her two weeks after she first flew. "It is my turn to oversee the territory. You're coming with me."

She looked up from where she was polishing her brand-new knives, barefoot and in pajamas, her choppy hair tucked carelessly behind her ears. "Yes, Your Archangelness." A tug of her lips. "I can't let you out of my sight, either."

Raphael wasn't certain he'd ever reach that point.

"My endurance isn't as high as yours," Elena added as he removed the top of his leathers. "I'll probably need to land in places—but if you dare set a single foot on that poisoned land, I'll shoot you."

"I have no desire to be infected by whatever Lijuan left behind." Bare to the waist, but with his pants and boots yet on, he picked up one of her knives, testing the balance. "You have a piece of my heart. You may be susceptible."

"If I am, let's find out while you're full of wildfire that can burn out the poison." She slipped a blade into a thigh sheath. "But, the toxin is keyed to archangels and I'm a weirdo hybrid. Never thought that'd be an advantage."

"Get so much as a scratch on your body and I will lock you in a steel-reinforced room for the rest of your life." He wasn't certain he wasn't speaking the absolute truth.

Rising, she hauled him close and took a kiss that was slow, deep, defiant. "I'd just break out." Another kiss. "I know you're freaked out. So am I."

"Archangels do not get 'freaked out.'" But he kissed her anyway. "Pack a gown. Mother has been making noises about an evening event to celebrate our 'triumphant return.'"

Elena groaned and banged her head against his sternum.

The anger and fear knotting up his insides softened. "Your favorite angel, Tasha, will be present."

"I'll get you back for that." A glare. "But your taunt has found its mark, curses on you. I'll now have to rustle up a fabulous evening gown so Tasha McHotpants can't show me up by being all gorgeous and competent."

That, he thought, was what annoyed her the most: Tasha was someone Elena might actually like if not for the fact that Tasha had made it clear she'd enjoy picking up where she'd left off with Raphael. It had been foolishness on Tasha's part, with no chance of success, but it meant Elena and Tasha would never be friends.

"Montgomery has no doubt already assembled a suitable wardrobe for you." Most of what his consort called her "fancy clothes" had burned up in the inferno of Raphael's power. "Speaking of which—Maeve is asking if we'd like the house rebuilt as it was, or if we want changes."

"It was a spectacular house."

"How about a special room for all your knives?" he said in a small joke between an archangel and his consort, but Elena lit up like a candle.

"Really? You don't think that's excessive? It could be a small room. Just with lots of wall space." A sudden frown. "Were you making fun of me?"

"A little, but now I will build you the best knife display room you've ever seen."

Elena's lips twitched. "Don't forget the spot for my crossbow."

"It will have a podium of its own with a dedicated spotlight."

"As it should." Feet bare and grin wide, she stood on his booted feet. "Talking about blades makes me hot."

"Any more sharp objects on you today?" he murmured against her ear.

"You're safe." Her mouth was wet and soft on his chest, her tongue licking him up in tender flicks.

His blood felt so cold at times these days, but never when he was with her.

Hand pressed against his heart, she threatened a playful bite . . . then paused, her head cocked slightly and tiny lines flaring out at the corners of her eyes. "Put your finger on the pulse in my neck."

"I have never partaken of this deviant sexual act."

"Funny man. Fingers, neck."

When he obeyed, she said, "Listen. To your pulse and mine."

As with most living beings, Raphael wasn't aware of his pulse in the course of normal day-to-day life. It took him a second to tune in to the sensation. "Our hearts are beating in time." In perfect synchronicity.

"It can't happen all the time, or we'd be constantly out of tune with our surroundings." A kiss pressed to his skin. "Must be a resting-state effect. I like it." The eyes that lifted to meet his were liquid silver, haunting and immortal.

But her kiss . . . it was Elena. Mortal, courageous, untamed.

She would not be taken by the Cascade, would not be broken. Raphael wasn't so certain about himself. Because the frigid cold of his new power, it was seeping deeper and deeper into his cells with each day that passed. The more he owned it, the more it became a part of him . . . and the more he had to fight to be Elena's Raphael.

Yet without that power, he could not make enough wildfire to defeat Lijuan.

For she would rise into her reign of death.

Cassandra had foreseen it. And Cassandra was never wrong.

26

They flew first to Amanat, their plan to rest the night, then head to China in the morning. Because Elena needed to conserve energy, after the Tower jet landed at a major airport in Kagoshima, she got into a helicopter for the rest of the journey to Amanat, while Raphael rode the wind.

The sunlight danced off the fire of her archangel's wings as they moved over Kagoshima's green and mountainous landscape. He was far enough not to be affected by the chopper's blades, close enough to respond should the craft suffer technical difficulties. It didn't matter how often she saw him fly, she felt the same sense of possessive awe—he was hers and he was magnificent.

"Does it burn?"

Startled, she glanced at the pilot, not sure she'd heard him correctly through the headphones. One of Caliane's people who'd returned to her after his lady rose again, he'd told Elena he'd spent years flying commercial jetliners before switching to helicopters. His skin was as deep a hue as finest dark chocolate and as smooth as silk.

He was old, this one. Old enough that vampirism had begun to refine his features into a kind of ethereal beauty that no mortal would ever possess. The odd thing was, Dmitri was older, but he remained as hard-edged as always. So could be, the change wasn't inevitable. Maybe, each vampire subconsciously influenced the shape of their features.

Dmitri, of course, would always want to look like a hard-ass.

"Burn?" she asked, as a family of wild horses raced the shadow of the chopper on the ground.

"The fire on Archangel Raphael's wings."

"No." That was no secret. Little Seth had touched Raphael's wings, the sight caught on camera by a resident in a nearby building. He'd no doubt find himself the focus of childish curiosity in Amanat, too.

Caliane's beloved home was no longer a Sleeping city, and its people had begun to have children. The first born would be toddlers by now. Maidens become maids often carried a child propped on their hips, while warriors and others flew babies into the sky to soothe them when they wouldn't stop crying.

Most of the children were born of mortals or young vampires, but two angels had also recently given birth. As far as Elena was aware, Amanat was the only place outside of the Refuge where you could see angelic children. And that was because it was a closed city. The only people who could penetrate its shield were those welcomed by Caliane.

Raphael's eyes met hers across the distance that separated them and he pointed down. When she followed his gaze, she found the local band of monkeys waving and hollering up at them from their perches in the forest outside of Amanat. Laughing, she waved in return; she was certain the band recognized her and Raphael.

The cheeky creatures hooted and clapped and no doubt made a racket.

And there, in the distance, was the shimmering shield that encased the jewel of Amanat. It glowed a pink-tinged blue in the soft pre-sunset light, eerie and beautiful. Looking at that symbol of enormous power, Elena was hit by the realization that Caliane could do it all over again—simply disappear into Sleep, taking her people with her.

The chopper began to descend, the landing site within walking distance of Amanat but not so close that the noise would breach the city's peace.

"Thanks," Elena said after they were on the ground. "You coming into Amanat with us?"

A slight widening of the pilot's eyes before he inclined his head and body as much as his harness would allow. "I would be honored to walk together with an archangel and his consort but I will be doing a return trip. Here is my passenger now."

Walking toward where Raphael had landed was a woman with brunette curls and pearlescent skin. *Vampire.* No human had skin like that. "She's definitely not one of Caliane's maidens." No filmy gowns or pretty dresses for this woman. She was clad in a razor-sharp black skirt suit paired with spiked red heels, a smartphone to her ear, but the real difference was in the sense of danger that clung to her.

Another old one. Older than Dmitri. So old that she made Elena's teeth ache.

"It was before my time," the pilot said, "but legend is that Celesta *did* enter Caliane's court as a maiden. Our wise lady soon realized she did not have the temperament for it. She is far better utilized as a huntress."

"I'm guessing she stayed outside Amanat while the city Slept."

"Lady Caliane sent Celesta on a hunt before she took the rest of our people into Sleep." His jaw worked. "She sent me away, too. She has said that we are strong and she knew we would survive without her—I am glad to have grown and come to her with skills needed for this new world, but I would not have her leave me behind again."

Such devotion . . . it wasn't so different from what Lijuan's people felt for her. Elena's skin prickled. Not at the pilot's loyalty, at her renewed awareness of how hostile China remained to anyone who would stand against their goddess—even when their goddess made shambling reborn who fed on flesh.

That cold thought chilling her blood, Elena saluted the pilot before she jumped out with her head lowered and ran to join Raphael. Celesta had stopped beside him, was bowing deeply. There was nothing obsequious about it; Caliane's huntress managed to infuse the act with respect without making herself appear weak.

Spice hit Elena's nostrils, hints of cinnamon entwined with bark, earthy and hard. Celesta's scent was shockingly intense, mature in a way that coated the back of Elena's throat. *Archangel, you have any idea of her age?*

When I was a boy, Celesta told me stories of my mother's first court. Out loud, he said, "Why are you bowing to me, Celesta? I distinctly recall you throwing me into a pond to cool down after I indulged in a childish tantrum."

The huntress's lips twitched. "It has been many years. I thought perhaps, the archangel you have become would not remember the highly unsuitable babysitter who sometimes watched over you."

"You are not a woman anyone forgets." Raphael gripped Celesta's forearm in the way he did with his warriors.

Smile deepening, the vampire moved into Raphael's embrace. "Consort," she said afterward, with another bow. "I welcome you and Raphael to Amanat. My lady awaits."

"Good hunting." Elena inclined her head in a way Jessamy had taught her indicated deep respect; she knew that unlike Raphael, she couldn't simply tell this deadly woman not to bow to her—with an immortal this old, it could be counted as an insult. Better she respond in a way that meant something to Celesta.

Stupid angelic etiquette.

Celesta's responding smile seemed genuine. "I am presumptuous, but it pleases me that the wild little boy I taught to string his first bow has a fellow hunter for a consort," she said before continuing on to the chopper.

"Why haven't I met her before?" The earthy darkness of Celesta's scent clung to the air.

"My mother's favorite assassin and fixer—I believe that is the mortal's term—has been in Charisemnon's court until a half year past."

Elena's respect for the other woman took a nosedive. "Oh."

"Celesta knew her lady would need spies in the most terrible places when she woke." Raphael tugged on a strand of Elena's hair. "Why do you think she waited so long to return home?"

The respect blazed again—at twice its original strength. "It's official. I have a girl crush." Her eyes turned to the chopper as it lifted off. "She's got balls of steel if she embedded herself in that den and stayed." Charisemnon had caused the Falling, killing five of New York's angels. Not content with that, he'd created a virus that infected and killed vampires.

Raphael's wings stirred in a susurration of sound. "If you are good, I will tell you bedtime stories of Celesta the Knife."

As Elena laughed, a voice older than Celesta's entered his mind. *Come home, my son.* The hope in it was a painful thing, for he would never again think of Amanat as home. The last link that tied him to his mother's beloved city had broken as he lay bleeding on a forgotten field far from civilization while his mother walked away, her feet light on the grass speckled with his blood.

We are on our way, he said in response, because as his hunter had pointed out more than once, Caliane was trying. She'd come back sane. And she'd been staunch in her support of Raphael since then.

He knew his consort's response to Caliane was colored by her own deep grief. Her mother could never come back, could never try to make it up to her. And so his tough consort was far softer on Caliane than Raphael would ever be—he remembered the pain too well, remembered Caliane's madness as hundreds upon hundreds of tiny graves.

He'd helped dig those graves.

Days spent on a task no angel *ever* wanted to do, for children were a gift.

Instead of rising into the sky with Elena, he took her hand, and they walked through the waving grasses that separated the landing area from Amanat.

Elena ran the fingers of her free hand across the tips of the grasses. "There's such beauty here," she murmured. "Sometimes, I think Caliane has the right of it—just put a bubble around our city and dare anyone to try and get through."

But she was shaking her head even as she spoke. "Except what about the rest of our people, those scattered across the territory and the world? How could she have left so many behind? Was it because of her madness?"

This, too, was true—that while Elena was soft on Caliane, she saw his mother's flaws. "I worry, Guild Hunter," he murmured. "About the madness that took my mother and my father. It is in my blood." Indelibly a part of him. "There are indications it may be brought to life by the surge in power during a Cascade."

"Don't worry, Archangel. I'll shoot you between the eyes if you show signs of impending psychotic delusions." The near-white canvas of Elena's hair was licked with orange-red as the setting sun caressed her, her eyes liquid silver that burned. "Then I'll drag you to Keir. If he can't help, you'll be putting us both into Sleep. I'll figure out a way to make you."

"I am most assured." Lifting their linked hands, he kissed her knuckles, while behind him his wings trailed over the grass, leaving a dance of fire that didn't scorch.

"I'm serious." She ran her fingers through his hair, locked her gaze to his. "I'll *never* let you fall. We do this together."

She was a young immortal, with no power when compared to him . . . but he knew she would keep her word, hold him to account, not let the cold of immortal power win. "Always," he said.

A fierce kiss before she turned her attention to the shield less than fifty meters away. "Shall I?"

"My mother will be most disappointed if you do not."

A wicked grin. "Also, I want to show off." Light burst out of her back and in the colors of sunset sparked wings as extraordinary as his consort.

"Elena, they are no longer pure white-gold and lightning." Color had begun to bleed out into the fire. Black at her back that faded into indigo, deep blue, and the whispered shade of dawn. The same colors as the wings he'd been forced to amputate to save her from further pain—but lightning danced through them now, violent and beautiful.

Instead of looking back to see the change, she touched the fingers of her free hand to his jaw. "No brooding. We survived. And I got retractable wings out of it. I'm not sorry."

"Neither am I." If he hadn't done what he had, made the choices he had, she might not have returned as his Elena, with her own memories and thoughts and emotions. "But I will never forget slicing off your wings." It would haunt him forever, that image.

"I know it was a fucking nightmare." Both hands on his face now. "But those wings were dead already. Because of what you did, I was able to turn into a butterfly." She frowned. "Okay, I suck at metaphors, but you get what I mean."

"You are a butterfly with warrior's wings." He kissed her hard, holding that image in his mind, of her emerging from a chrysalis into a being of beauty and strength.

Light lived under Elena's skin when they parted.

At last she looked at her wings. "Guess these are my colors and I'm determined to have them." A satisfied look in her eye, she ran her fingers through the energy.

It was thus, both of them afire, that they walked through the shield and came face-to-face with the woman who was the template from which he'd been cast.

27

Caliane was no longer the oldest Ancient awake in the world—the Cascade had been stirring up many things, including Sleepers who had lain dormant in secret places for eons upon eons—but she was unquestionably one of the two most powerful.

She wore a gown of cerulean blue with bejeweled clips on the shoulders and sleeves that flowed down into cuffs embroidered with delicate care. Her skirts floated to brush the earth, her midnight hair soft waves down her back.

Seeing her this way, regal and elegant, no one would believe that she was a warrior angel. Her voice was renowned in angelkind, but Caliane could make music with her blade, too. The wings of purest white that sloped gracefully down her back were capable of split-second turns and rapid acceleration in battle, and her fighting leathers were as well-worn as his. She had been his first teacher when it came to the sword.

His mother was a woman of many faces, the one she showed him today luminous with maternal warmth. "My son. My Raphael."

He bent his head and she pressed her lips to his forehead, her hands on his biceps. "My heart sings to hold you thus, to see you standing strong and alive before me." She turned without warning to take Elena's face in her hands. His hunter's hand clenched on his, her body stiff. Caliane had softened toward Raphael's "most unusual consort," but she didn't treat Elena as a mother did her child.

Today, however, she pressed her lips to Elena's forehead and said, "And you, my son's heart, I feel joy to see you walk into my city as a warrior once again." She reached for Elena's hair, running the short strands through her fingers and examining the tiny feather at the end of one.

"There is nothing I despise more than those who seek to see a strong woman fall." With that cutting denunciation, she broke contact. "Come, you must be hungry after the journey. We will break bread, and I will tell you what has been happening across the water in China."

That sounds creepily ominous.

Even more so because my mother isn't known for being melodramatic. Caliane did not speak in twisted truths and mysterious lies. *We knew this wouldn't be easy—Lijuan is no simple foe.*

They followed Caliane deeper into Amanat.

His mother's city had its own microclimate, warm and temperate no matter if snow fell outside. Flowers bloomed in window boxes and trailed down walls of aged stone. Lush grasses grew against foundations. Vibrant green vines crawled up the sides of the houses, some blooming with tiny flowers. The colors of Amanat scented its air.

Elena took a suspicious sniff. "I'm in danger of fainting from the fresh air. Where're my exhaust fumes, my mishmash of cooking smells, that special eau-de-subway?"

"You will endure," Raphael said solemnly.

"I dunno, it's strong stuff." She stepped off the path, her intent to examine a particular vine. *Don't worry. I've practiced—no more accidentally putting trees on steroids.*

Caliane came to a halt, her expression indulgent when she turned to him. "You will build her a new greenhouse?"

"It was her favorite part of our home." Even more than her weapons, Elena cherished her plants. Today, she shifted away from the vine to say something to a passing maiden . . . and the vine began to bloom. Not in huge bursts, but in small, secretive flickers.

Caliane went motionless, the utter stillness of a very old being. "More secrets, Raphael?" A chill in the air.

Raphael made a decision at that moment—whatever her flaws, Caliane would never betray him and, by extension, Elena. "We do not know all of who we are after our waking."

"Such things for one so young . . ." Caliane's voice was soft. "This isn't good, son of mine. Power grows with age because age tempers us, makes us calmer, better able to weigh our decisions. Lijuan is a case in point—she gained too much power too quickly, lost herself inside it."

Raphael wondered what his mother would say if he told her of the cold storm inside him, insidious and vicious and hungry.

An hour later, after he and Elena'd had a chance to "wash off the road dust," they met Caliane in a leafy candlelit courtyard deep in Amanat. A table covered with a crisp white tablecloth and weighed down with food and drink sat in the center. Caliane's people had whispered away to leave them in privacy under a velvet blue sky studded with stars.

"Do you remember your first taste of mead, my son?"

Raphael found himself laughing, the memory unexpectedly bright. "A friend and I made off with a jug long ago, when we were boys in short pants," he told Elena. "We were curious about this drink we weren't allowed to have."

"Nadiel and I found the boys fast asleep in another angel's garden." His mother gave him a sternly affectionate look, and for an instant, it stabbed him in the heart, the family they'd once been. "Angel-mead is not meant for little ones."

Elena grinned. "Do you still see him? Your friend."

"We have a glass together every decade or so."

"He remains a rapscallion," Caliane said as she took a seat. "He has rejoined my court, but half the time when I send him out, I'm simply waiting to hear what calamity he's walked into now."

Raphael chuckled, but all their smiles faded soon afterward. An angel of old, Caliane waited to speak until after Raphael poured them all a goblet and they broke bread. "I am sure your black-winged shadow will have already told you of the refugees who have landed on my shores."

"Jason says they are well-behaved and go to great pains to keep their heads down."

"It's why I permitted them to stay when the exodus first began. That, and because none held high positions in Lijuan's court." Caliane took a drink. "Matters took an interesting turn a month ago, however. A high-ranking courtier moved in under cover of night and made a foolish attempt to blend in."

"A courtier who wasn't senior enough for Lijuan to take with her to wherever she's gone—or so senior that they were left behind as a spy?"

"You speak my questions." At that moment, Caliane was very much the Archangel of Amanat and not his mother. "I invited this vampire to my residence in a city an hour north of here." Cold, dark and deep in her voice as she added, "Amanat will *never* again open its doors to any of Lijuan's people."

"What did you learn?"

Elena held her silence while Raphael and Caliane spoke—Raphael's mother was old and not always predictable, and Raphael would get information from her the quickest. And it wasn't exactly a hardship to sit back under a glorious night sky with her archangel beside her and their trip to Lijuan's poisonous territory a future problem.

"I have seen terror in many faces over time," Caliane said, "and I have seen the slavish devotion evidenced by Lijuan's courtiers. I have never, however, seen such an entwined mix of worshipful devotion and bone-chilling terror."

She opened out her wings, then pulled them back in, the sound of feathers brushing against one another a whispering rush. Elena had retracted her own wings soon after entering Amanat—no point wasting energy right when they had a dangerous journey coming up.

"The courtier is no weakling and had often been in the presence of an archangel," Caliane continued, "but she shook when she spoke, sweat rolling off her, her eyes unable to meet mine."

Raphael's wing brushed the back of Elena's chair. "Afraid enough to leave China, yet enthralled with her mistress?"

"I believe she worships her idea of Lijuan while being terrified of the truth of her." Caliane finished off her mead. "The courtier's estate was in a rural region. Most of the people around her were poor farmers. She did not much notice when they began to go missing—especially as the vast majority were mortals."

No huge surprise there. Even Elena's archangel didn't always see the value of mortal lives. He'd come a long way from when they'd first met, but from an immortal perspective, mortals were fireflies—pretty things that blazed bright for a heartbeat before disappearing forever.

"Then," Caliane said, "members of her own household began to go missing. At first, she believed they'd run away, but when one of her most trusted staff members didn't return from a walk, she decided to investigate."

An angel winged his way high above, keeping watch over Amanat's borders.

"She found ghost villages, their people gone in the midst of living their lives. Pots left on stoves that had burned out, washing partially hung, gardens half harvested with the harvest left to rot in the open air. A baby's bottle filled and left standing to curdle, a bag of foodstuffs gone putrid on a kitchen counter."

The chilling recitation raised the tiny hairs on the back of Elena's neck.

"I will say this to her credit—she didn't turn tail and run at the first village. She went to five villages one after the other. She found not a man, woman, or child in nearly all of them."

Elena sat up straight, exchanged glances with Raphael. "Nearly all?"

"In one village, she discovered living people so emaciated it was as if they were made of dust. When she attempted to speak to them, they gave her blank looks and continued to shuffle about their business. The tasks they were doing appeared to be repetitive—familiar movements that didn't appear input from their minds. She says they achieved nothing, but continued to repeat the motions."

The candlelight caressed Caliane's face. "You have spoken to me of how Lijuan fed on her people during the last battle, how you found one of her half-absorbed angels in the aftermath. It appears she is now doing this from beyond Sleep."

"This confirms she is not in true Sleep." Raphael's voice was grim. "She must've gone deep enough that her power is no longer detectable by the rest of the Cadre, but not so deep that it will be a long waking."

"She's glutting herself," Elena said. "Our worst-case scenario." So many vanished people, all absorbed into her flesh. What would that make her when she rose?

"The unfinished ones may be from a day when she fed so much she could no longer finish them off," Raphael said.

Elena's fingers grew bone white around the stem of her goblet. "It could've been at the other end, Archangel. Early tests to work out how she could absorb and hoard power long-term."

Two pairs of eyes as dazzling as crushed sapphires crashed into hers.

"If you are right, *hbeebti*, the war that is coming will be for far more than territory."

"An archangel who can hoard lifeforce stolen from others . . ." Caliane's jaw worked. "She will be an unstoppable, rapacious power that consumes the world."

The dark echo of Cassandra's voice in Elena's head, ancient beyond compare.

Goddess of Nightmare.
Wraith without a shadow.
Rising into her Reign of Death.

28

Elena and Raphael left for China in the pitch-dark hours before daybreak.

The two of them caught the jet to the border of Lijuan's territory, then dropped out of the specially designed hatch. Raphael went first, so he could catch her if her wings didn't emerge, the glittering white-gold of his feathers brilliant in the dawn sunlight. The fire had begun to calm down, his wings mostly solid until he wanted them to be otherwise.

The frigid air rushed past her face as she dropped, the sensation of freefall exhilarating until she was brought up short by the lightning storm of her wings. Folding them back, she dropped even farther, Raphael by her side.

Dougal needed to maneuver the jet for his return flight to Japan without worrying about catching them in his drag, and they had to be able to see the details in the landscape.

At first glance, all appeared as it should be: lush green fields, small homes with smoke puffing out the chimneys, angels in the sky. Every single one of those angels acknowledged Raphael when they spotted him. The squadrons that currently patrolled China had been created out of soldiers taken from the armies of all of the Cadre. Including from the two previous Archangels of China.

The vast majority of Favashi's people had chosen to stay when given the option to stay or go. They were determined to husband the territory for their liege. Lijuan's people had joined the squadrons for much the same reason. Had to be some tension there, but this was as much their home as it was for Favashi's people. It helped that they were all ordinary angels. Lijuan had taken her deadly generals and commanders with her.

Population density increased the farther they flew inward. Small villages turned into towns turned into cities. *Raphael, I think I should land.* Her body was starting to protest the long stretch in the air without a break, but one thing had become clear today: her endurance had increased from pre-chrysalis levels, as had her speed.

On the hill in the distance. It is far from any of the houses. Remember—any sign of illness, and you rise.

Elena made the landing without problem, then refueled with energy drinks and snacks she carried in the pack strapped to her back. It was designed to fit like a normal angel's pack, flush against her spine. Otherwise her wings would've burned right through it, destroying her supplies in the process.

Raphael stayed close by, circling the town at the foot of the hill; Elena could see people scurrying about like ants. That type of scuttling fear? It came from the knowledge an archangel had his eyes on them—which was the whole point of the archangelic patrols: to remind mortals and vampires that the Cadre of Ten had the country in its sights.

The sky crackled with golden lightning that had all movement in the village coming to a quivering standstill.

Putting her hands on her hips, she looked up. *Showing off?*

A single demonstration can forestall catastrophic bloodshed.

Rested, she pulled her backpack on, then took off with startling ease. As if the more she used these wings, the stronger they got. Weird when there were no muscles involved, but she wasn't about to look that particular gift horse in the mouth.

I have a theory about the Cascade, she said an hour later, as they crossed a largely uninhabited expanse of rock and shale that was eerily beautiful in its starkness.

I am listening.

Sometimes, you sound so much like an archangel. She had to force the lightness, because just then he hadn't been playing. The cold and remote edge had been real, his new power pushing constantly to erase the humanity inside him.

It may surprise you to learn that I am, in fact, an archangel.

Elena's laugh held as much relief as amusement, because *that* had been her archangel.

At times, he said before she could respond, *I feel the cells of your heart inside me. Small pieces of mortality that are so weak, so vulnerable, that they should be eaten up by my immortal blood and yet they endure.*

I feel you in me, too. Energy shattered her skin less and less now, but it was there in the background, a constant hum of power. That power tasted of Raphael and it had the Cascade cold to it, but though she could access enough of it to heal, fly, it couldn't seem to find a clawhold in her, designed as it was for the body of an archangel.

She rode an air current over a field left fallow for the season, the moonscape of rocks now behind them. Raphael swept down beside her and they skimmed the rooftops of a small hamlet where nothing moved. *I'm getting creeped out, Archangel.*

They are all out in the fields. Look.

A line of hats, bodies bent industriously over a low-height crop. The wind carried across faint sounds of laughter and conversation. *Phew.*

Tell me your theory of the Cascade.

We decided it isn't sentient and I haven't changed my mind on that, but what if it's driven by the thoughts of sentient beings?

Raphael angled to catch a draft, creating a slipstream for her to ride. She did so until it whispered out, then rejoined him at his side. *Who could have such powerful thoughts?*

I know it's an angelic ghost story, but what about those Ancestors said to Sleep below the Refuge? Immortals so old they were beyond time, immortals who had slept through the rise and fall of civilizations, through the birth of mortals and the creation of vampires. Elena had even heard it whispered that they were a different subspecies, an earlier iteration of angelkind. *It could be a reset of sorts.*

If so, they do it in Sleep so deep they are invisible to our senses. The sun glittered off Raphael's wings as he swept right. *The idea of a reset . . . We are currently in a time of great turbulence. Already, we're down to only nine in the Cadre. If it is a reset, to what purpose?*

I haven't quite figured that out yet. Elena dug into her jacket pocket for a couple of plain brown hair clips; her damn short hair kept getting into her eyes. She should've listened to Ransom and worn a headband but ugh, they made her think of the torture of junior high.

The sea washed into her mind again as she clipped back the worst offenders. *There is another option.*

Gee, you're not sounding scary at all right now.

What if the Ancestors are real and this Cascade is so violent because they are waking?

Elena's throat dried up. *That wouldn't be good would it?*

They are said to be so powerful they built our world. They could as easily destroy it.

Nice cheery ghost story. Thanks Mr. Guild Hunter.

Raphael laughed and they flew on, taking in everything around them and resting when Elena needed it. This was only the first of multiple flights they'd be doing across the country. At no point, however, would they be staying in China. The jet would drop them off at different points through the country. It would then return to pick them up in the air.

If necessary, the two of them would stay nights in the territories that bordered China, those archangels having agreed to the arrangement, but actually being resident in China, even with wildfire rampant in Raphael, was a risk too far.

It was as they were reaching the far point of the day's quadrant that they overflew a village of silence and stillness. No people in the fields. No dogs excitedly playing with children in the streets. No smoke rising from hearths even though with the sun setting in a blaze of soft reds and lush pinks, the world had become noticeably colder.

Jason marked this ghost village in his reconnaissance map. It was one of the first he discovered. Raphael's voice was the sea on a bitingly cold day, shards of ice forming on the surface.

She embraced the sensation, accepting who he was and who he was becoming. *I want to land, look around.* When his expression turned to granite, she said, *I've already done it multiple times with no ill-effects.*

None of those times were in a village devoid of life. Lijuan's poison may be soaked into every inch of dirt, every square meter of every home. Raphael continued to circle the eerily silent village after making that point.

But Elena wasn't done. *I think there are things going on below that one of us needs to see. Jason's last surveillance flight over this area was probably a while ago.* The spymaster had spies all across China, but they couldn't see everything.

If we land, we do it together.

Elena's abdomen clenched. *The poison is aimed at archangels,* she reminded him, desperate to keep him off the land that had infected one archangel already; Raphael had given her all the dreadful details of how the contagion had turned Favashi into an adjunct of Lijuan. *I have strange DNA that—*

No, Elena. No give in his tone. *We cannot allow Lijuan to dictate to us from beyond Sleep. And if I am vulnerable to her, I must discover it now, before she rises in battle.*

Shit. She couldn't exactly argue with that—because if Lijuan had become immune to wildfire, the entire world was fucking screwed. *Let's do it.*

Their boots hit the earth moments later. Dust swirled up around them as Raphael folded back his wings. Elena retracted hers, and the two of them began to walk through the village accompanied by the sound of nothing. No life. Not even a squawking chicken or irritated cricket.

Spotting an open door, Elena knocked. "Hello? I don't mean you any harm," she called out in the very basic Mandarin Chinese she'd learned in the weeks before their departure. Mostly greetings and phrases like this one that she'd thought might be needed.

But her nose told her that attempting communication was a vain effort: abandonment had a dull, musty odor it was impossible to mistake. The taste of it coated the back of her throat as thickly as the dust that caked everything in sight.

She walked all the way inside.

Charred pot on the stove. Looks like it was left on until the element burned out.

The table is set in this home, Raphael replied from another part of the street. *The food on the plates has petrified under mold.*

The two of them checked multiple buildings, even a barn, and a garage where a car sat up on blocks with its bonnet raised, but aside from the unnerving lack of people and animals, there was nothing unusual to see. No mummified bodies, no indications of burials. It was as if the entire village had simply vanished in a single heartbeat.

Taking off in pensive quiet, their boot prints immortalized in the dust until the next wind, they turned to the right. Their flight path would take them over new territory before they met up with the jet. Below them passed more green fields and rural villages. The light was fading but hadn't yet affected visibility. Which was why unusual motion below caught Elena's eye.

There's something odd about those villagers. She couldn't quite make out the details from their current altitude, so she dropped lower. *They're all moving like old people.* No village this big was occupied only by the elderly.

She descended farther . . . and horror curdled her stomach. Shrunken and emaciated faces. Bodies of bone in a skin bag. Shuffling movements, limbs being dragged.

We land. Raphael went down first, Elena right after him.

The shuffling villagers didn't react at all.

Everyone who wasn't an archangel reacted to Raphael.

Elena caught the gaze of a nearby woman. Her eyeballs gleamed wet in a hollow bone frame. Pity and a need to render aid overwhelmed the cold bite of fear. "We're here to help."

No response.

"Raphael, do you speak the dialect in this region?"

Yes. I lived in China for two decades long ago. But the woman just stared blankly at him before shambling past. She was pushing a small cart, the type of thing on which you might carry vegetables or other goods you were taking to market.

Not far from them, a man banged a hammer up and down on a piece of wood, as if building something. Except he'd been banging at the same piece of wood since they'd landed. It was splintering, the nail long since embedded.

"It is as the courtier reported to my mother—they are going through motions so well learned that they are instinct." An arctic gaze, the blue a cold chrome. "Nothing but the most primordial part of their minds remain."

Elena struggled with the ethics of what she was about to say, finally made the choice. "Check, make sure." She'd asked him to never again invade a mortal mind, but what if these people were trapped and screaming within? The *only* person who might be able to hear them was an archangel.

"There is nothing there," Raphael said in a matter of seconds, his expression flat. "Broken sparks of memories that are already fading. No sense of personhood. No awareness of the outside world or of others as living creatures. Even a badly damaged mortal mind has a sense of personality; here, there is only a blank slate. I will see if any others are different."

They weren't. Vampire or human, all were empty.

Nausea twisted Elena's intestines. "If the Cascade had won, I'd be like this, an empty shell with no soul."

"Such an abomination would've never walked the world. I would've kept my promise."

Yes, he would have. Even though it would've destroyed him. Elena went to brush her hand over his wing in a silent apology when it struck her. "Archangel." Cold sweat along her spine, her leg muscles suddenly rigid. "Where are the children?"

Every single one of the shambling skeletons around them was an adult.

29

The young would've been too weak to survive such a catastrophic drain on their bodies," Raphael said with chilling pragmatism. "A small mercy that they died before being turned into mindless shells who would have starved to death."

Elena had dropped a knife into her palm soon after landing, now clenched her fingers around it. "She has to die, Raphael." Her voice trembled. "I don't care how we do it. If we have to cheat, lie, break every rule in the book, the fucking monster has to die."

"Yes. Today, we must gather as much information as possible."

Fading light or not, they checked the entire village.

Nothing but more shambling mummies, a number already on the verge of starvation. Crouching beside one particular male who sat propped up in a corner, his head tilted to the side, Elena used the flashlight on her phone to light him up. And stared. "He's wearing the battle uniform of Lijuan's army." Gray with a single red stripe down the left side. "Did he come home to visit at the wrong time, get caught up in a feeding?"

Raphael hunkered down beside her, his wings brushing the

dust and dirt on the floor. "Not just a soldier. A captain." He pointed out the red dots on the collar that she'd missed because of how the uniform fabric had wrinkled over the male's emaciated body.

"Her captains all disappeared with her." No one higher-ranking than a lieutenant had been left behind.

Raphael stared at the dead man. "One mystery in all of this is how she's able to feed across such a wide range. The ghost villages are dotted throughout China."

A creeping chill on the back of Elena's neck. "You think he's a vector?" She held on to her knife like a security blanket, even knowing this threat was beyond knives, swords, guns.

"A willing sacrifice sent to anchor her link to this place. There is no precedent for such, but there is also no precedent for a consort who can store power for her archangel. The rules are changing."

Neither of them spoke again until they were in the air, the empty husks of people who'd once had dreams, hopes, fears, disappearing into the dark of dusk turned to night. But they didn't fly on, hovering close enough to each other to speak. A decision had to be made.

Raphael, however, didn't immediately bring up the fate of the people below. He said, "Do you recall the thick coating of dust in the previous village? The one with no signs of life."

"Hard to forget it." It had been ash under their feet, their boot prints clear and deep from the air. "Why?"

"I do not think those villagers disappeared. I think they're still there."

Elena pushed a fisted hand against her stomach. "Oh hell." Bile was a nasty taste in her throat. "We walked through people's remains?"

Raphael's voice stayed cold, but his tone gentled. "In New York, we witnessed how the husks collapsed into dust after Lijuan was done with them."

A million burrowing insects under her skin, her entire body revolting against the malice of such erasure. "I hope you're wrong. I hope all those people turn up even if it's as reborn." It'd be better than knowing that so many people had been consumed so totally that all that remained was dust. No bones, no headstones, no memorials.

"I would put the husks below out of their misery." Lightning broke in Raphael's eyes, his wings glowing with lethal intent. "Else, they will starve to death. It will be a protracted passing for all but especially for the vampires. Starvation takes much longer to kill one of the Made."

Elena's hand clenched again, her mind flashing to the bloody footprints she'd seen earlier in the night. They'd been left by a villager who'd shredded his feet at some point and now walked on bone. "Is there any chance they can be helped?"

"No, the spark that is life is gone from their shells. I know of no one who can bring it back." He ran his hand over her hair. "I'll tell one of the squadrons to keep watch, drop down food and blood."

Elena struggled against the only two choices. Raphael had chosen life for her, but again she remembered the bloody footprints. "Do they feel pain? Will they feed even if offered food?"

"I do not know the answer to the second question, but I sensed no awareness of pain—it is why they repeat tasks even when those tasks cause blisters to form or bones to break." A hand cupping her cheek, the pad of his thumb brushing over her cheekbone. "I will not fill your mind with the silent screams of the dead. We will give them a chance."

Sobs broke through her.

She didn't fight them. Someone had to cry for the lost.

Raphael wrapped her up in his arms, his heart beating in time with hers.

It wasn't until they were in the jet that they noticed the dot of black on the back of Elena's hand. Raphael immediately hauled his consort into the private room in the back so she could strip to the skin. She didn't protest his resulting examination.

"Just that one," he confirmed. "I'll take care of it with a whisper of wildfire."

"No, wait. It's tiny yet. Give it until we get to Japan—I want to know if I have any immunity." Elena pressed her unmarked hand over his heart, holding him back. "I have tendrils of wildfire inside me, too. If I get hit in battle, I have to know my tolerances."

Raphael ground his teeth because she was right. "*Only* until the jet lands."

"Agreed. Now get naked." A hard swallow. "I need to be sure, too."

It was his turn to cooperate.

"Not a single blemish." A kiss pressed to his spine, her naked body flush against his as she held on with desperate strength.

He picked up her marked hand. "The dot is nearly too faint to see." A "pop" of wildfire from beneath Elena's skin even as he fought the urge to eliminate the threat. "It's gone."

Turning, he kissed her until neither one of them had any breath left.

30

Their first flight the next day was over a large city. *Things appear as they should.*

I'm not getting any vibes, Elena said from where she flew to his left.

Lijuan, however, wasn't the only threat. When he spotted a huddle of vampires in a small cobblestoned courtyard, their eyes glinting red and their fangs flashing as their bodies shivered, he knew he had only one option.

Because that shivering, it wasn't cold.

It was a primitive and overpowering lust for blood.

The kiss began to disperse the instant they felt the shadow of his wings, running and crouching and scrambling in a way that confirmed their degeneration from thinking beings into creatures driven only by an insatiable need to *feed*. No finesse, no care. Jugulars torn out and bodies disemboweled.

He began to pick them off with surgical precision.

His consort took down three with her crossbow.

Her eyes were determined when they met his in the aftermath. "They were too far gone to help." She nodded down at the skinny vampire she'd pinned to a wall with a crossbow bolt through his heart. "Even though he knew you were hunting, he couldn't resist temptation. He was about an inch away from ripping out a passing girl's stomach and burying his face in the cavity."

She reloaded her crossbow with grim efficiency, her eyes hunter-focused. "I don't know why they do that. So many of them go for the stomach."

Raphael finished off the vampires she'd hit; a single touch of his power and their bodies burned in a flash that left only scorch marks on the wall and in the street. A silent warning to those who would follow the same violent path. "Yet you feel sadness at ending them." He'd caught the regret beneath the focus. "What am I to do with you, *hbeebti*?"

"Too late to back off now, Archangel. You're in this for eternity." She strapped her crossbow back on. "I don't actually feel sorry for them. Vampirism is a choice and it comes with consequences. It's the entire messed-up situation. It's getting to me."

"At least our sojourn here is temporary."

"Thank the fuck."

They located three more nests of bloodlust-ridden vamps in short order, cleaned them out as quickly. "It's like you can sense them," Elena said after the final execution.

"My instincts tend to take me in the correct direction—it is a gift that comes with ascension." He didn't often have cause to use that ability—such vampires fell under Dmitri's purview and he was efficient at organizing their capture and execution.

Their next stop was the city citadel. *I expect no problems here. The city is under the stewardship of one of Favashi's senior courtiers.*

Actual working courtier, not a pretty ornament?

Exactly so.

The citadel lay behind a wall and was a palace of lush adornment and bronze-streaked fawn marble; Favashi had converted the structure into a barracks for her soldiers and the Cadre used it for their combined forces.

Every single vampire, angel, and mortal in the vicinity appeared to gasp when Raphael landed in the citadel courtyard, but he felt no concern. He and Elena had run a test at dawn to confirm his immunity to the poison that had taken Favashi; they'd landed in a ghost village and Raphael had deliberately cut himself so the ash could get in.

Wildfire had erupted at once around the wound. His body would not allow the infection to get in, and if Elena didn't have enough wildfire to fight anything that managed to cling to her, he could give her what she needed.

Striding through the courtyard with his hunter by his side, he was met halfway by one of his own people, a senior angel Dmitri had seconded to China as part of Raphael's contribution to the Cadre's combined forces. "Sire." Gadriel went down on one knee in front of Raphael, his head bowed. The sword on his back had a weathered and old hilt, but Raphael had no doubts the blade was razor-sharp.

"Gadriel," he said. "Tell me what is happening here."

The angel rose to his feet, and inclined his head at Elena before he spoke. His eyes were a haunting gray mixed with green, his height an inch below Elena's, his skin pale with an edge of pink, and his body tautly muscled. "Riva has become erratic over the past week. He was doing an excellent job of managing the city before then."

"You've sent through a report to Jason?"

Lines flared out from the corners of the angel's eyes. "No, sire. I thought to give Riva a little leeway—he mourns Favashi's disappearance yet. He was not simply a courtier but one of her closest lieutenants."

"I would've made the same choice." Raphael clasped Gadriel on the shoulder. "He is nine thousand years old and not apt to fall down in his duties. Still, these are strange times. Tell me of his actions just prior to the alteration in his behavior."

"He rode out on his motorcycle to do a routine sweep of the city, but came back hours later than he'd indicated." Gadriel's wings were a deep brown with hints of bronze woven into the filaments and they glimmered under the late afternoon sunlight. "At the time, I thought nothing of it. All of us need time alone to shrug off the cobwebs. Especially here, with the constant screaming tension under the surface."

The steel and wildfire of Elena in his mind. *You think something got to him?*

The dead captain in the ghost village preys upon me. We do not know how many operatives Lijuan has in the world and what she can do with them.

Aloud, he instructed Gadriel to lead them to Riva.

"Sire."

Elena had met Gadriel once before—in the Refuge. Though he was named after a legendary angelic painter renowned for the sumptuous sensuality of his works, the gray-eyed angel with chestnut hair was a bit stuffy and set in his ways. More importantly, however, he was deeply loyal to Raphael. Now, she took in everything around them as he walked on ahead, his comment about the "constant screaming tension" resonating.

Lijuan might be gone, but the echo of her presence lingered in the air. It was stares on the back of Elena's neck from people in the courtyard, dust in the air that tasted of distant death, electric sensations beneath her boots—as if tiny insects were attempting to penetrate the soles and enter her bloodstream.

Favashi, she thought, had come into a tough situation even before the infection.

Shadows passed overhead right before they left the courtyard and entered the citadel, a wing of angels coming in to land. It was cool and dark inside, the stone walls smoothed by time. Elena felt the age of the building in her bones and when she put her hand against the wall, history itself spoke to her.

Nothing in New York was this old, this woven in time.

Gadriel led them to stone stairs far narrower than in modern angelic buildings, but still with enough span to accommodate wings. All the spaces in the citadel, she came to see, were built for angels. But it wasn't an angel who sat in the center of the large chamber into which Gadriel showed them.

The vampire, his scent cardamom crushed with ice and rippled with a thick treacly sweetness, sat with his head in his hands. His skin was ebony, his hair kinky curls darker than his skin. He wore battered leather pants, along with a black jacket and tee of faded brown, and when he lifted his head, his red-rimmed eyes proved to have irises of a stunning indigo.

Elena barely stopped herself from going for the long blade worn against her spine. Old, this one was *old*. Nine thousand years, Raphael had said, but this wasn't just age. This was the kind of power Dmitri would hold in another millennia or two. As for those eyes, she'd bet her new set of throwing knives that they hadn't begun that way. It was vampirism that had taken what might've been more ordinary blue or gray eyes and altered them to this startling and unearthly hue.

Why wasn't he Favashi's second?

Power alone does not a second make, but I think he was her third.

"Archangel." Riva rose to his feet in a clatter of limbs. His chair toppled behind him onto the thick Turkish rug.

Flushing, he bent to pick it up.

Gadriel whispered away at the same time.

"It has been an age, Riva." Raphael held out his arm. "I think two hundred years at least."

The vampire clasped his forearm, but the two didn't embrace as Raphael would've done with Dmitri. "Not so very long when one has lived nine thousand years." Riva's voice was melodious and deep, but his fingers trembled before he broke contact.

"Tell me what has happened." Cold and dark with power, Raphael's words weren't a request. "There is no use in lying. I can see it."

Shuddering, the vampire seemed to pull himself together with a conscious effort of will. He wasn't fully successful—his face quivered before he clenched his jaw, and though Elena couldn't see his hands because he'd put his arms behind his back, she could tell from the strain in his muscles that he was gripping the wrist of one with vicious force.

"I lost time." The column of his throat moved. "At least five hours. I have no memory of where I was or what I did during that time, but when I woke . . ." His voice broke.

"At this time," Raphael said, "I am your liege. Speak."

His entire body trembling, Riva began to shrug off his jacket.

Raphael, Elena murmured mind-to-mind. *Should I step out?* This wasn't about humiliating the guy after all; no one this powerful would want to be seen as weak, much less by the consort to an archangel.

Raphael spoke directly to Riva. "My consort asks if you would prefer that she step out."

The vampire's eyes flared before he inclined his head in a deep bow. "No," he said. "I thank you for your consideration, Consort, but I am too old to be shy in such matters." Words spoken with a courtly grace and innate confidence that showed her a glimpse of who he was when not under such strain.

Jacket off, Riva reached down to pull off his T-shirt, revealing a ridged abdomen hard with muscle. Nothing unusual about that in a warrior vampire his age—what *was* unusual were the lines of black that snaked under his skin from the right side of his abdomen, so dark and oddly *liquid* that they were striking even against the rich hue of his skin.

Elena sucked in a breath. "Are they moving?" Tiny, incremental pieces of motion.

Face twisted and hands fisted at his sides, Riva's words were shards of glass. "I kept telling myself that I was imagining it, but it's a lie I can no longer swallow. At first, they were nothing but scratches. I thought I must've fallen from my bike and hurt myself. I believed I had hit my head, and that was why I couldn't recall the lost hours."

Riva's words tumbled out atop of one another; Elena could almost hear how he'd convinced himself that it had been nothing, just a stupid accident.

"Where in the city did you come to consciousness?" Raphael asked, while Elena continued to watch the viscous black lines, her fingers itching to cut them out. She couldn't get it out of her head that the fucking things were *eating* Riva from the inside out.

"Not in the city—two hours outside of it, with my bike fallen on the ground beside me." His shoulders slumped. "I knew even then that it was all wrong; that area was nowhere in my plans for the day."

Pain in eyes too bright to be real, eerie in a way that meant he'd never be mistaken for human. "It's clear I'm no longer fit for my duties." Words spoken directly to Raphael. "You must replace me. Gadriel is more than competent enough to take over. I . . . I . . . Sire, I do not know what to do, where to go."

Raphael raised a hand flickering with wildfire. "There is a risk this will kill you." A deadly remoteness to him, ice in his tone. "Wildfire is not meant for vampires. It may, however, be the only thing that can kill what is inside you."

Riva shivered but gave a crisp nod. "I am ready."

"Sit."

A snap of the vampire's spine. "I cannot sit in your presence."

"If you manage to remain conscious through this, I will be very surprised. *Sit.*"

Riva still looked uncomfortable, but obeyed. Elena, meanwhile, put her hand on Raphael's arm. His skin was cold. *Tone it down—that's angel-level wildfire.*

Raphael didn't reply, but the wildfire faded until only the tips of his fingers burned. He touched those fingers to the living infection. Riva's entire body arched, his hands clamping on the chair arms and his muscles straining as he gritted his teeth against a scream. Wildfire crackled over his skin, burning him alive.

The scent of cooked flesh hit Elena's nostrils. Her gorge rose.

31

Jerking forward on the instinctive desire to help, Elena reached out a hand . . . and the wildfire jumped onto the back of her hand, a shocking bolt of energy. Power burned over every inch of her, the surface of her skin cracking open to display veins of gold before they sealed over again.

"Elena." Raphael's hand on her nape, hauling her close.

"I'm fine." Her chest heaved. "It was just one hell of a rush. Too much power inside me." Energy arced from her heart to Raphael's. He took it with no outward effects—and she was no longer choking on wildfire.

Sucking in gulps of air, she pressed her forehead against his chest. "That was weird."

"As always, *hbeebti*, you are a mistress of understatement."

"Riva?"

"Unconscious but alive." His next words raised every hair on her body. "It is as well that he lost consciousness before the wildfire jumped to you. Else, I would've had to take his memories, and that is not always a simple thing with vampires this old. It can leave them with permanently broken minds."

Drawing back, Elena held a gaze as cold as the heart of midnight, devoid of humanity or mercy. "Remember your promise, Archangel." She'd told him to check the villagers' minds yesterday; had that led to this?

"You would hold me to that even for a vampire who belongs to another archangel?"

Elena narrowed her eyes. "As long as I exist, you don't get to fall into that particular black hole." Of a power so violent it sought to reshape his very soul. "I'll never let you become cruel or heartless. Violating minds is a step on the wrong road."

Ice glittered in his expression. "This power, it tells me I would be better off without the weakness of you."

Elena folded her arms, set her feet apart. "And what do you think about that?"

"That regardless of what I believed about my hold on the power, this battle has just begun." Cupping one side of her face with a hand frosted in ice, he said, "It seduces with its strength, makes me want to alter myself to better host it."

Turning her head, she kissed his palm though her skin was numb from the cold of it. "Just remember what happened to Lijuan. Do you want to be His Creepiness?"

"I would much rather be your archangel." Dropping his hand from her face, he looked at Riva again, and though it was with the calculating gaze of an archangel weighing up a threat, his voice held a hint of warmth when he spoke. "Riva will be fine, but we have a problem."

Elena deliberately leaned her body against Raphael, using her own heat to warm him up. "This is no simple infection."

"No. It's too much of a coincidence that it attempted to take the leader of this city—the intent must've been for it to grow strong enough to control him. As Favashi was controlled."

"Why not go straight for the brain?" Gruesome as it was to consider, a worm in the brain would be an efficient shortcut.

"Too likely to end in death?" Raphael suggested as he opened up his wing to curve it around her, warm and heavy. "It's also possible that what matters is a critical mass, not the location of it."

"Did it feel the same as the stuff in Favashi?" An archangel and a vampire were two very different beings.

A pause, Raphael absently brushing his hand down her spine. "No. That poison is designed for archangels; it would lead to immediate death for ordinary angels and vampires. This is a softer thing, but I sense Lijuan's hand in it."

"You planning to speak to the Cadre?"

"I must. Each and every individual in a position of power in China must be checked for signs of infection. I can use wildfire to clear it from their bodies while I'm here, but that is a short-term measure." His next words were hard. "Let us hope it is confined to the vampires. Because if angels can be controlled thus, there is only one option: annihilation."

Because free of *any* angelic oversight, vampires across China would inevitably give in to bloodlust. They would torture and murder, rend and tear. They would become a horde that spilled over into neighboring territories. The Cadre would execute every single living being in China, stain its soil a permanent red, to prevent that outcome.

Kill it. Burn the entire territory down to the ground." Charisemnon bit out the words, but even the Archangel of Northern Africa had a grim look on his handsome face at the idea of such a death toll.

"If only that were a viable choice," Astaad murmured. "It will not end the threat posed by Lijuan."

"And death on such a scale?" Neha's sari was a deep yellow with a rich pink and gold border and the silk of it whispered as she moved a hand in a strong negative. "It will leave a stain across eternity."

"You are all being very careful not to look at me," Caliane murmured in a quiet voice that held the echoes of hundreds of crying children; they were ghosts of the dead that his mother carried within and would into her final Sleep. "But of all those here, I am the only one who understands the toll it takes to wipe out thousands of innocent lives—I cannot be permitted to hide from my knowledge."

It was a bleak truth. Alexander had killed in battle, as had Raphael and many of the others. Some of their number had murdered in cold blood, but none had unleashed wholesale slaughter. Caliane had wiped out the thriving populations of two cities.

She'd spared the children, but their fragile hearts had broken under the trauma. Most had simply curled up and died. Angelkind had fought to save those tiny human lives and failed. Raphael's palms curled inward, his skin remembering the calluses that had formed from digging grave after grave.

It hadn't been in penance for his mother's horrific crime. *Nothing* could be penance enough for that.

"Such an action is a burden that will haunt you through time." Caliane spoke with no self-pity, with potent directness. "Atonement is an impossibility. The ghosts of the lives I took have become my constant shadows. I hear them in the gray hours before dawn, when the world is quiet, and I have no answers for them when they ask me why they had to die."

Raphael's shoulders bunched, his gut tight. This was the first time he'd heard his mother speak of her terrible act, the first time he'd understood that she'd not only come out sane after her long Sleep, but with all her memories intact. In the bleak lines of her face, he saw the truth: his mother remembered each and every soul she had condemned to the pitiless ocean.

"But what I did," she continued without mercy to herself, "would pale in comparison to eliminating the people of an entire territory. We would not survive the weight of the dead on our conscience. The Cadre will fall and Lijuan will rise again from beneath the bones of her dead."

Raphael stood in a pool of silence, the screens around him showing faces gone motionless. Each of the archangels had responded quickly to his request for an emergency gathering.

Michaela had done so from deep in Hungary, the face that had been the muse of artists through the ages even sharper in its beauty. She'd lost weight. Where others might've appeared haggard, she looked refined down to the very core.

Astaad had called from a Pacific isle, his skin damp and his hair windswept, his goatee rougher than usual. He'd been the first to make the connection and they'd spoken privately for a minute or two. "I've had to clear this island of all its citizens—my own abode here is in the process of being dismantled."

It turned out that the calm waters around the island had become violent to the point of causing tidal waves. Astaad had already lost ten people who'd been caught unawares by the first wave, and was taking no chances.

Neha, the archangel currently closest to Raphael, had responded to his request from the room she most often used for these meetings. But while she wore a sari and sat on a throne, her hair was not in an elegant bun but simply braided. The braid sat over one shoulder, the black strands entwined with copper thread. Kohl rimmed her eyes.

Titus, Alexander, and Elijah had all appeared at the same moment.

Now, Caliane's closest compatriot in the Cadre stirred. "I hear you, my friend." Alexander's golden hair glinted in the early evening sunlight where he stood, a general at rest. "Wiping out China is not a viable option unless we fail to contain the spread of this contagion." New lines in the face he turned to Caliane. "If that is the case, we have no choice and must bear those deaths on our souls."

"If the Cadre is agreeable," Neha said, "I'll send a medical team to begin the examinations." A pause before she locked gazes with Raphael. "I can take over your aerial sweep so you can assist on the ground, but China is currently yours."

"I would be glad of the help." Whatever their differences, he had no argument with Neha's commitment to the goals of the Cadre. "I cleared the medics at this citadel and sent half of them to check on the leadership in the next major hub." He'd also made sure they had a heavy escort and that those escorts were clean of infection. "The other half are in the process of examining Riva's closest advisors and associates."

"We may hope this isn't widespread." Astaad stroked his damp goatee. "You say the tainted vampire disappeared for a number of hours. It seems he must've been taken to a secret place to be infected. The contagion may not be in the air or in the soil."

"I am in agreement with you." Riva's infection had been a purposeful act.

"As only Raphael has the wildfire," Elijah murmured, "our options are limited."

Discussion ensued. The final consensus was unanimous: should the healers discover that Lijuan's scourge had only affected vampires who held cities and not their angelic brethren, the vampires would be pulled out. The angels who remained would commit to a checkup once a week as a safeguard.

And if angels were shown to be infected . . .

None of them wanted to face that, not until it was unavoidable.

Four days later, and the official count of infected commanders was at five. All vampires. After Raphael used wildfire to eradicate the scourge in their bodies, he ordered the exodus of all vampires who'd been sent into the territory by the Cadre. That included the senior vampires of Favashi's court.

All of Lijuan's people chose to stay and as they were of this land, and already loyal to Lijuan, with no need for her to take control of them in other ways, there was no reason not to permit the decision. As a precaution, however, any vampire in a position of power was demoted to a lower rank.

Angels would now run the cities, with Gadriel taking over Riva's citadel.

The Cadre also decided to speed up their rotation cycle after Raphael reported the signs of rising bloodlust. Michaela was meant to follow Raphael—she was actually down to do a double shift, as she'd been unable to make her last rotation. Titus had agreed to cover for her. Prior to that, she'd talked Charisemnon into taking her place.

Raphael was expecting the call he received from her the night before he and Elena were scheduled to make their last flight over China. Exhausted from the long day, the two of them had just showered in preparation for a late meal in their rooms, when the screen in the living area chimed.

Elena paused in the midst of pulling on her pajama shorts to throw clothes at him. He pulled on the loose sweatpants and T-shirt, sealing the wing slits shut with the ease of long practice before he answered the call, while his consort stayed out of view.

"I need to return to my own territory," he said the instant Michaela's face appeared on the screen. "That is nonnegotiable."

Elena, having tugged on her tank top and shorts, began to sharpen one of her knives.

"I know." Michaela's rich brown skin held a shimmer that turned her sensual beauty ethereal. "I was hoping you could speak to Lady Caliane on my behalf."

Raphael had no time for the games of the former Queen of Constantinople. "Michaela, I'm already scheduled for extra shifts as a result of my absence and I had a good excuse. I do not think my mother will look kindly on your shirking of this duty."

Michaela lifted a hand to rub her face, the lush tumble of her hair a mass of dark brown and bronze with traces of other colors. "I convinced Charisemnon by hinting I'd allow him to put his hands on my body. I convinced Titus by feigning illness—he is so soft about such things."

Hbeebti, I can feel the laser burn of your glare.

She doesn't sign off soon, I'm telling her to get her ass lost. Screw archangelic etiquette—you need to rest and she needs to do her job.

"For you, however," Michaela murmured, "it must be the truth." A faded smile that actually managed to look truly tired, but Raphael didn't soften; Michaela was a master manipulator with a hundred faces.

"I know you will not believe a word I say," she added, "not after the last time, so I will simply show you. And trust you not to use it against me." Michaela rose from her chair . . . and the gauzy sides of her gown split over the tautly rounded curve of her abdomen.

32

Oh. My. God.

Elena's mental imprecation echoed Raphael's own shock.
There was no way the Archangel of Budapest could be faking
that. Not when the rest of her body also evidenced signs of
advanced pregnancy now that he knew to look for them. The
sharpness in her face, the shimmer in her skin, her slower rate
of respiration and the way her hair appeared thicker, even
more luxuriant.

All were common in angelic pregnancies.

Cupping the mound with both hands, Michaela looked
down, her expression vulnerable in its softness. "Now you see
why I can't do my scheduled shift."

"You appear close to full term." Raphael forced himself to
stay calm—as if an archangel being pregnant wasn't an extraordinary moment in time. The last time this had happened, it
had been his mother.

"Less than a month remains." Michaela took her seat again,
her movements unwieldy in a way he'd never before witnessed
in the stunning, capricious woman who'd brought emperors
to their knees and led another archangel into blood-fueled
carnage.

"Why are you not at the Refuge?" Angels didn't give birth outside of the Medica; Amanat was the sole exception to that rule.

"I trust very few with such a precious gift." Michaela's face hardened. "Keir has been aware since I first knew, and he will attend me. Even now, he prepares to come to Budapest. The only others currently in my stronghold are those who would allow me to cut their throats should I ask—they will defend me and my babe to the last."

"Is the babe's father among them?"

A flick of a hand that was very Michaela. "The father is of no consequence. This is my child, an *archangel's* child." She placed her hand below the screen and he guessed she was cradling her belly again. "I know you will not betray me in this— you are too human now. I never thought I would consider that a gift." She exhaled with slow care. "Your mother has borne a child. I trust her to honor my truth."

"Why didn't you speak to Caliane directly?" A pregnant archangel was the weakest she would ever be—should Raphael want to kill Michaela, he would never have a better opportunity. "Why expose your weakness to me?"

"Lady Caliane intimidates me. You, on the other hand, are my compatriot." Her smile was lush, deep, reached her eyes— and would've dazzled had he not been immune to her methods of getting what she wanted. "Even if you have refused to be my lover."

I see pregnancy hasn't altered her winning personality.

Resist the temptation to throw that blade at the screen, warrior mine. It would be awkward to explain to Mother. "The child is safe?" he asked Michaela.

Her practiced mask crumpled, her throat moving. "Keir has sensed nothing amiss. No remnants of Uram. The child in my womb is healthy in every way and he is mine."

"A boy child?"

"I couldn't wait. I asked Keir to ascertain it for me." Her smile was a dawning light, real in a way that couldn't be counterfeited.

Wow. Elena's voice held wonder. *That kind of beauty . . . She could own the world if she stopped trying to manipulate everyone.*

"I am to be a mother again, Raphael." A whisper. "At long last, my pain will end. He is my redemption."

"I will talk to Caliane. I can promise nothing—she will make her own decision."

"So," Elena murmured after Michaela ended the call.

"She's manipulating us."

"Of course she is— that's status quo for Michaela." Elena played a knife through her fingers. "But she *is* also super pregnant."

"If Keir has confirmed all is well, then we do not have to fear this will be anything but a child."

His consort shuddered at the reminder of Michaela's last "birth." "No argument that she loves her kid already, but all that 'my redemption' stuff rubs me up the wrong way." She made a face. "Maybe it's because I don't like her—and jeez, now I feel like shit."

"No, Elena. I feel the same." Walking to their balcony with her by his side, he leaned on the railing and looked out over the night-blooming flowers of Amanat. "She is making this about her and not the child."

"I guess it's understandable since she once lost a child."

His hunter's soft heart was there in every word. And it *was* hers now. His own had never been that empathic; what compassion he had, what humanity, it came from her.

"Kid's probably going to be overprotected all to hell," Elena said, "but I don't think Michaela would hurt her baby."

"To my knowledge, Michaela has never caused harm to a child." Raphael watched a firefly flicker in the lamplit dark. "She is not the threat that concerns me."

Sliding away her weapon, Elena leaned against the railing next to him, her body brushing his. It was instinct to spread his wing to cover her. She ran her fingers over the sensitive inner surface. "You're worried about Uram?"

"I'm certain we destroyed his lingering phantom." The dead archangel had somehow managed to leave behind a "ghost," an energy echo that had sought to possess Michaela. "I'm more worried about whether she sustained any permanent damage as a result." He shook his head. "It's a foolish worry—archangels aren't so easy to scar."

"Yeah, but the rotting meat 'baby' . . . Nothing about any of that was normal even for the Cadre." Worry wove through the compassion. "Do you know what happened to her first child?"

"The babe simply stopped breathing one day. Such a thing is extremely rare among angelic infants—in my entire life-time, I have heard of only two cases, and Michaela's infant was the second." Memories flowed through his mind, of a tiny flower-laden bier, of Michaela's severe, silent beauty.

"It is the only time since I have known her that I remember Michaela as a creature of icy silence. She did not speak for a year after her babe's death."

"Man, that's so sad."

"Michaela's lover at the time, the babe's father, was found dead two days after the infant's burial. He'd been flayed alive, then beheaded."

Elena's hands clenched on the railing. "Michaela?"

"No one knows, but she didn't demand an investigation into the incident, showed no anger, didn't appear to feel any grief. And though he'd been her lover for half a century, she didn't attend the ceremonies we hold for our dead."

Elena had the feeling she'd never figure out Michaela, not if she lived to be as old as Caliane. "An act of grief because he reminded her of her lost baby? Or a scapegoat for her anger at being unable to protect her child? Could also be that she didn't do it but was too numb from the first loss to process a second."

"Only Michaela knows the truth and she's never spoken of it—I tell you this so you remember that even with child, Mi-chaela remains Michaela."

"I guess it's hard for me to see her intense love for her baby and separate that from who she is the rest of the time." She shrugged her shoulders in a sharp movement.

Folding back his wing, he ran his hand down her spine. "What is the matter?"

"Just this weird sensation." Her energy wings exploded out. "That's better. It felt as if the lightning was building up under my skin."

Raphael played with the lightning in wings that now held all the hues of her. Midnight and dawn. "You're becoming stron-ger." She'd flown all day today and yet she had excess energy.

A smile so brilliant that Michaela's could never compete. "Hot damn. I might not have to ration my hours in flight anymore." She jumped into his arms, kissed him all over his face, her joy an irresistible lure.

Their lips met in the stormlight of her wings.

After a quick meal, Raphael left his consort in an enclosed external courtyard bathed in the moon's silver beams. She was planning to speak to friends in the Refuge, including a little boy who adored her; it had been her idea that he go to Caliane alone. "You know how she misses you."

Such a soft heart.

"Raphael." Caliane's face bloomed when he entered her favorite garden.

She sat on a stone bench that faced a pond with water so motionless it was a mirror. Her joy in seeing him was an open incandescence that outshone the moon. Raphael's heart clenched. The same woman who'd left him broken and bloody on a forgotten field had also sung to him as a child, songs so heartbreaking in their beauty that the entire Refuge had stood still to listen.

She was also the woman who carried thousands of dead souls on her conscience. Did she hear them in this space, quiet and lonely? Was that why she so often sat here? To listen to the recriminations of the dead? To remember their faces?

He held out his arm. She took it with a smile of pure happiness and allowed him to help her to her feet. Her gown was a glittering ice white and it flowed around her like frozen water as they walked the garden paths. It was Raphael who spoke first. "I know it hurt you to speak about the past to the Cadre."

"I cannot pretend it didn't happen, that I didn't do a monstrous thing." Pain scored each word. "I must bear witness to all the lives lost." She squeezed his forearm. "I have asked Jessamy to bring the records here, so I can read a full account of what happened during my worst madness."

So many children had died, the two cities become a tomb. In the end, the horror of it had been too much and the Cadre of the time had razed the cities to the ground. No new buildings sat on that land to this day, the area taken over by wild grasses that thrived in the sandy soil near the ocean.

"Are you certain that's the right decision?" Jessamy's histories could push Caliane back over a dark edge.

"It haunts me. I must know all of it." Long minutes passed before she said, "I will not become mad again, Raphael. I know the signs now. If they appear, I will go back into Sleep."

He believed her resolve, but he also knew that madness had a way of eating away at rational thought. He'd witnessed it firsthand in both his mother and his father.

"At times," Caliane murmured, "I think Lijuan and I are not so very different."

"If she had stuck to mortal victims, perhaps." Heartless as it was, the Cadre didn't interfere in such things in another archangel's territory. "But she has managed to infect an archangel. That threatens our very civilization."

"Should she come back sane?"

"Then we will have another conversation." Raphael didn't believe sanity was a possibility, not when Lijuan continued to stretch her arms across China. Sanity came from a long Sleep and she was, at best, in a light doze.

"Where is your consort?"

"She thought we needed time alone to be mother and son." What his Elena would give to be able to take a midnight walk with her mother, talk to her one more time.

"She has courage," Caliane said. "I see it and I am glad for you that you have such a consort, even as I worry about how her humanity changes you."

Raphael didn't reply; he'd made his choice and he had no regrets and never would. He would fall again and again with Elena. "I have another matter to discuss with you." He told her Michaela's secret.

Sucking in a harsh breath, she stopped on the path. "You are certain?" Wings limned with light against the night sky, her eyes blue flame.

"Yes. I was able to get in touch with Keir before I came to see you." The healer had stopped at a waystation set up for travelers who were passing through a territory. "Michaela had given him permission to confirm the news should you or I ask." And the healer did not lie, not for anyone.

Caliane began to walk again, her hand in the crook of his arm. "I noticed her tiredness and lack of interest in Cadre business, but I put it down to a period of ennui as happens to so many of us over time."

Raphael hadn't yet experienced such. Even when he'd begun to go cold before he met Elena, empathy fading into cruelty, he'd still been interested in the world. "Will you cover Michaela's sweep of China, Mother?"

"Of course—she cannot risk any kind of infection. Is she protected? A babe is a strong drain on an archangelic mother's energy." A smile, a pat of his forearm. "I never minded, but I had Nadiel to watch over me and our gorgeous black-haired babe. You say Michaela claims the child alone."

Memories from a distant corner of his past, of splashing in a bath while his mother laughed, of how she'd wrapped him up in a towel and carried his wet body close, uncaring of her pretty gown. "If no one has revealed Michaela's secret till now," he said through the heaviness in his chest, "then I think she has the right people around her."

"Good. I will speak to her of such things as only an archangelic mother can understand." Her hand rising to brush his hair off his forehead, as if he were a youngling. "We must be creatures of power while our hearts are on display to the world. It is a good thing that among our kind, to kill a child is an unforgivable offense. Else, I would've burned the world to the ground to protect you."

"Did it take you a long time to recover your strength after my birth?" He'd been a youth when she'd left him broken and bleeding on that verdant green field. Such questions hadn't come to him then.

"No, not so long. The archangelic body heals quickly. But I had a wound all the same—and I have it to this day." The depth of her smile told him she was quite content with that. "You will always be the babe I rocked in my arms. When you hurt, I hurt. And I would still burn down the world for you."

"No, Mother, you will not."

A deep stillness to her. "You fear my madness even now."

"Time is a winged beast for mortals, but for us, it is a creeping tide." It would take him centuries, longer, to accept that Caliane's sanity was here to stay. "You have been awake but a heartbeat."

"When did you get so philosophical, my young Rafa?" A childhood pet name he hadn't heard for an eon. "I left behind a wild, impulsive boy who wore his anger like a second skin, and came back to an archangel in firm control of his world but for his fascination with a mortal." Laughter broke her motionlessness. "So . . . I think the wild boy remains in the man you have become. Still tweaking the noses of the stuffy and the rigid."

For an instant, they were just mother and son. "According to Elena, half of angelkind thinks I have lost my mind and are waiting to see if I will regain it."

They spoke of small things in the ten minutes that passed; of the newborns in Amanat, of the homes being repaired, of how his mother wished him to admit a vampire maiden into his Tower. "She is too fierce a thing for Amanat. If she wishes to return later, I will welcome her home, but I think to force her to stay here would be to smother her."

"I will ask Dmitri to organize a transfer."

Caliane's next words were far more pensive. "A strange thing, is it not? That an archangel's womb becomes fertile during a time of catastrophic change?" She looked up at the moon. "I think before this is over, the world will be altered in more ways than one."

The words held the ring of a prophecy, raising the hairs on the back of Raphael's neck, but he reminded himself that his mother was no seer. She wasn't Cassandra, who'd once dreamed of a mortal become an angel, then risen to see her dream in brilliant, living color.

He deliberately changed the subject. "Elena mentioned today that she has never seen an image of Father." The ones in the ancient stronghold of Lumia didn't count; all those had been of his father's death as witnessed by a traumatized young angel. Hair of fire, eyes of flame. All his colors had been submerged in the angelfire that was his death.

Sadness draped around Caliane's shoulders like a heavy cloak, but intermingled with it was a smile drenched in love. "I keep my favorite portrait of Nadiel in my quarters." She squeezed his forearm. "Tell Elena to join us. We will go see your father."

33

Elena had never before been in Caliane's private quarters. Raphael met her outside, told her his mother was waiting within. She wasn't sure what she'd expected; what she got was both surprising and not. The space was exquisite in the way of a being who had lived millennia upon millennia and could choose from an endless number of cultures and designs.

The palette was white and a pale gold for the most part, the high walls of the hallway in which she walked covered in a wallpaper that stole her breath. Delicate and lovely, the design proved to be lovingly hand-painted. The floor wasn't glossy marble but a warm glowing wood of pale honey, the curtains that hung over the large windows a white muslin so fine it was air.

It was a warm and welcoming space . . . until you got to the floor-to-ceiling doors that blocked the way to Caliane's inner sanctum. Heavy iron, they bore the emblem of two crossed swords. Elena stopped far enough away that she could take in the entirety of the massive block of metal, and after a while, began to see elements hidden within the initially bold design.

Each of the swords, for one, was unique, the hilts boasting

intricate designs that had nothing in common yet were somehow complementary.

"My father's." Raphael pointed to the right. "My mother's." The one on the left. "His burned up during his death and she broke hers into pieces and threw it into the ocean."

A stab in Elena's heart. She couldn't even begin to comprehend what it would've cost Caliane to execute the man she loved so deeply, a love she hadn't found until an eon into her long existence.

She deliberately brushed her body against Raphael's as they took several more steps. *Oh.* "I almost missed all the other designs." Intricate pieces that made no sense until you were close enough to see the details.

Raphael touched one particular panel. "My birth."

She saw the child then, cradled within two palms, one masculine, one feminine. It was a stylized image, the infant not visible except as soft curves and a hint of wings on the back, but she put her fingers on the panel and smiled. "Finally, I get to see baby photos of you."

No laugh from her archangel, his eyes on two panels high on the right-hand corner that seemed shinier than the others. "Those were not there before."

Squinting, she tried to see what he had . . . Her skin tightened. A blaze of light. A falling angel, his wings broken and fire licking up his body. Nadiel's fall. Right below that was a panel with the collapsed body of another angel, his wings crumpled and his body shattered until his limbs twisted into the wrong shape.

Raphael's last encounter with Caliane before she woke sane.

"This is her history," she whispered, realizing that these doors held the eternity of an archangel's life. Even the broken and bloody pieces.

"I did not think she would choose to remember that." Raphael's gaze remained locked on the two painful panels. "Sometimes, Elena, I do not understand my mother."

"Well, don't ask me for advice about how to deal with parents. You've seen the stellar state of my relationship with Jeffrey." But she leaned into him and when he spread his wing, she moved her hand to brush over the inner surface. And froze. "Um, Archangel?"

"Hmm?" He was looking at another panel.

"Did you forget to mention acquiring black and purple feathers?"

That caught his attention. Looking down, he took in the black feathers that came out from the curve of his wings, as if growing from where his wings emerged from his back.

Those obsidian feathers faded into indigo and a deep blue before the white-gold of his wings took over. "It appears you have marked me once again." He flared out the other wing, which bore the gunshot scar. "The underside is the same here."

Shifting, Elena took in the top of his wings. "No change up top."

"Show me your wings."

Stormfire erupted out of her back. She saw the midnight and dawn of herself but alive within it was his golden lightning. "I thought the blending only went one way." He was one of the Cadre, while she'd been a baby immortal when she went into the chrysalis.

"It appears not." Not sounding worried in the least about that, he folded in his wings. "My mother has just asked if we intend to come inside or stand here all day."

Despite the constant changes happening to both of them, her shoulders shook at his impression of Caliane's regal tones. "Behave." Turning as one, they pushed through the doors . . . into moonlight.

Elena's breath caught.

The living area had no opaque walls excepting the one that led deeper into Caliane's suite. The rest of it—roof included— was glass. Vines crawled over the roof, thick enough to provide dappled shade in the daytime. Set out below the vines were white velvet sofas that featured curved legs; the seat cushions had buttons on them.

"Come," Caliane said, her face difficult to read. "I will take you to Nadiel."

Elena fell into step beside the Ancient, while Raphael took the rear. Caliane led her through another set of doors into a large bedroom. The lighting here was soft rather than harsh, curtains pulled over the windows. The bed was a four-poster made up in white-on-white sheets with the bed curtains a pale gold and the carpet underfoot a rich brown.

"There." Caliane shifted to face the wall *behind* them . . . the wall she would see when she woke each morning.

Chest tight, Elena turned, too.

The painter had caught Nadiel in an informal moment. He was shirtless, his legs covered in a warrior's leathers, and his sword held across his thighs. A rag was crumpled in his right hand, and he was laughing, his eyes turned to someone just off to the left of the artist.

Caliane, it must've been Caliane. There was a potent intimacy in his laugh, in his eyes. The artist had captured a moment between lovers, been talented enough to put that moment on canvas.

"The Hummingbird," she murmured, and it wasn't a question. She knew only two angelic artists with gifts so incredible and Aodhan hadn't yet been born when Nadiel died.

"Yes." Caliane's voice held an age that pressed on Elena's bones. "She dropped by for a visit, and as always with Sharine, she had her sketchpad with her. Nadiel was outside cleaning his weapons, and I was laughing with him about something or other, and Sharine was sitting there sketching and it was such a normal thing that we didn't really notice. A year later, she gave me this."

It startled Elena to hear of the mysterious, haunted Hummingbird spoken of as just Sharine—a friend, a compatriot. But she was too fascinated by the portrait to follow that line of thought, to ask about the woman who was so very talented and so very broken.

Raphael had told her once that while he had Caliane's colors, he had Nadiel's bones. She'd glimpsed that truth in the angelfire portraits in Lumia, now saw the totality of it: the shape of Nadiel's face, the width of his shoulders, the height she could see even with Nadiel seated, it was a mirror of Raphael's.

Your father's eyes were green. An astonishing green caught between emerald and aquamarine. So clear they were striking even caught in paint. She didn't know why she'd never thought to ask about Nadiel's eye color. Probably because Raphael's father's eyes had been pieces of angelfire in all the paintings she'd seen in Lumia.

The man in this painting wasn't burning from the inside out. He was tanned and muscled, his cheeks creased, and his wind-tumbled hair a lush brown that faded into gold at the tips. In his right earlobe flashed an amber earring and she knew it for Caliane's mark.

"He had such wicked laughter in his eyes." Love was an ache in Caliane's voice. "I knew him as a new member of the Cadre, but that was what first drew me to him as a man—his laughter. I heard it across a crowded marketplace and I had to know who it was that laughed with such open, unashamed happiness."

A glow suffused her face, her eyes luminous. "He had mischief in him, too. He made me remember the girl I'd once been, the woman beneath the archangel." The next words she spoke were in a language Elena didn't understand.

When she glanced at Raphael, he shook his head. *I do not know this tongue,* hbeebti. *It was one shared between my parents in their private moments and I have only a vague recollection of it in my memories.*

I don't really need a translation, I guess. Piercing love had a flavor, a hidden song within. *She really misses him.*

Their love is the one thing I never doubted. He'd grown up in the arms of that love. *Even when they couldn't be together, they would write letters, send each other small gifts, make comments many times a day about a thought they had to tell the other.* The constant presence of that love had made it easier for Raphael to be apart from one parent during the periods when Caliane and Nadiel had to separate.

For two archangels couldn't coexist in the same territory for a long period without their energies leading to an inevitable conflict. That Nadiel and Caliane had managed it as much as they had was a testament to the agonizing depth of their love.

Did you stay with both of them alternately?

When I was a babe, I stayed with Caliane. But later, after I was grown enough to understand how things must be, I would go with my father at times, remain with my mother others. Old memories stirred awake at the corners of his mind. "Mother, do you remember the time I returned home with no hair?"

Caliane's sadness fractured in a waterfall of startled laughter. "Nadiel was so afraid of my wrath that he sent me buckets of flowers in the days before your arrival." She still had her eyes on the portrait, but her next words were directed at Elena. "Our son had somehow gotten into a vat of tar. Nadiel managed to clean his skin and his wings but his beautiful hair was a lost cause."

Elena grinned and glanced at Raphael. "I'm trying to imagine you as a kid and failing, despite that baby portrait in the door."

"I can show you." Caliane brought her hands together as if she were a young maid and not an Ancient; her smile was of pure delight. "I have portraits."

"Mother."

But both his mother and his consort were intent on ignoring him. Giving in to the inevitable, he trailed after them through another door. And into a room that had him groaning.

It was a lovingly lit gallery.

Of him.

As a naked babe in his father's arms.

As an equally naked toddler caught climbing up the side of the house.

As a boy—with pants at least—trying out his wings.

As a fully dressed youth sitting beside his mother while she played the lyre.

And more, so many more.

"He would *not* sit still," Caliane told Elena. "Sharine did most of these after managing a quick sketch while he was up to mischief." She pointed at the painting with the lyre. "That one was the easiest. He liked to hear me sing and so he'd be quiet and in one place for that time."

"This is amazing." Elena had a hand pressed to her chest. "Can I take photos?"

"No." Raphael glared at her. "Else I will contact your father and create a public gallery in the Tower of your childhood self."

A narrow-eyed look from his consort. "Fine. Be that way." She turned her attention back to the paintings.

Caliane held her wings with warrior strength, but her lips were soft and her face warm with affection as she told his consort the stories behind the paintings. Her memories were precise, detailed.

"Why didn't I ever know about this gallery?"

Caliane laughed. "Ah, this is a thing for a mother. You were busy being a boy, a youth."

Raphael found himself drawn to the single family portrait in the gallery: Nadiel stood with his arm around a young Raphael, while Caliane sat in front of them, but she was glancing back with a smile on her face, as if distracted by whatever the two of them had just said. Father and son were in the midst of a laugh Raphael could almost hear.

"She has such hands, Sharine." His mother came to stand beside him. "Did I tell you that I visited her? She has settled well into her new role in Morocco." A touch on his forearm. "That is a good thing you did, Raphael."

"The Hummingbird was the best person for the task." The Cadre had needed a neutral party to take over the running of Lumia and its surrounding village, and no one in angelkind had a bad word to say about the Hummingbird. "She is outside politics and alliances."

"But for her son," Caliane reminded him.

"Yes." For Illium, the Hummingbird would do anything . . . but even Illium hadn't been able to hold his mother fully to this world. The Hummingbird existed in one of her own; she was a broken instrument, a lovely shattered piece. Raphael had never seen so much of her work in one place—and in doing so, he mourned her all the more.

The woman she'd been had understood life and love, understood what it was to be part of the world. Part of a family. But the family she'd painted with such tenderness was now as splintered as the Hummingbird's mind.

34

While Elena's stormfire wings continued to attract attention in the weeks after their return to New York, Raphael's consort got off much easier than expected—the entire world was watching China. Not because anything had happened, but the opposite. Gadriel had reported a sudden and eerie calm among the residents, including vampires formerly on the verge of bloodlust.

"Nothing I can put my finger on, but . . . my skin creeps."

Other commanders had reported much the same.

That might not have been enough to keep the Cadre distracted had Michaela not caused short tempers three weeks later with her outwardly petulant refusal to attend any meetings of the Cadre, even via a screen.

"The birth was a difficult one," Keir murmured when Raphael and Elena called to check on her welfare. "I tell you this only because she has authorized it—but it must remain between you and Caliane."

"You have our word." This was not a thing of games or manipulation.

"The babe is strong, healthy," Keir told them. "Michaela

recovers with archangelic speed but even that is not instantaneous after a birth." The healer's ageless eyes held theirs. "She will not move to the Refuge. She is convinced her child will be safer within the walls of this stronghold."

Raphael saw no real cause for concern, not with Keir overseeing the newborn's health as well as Michaela's convalescence. "It's unusual for a child to be raised outside the Refuge, but it's not an unheard-of choice—I spent much of my time in either Nadiel's or Caliane's territories."

At first, his world had been confined to the safe spaces behind the walls of forts and citadels. To a small boy with wings he could barely control, it had been a vast play area full of secrets and challenges. He'd grown under the watch of honed warriors and highly educated courtiers who'd taught him the responsibilities that came with freedom. By the time he grew strong enough to fly over the wall for the first time, Nadiel had gifted him his first sword, and Caliane had taught him how to fire a bow.

"I do not worry about the babe's safety but its development." Keir ran a hand through his hair in a rare restless gesture. "You attended the Refuge school for many a term, enough to make friends and to learn to be a child with other children. Jelena and Avi always took Tasha out of school at the same time Caliane did you, so the two of you could be playmates."

Such wild games he and Tasha had played. Two small sunbrown angels left to run riot across a vast court. *I wish Tasha had not been so foolish as to attempt to come between us,* he said to Elena. *You would be most amused at the stories we could tell together.*

Give me a decade or two. Wings of storm and lightning brushed his in an electric caress. *I might have calmed down by then and no longer want to fillet Ms. McHotpants.*

As he fought his smile, Keir said, "Nadiel was more lax in such matters, but his citadel was home to the mortal children of his youngest vampire soldiers. You were never isolated. I fear this babe will be brought up in a pretty prison."

"There is time yet." Angelic babies developed very slowly; the child would need nothing but its mother for some time.

"Yes, perhaps I am borrowing trouble without need."

After Keir signed off to go attend the infant, Raphael turned to his consort. "Would you like to fly? The skies are clear." A welcome change after two heavily cloudy nights.

"How about Cassandra's site?"

Raphael nodded. Squadrons of senior angels overflew the site several times a day on their way to or from other tasks, and sent through a report, but he wanted to put his own eyes on the location where Cassandra had disappeared with Favashi in her arms.

No one else was around when they landed outside the fence that had once ringed a lava sinkhole. Today, when they walked to look through one of the windows in the fence, all they saw was a sheet of unbroken white.

This early into December and Manhattan hadn't yet seen any snow. But here, it crunched under their boots, a glittering carpet lit by starlight.

A set of snowy wings drifted into view a second later, the owl coming to a graceful landing. Its mate landed moments afterward, and the two birds looked down, their gazes intent.

"They miss her," Elena murmured. "I can feel it the same way I can feel their minds, know they're mine for the moment." She pressed her hand to the glass. "I hope she's found a semblance of peace."

The wind swirled around them, the snow rising. The owls took off in a silent burst, while Raphael and Elena stood in watchful quiet. Elena held her breath, not sure what she wanted. The last time Cassandra had risen, it had nearly meant the end of her world. Yet when it counted, the Ancient haunted by visions of the future had come through. She'd helped Elena—and she might've helped Favashi.

But the wind calmed as swiftly as it had risen, leaving only flecks of snow stuck to Elena's winter-weight leather jacket. "Nope, that wasn't great for the blood pressure."

"A moment, *hbeebti*." Stepping back so he wouldn't buffet her, Raphael took flight. She watched as he swept over the former lava sinkhole from high above, the owls circling with him. *See anything?*

Yes. Come.

She rose to join him. Her heart tightened. Drawn in the snow was the body of a huge white owl, its wings spread wide.

"She's still partially awake." Enough to know they had come to see her. Enough to reply. "Should we increase patrols?"

"There is no need." He nodded at the owls who'd dipped lower, closer to their mistress. "If there comes a day when her owls leave you, we will know."

"Yes." The beautiful creatures were borrowed treasures, lent to her by an Ancient who had seen her birth millennia ago. "It's not good that she's still half awake, is it?"

"We all agree that Lijuan is also partially awake, so the Cascade energies may be disrupting their Sleep."

Cold fingers on Elena's spine. "Let's hope they're the only two Sleepers affected."

That hope was dashed two hours later, when Astaad convened an emergency session of the Cadre. Raphael had dressed quickly for the meeting, while Elena sat out of shot naked but for the blanket she'd wrapped around her body.

The Cadre responded within a matter of two minutes—surprisingly enough, Michaela's face was among them. Her razor-sharp beauty took center stage, but Raphael saw the lack of color under the skin, the slight puffiness around the eyes. If anyone else noticed, they'd put it down to having been woken out of a sound sleep.

The world had forgotten that Michaela had once been a mother; no one thought of her as maternal. He hoped for the sake of her babe that continued to hold true. Not everyone was a fan of the Archangel of Budapest and attacking her while she was weak could be a temptation.

"I hope you have a good reason for this," she muttered now, her words knife blades sinking into unguarded flesh. "Emergency calls are not to be made lightly."

Astaad had on a rumpled tunic, his hair windswept. "You must all see this."

His feed altered to show a turquoise blue ocean under a Pacific sun; that ocean was choppy, the water foamy. From the jerkiness of the image, one of Astaad's people must be flying overhead with a recording and transmitting device. As they watched, the foaming of the water turned into a whirlpool so powerful that Raphael hoped the angel involved was high enough up not to get caught in its drag.

"Astaad, my desert territory is currently suffering its twentieth ice storm." Alexander pressed two fingers to the bridge of his nose, his words clipped. "Such a phenomenon is not reason enough to—"

"There!"

Raphael's entire body stopped moving. Because the water had just erupted up and outward, and Astaad had frozen the image.

Archangel, am I seeing things or is the water spout in the shape of a face?

His gut tensed as he recognized that face. *You are not imagining it.*

Water god?

Just an archangel of arrogance. Mortals have called him by many names over time, but he is said to prefer Aegaeon.

You sound like you know him.

He took a short sojourn from his Sleep during my lifetime. All of the Cadre here but for my mother would've met him at that time—and she is likely to have known him during another waking.

"How long has this been going on?" Neha, her hair unbound and held back with jeweled clips, but her body clad in warrior's leathers as she stood in a room with rough redstone walls.

"Three or so hours, but initially, I thought it a weather phenomenon as suffered by Alexander."

"My apologies, Astaad," Alexander said, the edge in his tone different this time. "Aegaeon went to Sleep roughly a century before I did. I had forgotten his penchant for drama."

Alexander's not a fan.

Neither was Raphael. If Aegaeon woke, it would destroy the lives of two people Raphael cherished.

"He's what, fifty thousand or so?" Charisemnon's tone was offhand. "Not an Ancient in the same way as you or Lady Caliane then."

Caliane raised both eyebrows. "Is that what he spread around? He did always have a strange vanity about his age.

The truth is, he was born when I was a youngling. He is of an age with Alex and me."

I did not know he claimed to be fifty thousand, Raphael said to Elena. *Perhaps he never tried with me because I had one of his compatriots for a mother.*

"Aegaeon's overall level of power in comparison to the current Cadre is impossible to calculate," Alexander muttered.

"He will be a power in age and experience alone," Neha pointed out. "I remember him from his last waking—he did not enjoy that time, did not stay long—but he was an impressive being while he walked the Earth."

Meanwhile, Neha is a fan.

Aegaeon had a way with women—though I would not call it charm. It had been too rough for that, too reckless.

Raphael? Why are you so angry at him?

I cannot speak of this, Elena. It is not a promise . . . but a trust I hold dear.

Elena didn't force the issue; she was a warrior, understood the import of such things.

"The Cadre is missing a member." Elijah, calm and thoughtful. "It may be that we are being brought back into balance."

"I will inform you of any further signs of waking," Astaad said, white lines around his mouth.

Astaad had reason for his tension. Should Aegaeon indeed rise, the Archangel of the Pacific Isles would have to share his territory, as Favashi had initially shared with Alexander. Astaad, however, was in a better position to hold on to the Pacific than Favashi had Persia—while Aegaeon had no doubt ruled that territory at some point during his long existence, the last time he'd woken, he'd held dominion over the lands Michaela now called her own.

Not only that, but if he was as old as Caliane had said, then most of his people had to be dead or in a long Sleep of their own. Maybe that was why Aegaeon hadn't stayed awake for an extended period the last time. Just long enough to irreparably break a precious gift to angelkind.

"Since we are all here," Neha said, her hands on her hips, "what is the situation in China? Lady Caliane, you have been there most recently."

More than one head turned toward Michaela; she ignored

the pointed looks. Caliane, by contrast, was too well respected for anyone to ask why she'd stepped in.

"No new infections among those who watch over the territory for the Cadre. The half-consumed discovered by Raphael are all dead—they would not feed, even when sustenance was placed into their hands."

"So nothing has really changed. Good." Michaela logged off.

"So nice to have the princess back in the fold." Charisemnon's tone was pure poison before his screen, too, went black.

The others followed one by one.

Elena's face was forlorn when he turned to her. Crossing the carpet, he ran his fingers through her hair. "We did what we could to save the villagers. But they were doomed at Lijuan's first touch."

Leaning her head against his thigh, his hand curved over her nape, she looked out at the soft rain that had begun to fall. Manhattan glittered beyond the veil. "You didn't mention the snow owl."

"Let us allow Cassandra to Sleep in peace as long as she is able." The two owls who dozed in one corner of the room, on a low perch that Dmitri had used long-rusty skills to make, rustled their wings as if in a dream. "One more Ancient, the Cadre can absorb, but two?" He shook his head. "It may tip the world into an archangelic war."

35

His fears proved groundless.

Three days after the meeting, Cassandra's site was dead calm and Astaad reported the same of his territory. "It is as if Aegaeon had a nightmare and cried out in his Sleep, then laid his head back down."

Raphael took a silent breath at that. He'd been weighing up how to share the news of the Ancient's possible awakening with the two people who'd be most affected by it, all the while aware that, by speaking, he would devastate both their lives at a critical time. He would hold his silence now, speak only when a waking was confirmed.

The violent weather systems had also settled, including Alexander's ice storms as well as the geothermal activity in Raphael's territory.

"It almost feels like the prelude to a tsunami," Elena said one night as they stood atop the Legion building after Elena had spent the day getting her hands dirty. "How everything goes still and the water retreats and retreats from the shore . . . only for a huge wave to return and pummel everything to death."

"Your positive thoughts overwhelm me." Raphael watched

the purple-hued horizon as day fell into night, almost expecting to see the wave crashing.

"That's me, chipper as a spring bean." Lightning dancing through her wings, she threw a blade at him without warning. "You gonna tell me what was in that package from Amanat?"

Raphael lobbed back the blade through the frigid night air. "Another portrait of my father." The words came out even, without emotion. "My mother wants me to have it."

Tilting her head to the side after slipping the blade back into its sheath, Elena crossed the space between them. "Hey." A hand pressed to his heart. "Talk to me."

His pulse speeded up to beat in time with hers. She was now a full immortal, but she remained fragile in comparison to him. Breakable. Lijuan could end her with a single blow . . . yet his Elena would fly into battle at his side. Courage was writ on her soul. As defiant as the stormfire wings she'd clawed from the Cascade.

"My mother remembers all the good about my father," he said, his mind filling with thoughts of another pair of lovers. "I wonder if she has forgotten the rest, or if she chooses only to focus on the light."

Time rolled backward.

"That he loved her is beyond question. He was a huge power and women gravitated toward him, but he never looked at anyone else. Even when they were apart for months at a time, he never fell to temptation, never even saw it—I witnessed that with my own eyes." Raphael caught lightning from her wings. "In that, I am my father's son. It will only ever be you for me."

Near-white strands of hair flirting against her neck, Elena reached up to brush her fingers over his cheek.

"But he was also . . . irresponsible." Laughing and bright-eyed and not as adult as he should be. "A strange thing to say of an archangel, but there was a boyishness to him that I can see clearly when I look back at my memories. He would take me on wild adventures and it was all wonderful—until I fell and broke a wing or a leg.

"*I* loved the adventures, loved the danger. But it bothered my mother and yet, he wasn't careful. He loved her desperately, but he wasn't careful with her heart." Raphael tried to find the words to explain. "He was always taking risks, always riding the edge. When the madness first licked at his mind, the healers told him to Sleep, that often, a long Sleep cured that which was broken."

Memories, hard and loud in his head. "I heard them arguing. I wasn't a child any longer, and I understood. She begged him to Sleep, promised she'd be waiting when he woke. But my father refused to 'give up on life.'" So stubborn and arrogant and believing he knew best.

"In the end, he forced her to execute him." It had broken Caliane in ways Raphael didn't think would ever heal. "The woman you know, that's not all of her. Parts are missing." Would *always* be missing.

"I saw it in the portraits." Elena's eyes were more gray than silver today, her mortal heart right out in the open. "She had a candle inside her that's dimmer now, quieter."

"She was so old when they met. Old enough to be considering an endless Sleep. He brought her to life—that's what she always told me."

Sliding her arms around him, Elena held him tight as the wind wove around them, bringing with it a chill that promised snow not too far in the distant future. "I wish I could've met them when they were together and happy. I wish you could've met Jeffrey and Marguerite when they were the same."

But the past was gone, leaving only broken shards at their feet. All they had were memories and a perilous future in which everything was shifting. Including the turbulent power inside Raphael that had become fused into his cells.

HUNTER ANGEL RETURNS TRIUMPHANT!

Elena glared at Demarco when he waved his tablet in front of her face a week later, that headline blaring across it. "Take that away or I'll use it for target practice."

Her fellow hunters had freaked out at first sight of her stormfire wings, but by now it was old news. Alas, the same could not be said for the local papers and magazines. They were *obsessed* with her wings. A new article every damn day. It wasn't a security threat since they mostly printed photos snapped by citizens along with gushing headlines like today's, but she was starting to feel like New York's prize poodle.

Demarco, dressed in his now-faded Hunter Angel T-shirt and worn blue jeans—and smart-ass smile—began to read out the article while Elena, Ransom, Ashwini, Honor, Kenji, and Rose lounged around the table in the Guild HQ break room. "Elena Deveraux," he intoned, "has returned from the dead not once but twice!"

"I wasn't dead either time," Elena muttered. "I was just mostly dead."

Kenji snickered, and Demarco read on. "In this incarnation, she's made the city proud with her retractable stormfire wings—"

"Wait a minute!" Having been leaning back in her chair, Elena slammed it to the floor now. "Those are *highly* specific words." Words she'd used to describe her wings. "Is there a mysterious anonymous source in this article?"

Demarco blinked innocent eyes at her. "Do you want to hear the rest or not?"

Balling up a paper napkin, she threw it at his tousled head of streaky blond hair, while the others cracked up.

"Where was I before I was attacked?" He ostentatiously found his place again. "To those who doubted her, it's a slap in the face. But to New Yorkers, it is confirmation of what we already knew: our hunter angel is unstoppable."

Elena groaned, her head in her hands. "End this torture. Please, I beg you."

But Demarco was relentless and her other friends egged him on. At least Ashwini threw her a chocolate bar as a consolation prize and she soothed herself with sugar and cocoa until the entire excruciating exercise was over—complete with the mysterious anonymous source who gave nothing away but added to the legend of the hunter angel.

Her favorite quote was: "I've seen her wings zap people stone-dead."

"I guess I should thank you for that." She threw another balled-up napkin at his head. "Hopefully it'll stop the ones who can't resist attempting a touch." Unwanted touch had been uncomfortable on her old wings and it was the same now.

"I have no idea why you'd thank me," Demarco said piously. "Thank the anonymous source."

"Did I show you guys my new Hunter Angel T-shirt?" Kenji unzipped his jacket to reveal a cobalt-blue tee with Elena's silhouette in black . . . with glitter for wings.

"I got the pink one," Ashwini said, her booted feet up on the table and big silver hoops dangling from her ears. "Bright pink with the Hunter Angel in gold and gold glitter for the wings."

"Honor and I went for yellow." Rose bumped fists with Honor.

"Mine's black with white. Classic. No fucking glitter in sight." Ransom's phone beeped before Elena could threaten to murder the whole lot of them. Her hardass friend went sheet white under his coppery skin. "Now?" he blurted out. "I'm on my way."

He got up so abruptly that his chair clattered to the floor. "Where's my helmet?" Manic expression, head swiveling this way and that.

"Right behind you." Elena frowned. "But I don't think you should be driving in that state. What's wrong?"

Everyone but Ransom had gone quiet and watchful, a group of lethal hunters waiting to spring into action for a friend.

Ransom stared at her before throwing out his hands as if it should be obvious. "Nyree's having our baby!"

A collective intake of breath, then they moved like a well-oiled machine. Demarco took charge of Ransom, shoving him into a Guild vehicle; Kenji and Rose piled in the back. Ashwini got on Ransom's bike, Honor behind her, and they roared off in the wake of the vehicle, while Elena took to the air.

Nyree was already in the maternity suite by the time they arrived at the hospital and they made sure they got Ransom to the right place. Elena had never seen him so shell-shocked—but his shoulders straightened as he went through the doors of the suite, his expression shimmering to pure calm.

The rest of them waited like anxious parents themselves. Elena drew a bit of attention, but all the weapons bristling on their bodies kept the curious at bay. Or maybe it was the whole group that was drawing attention. Demarco was wearing a sword in a spine sheath, while Ashwini's gun hung at her hip; she played throwing stars around her fingers—the light glinted off the viciously sharp edges.

Kenji had taken a seat and begun to snap a garrote between his fisted hands, while Rose was practicing throwing a pretend knife. A passing doctor ducked as she sent one invisible missile flying. Honor, meanwhile, was "catching" Rose's throws and sending them back.

"Did he spill yet if it was a girl or a boy?" Demarco wrapped one arm around Elena's waist, careful to keep his forearm away from her wings.

Elena shook her head. "Said they don't know. Wanted it to be a surprise."

"I'm going to kill all of you." Sara rushed into the waiting room on black high heels, her outfit today a fitted dress in deep plum and her hair swinging glossily across her shoulders.

"We know you're magic, boss." Demarco, with no regard for his life, sent Sara a quick salute. "Had zero doubts you'd make it here in time."

Sara glared at him. "Any news?"

"No." Honor brought up her legs to sit cross-legged on the hard plastic chair. "Doctor said since it's Nyree's first, it might take a while."

But it was only two hours later that Ransom walked out with a shit-eating grin on his face. "I'm a dad."

They swarmed him with hugs and congratulations and questions. After Sara corralled the lot of them into order, they snuck in to see mother and baby in groups of two or three. Nyree had already told Ransom it was all right.

Elena entered with Demarco and Rose to find Ransom on the bed beside his wife, his arm around her back and his hand stroking the tiny head that lay nestled against Nyree's skin. The new mother looked a little tired, her dusky skin paler than usual and her black curls wildly tumbled. Her smile, however, was radiant.

"He's so tiny." Demarco's tone was awed; he kept his hands scrupulously behind his back. "Jeez, Ransom, how're you going to handle him without breaking him?" Not a smart-ass question, an honestly petrified one.

Ransom ran the pad of his finger over his son's head again. "You have no idea of my current level of fear." His grin didn't fade an inch. "But I can't wait to do the dad thing."

"Nyree," Elena whispered, "you grew a human." With miniature fingernails and skin so new it was dewy.

"I can't believe it myself." Ransom's tough little wife pressed a kiss to the downy hair on top of the baby's head. "You'll all be babysitting so start studying up."

A collective spike of terror shared between her, Demarco, and Rose.

Nyree's laughter filled the room.

At that instant, all was right with the world, Lijuan's reign of death forgotten in the gift of this tiny new life. But things deadly and violent were stirring awake even as Elena dared touch a careful finger to the baby's fragile hand.

36

Archangel! I have the best news!

Stepping out onto the balcony outside his office to meet his consort, Raphael went to ask the reason for her joy when a lightning strike speared out of the sky. Elena jerked out of the way just in time, and the bolt hit the balcony beside her.

The surface cracked, fine fault lines spreading across the entire space.

More bolts appeared out of the cloudless sky on the heels of the first, deadly arcs of energy that could fry an angel's wings and crash him to the earth.

LAND! NOW! He sent the mental command to the edges of his ability, saw angels begin to arrow down to land wherever they could. A number of the Legion did the same, but one of them couldn't avoid a strike.

His body disintegrated.

At least the Legion would rise again, unlike an angel who was hit. "Stay down, Elena. I must see if I can protect them." The strikes were coming faster together now and many angels had been high, couldn't drop fast enough.

Be careful! A mental shout as she got to the shelter of the doorway and he took off.

The lightning altered direction to angle toward him. He permitted a small bolt to hit him so he could gain further information, absorbing the impact with the strength that made him an archangel.

No strange Cascade energy. This was simply weather run amok.

But, for some unknown reason, he drew the violence like a lightning rod. Maybe because the energy that danced on his skin was akin to the lightning. Instinctively creating a shield around himself, similar to the one he used when he and Elena dived into the ocean together, he headed out toward the sea.

Guild Hunter, do not take to the air under any circumstances. You carry enough of my power to attract the lightning. It wasn't chance that the first bolt had hit the balcony next to her. *I'll survive it. You won't. Not at these levels.*

Don't you dare get hurt!

Wings floated in the ocean below him as he left the skyscrapers and high-rises of his city behind him; the squadron must've been flying home when he gave the landing order. All appeared uninjured, including an angel with wings of wild blue.

Sire? Illium's voice. *I can join you.*

No, stay in the water until I give the all clear. The lightning continued to strike at his shield; he couldn't guarantee the safety of anyone flying beside him.

He flew until he was far enough away from the downed squadron that the water wouldn't conduct any energy release to them. Dropping low enough to the blue that he was just touching it, he pointed his feet and his hands downward . . . and dropped the shield.

The lightning hit him in a rapacious burst, jetting through his body and over his skin in arcs of fire that arrowed into the sea. The water boiled and surged, mist curling up into the air. Cold fire burned him from the inside out, but he knew it wouldn't cause permanent harm.

Gritting his teeth he rode it out.

It was only after the sky went quiet at last that he realized the state of his clothes. Elena would not be happy. *Have the skies cleared?* he asked his consort.

Yes. Are you all right?

My clothing is a touch scorched, but I sustained no damage.

I'm homeward bound. He told his angels it was safe to get in the air as he headed back.

Illium met him halfway.

It was no surprise the young angel had headed Raphael's way; headstrong and loyal, Elena's Bluebell was an angel Raphael was proud to have in his Seven. The icy Cascade power in his veins agreed; Bluebell was an asset. Not only because of his fidelity but because of the potential that burned in his body.

Raphael didn't fight the cold calculation of that power head-on. He'd begun to understand that he had to stamp this power with his mark rather than attempting to leash it. So he stirred his memories, bringing the past to the fore. A past in which he'd given a toddler with nascent wings of blue a piggyback ride before taking the thrilled little boy on a flight through the Refuge gorge.

Rafa! I fly!

Illium would never be just a source of power to him.

"Well," the angel said across the calm winds between them, "that was strange."

Raphael felt his lips twitch. It was not chance that Illium and Elena were such good friends. They had a way of taking the most eerie, most deadly events and making them somehow human. "It appears the Cascade was merely taking a breath before it pummeled us once more." The lightning strikes may have been nothing out of the ordinary as far as their composition, but their behavior had been distinctly abnormal.

"At least it seems to be maintaining a certain level and not increasing in power or virulence. I'll worry when the sea turns blood red."

"Should that happen, we will all have wine and watch the end of the world from a good vantage point."

Grinning, Illium peeled off as they hit the edge of the city, and there was Elena, coming toward him on wings of stunning stormlight, several of the Legion in tow. The lightning in her wings seemed stronger, more violent.

"A *touch* scorched!" she yelled when they were close enough to exchange words. "You don't have on a tunic anymore and your pants look like they were hacked up by a designer who charges five thousand dollars for his scissor skills."

Her scowl deepened the closer she got. "And the soles of your boots are smoking!"

"I acted as a lightning rod. I'm surprised I still have boots in any form." He'd half expected that they'd blow right off. "Whatever I did, I cannot explain the physics of it."

"Let's just call it Cascade weirdness and leave it at that." His consort flew all around him, then back. No one but Elena had ever worried so much about him.

"Will I do?" he asked when she finally came to fly beside him once more, as inside him, the Cascade power morphed under the sheer force of her love, the ice infiltrated by a tendril of wildfire and steel that flat out refused to leave. And he knew. This change was permanent, anchored in the pieces of her heart in his bloodstream.

"I can't see any burns, so I might forgive you for giving me a heart attack when you flew out with *lightning* chasing you."

"Immortals don't get heart attacks."

"Look closely. This is my *not*-laughing face."

Dismissing the Legion, Raphael wrapped himself in glamour while grabbing hold of his consort, so that she, too, was hidden from the world. Her wings danced stormlight over him, her lips meeting his as if they'd choreographed the contact.

It was a hard branding of a kiss and it held her heart.

He felt the thud of her pulse, tasted the bite of her fear. As she'd soothed him at times, he did the same to her now.

She broke the kiss at last with a suckling taste of his lower lip. "Okay, you're okay," she said, pure warrior strength and granite resolve. *"Raphael."*

He understood. She'd convinced the small, irrational part of her that worried about an archangel's hurt that he was all right. She could breathe again. Her heartbeat could turn normal again.

He flew her the rest of the way home. She didn't protest, just wrapped one arm around the back of his neck and watched their city grow closer and closer until it was steel and glass and life beneath them. No one saw them, the glamour one of the greatest tools in his arsenal.

Sire. Dmitri's voice. *Jason's just sent through a disturbing video captured by one of his people in China. I think you should see it as soon as possible.*

"Dmitri has more weirdness for us, *hbeebti*," he said aloud while mentally acknowledging Dmitri's words. "This time from China."

"Oh yay, my excitement knows no bounds." A distinctly unenthusiastic tone. "I think immortals should make a rule—once you get to be a certain age, it's time to go Sleep off the crazy. Not an option. Compulsory."

"You should discuss your thoughts with my mother."

"You are a horrible man sometimes." She was yet scowling when he landed on the balcony outside Dmitri's office, but the first thing she did was run her hands over his chest and arms, then go behind him and do the same with his wings and back.

"Uninjured." Hands on her hips in front of him, she nodded. "You're permitted to talk to Dmitri."

"So much concern, Elena. I will worry you have no faith in me."

A tightness to her jaw. "Don't mess with me, Archangel. I am not in the mood." Turning, she strode toward Dmitri's door.

It was only when he saw himself reflected in the glass surface of the large window that was the back of Dmitri's office that he understood her rattled response. His hair was singed at the edges and still smoking a little. His chest was covered with streaks of black smoke and his skin opened and closed in random spots with bursts of golden lightning.

Smoke curled out from the bottoms of his boots.

His eyes glowed. So hot it was as if he had a blue flame in his irises.

Elena walked through the door Dmitri had opened; Dmitri was momentarily silent when Raphael followed. Raphael picked off a shred of tunic that was somehow still stuck to his biceps, and dropped it in the wastebasket by Dmitri's desk.

"I blame you," his second said to Elena. "He didn't think about frying himself in lightning bolts before you."

Raphael waited for Elena to snap a quick comeback at Dmitri. He had the sneaking suspicion the two of them thrived on their animosity toward one another. He also knew that if push came to shove, they would fight as a battle-hardened unit. This was an amusement, nothing more.

Today, however, Elena pressed her lips together and looked

down at the carpet. Frowning at the unexpected response, Dmitri went to the large screen on one wall of his office and played the recording he'd already cued up: waves of black smoke engulfed a village.

"A fire?" Raphael murmured, right as the recording panned out. The black fog was emerging from the ground about a quarter of a mile out. It wasn't moving at dangerous speed, but the people in the recording did nothing to get away. As it brushed over them, they just waved at it as you might at an insect that was annoying you.

It was clear the villagers believed the fog would soon retreat or be blown away, but what happened was something else altogether. Once the strange fog had spread across the entire village, it hunkered down and turned opaque. The camera could no longer see through the thickness of it. No more faces. No more waving hands. Nothing but an endless night.

Expression grim, Dmitri brought up another file. "This was recorded the following day." The fog had all but dissipated, but when the angel holding the camera flew down to take a closer look, he found only silence. Oranges rolled out of a bag abandoned on the small deck attached to a house. A barn door flapped open, no animals within. A bowl of food sat in front of a doghouse, but no puppy barked up at the angel.

No villagers. No bodies. An entire group taken without a trace.

37

Elena broke the chill silence. "At least now we know how she's doing it." A glance at Raphael. "Could be in conjunction with another volunteer acolyte . . . or maybe she's gone beyond that."

"I will send an alert to those in charge. The people of China must be warned to get out of the way should they see such a fog." Doing nothing in these circumstances wasn't an option. "Dmitri, send the recording to others of the Cadre, under my seal."

His second nodded and turned his attention to the task.

Raphael, meanwhile, asked Elena to walk outside with him.

Only once they were out on the edge of the railingless balcony, their city spread out below them like a toy creation, did he say, "Why did you allow Dmitri's jibe to get to you?" It had disconcerted his second, too. Dmitri only acted the way he did with Elena because she gave as good as he dished out.

"It just struck me." She stared out at the steel and glass and vibrancy of their city. "This craziness began with me—with a mortal turned angel. What if I was the catalyst for the Cascade? All this death and darkness and horror, it'd be on me."

"It could as easily be said that Uram was the catalyst." Raphael felt sorrow for the archangel he'd had to execute, an archangel who'd once been his friend, but he also knew that it'd had to be done. Uram had become a monster, one who gorged on death and whose murderous appetite would never be satisfied. "It's what brought you into my life."

Elena played a throwing knife through her fingers, the fading winter light glancing off the shining surfaces. "I try to tell myself that, but . . . I'm the wild card element in all of this. Archangels, angels, mortals, vampires, that was the world before me. Now we have an angel-Made."

"Naasir would be most annoyed at you for forgetting him."

But Elena's gaze remained solemn. "Naasir and I should begin a club for all the ones who don't quite fit on the taxonomic tree."

"You were just the first whisper of the Cascade, Elenamine. Not the catalyst, for no one can control such powers as are currently smashing the world, but the first sign that the Cascade had begun."

Allowing him to haul her close, Elena stroked his skin . . . and jumped. "You're a little electrified, lover," she informed him, while continuing with her caresses. "I don't know if I like being the first sign of impending doom any better." A scowl. "Still, it beats being the cause."

"What arrogance you have, Guild Hunter, to think you are the reason behind a tumult of power such as the world has never seen."

"Jeez, you're right." She bumped her forehead against his chest. "I must sound so full of myself."

He went to reassure her that he'd meant nothing of what he'd said, then paused. His words had worked. Not in the way he'd wanted, but they'd broken through the shadowy miasma that had threatened to encompass Elena. So he curved his hand around the side of her neck and said, "It is the curse of immortality. You must watch against further development."

She tilted back her head. "Fiend." She "punched" him in the side, the touch featherlight. "Also, Dmitri's now one point up on me. Ugh."

"You've forgotten the kiss."

Her eyes brightened at the reminder of Dmitri's utter horror. Satisfaction curling her lips, she pressed a kiss to his chest, shivered. "Yep, still electrified."

"And filthy. Come." He rose up into the air as night licked the horizon. "You can wash my back."

Elena put on soft gray pajama pants after a delicious bath with Raphael, topping them with an equally soft tank in a darker gray and a deep blue hoodie—both designed with wing slits. The hoodie boasted a sparkly silver unicorn on the left breast, while on the back were printed the words: *Wait, I have to park my unicorn.*

"I miss the time when unicorns roamed the earth."

"Very funny, Archangel." She knew that glint in his eye by now. "Beth got this for me after Maggie picked it out."

"Talking of gifts." Wearing only a pair of faded sweatpants that hung precariously on his hips, Raphael plucked out a small box from inside their private weapons locker.

Elena's breath caught. Slipping a hand under her pillow, she withdrew her own small box. "I was going to spring it on you in bed."

Raphael's wings began to glow.

Opening his box, he held it out. The last time, it had been small amber hoops appropriate for a working hunter. This time, it was studs: one an amber crossbow bolt with a heart of white fire, the other a tiny crossbow that must've taken an artisan days to craft. She held her breath as he inserted first one, then the other through ears she'd had pierced a couple of weeks ago.

Neither of them spoke as she opened her own box. A ring because Raphael wasn't much for other forms of jewelry. A heavy titanium band scored with a pattern that echoed the gunshot scar on his wing, a roughly square chunk of amber in the center. An explosion of white fire had been caught in the amber, the edges pale gold.

The one thing that wasn't new was the word inscribed on the inside: *Knhebek.*

Raphael held out his hand and she slipped it on.

A sigh whispered out of her. She hadn't known how much she missed this small sign of their entanglement until now. "I saved the rest of the amber."

"For the next time we blow up ours?"

"The rate we're going . . ." That was when she caught a glow on the horizon out of the corner of her eye. "Don't look now but I think something's happening."

Of course, they both headed outside. Elena hugged her arms around herself as they stepped out into the cold. Her hoodie wasn't meant for outdoor temperatures. Raphael, bare chested, tugged her against that chest and the two of them stood in the winter cold night while an eerie light came to life over the water, the colors of it blood red.

"Illium told me that at least the sea wasn't turning blood red."

"Now he's jinxed us." She watched transfixed as the light came closer and closer. "Shall we—"

"No, your Bluebell has already taken a squadron out for the initial reconnaissance."

Raphael kept thinking he should know about this light, a faint whisper of memory at the back of his mind.

Sire, Illium said. *The water around the light is clear and I just saw a bird fly into it and return with no apparent ill effects. The light isn't coming from the sky but rising from the ocean.*

Continue to watch. Raphael trusted nothing about the Cascade. *Do not enter it.*

Elena's owls are dancing around in the colors of it.

"Guild Hunter, you will have to unpark your unicorn. It appears this is for you." He told her of the owls.

"Cassandra?" A quiet tension in her voice. "Let's go find out."

It took them only a short time to get into gear more suitable for a night flight and head out. Elena took only minimal weapons—which for her meant her crossbow, the bolts, and enough throwing blades to set up a knife shop.

When Raphael saw how many other curious angels were heading toward the luminescence, he ordered everyone but the squadron to fall back.

Obedience was immediate.

Wow.

Raphael had to agree with Elena's awed whisper. He'd been alive an eon longer than her and he'd never seen such a sight. What had seemed blood red from the Tower proved to be a complex blend of colors, true red only at the very top edge. Even there, it wasn't blood red but a deep pink red.

That shade faded into a softer pink; the colors that rippled below it were blues and greens and golds and so many other hues that he didn't have names for all of them. *It is like an aurora on the ocean.* A lovely vision thrown up from the depths.

How high does it go?

Raphael flew up, and up. *As high as the Tower.* Arrowing back down to hover beside Elena, he watched the owls dance over and through the light and, despite his suspicions of the Cascade, could find nothing threatening in the sight. It was an artwork given life, a song painted in color and light.

Raphael. I have Jessamy on the line. Dmitri's confident dark-edged voice. *I've asked her if she's heard of this phenomenon.*

Tell her that it appears peaceful at first glance. The owls are certainly happy with it. It may be linked to Cassandra.

A pause, during which he and Elena winged along this side of the sea aurora. Bathed in that light, Elena's wings shimmered a stunning array of color, a mix of her own and the aurora. When she reached out a careful hand toward the light, he went to stop her, but it was already too late.

The light painted the canvas of her skin but it didn't stick, her hand unblemished when she drew it back. *Sorry, I shouldn't have done that but I felt so safe.* A glance at the owls. *I think they know this isn't harmful.*

Raphael sliced his wing through the light. *There is energy here. A power.* It resonated deep within him. *But I sense no malevolence.*

The sea aurora was moving steadily toward his city. *Dmitri, do you have anything?*

Jessamy just found a reference to a "dream of light and color over the ocean." It's in an ancient text that vaguely mentions Cassandra—Wait. Thirty seconds passed. *Here's the quote: "And in that dream of light and color over the ocean danced the seer's wings. The two are ever entwined and never together. One of light and dreams, the other of blood and prophecies." Make sense to you?*

I'm afraid it might.

Elena, now close to him, said, "Why the look?"

He told her what Dmitri had just said and watched her work
it through. A tiny frown dug its way between her brows. "*One*
of light and dreams, the *other* . . ." A widening of her eyes.
"Shit. Another waking Ancient?"

"That seems to be the unavoidable explanation."

"Fuck."

"Yes." Aegaeon had stirred in Astaad's territory, Cassandra
was in a fitful Sleep at best, and now this. "For the time being,
however, it doesn't appear to be dangerous. I will allow our
people to view it as long as they follow the squadron's orders."

Angelic silhouettes lifted up from roofs and balconies and
streets all over the city as Elena and Raphael flew back. A
number of seacraft began to chug their way toward the light.

Dmitri and Venom were waiting on the Tower roof and Raphael angled that way, Elena beside him. The snow on the roof
softened the sound of their landing, and the light, when they
turned to look back at it, remained as beautiful and as eerie.

Venom came to stand beside Elena, Dmitri beside Raphael.

"I took a call while Dmitri was talking with Jessamy."
Venom slipped his hands into the pants pockets of his deep
gray suit. "It was from Charisemnon's second." His lip curled
up at the mention of the archangel who'd caused the Falling,
crashing angels to the ground all over New York. "Images of
the light phenomenon have already spread around the world.
He called to ask if we believed an archangel was waking."

Raphael spread his wings, closed them with slow deliberation. "That's a highly specific question."

"I pointed that out. Response was that a remote lake in
their region has just frozen over—within it are millions of
translucent bubbles, the colors intimately similar to our aurora
over the sea." He passed across his phone. "Pure luck anyone
found it—a senior angel decided to take the long way home."

"Wow again," Elena said.

"Indeed." The water was a glossy sheet, the bubbles below
pristine and perfectly formed. Air caught in ice. "Do they
know if this occurred at the same time as the sea aurora?"

A shake of Venom's head. "I got the impression they discovered it a couple of days ago, but kept it quiet." No surprise
in his tone at such behavior from Charisemnon's court.

"I can see why they think the two incidents are connected." Elena handed back Venom's phone. "Those are distinctive colors in the bubbles and in the light."

"How many Ancients can the world sustain?" Dmitri folded his arms across his chest. His black shirt rippled in the cool wind coming off the water in the distance.

"We are currently nine. The tenth should be an archangel not an Ancient, but the world will not break if we are three Ancients." He seemed to recall a long-ago history lesson in Jessamy's classroom that mentioned a Cadre with three Ancients.

"After that, Ancients who awaken will cause major disruption and chaos *unless* we lose several current members of the Cadre." Their powers would be too close together, the energies too violent—and the old tended to be set in their ways, not ready for this new world. "It'll make the Cascade look like a training run."

Elena sucked in a breath. "That bad?"

"We survived with eleven before because Mother did not want territory and China is so huge that Favashi was far distant from her. We can rely neither on a lack of territorial desire nor geography with any new archangels or Ancients." His mother was a unique case in not wishing to rule a vast area.

"You've seen how much violence two archangels can do in battle." Raphael and Uram had nearly destroyed New York. "Now imagine that happening between more than two archangels, the battles taking place in multiple locations around the world at the same time."

Elena's gaze returned to the sea aurora. "You can be an Ancient and not be an archangel, right?"

"Yes. But any Ancient who awakens with natural phenomena such as this is an archangel." The light continued to hang over the sea, seeming to ripple in the wind, a gentle music.

Dmitri's phone rang. He glanced at it. "It's Rhys."

A senior general in Neha's territory.

He stepped away to take the call, returned to say, "Delhi is glowing. Some kind of bioluminescence. Rhys is sending me images."

"If this is all the same Ancient," Elena said, "then I kinda like them already. I mean, pretty lights, cool bubbles in a lake, glowing cities, seems pretty mellow to me."

Raphael stared out at the water, not certain it *was* all connected to one Ancient. "The bioluminescence strikes me as different from the two water-based phenomena."

"Rhys has understatement down pat." Dmitri flipped his phone in their direction.

"It looks like the aliens came and irradiated everything," Elena whistled through her teeth.

When Dmitri's phone rang just as he drew it back, Raphael said, "Which second is it now?"

"Not a second but might as well be—it's that creep, Riker. I don't know why Michaela keeps him around. He's a vicious fucker."

"He's also viciously loyal to her," Raphael said as Dmitri stepped away again.

His second just held out his phone when he returned: on it was the image of an old European city, possibly Prague, backed by a sky in which swirled a slow spiral of stars. A new galaxy being born.

It wasn't the final portent.

By dawn, New York was in the grip of a huge storm that coated the city in ice, and the list had grown to include intricate crop circles in Titus's land, a rainstorm in Japan that turned the country a bright magenta, large standing rocks erupting out of the earth in Alexander's territory—some through the floors of buildings—and last but not least, an impossible blooming of wildflowers across frozen Siberia.

If each represented an Ancient—or even simply an archangel . . . Death. It was death.

38

The vortex of ice finally began to thaw seventy-two hours later, but Elena wasn't breathing easy. Not only had the bitter cold caused a number of deaths, the volcano that shouldn't fucking exist had blown with a vengeance. Andreas was in charge of disaster cleanup and his people were still counting the dead.

Raphael's territory wasn't the only casualty of the wave of catastrophic events.

Hundreds, maybe thousands, had been washed away in floods in India, while plagues of locusts had poisoned countless people in Titus's and Charisemnon's territories. A massive landslide in Alexander's territory had buried a remote village, while a rampant fire had rioted through the ancient city of Xian, China.

Michaela's territory was in the midst of a deadly heat wave in the depths of winter, while food crops designed to feed many of Elijah's people through the winter months had begun to rot and degrade without reason.

With all that going on, Elena barely felt the chill of the drizzling rain as she paced along the cliff-edge of their Enclave land. "What did Astaad say?"

Raphael thrust his hand through the damp strands of his hair. "He just lost two more of his islands under the turbulent water. Low casualties because he'd already given the evacuation order, but a large ship capsized at the same time deep in the ocean. Over forty mortal lives taken by the sea."

Numb from the constant wave of disasters, Elena went to ask about Japan when her body swayed on a rolling wave Across the ice-encrusted waters of the Hudson, the Tower *moved*. "Archangel, the Tower."

"It is designed according to modern ways of building. It will flex not fall in a tremor."

Elena jolted as another tremor hit, this one much harder. Lifting off was instinct. She and Raphael headed directly for Manhattan, hitting the edge of the city just as a skyscraper in the distance, its windows a reflective blue, began a stunning and deadly show. Sheets of windows dropped like water to shatter onto the sidewalk and street far below.

Raphael's wings turned to white fire, Elena flying as fast as she could in his wake, but it was too late to save the pedestrians who'd been under the glass when it first fell. The world wasn't shaking anymore by the time Elena landed, the entire sidewalk covered with unyielding snow created from shattered blue glass.

It was safety glass, but the amount and velocity of it had been catastrophic. Racing to where she could see an outflung hand with nails painted a soft pink, she began to clear away the glass. Raphael was already pulling another body out of the glass rubble behind the woman.

She barely noticed slicing her hand on a piece of metal wire hidden in the glass debris, the red smearing across the squares of blue. It wasn't until later, after she'd delivered a small teenage girl to the hospital, that she wiped her palm on the side of her pants . . . and remembered that a cut that wouldn't heal had been one of the first signs of her "devolution."

Gut twisting, she lifted her hand to examine the cut.

Her palm was smooth, unmarked by anything except dried remnants of blood. Disbelieving, she pressed down on her flesh. No bruising, no indication she'd hurt herself at all. She was still staring at it when her phone rang. It was Vivek, directing her to another area where someone needed assistance.

New York was built strong, but it also had a bunch of old buildings.

Regardless, it was only two hours later that she and Raphael met in the sky above the city. "It's not as bad as we thought at first."

The vast majority of the city had come through with no ill effects. Yellow cabs zipped along the streets, exchanging insults with kamikaze bike messengers, while food carts that had closed up shop after the shake were all back to doing a brisk business.

"I'm more worried about other consequences." Raphael stared out at the ocean. "Our sensors are reporting a deep-sea disturbance."

As if on cue, the ocean began to boil . . . and the sky, it turned a violent bruise purple. As they watched, the water parted as if over a great beast from the deep. However, what emerged from that water wasn't a mythological beast but a slender man dressed in a white tunic and black pants, his hair tumbled dark brown and his skin tawny.

His eyes were a dazzling gray, his bones perfect.

I am Antonicus! Who dares wake me?

Elena winced at the hugeness of that voice.

Showing no outward response, Raphael flew toward the other archangel. *I am Raphael and you are in my territory. This land is not yours.*

The Ancient stared at him, his gaze flat. *You are a pup.* He threw out a hand ringed with angelfire.

Easily dodging the bolt, Raphael returned the hit with a bolt of his own. Antonicus managed to evade it, but it singed the side of his tunic. Hissing, the other archangel stared unblinking as Raphael came to a stop across from him. "Why disturb my rest, pup?"

"I do not wish for you to be awake," Raphael said bluntly, in no mood to go gentle. "A Cascade is in effect and it's having an unpredictable impact on all the Cadre, even those who Sleep."

The Ancient's shoulders knotted, fury distorting his beauty. "I have lived through my Cascade. It is my time to rest."

"I do not believe this particular Cascade will let you sleep until it reaches its crescendo." At the same instant, he contacted Illium, asked the angel to join him and Antonicus.

"I am tired." Antonicus looked around on that absolute statement. "What is this place of steel and glass and towers that touch the sky?"

"I will explain. For now, we have recently had an earth tremor and I must ensure my city is safe." Raphael realized he'd gotten lucky—despite the initial exchange of angelfire, Antonicus seemed stable enough. "You are welcome in my Tower. We will speak again once I return."

Antonicus didn't budge, wings of charcoal gray spread in a hover. "You have eyes such as I have seen on only one other being in all my existence. But Caliane had no offspring when I went to Sleep. She did not even have a mate."

"Caliane is my mother." Raphael cut the Ancient off before he could speak further. "My squadron leader will show you to the Tower." He nodded at Illium, who'd stopped at a respectful distance beyond them.

"Another pup." The Ancient snorted. "What has the world come to if only the young are awake?" He was yet muttering as he flew off with Illium.

At the same instant that tremors hit New York, the sky turned a silver-dusted aquamarine in the depths of the night in the Pacific, as geysers of water shot up from one of Astaad's newly submerged islands, and the heavens opened up.

It was pure luck he was nearby at the time.

According to Plato, the vampire his oldest philosopher, it was almost as if the bones of the world itself had shifted, putting things out of balance. Astaad enjoyed speaking with his historians, philosophers, and scientists, appreciated the gift of intellect, but he had no patience with such explanations in the midst of a Cascade. He needed hard facts to prepare himself and his people.

The enraged Ancient who erupted out of the submerged island on a roar of sound was Astaad's exact opposite. Known for his temper and his infamous harem, Aegaeon had been born with a weapon of war in hand.

Astaad, too, kept a harem, but his was a family. His women saw one another as sisters. He rarely took mortals into that harem, but the infrequent times he did, he loved and cared for each to the end of her life—as did her sisters. His harem mourned when one of the family was lost.

Aegaeon's harem by contrast, had been a place of lust and ambition. Even during his short waking in Astaad's lifetime, many of his lovers had died at one another's hands. Aegaeon had rewarded the most deadly members with his favors while discarding those he considered weak.

Sound boomed from the throat of the heavily muscled archangel with skin that held the sunshine, and hair of a shocking blue-green. His eyes were the same blue-green, his fists huge mallets and his bare chest marked with a silver swirl that echoed the pattern in the sky. In his hand was the scythe that had become his weapon of choice, the implement from which he so often released his power.

The wings that spread out behind him were a darker green with streaks of wild blue.

"I am Aegaeon!" he roared. "I am not to be disturbed!"

Astaad wished he weren't drenched, his tunic filthy from the work he'd been doing to save as many of his people as he could, but that was how things had fallen and he was an archangel. "I am Astaad!" He made his own voice boom, for yes, he was capable of such—he just preferred to be more refined. "You encroach on my territory!"

The scythe caught the silver from the sky, its edge glowing. "Why do you wake me?" Aegaeon's eyes gleamed hard as gemstones. "I am not ready to wake!"

"We are in the midst of a catastrophic Cascade." Astaad had no more answers for him than this. "It is why your island is submerged."

Aegaeon looked down, his hair falling around the square lines of his jaw, seemed to notice the water for the first time. A curl of his lip. "Can you not clear such things?" A wave of the scythe and the water retreated.

"I prefer to save my energy for the lands that remain inhabited." Astaad would not allow an interloper to make the rules in *his* lands; he would however, make use of Aegaeon's penchant for flaunting his power. "My people are dying and islands are being submerged faster than we can evacuate them."

"Show me!"

Every word out of the man's mouth was headache-inducing. "Come."

Aegaeon flew after him without argument, but Astaad knew the cooperation would soon devolve into aggression, Aegaeon was not an angel who would be satisfied with anything but a full territory.

Even as Astaad saw the first geyser of water on the island, a wave of sound hit Alexander's territory while he stood ankle-deep in snow. The clear sky turned into a moonless night, ebony and without end.

"Zanaya is rising," he said to his second.

Taking to the air, he soon spotted snow-covered sands in the distance from which emerged a mirage of light and darkness, a woman colored in starlight. Waist-length curls of silver washed with purple until it was a hue he'd seen on no other, skin of night, eyes huge dark orbs that he knew flickered with silvery light and lips so plush a man could look at them and think himself lost.

Until she cut out your heart and fried it to eat with her most prized wine.

Shorter than him by several inches, Zanaya wore her sword across her back because of course Zanaya would go into Sleep with a sword. It was her most beloved lover.

Her body was clad in a short wrap that hugged every curve and valley. A glittering starlight creation that covered her breasts and thighs and yet left her more alluring than if she'd been unclothed. Though, as Alexander was personally aware, Zanaya was beyond alluring when bare to the skin.

He landed in front of her with a feeling of inevitability in his gut.

"Xander." A purr of sound, the language one he hadn't heard for millennia even before his Sleep. "We meet again."

"That is my grandson's name now."

The sparks of moonlight in her pupils grew brighter. "You

jest? You are a grandfather?" A slow seduction of a smile. "I have Slept long."

"That is a matter of opinion," he muttered under his breath.

Throwing back her head, she laughed and the sound wrapped around him as it always had, luscious and drugging and Zanaya. "Oh, Alexander, do not say you are not happy to see me. I am crushed."

She stretched her arms to the sky, back arched and toes digging into the snow, and it was like watching a lioness wake to the sun that even now chased Zanaya's sudden night from the sky. "It did not snow in this desert when I went to Sleep." She crouched down, lifted a handful of glittering ice crystals. "Does my Nile yet flow, or is it ice?"

"It's begun to ice over," he told the deadly, lovely archangel who'd preferred to be called the Queen of the Nile over any other title. "We are in a Cascade. You are the only Ancient I know who has woken with such suddenness, but there are signs Aegaeon is also stirring. Caliane woke before I did."

No smile as she rose, regal and so beautiful that he had never comprehended why the world considered Michaela the epitome of beauty. "I will Sleep," she said, because infuriating and half insane she might be, but Zanaya was also an archangel who'd been beloved by her people—and once, by Alexander.

"I do not think the Cascade will let you Sleep." He folded his arms with rigid tightness to stop himself from stroking his fingers over her shoulders, down her arms, as he'd done a thousand times in another age. "I will call a Cadre meeting about you, but first, I have to rescue a village buried under ice and snow."

"Why so bad-tempered, lover?"

"I am an Ancient. Treat me as such or . . ."

"Or what?" A wink, long lashes coming down like a fan. "So, tell me what you've been doing since I decided I'd caused enough mayhem for ten immortal lifetimes."

As if they had not been apart a hundred thousand years. She had gone into Sleep ten years after their last fight, while he was still half furious and half in love with her. Not because of him. Zanaya had never been tied to the decisions of others and it was part of why she'd so bewitched him.

"I have work to do." He rose into the air.

She followed with a laugh, her wings rippling black with flecks of silvery white.

That was when the world turned black in a way that was nothing akin to Zanaya's luxuriant darkness. The silence that descended was oppressive . . . until it was broken by screams that drilled into the ears and shrieked.

"What is this cacophony!" Zanaya yelled. "No archangel I know wakes with such darkness!"

"You do not know her. Her name is Lijuan."

39

Neha watched Lijuan's return from a border fort in her own territory, Nivriti by her side. She and her twin had declared a strange, unsteady truce in the face of the chaos fostered by the Cascade and when Nivriti stood with her this way, the peacock hues of Nivriti's wings nearly touching the white and indigo of hers, Neha remembered all that she'd lost and wondered if it was her time to Sleep.

Everything hurt. Her heart. Her soul.

She was so tired.

But none of them could Sleep now, with Lijuan rising once more. The screaming blackness that had announced her waking had finally withdrawn its suffocating presence from Neha's lands, but it stayed solid over and around China. "Do you think the people within see any light?"

"I think that one likes to keep her people in the darkness."

The wind brought scents across the border, all the way to the top of the fort. Tiny hairs rising on her nape, Neha sent out a mental order to her generals to mount a permanent guard across the entire border. She would not be taken by surprise, would not be a prize for Lijuan to claim.

Yet even as she thought that, she knew that Lijuan had

come back different from the Cadre. The Archangel of China had already been able to go noncorporeal prior to her disappearance, and now she was back after no real Sleep at all—with the power to opaque her entire territory from the rest of the world.

The black fog hovered over China, only to curve down to meet the earth at the border. As Neha watched, a bird disoriented by the sudden changes in the sky flew into the wall of fog. Its small body tumbled to the earth a heartbeat later. Jumping off the roof of the fort, strands of hair that had escaped her braid sticking to the sides of her face, Neha flared out her wings so she could make a soft landing on the dirt below.

Nivriti was already down. She'd always done that. Tried to be faster, better, stronger. Not that it mattered any longer. Sliding her sword from the sheath at her hip, Neha nudged the bird's small body out of the danger zone. "Do not touch it," she said when Nivriti hunkered down, the emerald and cobalt and black of her wings spread out behind her.

"I am not a fool, sister." Rote bitten-out words, Nivriti's attention on the dead bird. "It is hard to say if the marks of violence on the body are as a result of the wall, or of the bird's fall."

Neha hunkered down beside her sister, their wings overlapping. "See those, Nivi." She pointed to the wing area.

A hiss. "Cuts. Yet there are no stones on the ground that could've done such damage."

"Lady!" One of Neha's senior vampires ran toward her, was breathless by the time he arrived. "A dog ran into the dark fog and it fell where it stood. When we dragged it out by the visible hindquarters, it was cut all over and bleeding."

"Dead?" She had to know if survival was possible.

"All but," the vampire said. "We gave it mercy."

"Mercy was the right choice." She rose to her feet. "Spread the word that no one is to approach the border. I will warn Lady Caliane's people. If anyone does fall in, haul them out as fast as possible."

"Yes, my queen."

Nivriti got to her feet as the vampire ran to action Neha's orders. "No archangel in history has been able to so surround their territory."

"Caliane can do it," Neha murmured. "But Amanat is the size of a large village. To encompass China . . ."

She stared at the dark fog and told herself it was her imagination, that she couldn't see the trapped and screaming faces of the lost villagers staring back at her.

All those souls imprisoned forever, their teeth and nails Lijuan's weapons.

40

"Talk about hell on earth." Elena's mutter had Antonicus shooting her another riveted look. She tried to ignore him. He'd been staring at her since she returned to the Tower.

He *should've* been staring at the screen in front of them—on it was a live broadcast from Neha's territory, of the border with China. Neha's second had sent it out to all of the Cadre before Raphael could initiate a meeting about Antonicus.

"Hell is a mortal concept. This is very much an immortal nightmare."

Elena couldn't disagree, but that wasn't why the back of her neck was prickling. *Why does Antonicus keep looking at me as if I'm an interesting new bug?*

He has no idea what you are and that is a strange thing for an immortal. He ran his fingers through the stormfire of her wings.

Shivering inwardly, Elena said, *Stop that. I have to look hard-ass so your new friend doesn't try to chop me open and examine me.*

He is not a friend. Raphael's features gave nothing away as he turned to the Ancient, his presence remote in a way that reminded her of the archangel she'd first met. "You have been most patient. It is time, however, that we had a meeting of the Cadre."

"It has been no trouble," Antonicus replied in a language that Raphael could just understand. He knew the other archangel had chosen that language on purpose—because he must've already picked up modern English. That was a skill that seemed to sharpen with age and knowledge, as if once the brain had a hundred languages inside it, new ones were simply absorbed.

Antonicus's eyes returned to Elena.

"Unless you wish to start a war," Raphael said in the same ancient language, "you will treat my consort with respect. Or she will be forced to excise your eyes from your head."

Clearly comprehending his tone if not his words, Elena began to play a sharp blade through her fingers.

Antonicus remembered his manners at last—he even had the grace to flush. Raphael knew the change was unlikely to last. Angels this old, archangel or not, had a tendency to believe age gave them the freedom to discard accepted rules of behavior.

"Consort." The archangel spoke English with a liquid accent. "You are the most unique being I have seen in all my life."

"Guess you don't know Naasir," was Elena's cool riposte.

Antonicus's wings opened in a wave of charcoal gray, snapped shut. "Who is this Naasir? Is he like you? An angel-Made?"

Elena's smile was slow and as sly as Naasir's. "You'll have to ask Naasir what he is."

Amusement slicing through the ice of his anger, Raphael touched her mind. *Attempting to break Naasir's secrets through others?*

Never! I'm going to find those answers myself. I just want Antonicus to beat his head against that particular brick wall, too.

"Sire." Dmitri stepped into the office. "Archangel Neha has convened a meeting of the Cadre." Words of perfect politeness that gave away nothing of the reality of Raphael and Dmitri's relationship. His second and friend had met enough Ancients to understand how to manipulate their perceptions where it mattered.

Antonicus paid no mind to Dmitri. The old were often foolish.

"Keep an eye on this feed." Raphael indicated what was occurring on Neha's border. "Interrupt us if there is a major change." With that, he led Elena and Antonicus into the large room set up for these meetings and initiated the link.

Antonicus reared back when he saw Neha's face appear on the central screen, Caliane's on the screen next to hers. "What is this? You have trapped the Cadre within these black boxes?" His wings began to glow.

"Antonicus, I would know that voice anywhere." Caliane, her white leathers dusty and her hair damp, shook her head. "Still acting before you think, I see."

"We do not have time to explain the modern world to you," Neha snapped at the much older archangel. "Suffice to say that these are communication devices."

More faces appeared on the screens around them. Alexander also had an unknown archangel with him. Raphael's gut tightened. Each waking should've sent a wave of color or light or sound across the world, alerting the entire Cadre as to what was occurring. In New York, aside from the disturbance caused by Antonicus's waking, that had only happened with the death screams that announced Lijuan's return.

Unless . . . was it possible the others had woken all at once?

He waited for Astaad, his spine rigid. The Archangel of the Pacific Isles was the final member of the Cadre to appear. With him was an archangel with massive shoulders and hair of blue-green. *Elena, I need you to go to your Bluebell. I want you with him when I give him some news.*

Elena slipped out of the room in silence and without questions, and he knew she'd felt the urgency pulsing through his veins.

He spoke next to Dmitri. *Find someone we trust in the village by Lumia. No, someone* the Hummingbird *trusts. That individual's task is to keep her away from any news feeds until given further orders.* Illium's mother was at least isolated enough that he could give her time to become used to this turn of events on her own terms before the world started coming at her.

Raphael forced himself to pay attention as Alexander introduced Zanaya, then did his own duty by presenting Antonicus. Astaad was commendably calm in his presentation of Aegaeon.

The Ancient scowled. "I did not intend to wake yet. I have barely Slept."

A surge of violence inside Raphael that had his hand curling into a hard fist by his side. Better that this particular Ancient had Slept forever.

Raphael, I'm with Illium. He's exhausted after the training maneuvers he's been running all day.

Stay with him. No matter what. He couldn't tell Elena why—this news must go first to Illium.

I won't budge from his side.

Raphael touched Illium's mind without effort—all his Seven were permanent imprints in his mind. *Illium.*

Sire. Do you need me? I'm with Ellie. I was on my way to bed but she lured me over with a full tray of Sivya's delectable treats.

Raphael hoped Illium's bond with Elena would help him weather this. *I have bad news for you.* He gave the younger angel the information with no attempt to soften the blow—there could be no softening it. *Your father has awakened.*

Elena knew the instant Raphael told Illium whatever it was that had put that deadly yet protective tone in his voice. Illium froze in the act of reaching for another tart, suddenly as motionless as a marble statue. Seated beside him, she slipped her hand over one of his brutally clenched ones. He didn't react, his jaw rigid and his wings held precisely to his back.

Elena just held on.

It felt like forever before he said, "I have to go to Morocco." Each word was harsh, full of grit.

Acting on instinct, Elena said, "You're fast, but you're tired. The jet's ready." It was always ready and waiting to go when Elena, Raphael, or any of the Seven were in New York. "It'll have you at the private airstrip in Morocco in eleven hours."

Illium's nod was jagged, his expression dangerously flat.

Raphael, Illium's heading to Morocco. I want to go with him. There was no way she was going to put Bluebell on that plane alone, not in his current condition. *Will my being absent throw a spanner in the works?*

That was a question she wouldn't have asked after first falling for her archangel, but their relationship had grown and matured. It was no longer about her fighting for her freedom and Raphael wanting to wrap her up in cotton wool. She was his consort and not only did he need her by his side at certain times, their enemies wouldn't hesitate to use her to make a point against him.

Go, he said. *Protecting you will snap Illium out of his shock. Aodhan will fly from the Refuge to meet you in Morocco. The current situation with the excess number of archangels will keep the Cadre distracted in the interim.*

Elena's shoulders grew less tight. Aodhan and Illium currently had a rocky relationship, but their friendship was centuries old. It might be under strain, but it wasn't going to fracture anytime soon. *I'll be back as soon as Illium's doing okay.*

The crashing and ice-kissed sea in her mind, her archangel's embrace dangerously more powerful.

"I'm coming with you."

Illium snapped up his head, the blue-tipped black of his hair shifting with the movement. "You need to be here, with the sire."

"We've spoken—it's fine. I'll call the flight crew to let them know we're on our way."

"Ellie—" Eyes of beaten gold dark with torment and confusion.

"Decision's made." She rose. "Do you need to grab clothes from your suite?"

Making a frustrated sound, he said, "This isn't over," but left at a run.

She alerted their most senior pilot—the grumpy but brilliant Dougal—then ducked into her closet to grab a change of clothes for herself . . . and saw a brand-new canvas duffel bag sitting there, packed and ready. Her battered old bag that had survived many a hunter trip had been at the Enclave house when it went boom.

This one was an identical match, down to the padded shoulder straps.

"Montgomery, I love you more than is natural." Grabbing the bag and pausing only long enough to throw in her laptop and some underwear, she was out in the corridor when a thought struck her. *Raphael.* She waited for an acknowledgment of the contact; she wasn't about to distract him when he was in a discussion with ruthless immortals who'd take advantage of any sign of weakness.

You can speak, hbeebti. *Right now, matters are civil and calm and icy. With Lijuan awake, there is no room for these newly awakened ones in our world. It is not their time.*

Elena's skin prickled, his words reminding her of Cassandra, who lived always out of time. *The Hummingbird—*

It is done, Raphael interrupted. *Dmitri has asked one of our toughest warriors in the region to have an emotional crisis. The Hummingbird has a soft heart—she will stay with the seemingly heartbroken warrior for as long as it takes. He has promised to cry if she tries to stir.*

We have good people. And the Hummingbird inspired devotion; Illium's mother was so gentle, so kind, and so broken that Elena'd punch anyone who was mean to her in any way. *Good luck with the meeting.*

At the rate it's going, I may be here when you return—Antonicus is orating as if in an amphitheater of disciples, while Aegaeon and Alexander gnash their teeth and Charisemnon snipes.

She blew him a kiss with her mind just as she caught silver blue in her peripheral vision. Illium was back, his bag held in one hand and his facial muscles taut. They didn't speak as they strode to the nearest balcony to take off. The wind was a frigid slap, icicles still hanging from a multitude of buildings and the Hudson boasting the odd iceberg.

"You should go back!" Illium yelled across the space between them.

"I can't hear you!" she yelled back in a singsong voice.

"How can I focus on my mother if I'm worried about you?"

The attempt at a guilt trip might've worked if she hadn't been aware that Aodhan was also on the way and that she'd be returning to Manhattan as soon as Illium had another trusted friend by his side. "We'll both focus on her!" She winged to the right to get around a skyscraper.

Hands pressed against the windows, the office workers waved at her. She waved back on a bolt of incandescent happiness. To lose flight, then regain it . . . Her throat grew thick, her eyes hot.

Elena. Aeclari. *We fly*.

Countless numbers of the Legion flew up from various buildings to join her and Illium, an enigmatic escort on silent gray wings. The one nearest to her still had frozen eyelashes from the recent storm, his hair glittering with ice. He must've been sitting in a shadow the sun hadn't warmed. She just shook her head; the Legion kept their home warm for their plants but didn't seem to mind being frozen into statues.

The beings from the deep stayed aloft when Elena and Illium landed at the Tower airstrip. "Hi Mack!" She waved cheerfully at the heavily built man of medium height who'd just come around the plane—it looked like he was doing a safety check. Probably his tenth one so far. Dougal Mackenzie was a teensy bit detail-oriented. *Exactly* what Elena wanted in a pilot.

"Consort." Dark eyes met hers before he inclined his head, his hair a rich mahogany that suited the warm cream of his skin and his facial structure's hard angles and squares.

"I heard about your drunken weekend in the Caribbean! Go, Mack!" She'd heard nothing of the sort, but provoking a rise out of the vampire had become a calling.

Dougal looked at her stone-faced.

Taking her hand, Illium dragged her to the plane. "I apologize for the consort," he said to Dougal, so polite and proper that Elena felt bad for surrendering to her urge to tweak the vampire's nose. Dougal couldn't help being so stiff.

Then Bluebell grinned. "Next time, we'll do one of Astaad's tropical islands—heavy on the tequila. No more doe-eyed maidens, though. I can't keep up with you."

Dougal's lips actually gave the vague approximation of a smile.

Elena was still gaping over it when Illium pushed her up the stairs to board. She moved quickly so they could get underway, but the instant they were both in their seats, she poked him in the ribs. "Do you and Dougal really hang out or were you messing with me?"

"What do you think?"

She gave a prim sniff and folded her arms. "Ever since I

learned that you and Andreas are buddy-buddy, I feel like I don't know you anymore."

He laughed, though it did nothing to budge the intense darkness in the depths of his gaze. "Dougal and I have been friends since he joined Raphael's service. The laird can—" A sudden halt, followed by pursed lips. "But Dougal's secrets aren't for me to tell." A flutter of black lashes dipped in blue.

"One of these days, Bluebell . . ."

Dougal entered the plane, with his copilot following. The petite female vampire shut the door with professional speed before slipping into the cockpit to join Dougal. The two had them in the air much faster than with a commercial flight.

Elena's eyes went to the window, her gaze searching for the Tower. *I'll see you soon, Archangel.*

41

Elena'd been working on her laptop for a half hour when Illium poked his head over to look at the screen. She bit back the force of her relief at the interruption—Illium was *never* as painfully silent as he'd been since takeoff.

"What are you doing so fiercely?" He propped his chin on her shoulder, his breath warm against her skin and the strands of his hair mingling with her own.

"Reigning over my blood-café empire." It actually *was* turning into an empire, mostly thanks to Marcia Blue, the shy vampire who'd come up with the idea. Though their financial manager, Jonas, had also proven his worth.

"Is sweet Marcia still besotted with Jonas?"

"The besotting is mutual, but Marcia's too wary after her Contract period." Marcia's angel had been a cruel fuck. Immortality didn't always bestow empathy. It tended to wear that empathy away, until many immortals treated humans and young vampires as nothing but toys, to be used and discarded.

"Don't ever become like that asshole." She reached up to pat his cheek with one hand while scanning a financial report. "I want to kick him in the face anytime I see him. Too bad even consorts can't go around kicking asshole angels in the face."

"I'll help you hide the body if you ever want to do away with him." Playful words, but she felt the rigid tension that continued to grip his body.

She closed the lid of the laptop—she'd only opened it to give him space. "Want to raid the liquor cabinet and see if we can get you drunk?" Angels had such high metabolisms that alcohol did nothing for most. The only angel she'd ever seen even a little drunk was young Izzy, and he'd been badly injured from battle at the time—he'd also been sipping on Illium's lethal secret recipe.

"I'll grab the whiskey."

He came back with a full-size bottle and two tumblers.

Elena had no idea if she'd become impervious to the effect of alcohol, so she was careful with her sips. "Whoa." It hit her bloodstream with a punch of heat.

Illium threw back his own drink, then poured another one—all the way to the top of the crystal tumbler. He drank with methodical calm and was three quarters of the way through the bottle when he said, "My bastard of a father is awake."

Elena's muscles locked. She knew nothing about Illium's father except that the topic must be a sensitive one. He had such an openness to him—even when speaking of hurtful things like his lost mortal love and Aodhan's retreat from the world—that it was obvious when he didn't talk about something. And he never talked about the man who'd sired him.

"He's an archangel?" Raphael *had* once mentioned that Illium had an Ancient for a parent, but Elena hadn't made an automatic connection to the Cadre. As for the Hummingbird . . . she'd already been a gifted painter during the time Nadiel and Caliane were lovers, so she wasn't young—but either she wasn't old enough for Ancient status . . . or she occupied a position in the angelic world that was matchless, beyond age or time.

"Everyone knows that Raphael is the beloved son of two archangels. My parentage is a question mark." His lip curled. "I know he's my father, but the rest of angelkind began to whisper questions after the bastard left us to fend for ourselves when I was too small to fly straight.

"*Raphael* was the one who taught me how to lift a sword,

how to be a man of honor. He was the one my mother relied on to protect her boy. Aegaeon just took his pleasure of my mother and left. No archangel ever just abandons their child, that was what the cruel said. The Hummingbird must've been unfaithful, the boy another angel's seed."

His hand clenched so hard on the tumbler that it cracked. Abandoning it, he picked up the bottle of whiskey and slugged it down. His eyes glittered in the aftermath, but she knew it wasn't the alcohol. It was anger so deep it cut. Elena didn't blame him, but she couldn't let it poison him.

"Clearly, your father and Jeffrey share the Great Father of the Year Award."

Illium stared at her for a second before starting to laugh hard and deep. It hurt, that sound. There was no joy in it, but perhaps there was a release of pain. Because when he stopped at last, he reached over to tug on one of the tiny feathers at the ends of her hair.

"Aegaeon's the reason the award was invented." Settling back into his seat, Illium put down the whiskey bottle and stared up at nothing for a while. "Bastard was a good father while he was around. Taught me how to get myself in the air, picked up and kissed my mother with this bold hunger that made her smile and blush, told me to be courageous and to explore like a warrior."

He flexed his fingers, curled them in again to bloodless tightness. "But he broke my mother with his selfishness, and I'll never forgive him for that."

"Your mother is a gift." A being lovely and unique and old. "Whatever he did, he didn't steal her soul."

But Illium shook his head. "You've only ever met this Hummingbird." Such sorrow in his words. "My mother used to be so *young*, Ellie. She had me when she was many eons old, but I never felt as if I'd been birthed at the twilight of her life."

A haunted smile. "She'd play hide-and-seek with me through the Refuge, and when Aodhan and I got in trouble, she'd discipline us with the sternest expression, then hug and kiss us when we got sad.

"We'd make sweets together. We'd throw paint at canvases just to see which patterns emerged. We'd sneak into the Library at night to read by candlelight. She used to dance to any music that was in the air, this vibrant sprite that I'd sit and watch."

Elena couldn't imagine Illium's mother doing any of those things. The angel she knew was a luminous talent, an artist revered and cherished, but she was also ethereal, existing in her own world. Often, she didn't seem to remember that Illium was an adult, instead treating him as the boy he'd once been. But Sharine wasn't mad, not in any sense of the word as the world used it.

She was, as Illium had said, broken. No, fractured was the better word. Cracks in her psyche, cracks in her emotions, her sense of self damaged. That didn't stop her from being well-respected and, as she'd shown since being appointed to her present duty, she had the self-possession, intelligence, and sheer *kindness* to take over a place traumatized by evil.

"That he's risen now, when my mother is coming into her own again?" Illium ground his teeth. "I will kill him if he damages her a second time. I swear it . . ." Flat, deadly words that allowed no room for doubt.

Raphael knew Elena was vulnerable away from him, but he also knew Illium would lay down his life for her—and he was an angel very few in the world could defeat. Most of those who *could* defeat him were preoccupied with the catastrophic emergence of three extra Ancients on top of Lijuan's return. If they were lucky, no one would even notice Elena's absence.

Around him, the Cadre meeting continued on unabated.

He'd held his silence since soon after the start. First, he'd given Aegaeon and Antonicus time to stop complaining about being so summarily woken, then he'd given the rest of the Cadre time to announce that *no one* was about to seize their territory from them. Zanaya'd had an amused smile on her face throughout, her contributions to the discussion cleverly designed verbal grenades.

At this moment, his mother was updating the new Ancients on the central events of this Cascade.

"Are you saying this Lijuan believes she is better than *us*?" Aegaeon snorted. "Show her to me and she will soon lose that belief."

Titus was having none of it. He slammed down his staff; the resulting percussive thunder succeeded in claiming everyone's attention. "Before you make rash promises, perhaps you should watch the recording made by Neha's people." He initiated a replay of the black fog that swathed China.

Antonicus had not paid much attention while Raphael was viewing it, now watched with engrossed concentration. To Zanaya and Aegaeon, it appeared new.

"She is the Archangel of Death." Zanaya's features held a repulsion that made her starlight eyes flow into obsidian. "I see this now." She turned to Antonicus and Aegaeon. "Do you not see?" It was a demand. "We wake before our time to take care of this menace. We are not meant to live in this world. It is *not* our time."

Raphael felt a reluctant liking for the Ancient. She might delight in stirring the pot, but she also saw with more clarity and less arrogance than most of the Cadre.

"Why would the Cascade do this?" Michaela's cheekbones sliced against her skin. "Why give us a way to defeat Lijuan?"

"Because the Cascade wants chaos," Raphael said, repeating words the Legion had dredged from the depths of memory so old that it began before the birth of mortals. "There is no chaos in only one power."

He gestured to the frozen image of a blanked-out China. "A being who can do this, who can hide a landscape as vast as China, is no longer an archangel. She is beyond that, and we will need all our strength to defeat her should she prove a threat."

"What do you mean, prove a threat!" Charisemnon brought his fist down on the ornate table in front of him, veins pulsing at his temples and splotches of red on his neck. "Do you not see what she is doing?"

"She is the goddess of her own territory," Neha reminded him, her tone frigid. "As long as she remains in that territory, we cannot and will not touch her."

"To do so would be to breach the laws that keep peace in the world," Astaad said. "We do not interfere in territory that belongs to another."

Elijah looked to Neha. "Do you have any further news of China?"

"Death." Neha's answer rang in the silence. "Anything that flies into that fog dies." The jeweled green viper on her shoulder twined itself sinuously around her upper arm. Touching her fingers to its triangular-shaped head, she said, "We did not have to sacrifice any creatures—Lady Caliane and I both witnessed disoriented animals wander in and die."

"This is so." His mother's voice was somber. "Thus, the talk of making war on Lijuan is moot for the moment. We cannot enter that dark fog."

"We are archangels!" Antonicus pushed out his chest, his wings spread. "We cannot be brought down by *fog*. What feebleness has permeated the Cadre that you act akin to scared prey?"

"Raphael." A tic in Neha's jaw, her gaze hard as stone. "Do you have any recordings of what occurred in your territory when Lijuan made war on you? I do not think our awakened brethren will believe us until we show them evidence of—"

"This is foolishness!" Antonicus's wings glowed. "I do not need to see more of your moving images. I will end this once and for all. I am going to China."

"You have no invitation," Caliane reminded him with commendable calm. "Entering another archangel's territory without permission is a breach of protocol."

"Once I find this Lijuan, I will make my apologies." He unsheathed his sword. "And if she is a threat, I will neutralize her."

Raphael and the others of the current Cadre attempted to talk the egotistical Ancient out of a project that could have no good ending, but he was adamant.

"In that case," Raphael said when it became clear that Antonicus would not see reason, "will you agree to wear a device that records and transmits images back to us? We must know what is happening within the fog."

Antonicus flicked a hand. "As long as it does not interfere with my ability to use my weapons." Pure contempt in the look he gave the Cadre. "I must have a day to rest after my premature waking. I will make the attempt directly afterward."

"We must all bear witness," Caliane murmured. "Neha, I would ask permission for the Cadre and the awakened ones to gather on your border to watch Antonicus's flight into the fog."

"I will be gracious." Neha was very much the Queen of

India at that moment. "You are to leave immediately after Antonicus's attempt, unless there is reason for another meeting of the Cadre. If so, we will hold that meeting at the border fort."

"Agreed," said every archangel in the space.

All twelve of them.

Add Lijuan and there were thirteen archangels in the world, *five* of them Ancients.

War was a certainty.

42

Elena took a deep breath. The orange-red of the Moroccan landscape was a familiar embrace, the sun kissing it with warmth even in winter. She'd wondered if her response to this land would change now that she knew the horrors that had befallen her grandparents here, but no, it continued to feel a little like home. The lilt of people's voices, the scents in the air, the grit between her teeth as the sand got in, none of it was alien.

"Does it hurt you to be here?" Illium asked while they were stretching out their bodies after disembarking from the plane.

"No. My strongest sense of Morocco is love." Raw and deep and constant. "Jean-Baptiste's love for Majda and hers for him. Majda's desperate love for her daughter." This was where Elena's history had begun. "How are you doing?"

His eyes shimmered even more golden under the light of this place full of mountains and sky. "I worry for my mother's heart. It is so fragile, Ellie." Muscles hard as rock, he said, "I long-ago ceased to have any hopes of my father, but she's been waiting for him all this time."

He spread out his wings. "I would delay this forever, but I can't. My mother deserves to know."

The village was just stirring after the languid time following lunch when they reached it, the merchants reopening their stalls and shops, while neighbors stood talking with steaming cups in hand. Mint tea perhaps. Or coffee so strong it was a kick to the system. But the most welcome sight was in the distance, on the flat roof of a dual-level house not dissimilar to others in the village except that its balconies had no railings.

Light broke on the glittering hue of the angel's hair—as if each strand was encrusted with diamonds. It caressed the warmth of his skin. Such flawless pale skin, but one with an inner glow that made it clear he was flesh and blood, not a statue. And his wings . . . each filament of each feather appeared a jeweled construction.

To look at him was to think of light and beauty and a sense of innate distance.

All were true.

"*Aodhan.*" Illium's voice was choked. "What's he doing here?"

Not answering, Elena flew toward Aodhan with a smile. She landed first because Illium was lagging—on purpose. Elena could never outpace him, not on any planet. "Sparkle." She held out her hands.

Aodhan was okay with her touch now, but she never took it for granted. Today, he didn't scowl at her for using that nickname, just closed his hands over hers while meeting her gaze with the extraordinary beauty of his own. A black pupil with shards of crystalline blue-green breaking outward from it. "How is he?"

"Angry," she said as Illium took his time descending. "Worried about the Hummingbird."

Illium landed beside Elena before Aodhan could reply. His face, with its clean lines and warm gold skin, was set, unwelcoming. "Why are you here? You should be in the Refuge helping Galen and Naasir." He held his body with such fierce control that it hurt Elena to witness.

Aodhan walked over to his best friend without a word, hauled him into an embrace, one of his hands cradling the back of Illium's head, his other arm locked around Illium's shoulders. As if he had never shunned touch, never turned away from even the angel he most trusted.

Illium remained stiff, his wings folded tight to his back, but Aodhan was having none of it. He wrapped Illium up in his own wings and Elena was close enough to hear him say, "I am here for you," in a tone as unbending as stone.

But Illium hadn't thawed in the least when Aodhan released him. "I have to speak to my mother before—"

The Hummingbird walked out through the wide doorway onto the roof, her hair a river of gold-tipped black down her back and her wings a startling indigo dusted with shimmers of a shade so pale it was kin to sunlight.

The champagne of her eyes softened into pure sunshine when she caught sight of Illium. "I believed I was imagining my heart's ache; it only ever does so when I am close to you. My baby." She glided across the roof, the airy lightness of her pale yellow gown a silent testament to her grace.

At only five feet tall, she was the smallest person on this roof, but she was radiant.

Reaching Illium, she raised a delicate hand to his cheek. He bent instinctively to make it easier for her, this tall and strong angel who towered over his mother. "Yes, it's you." Joy so deep it cut at Elena.

After a moment, she turned toward Aodhan with a smile as luminous and happy. "And my borrowed baby."

Elena held her breath but Aodhan bent his head the same way Illium had done. Elena saw no tension in his body, no indication of discomfort with the Hummingbird's touch. Illium's mother looked at him with the same maternal love she'd done Illium.

"Is he getting you in trouble again?" A smile that was starlight. "Always, I knew he was the instigator. But you would never admit it, adamant that you receive equal punishment. My babies, grown so strong and tall."

Elena frowned; there was something different about the Hummingbird today. She was speaking of the past in past tense. It wasn't a given with this lovely woman. Her sense of time had fractured long ago, and often, she switched back and forth, sometimes believing that Illium was a child, other times acknowledging the man he'd become. Today, despite her use of the word baby, she seemed very aware that she was talking to two grown men.

Aodhan's smile was a thing that stopped Elena's heart. "You must believe me, *Eh-ma*, I was the instigator three times out of ten, but no one ever thought to point the finger at me."

When Elena glanced questioningly at Illium while the Hummingbird laughed, he said, "It means 'second mother' or 'mother who is my friend's mother but also mine.' It is more than respect. It is affection and love." His eyes shone wet for a second before he blinked the moisture away. "The years he spent isolating himself, she was the only one permitted to visit him whenever she wished. They'd paint together for hours."

"I can believe it." Love glowed in the moment framed in front of her. "Do you have the same relationship with his parents?"

Illium shook his head. "They aren't as old as my mother, but they always felt older. Kind and loving, but sedate. Not the type to go out at midnight with two little boys and watch a winged race through the Refuge, or to teach them how to dance to the beat of a bass drum."

The Hummingbird moved from Aodhan to Elena. "And you have come, too, my Raphael's love." A voice so warm it twined itself around Elena like a hug. "Is he well?"

"Yes, Lady Sharine," she said, using the name Illium's mother had given her on their first meeting. "He thinks of you often."

The Hummingbird kissed Elena on the cheek—because Elena, too, had bent her head to make it easier for the diminutive angel to reach her. Her scent was soft and warm and it caused Elena's eyes to go all hot. Marguerite had preferred gardenias, but below that had been the same unconditional love.

"I will come again to your city of metal and glass and noise and color."

Stepping back, the Hummingbird took them all in with an acute eye. This was definitely *not* the angel Elena had first met in New York. This Sharine was anchored to the world and confident in her strength. That she showed her strength gently made no difference.

"Now, my children," she said in a tone that was the epitome of steel encased in velvet, "tell me why you are here."

Bones hard against skin, Illium said, "Mother, the Cascade is waking Sleepers before their time."

The Hummingbird's face became a living monument, unmoving and unreadable.

Stepping closer, his wings agitated, Illium said, "Father is awake."

Silence reined. The desert seemed to go still in its whispering roll. The bright, active sounds of the people in the streets disappeared. The angelic warriors who'd been running a training exercise in the distance faded from view.

Only Illium and the Hummingbird existed, their pain a tableau.

Panic scrabbled inside Elena, and when she caught Aodhan's gaze, she saw the same dread in him. Fault lines already existed inside the Hummingbird. If this blow shattered them open again, it'd break her—and destroy Illium. His anger would eat him from the inside out, killing the heart of their wild Bluebell.

Then something extraordinary happened.

The Hummingbird drew up her shoulders, pinned her son with an unblinking gaze, and said, "*This* is why that poor squadron leader has been pretending to be so heartbroken he can't function for most of a day?" She did not sound impressed. In fact, she sounded like a mom who expected them to explain themselves. Right *now*.

"Er." Elena had never seen Illium so without words. Reaching back, he scratched at his nape. "I wanted to be here," he said at last.

A softening in his mother's expression. "Always watching after me, my son strong and beautiful. When I should be the one looking after you." Her hand on his cheek again, so gentle. "Will you forgive me this, Illium?"

"There is nothing to forgive." He turned into the touch of her hand, a son who loved his mother.

"There is much, but we will talk of that later. For now, Elena will teach me how to throw knives."

It was Elena's turn to be struck mute. "My lady Sharine?" she finally managed.

"I am not mad." She shook out her skirts, her voice as haunting and beautiful as ever. "I wish to learn to throw knives so I can sink those knives into Aegaeon's worthless chest should he dare show his face here."

Illium's jaw dropped. Aodhan appeared to have lost the ability to speak.

Elena grinned and bent in a deep bow. "It will be my pleasure."

43

Raphael had to read Elena's report twice before it sunk in. The woman Elena was describing was the Hummingbird of old. The one who'd come to tea in his mother's Refuge stronghold and taken him away for an afternoon of painting. He'd been a small boy with far too much energy and she'd been delighted with him.

She'd let him dip his hands into pots of paint and smear them over canvases. Afterward, she'd helped him color in the white spots, add in more paint and texture, and later, beamed proudly as he presented the art piece to his mother.

That Hummingbird had been a creature of delight and laughter.

She had, however, never played with knives.

Yet Elena assured him the Hummingbird was quite sane, and he wasn't to worry. She'd ensure Illium's mother stayed safe while she worked out her anger on various hapless targets of stuffed straw.

I'm also having to hug Bluebell a lot and pat Sparkle on the hand. Sharine's poor boys are having trouble processing this turn of events.

The tone of her missive would've made him smile if the situation in the world hadn't been so dire.

Less than two days after she'd left for Morocco, he soared in the skies above Neha's territory, on his way to the agreed meeting point on the China-India border. A portentous weight hung in the air. So many archangels in one place—it was inevitable that it would bleed into the world. The pressure against his skin reminded him of their family home when Nadiel and Caliane had both been in residence. Often, as a child, he'd felt as if his hair was standing on end.

His own power roiled and surged, an instinctive response to the potential threat. Jason had confirmed that Charisemnon had left his territory—at the same time as Titus. The two archangels didn't trust one another an inch and would not leave their lands while the other was in residence. Raphael had every faith in Titus's honor. He had none in Charisemnon's.

Neha was already at the border fort and had been since the fog first descended. The rest of the Cadre as well as the awakened ones were en route. Antonicus had gone half a day ahead of Raphael, wanting more time to take in the situation. Now, Raphael dropped below the cloud layer that hung in the night-dark sky. Stars glittered above the clouds, but below was a leaden gloom through which he spotted wings of bronze.

Michaela, he said in greeting.

The bronze wings angled into a hover, Michaela's face breaking out in what might've been a genuine smile. With skin the color of milk chocolate, a body that held all the curves necessary to bring her targets to their knees, and hair that tumbled down her back in a multitude of brown-gold shades, the Archangel of Budapest had been the muse of artists through the ages. Emperors and kings had worshipped her. Mortals and immortals alike were in awe of her beauty.

Raphael was thankful he'd never felt the allure. The lovers of the former Queen of Constantinople tended to end up dead and buried sooner rather than later. The only significant one to have survived was Astaad's second Dahariel. Perhaps because Dahariel, too, was a master game-player; he also happened to be a man who never put a woman first—he had other priorities.

It had always been a peculiar coupling: a woman who demanded obsession from her lovers and a man so jaded that he needed ever more extreme acts to feel any pleasure.

Raphael. Michaela's bronze skinsuit was textured to make it appear as if she were encased in a thin coat of bronze stone. While the neckline was a sedate curve, he'd seen how the back plunged deeply between her wings.

You are well. So soon after giving birth and notwithstanding the exquisite beauty she used to blind others, she had to be exhausted.

It is good to be known as demanding and self-centered. A twist of her lips. *Neha didn't blink an eye when I requested landing clearance for my jet.*

Clever. Using the jet would've left her with reserves of energy she could use to conceal her weakness. *Nothing on the outside gives away your true physical state.*

I have worked hard to make it so.

The two of them flew on. Michaela was uncharacteristically quiet.

Raphael thought she must be further conserving her strength, but when she spoke, it had nothing to do with power or the threat in China. *I have brought a child into a world where an archangel of death reigns over the biggest territory on the planet. I do not know what awaits my son.*

Raphael caught a wind, rode it. *We can only live in the time into which we are born.* As he'd been born at a time when two archangels, one old, one younger, struggled with the caress of madness.

A hint of a bruised darkness on the horizon, licked with flame. Neha had ordered flaming torches placed along the entire China-India border, as warning to her people not to cross.

Raphael, my friend! Titus's mental voice was as much a thunderclap of sound as his physical voice.

Raphael looked to the left. *Well met, Titus.* The three of them flew on without further conversation. All the talk had been done and done again.

Antonicus had made his choice and today, they would see the outcome. Still, after landing atop the roof of the border fort, Raphael made his way to the Ancient and said, "You are resolved to do this even now that you see the darkness of what you face?"

"Yes, pup. I do not know how you do things, but I hold to my convictions."

Those convictions had been set with little real information, Raphael thought. But all he said was, "So be it." Antonicus was no youth; he was an Ancient and he was making this call while staring at what awaited.

"I have seen nightmares you can't comprehend," Antonicus added. "A jumped-up faux-goddess is no threat to me."

Raphael gave a nod of acknowledgment before making his way to an angel with wings of pristine white. "Eli, you have beaten me here." He and the Archangel of South America had planned to fly together, keeping company on the long journey, but then a quake had hit Elijah's territory, and he'd had to remain behind for half a day to deal with it. When Raphael offered to assist, Elijah had told him to go ahead as Raphael intended to stop in at Amanat to speak to Caliane.

"I was lucky, my friend. My work was done within two hours, not half a day. Then I was able to catch wind currents so strong I feared a cyclone was building. I looked for you in the sky as I flew but you must've been far distant." Eli scanned the rooftop. "Lady Caliane?"

"She broke away to go to Neha's palace atop the hill." His mother had wished to have a private conversation with the Archangel of India. "I see her now."

"Neha flies with her."

Several others arrived at that instant. Including Aegaeon. "I hear my son is part of your court, Raphael," he said, his feathers a deep sea green that flowed into blue and his face a harder, craggier version of Illium's—no one would've accused the Hummingbird of deceit had her son been full grown when Aegaeon disappeared into Sleep.

That he was Illium's progenitor was impossible to miss.

"Illium is one of my Seven." Raphael forced himself to be civil; if there was to be a confrontation, it belonged to Illium.

"Wild still is he?" Aegaeon's eyes gleamed with laughing pride. "Always playing tricks, my son."

"You will excuse me. I must greet my mother." Raphael had to get away from the angel before he punched him. Not many people aroused such primal anger in Raphael, but Aegaeon stood in first place.

Both for what he'd done to the Hummingbird, and what he'd done to Illium. As if they had no more importance to him than any other angel in his harem. Raphael would never forget finding the Hummingbird's mischievous, laughing boy curled up in a heap behind a tumble of rocks, crying in heartbroken silence. Aegaeon had left without warning, with no care for the small heart that worshipped him.

He came to a stop near where Caliane and Neha had landed. "Mother. Neha."

Neha gave a nod of acknowledgment, but her eyes were on the fog. "Do you feel it?"

"Yes." A heavy sense of oppression, a near-physical touch. "Is it causing weather changes in your territory?"

"My weather scientists say it has to do with how the fog is disrupting the ground to sky flow in Lijuan's land." Dressed in the faded leathers of a warrior, she spoke to Raphael without anger, her only focus the dark fog. She didn't seem aware of the thin snake wrapped around her left wrist, a living bracelet in tones of dark orange and copper.

Caliane was dressed much the same except that her hair was out while Neha had braided her own. The three of them moved to the edge of the fort roof. The others soon joined them.

"Did any of you fly over China on your way here?" Neha asked.

"It was not on our route, but Zanaya and I deliberately detoured there," Alexander said.

"We have sent mechanical devices that fly and take pictures above the fog," Neha said, "but they can only go a certain distance before their energy runs out. Did you see anything unusual during your flight?"

"Darker patches in certain sections."

"It seemed thicker," Zanaya added, "more viscous."

"The mechanical devices also sent us such images." Neha's face was thinner than Raphael was used to seeing, her bones sharp.

"Has anyone come out of the territory since the fog descended?" Michaela's voice, her body held with a familiar languidness where she stood next to Titus. "My sentries have reported none on the Mongolian border."

"I have had no new refugees," Caliane said.

"Nothing alive has crossed this border," Neha said. "Not even a bird. The ones on this side are now avoiding it, as if they have heard the death screams of their fallen brethren." She pointed down. "My people would normally clean that up, but I wanted you to see."

Raphael's blood went cold at the sight that awaited: a row of birds, all fallen at the edge of the fog. Tiny corpses that told a story of cold, sudden death.

"How long between contact and death?" Astaad asked, a smear of dust on his sleeveless black tunic.

"As far as we can tell, it is instantaneous." Neha looked to Caliane.

Raphael's mother nodded. "The birds touch the fog and they drop, already dead. It is not the fall that kills them, that we have determined. Smaller animals, even snakes, have been found dead with their heads just inside the fog and bodies outside."

"Enough." Antonicus stepped back from the group on that single contemptuous word and spread out his wings. "It is time I do what must be done—I am not a child to be scared by ghost stories. I will see you all after I return from speaking to this Lijuan who believes herself a goddess even over immortals."

The Ancient lifted off. He'd initially intended to fly to the part of the fog over Lijuan's stronghold before he dropped down, but that would put him far from sight and they needed to know what would happen to an archangel who flew into the fog.

Antonicus had finally agreed to do a short flight into the fog within their line of sight, rise up to show them he was well, then make his way to the coordinates of Lijuan's former stronghold—in that at least he'd accepted assistance, and was wearing a watch that would help him find the correct location. He also wore a small camera on his left shoulder that would transmit images back to a unit that sat to one side of the roof.

Antonicus crossed the border. No one spoke. Not even when the Ancient reached the test location deep within the fog area but still visible to them.

He lifted an arm, and Neha raised hers to show him they

could see him. That hadn't been guaranteed given the darkness, but enough torchlight leached out that far to make Antonicus a clear silhouette.

The Ancient flew down into the fog.

One.

Two.

Three.

No one looked at the transmitted images; those were being recorded, could be gone over at will.

Four.

Five.

Antonicus should've emerged by now.

"He's dead," Neha said, not coldly but with the conviction of belief.

An arm erupted out of the fog, the fingers locked into a tight fist. It was followed by a head, then a torso, then wings, and suddenly, Antonicus hovered over the spot where he'd gone in. Raphael's gut clenched against the hard punch of relief. If the Ancient could survive this, they had a chance against Lijuan if—*when*—she made war on the world.

Antonicus wobbled, his wings dipping this way then that.

"What is he doing?" Michaela asked, but Raphael was already lifting off.

Stay here, he told the others. He flew on wings of white fire across the short distance.

Antonicus was attempting to fly toward him, but his wings were listing heavily and he was halfway back inside the fog when Raphael reached him. Grabbing his visible arm, Raphael fought to stop Antonicus's momentum from dragging them both down into the darkness.

44

Raphael's arm jerked in his shoulder socket, and then he had control, Antonicus's weight less than he'd expected. Raphael hauled him out. The Ancient's face was skeletal, his eyes glistening orbs infected with lines of liquid black.

Raphael had been hit by the same energy once, had gone blind from it before the wildfire forced it out. Seeing Antonicus's wings crumple, he shifted his hold so the other archangel was in his arms.

He was light. So light. His clothes hung off his frame, his dark brown hair thinning in the wind before Raphael's eyes. "Hold on."

The archangels gathered on the roof parted for them. Raphael landed in the center, placing Antonicus on a plush blue rug Neha must've had brought up. Kneeling down beside the other archangel, he placed his hand on Antonicus's chest and said, "I am going to attempt to fight this infection." He thrust wildfire into the Ancient.

Antonicus's eyes burst with light from within before the black retreated to reveal the gray of his irises. "Death," the injured archangel rasped. "It is pure death."

The liquid black began to creep again. Raphael pulsed more

wildfire into his system; Antonicus clutched at his hand as the bolt arced through his body. His eyes cleared once more.

"What did you see below the fog?" Neha asked from the fallen angel's other side. "The recorded images are blurred by severe movement." She closed her hand over Antonicus's.

Raphael noted the contact, noted also that the infection—or whatever this was—didn't seem to be crossing over. At the same instant, he saw that Antonicus's wings were turning black from the edges in. The Ancient's primaries began to curl inward. One detached to lie on the rug. Favashi had shown similar symptoms, though she hadn't been as far along. He calculated rapidly as Antonicus began to speak.

"No life. No lights," he rasped. "Death." Liquid black crawled over his irises.

"Raphael." Caliane's hand on his shoulder.

Raphael spoke directly to Antonicus. "I could kill you. The wildfire is a blunt weapon designed to attack Lijuan's power and you're riddled with it."

"It is killing me anyway." Antonicus coughed and what came out was a thick black slime—his insides being liquefied in front of them.

Raphael thrust two more bolts of wildfire into the Ancient. The second surge crackled all over him in a violence of white-gold and electric blue, clearing his eyes and putting a shine back in his skin, and for a moment, Raphael thought they had defeated Lijuan's brand of death.

Then the signs of Lijuan's poisonous power surged back faster and more virulent than ever. It covered his irises, ran through his skin, blazed across his wings. Further jolts of wildfire had no effect.

Titus crouched by Antonicus's head and put a hand on his shoulder in a grip that told the archangel he wasn't alone. Raphael held on to Antonicus's left hand as Neha held on to his right. The others all crouched down, their wings trailing on the dusty roof, and together, they watched the final breaths of an archangel who had lived millennia, only to be brought down by a death that was beyond anything this world had ever seen.

"He is gone," Caliane murmured when Antonicus's breath had ended, no sign of a heart beating in his chest, and his skin holding a putrid greenish cast. It was a decaying corpse that lay before them in place of a powerful Ancient who had blazed with life and arrogance only an hour ago.

"We must burn him—we do not know what he carries in his blood." Neha's words might've been harsh, but it was with a gentle touch that she reached out to close the Ancient's staring eyes.

"Are we sure?" A soft question from Michaela, who had understandably kept her distance. "We do not need to breathe or have beating hearts to live."

They all considered that. In front of them, the liquefaction process seemed to have stopped at the moment of Antonicus's final breath. His wings were shreds of rotted tendon and blackened feathers, his chest sunken inward, but nothing new had been lost since his apparent death. Either the process had halted now there was no living flesh on which the infection could feast, or the archangel was somehow fighting back.

"We cannot have this body in any of our territories," Titus said. "It pains me to reject a warrior so courageous, but we must care for our people. We cannot bring in a source of infection where it may leach from his body to poison the soil."

Raphael thought of Naasir, of the ice and snow where he'd been born. "There are islands in the Antarctic ice that are peopled by no one. They are also small enough that we can erect high fences around and above our chosen island to stop animals from coming in and spreading any infection."

"We will bury him deep," Elijah murmured. "We have enough power to dig a hole so far into the earth that only a living archangel will be able to force his way out."

Raphael and Titus began to roll Antonicus's body up in the rug on which he'd died, their faces solemn and their actions as respectful as they could make them.

"I will contact one of my generals to find large plastic sheeting and tape," Neha said, and went down to pick up the items herself, not wanting anyone less powerful than an archangel near the corpse. On her return, they sealed the rolled-up carpet in the sheeting, then locked it tight with the tape.

Three times.

No one argued or stated it was overkill. "I will carry him," Raphael said afterward. "I am the only one who has any kind of an immunity." That Neha and Titus had touched Antonicus in his dying moments was a testament to their heart and courage.

Neha locked the dark of her eyes with his. "But it appears even you cannot defeat this evil any longer and that chills my heart."

Not answering because Neha's words were the simple and cold truth, Raphael picked up Antonicus's body, a body made heavier by the carpet but not so heavy that he couldn't carry it. "I'll need to rest at times," he began, but Elijah frowned.

"We can all help with the passage without risk of infection. All we need are ropes. If we create a sling, no one of us has to bear the entire burden."

Neha added, "I will ask for the rope to be brought to the room below."

Raphael put Antonicus down while they waited. "Will you burn this building?" he asked Neha.

"Yes. I've ordered everyone but those bringing the rope to evacuate. I will send this fort up in flame as soon as they are clear and we rise." Her face was half in shadow as she turned her head toward China. "Lijuan has evolved beyond us. Archangels cannot be killed by anything but another archangel, yet she is killing from a distance with this dark fog."

"Cassandra prophesied that the Cadre alone would not be enough this time." He took in Zanaya's and Aegaeon's motionless, expressionless faces; neither had said a word since Antonicus began to die. "It is why you are awake."

"But if your wildfire has failed, Raphael, then I fear their waking will not matter." Caliane's hair flew back in the night breeze. "This time, our world may end."

The explosion boiled the sky behind Raphael as Neha incinerated the fort's roof before collapsing the building inward into a hole that Caliane had helped her create. He and the others had flown ahead, with Antonicus in a sling between them. Those with glamour used it to hide the body.

Anyone who looked up would see many archangels together, but that was an explicable thing given the deadly fog and other catastrophic incidents around the world. No one would see a body. No one would know that an archangel had died. Antonicus had gone into Sleep, that was all the world would be told.

If Antonicus's end caused havoc with the weather, as sometimes happened when an archangel passed, it would be believed to be part of the recent chaos.

When day broke, Michaela and Astaad flew down to wild fields full of flowers and returned with bunches of them to drop on Antonicus's body. The rope sling the Cadre had woven together was tight enough that the flowers collected around the body and by the time they left the fields, it was a flower-draped bier such as was their way and not just a makeshift coffin created to contain infection.

No one spoke as they flew. On the roof, there'd been some discussion of leaving half their number at the border with China, but in the end they'd decided that there was nothing half their number could do to stop Lijuan. Better they deal with this together, then go to their territories, to prepare in any way they could . . . and to mourn all those of their own who'd been trapped within when the fog crawled across China on a tide of death.

Gadriel, a little set in his habits but noble in a quiet way, hadn't made it out. Raphael had no body to take home to his family. The angel wasn't the only one who'd vanished into the murderous dark; Raphael had lost too many good people and the war hadn't yet begun.

It was a risk to assume nothing would change during the short time they disappeared to bury Antonicus, but the risk was a considered one. The more opaque patches seen by Neha's drones and confirmed by Alexander and Zanaya seemed to indicate that the Archangel of China was consolidating herself. How she might be doing so was a thing Raphael didn't like thinking about.

He remembered too well the pathetic half-consumed husks he and Elena had discovered. Lijuan fed from life to make death. There'd been millions of people in China before the fog. Now, no voices penetrated the dark wall and Antonicus had said the landscape was devoid of light.

The blurry green-tinged images picked up by the camera worn by the Ancient had shown the same: an endless wall of pitch black, so murky that even technology meant to penetrate night had failed.

Raphael did not want to see what remained when the fog retreated.

Resting one another by taking turns with the sling so they had no need to stop, the eleven archangels made a direct trek to an ice island that Alexander and Charisemnon flew ahead to scout.

Conscious of her vulnerable physical state, Raphael had checked in with Michaela multiple times during the trek. *I can ask for a break if you need it,* he'd said. *I will blame it on the output of wildfire.*

A little pale under the smooth richness of her skin, she'd nonetheless demurred. *We must do this if my son is to be safe. I cannot stand any delay.*

So they flew on. He noticed that Caliane stayed close to Michaela, not enough for it to be remarked on, yet enough to render assistance should it be necessary. But Michaela managed to stay airborne until they landed at their destination: a small, rocky island encased in clear ice.

Together, Zanaya and Elijah created the deep hole needed for the burial, then all eleven of them joined to lower Antonicus into it using the ropes. They took it slow, none of them wishing to simply dump him. Once the sling touched the frozen soil that was his resting ground, they dropped the ropes into the hole with him.

Caliane stepped forward to the edge of the grave. "Antonicus is gone from this world, perhaps forever, but before he went, he gave us a great gift. He showed us the enemy we must be ready to fight, the evil that may defeat us all if we are not ready. For that, he will be remembered forever in our histories. I will ensure the Historian knows of this, so she can share it with angelkind when the time is right."

Right now, Raphael understood, the knowledge of Antonicus's passing would only spread fear and terror. Archangels were not vulnerable. That was their legend and what kept the world in balance.

"To Antonicus." Caliane lifted a handful of shattered ice-rock.

"To Antonicus." Together, they threw the handfuls into the grave, then Raphael, Titus, and Astaad collapsed the grave inward before filling it with the material excavated during its creation. It left a depression over which they built a cairn using rocks taken from another small and distant island.

Then, while Michaela and Caliane kept watch, the rest of them flew toward a trawler anchored about two hours from the island. Each of them had contacted their seconds while yet in India, gotten details of any ships that'd be passing through the wider Antarctic area at the correct time.

Their target flew the flag of Elijah's land.

On it were the timbers, sheets of metal, wires, and other materials necessary to build a research station in a different area of this remote continent. Distant as the trawler was, there was no danger the crew would realize the archangels' flight path or final destination. That crew watched goggle-eyed as archangel after archangel flew down, before flying off with materials to build a crypt that would act as a cage for the infection.

I shall destroy the ship and its crew, Aegaeon said after the last pickup.

There's no need, Neha replied. *I wiped their memories. They know only that they have been ordered by their archangel to return to base and renew their supplies. Better to leave no ripple here, not even the small one caused by the loss of a trawler.*

Raphael knew his hunter would be horrified by Neha's unilateral choice, but those mortals could now live out their lives in safety. This secret was too huge, too deadly.

It had been decided they would embargo the entire area of the grave for fifty miles in every direction. No ships or flyers. As a final act, they would brand the crypt with each of their sigils.

No one in the world was suicidal enough to take on the entire Cadre.

Elijah, whose territory was nearest the ice island, would have his most trusted squadron fly regular patrols over that area, ensure Antonicus stayed undisturbed. Titus was farther, but he would also send out irregular patrols to make certain no one became complacent and decided to encroach on the graveyard.

With so many of them, the crypt was built by nightfall. They burned their sigils into the metal walls in silence. After his ascension, Raphael had chosen a simple marker for his name in the angelic tongue as his sigil, but he'd altered that to include Elena in the months after they fell, while he waited for her to wake.

The marker for his name now twined around a dagger.

Aegaeon sneered. "You broadcast your heart's weakness."

"The world knows well what I feel for my Elena, and I would not hide it." His words held cold judgment, but Aegaeon was too drunk on his own belief in himself to sense it.

Caliane was the last one to burn in her sigil. "It is done."

Eleven archangels rose up in silence from a grave that should not exist.

Cassandra's voice rang in Raphael's head, an echo from the final moments before he'd released the power that had shattered the chrysalis.

The future aligns. Paths are chosen. Death comes.

Such death, child of flames.

Goddess of Nightmare. Wraith without a shadow. Rising into her Reign of Death.

Wings of silver. Wings of blue.

Mortal heart. Broken dreams.

Shatter. Shatter. Shatter.

A sundering.

A grave.

I see the end. I see . . .

Was this the grave Cassandra had foretold? Or would there be more? How many of the Cadre and the awakened ones would be alive by the time this ended?

45

Elena hugged the Hummingbird, inhaling the gentle love that was her scent. "Are you sure you want us to go?" she asked after drawing back. "We can stay longer."

"Ah, child." The Hummingbird smiled. "I feel you missing my boy who did not come from my womb. I am quite capable of being left to my own devices." She glanced at Illium, who stood on the far edge of the roof having a low-voiced conversation with Aodhan.

He didn't look happy but he didn't shrug off Aodhan's touch when the other angel closed his hand over Illium's nape. His wings opened and closed restlessly, his jaw set in a rigid line.

"Care for him." The Hummingbird's voice was a melody of sorrow that tangled Elena's heart in melancholy chains. "My boy's heart loves too much and it hurts too much when it is broken."

"I'll keep an eye on him. Raphael's ordered Aodhan home, too." She returned her attention to the Hummingbird. "I never realized how strong you were, Lady Sharine, and I'm sorry for that. This week has taught me to never again underestimate you."

"You are flattering me, but I will accept it." A sparkle infiltrating the sadness, she dusted something off Elena's shoulder. "Thank you for indulging my need to get my anger out with knives. I know I am no warrior. I am also not who I once was . . . and my son, he has had a ghost for a mother for too long. It is enough."

The Hummingbird's beautiful pale eyes, champagne held up to moonlight, yet had an ethereal quality, as if she saw beyond the veil, but in her voice was determination. "I never thought I would thank Aegaeon for anything, but I will thank him for the roar of rage that woke me up from my own long Sleep."

While the Hummingbird went to speak to Illium and Aodhan, Elena looked out over the village and thought of how different it felt from when she'd last been here—people still flinched when they spotted wings, but they recovered quickly and many offered hesitant smiles.

If she walked with the Hummingbird, there was no flinch, only joy and adoration. Children ran to Lady Sharine with flowers clutched in their tiny, pudgy hands, while adults bowed down low when she passed, though she was not an angel to demand such things. She would take the children's sticky hands in hers and walk with them as she spoke to their parents. At times, she would touch the shoulder of a villager who had bowed, and ask them about their day.

The people of this village bowed not because they feared her, but because they loved her.

The Hummingbird's warrior squadrons were treated with respect and awe. She had chosen each warrior herself, from among the armies of the Cadre, and not one angel or vampire chosen had demurred at serving for a time in what was considered an unexciting post devoid of risk or danger.

Fear hadn't yet totally evaporated from the village, but it was no longer a noxious miasma in the air and she thought if she returned in another six months, it might be to clear air. These people were learning that they *could* trust angelkind not to be cruel and capricious and ugly of heart.

Such cruel angels existed in the world, always would, but not here. Not anymore.

"Ellie, it's time." Illium's face was sullen, an expression she'd never before seen on him.

The Hummingbird cupped his face in her hands. "Will you not smile at your mother before you go?" When Illium continued to look surly, his mother leaned in close. "I promise you I will not be a ghost again—you do not need to worry. Do not forget that despite all his power, I won the race."

Illium's eyes widened. "You remember?" A rough question.

"I am waking, my sweet boy." Tugging down his head, she kissed him on the forehead before rolling something off her wrist. "Wear this and remember who I once was. I will become her again."

Illium held out his hand on a hard swallow, and his mother got the stretchy bracelet over his larger hand and onto his wrist. The wooden beads were far more separated out on his wrist, but it looked like the strap was strong and would hold.

Illium hugged his mother, wrapping her up in his wings and holding on for a long time, his face tight in a paroxysm of hope. Afterward, he said, "You'll call if you need me?"

"I will call you," the Hummingbird promised. "But if Aegaeon dares come here, I will deal with him. This is a matter between me and your father." She stepped back—but not before she turned to Aodhan and pressed a kiss to his cheek. "Go home now, fledglings. I hear enough to understand that a terrible darkness threatens the world. And I know that Raphael needs his Seven and his consort around him at such a time."

Illium looked at Elena, nodded.

The three of them took off as one, with Aodhan going high as he preferred—that high in the sky, he was a shooting star or a spark of sunlight caught on an unknown object. Closer to earth, mortals and vampires gathered underneath, pointing and gasping. Drivers had been known to stop their cars without warning, distracted by the shattered light that was his body in flight under the sun or the moon.

Illium looked back one last time after they'd flown some distance. Following his gaze, Elena saw the Hummingbird's small figure on the distant rooftop, the creamy orange of her gown fluttering in the morning breeze. Elena raised a hand and the Hummingbird raised one back. Illium's mother became too small to see a wingbeat later, her home fading into a backdrop of desert and sky.

Raphael watched the jet come in from his vantage point on a nearby rooftop, the afternoon light hazy. Dougal was bringing the craft in smooth and steady, despite the high winds that had begun to buffet the area over the past hours. The weather scientists were forecasting hurricane-force winds and rains.

New York wasn't the only city affected; the entire Eastern seaboard was under threat. It was also snowing in Florida. Eli had returned home to find half his territory in the grip of a massive snowstorm. Michaela had contacted Raphael in a panic because she was having trouble fighting the winds in her own territory to get to her child, but it had eased enough that she'd been able to break through.

He hadn't heard from the other archangels, but he knew they were all apt to be dealing with things deadly and dangerous and unexpected, the Earth in chaos. Neha had the worst of it, her entire army on constant watch to ensure the fog didn't drift across her border.

"Though what I will do if it does encroach, I do not know," she'd said to him and Caliane before they all parted after burying Antonicus; shadows under her eyes, she'd rubbed at her forehead.

Elena-mine, I have missed you. Such simple words for the raw ache inside him. He'd nearly lost her too recently to be easy with such a separation.

I can see you. Her happiness came through in a wash of molten steel against his mind. *I plan to jump in your arms and kiss you stupid, so be ready.*

Feeling his lips curve in a way only his hunter could engender, he took off and paralleled the plane's descent from a short distance away. He could've gone much closer, but then Dougal might worry about catching him in the plane's draw and he wanted the pilot's focus to be on a safe descent. Because in that metal body was Raphael's eternity.

Everything changed a third of the way through the descent. The strong winds began to twist into deadly funnels. One newborn twister spun into a small plane parked near a hangar; the plane flipped against the hangar wall, the force of it breaking the craft to pieces. A second twister hit a much larger jet that had just finished deplaning its passengers and crew—all of whom were Refuge-based soldiers Raphael had called home.

The jet was shoved halfway back down the runway where it slammed into another twister; the huge metal body groaned as it flipped over onto its back with a spark of metal on asphalt. *Dougal, abort the landing!* The pilot had a better chance of avoiding the twisters if he flew straight through and into clear air—the deadly funnels seemed focused in and around the airport.

It's too late, sire! Dougal's mental voice was faint—the vampire wasn't as strong as any of Raphael's Seven, but he'd gained enough power over the centuries that he could reply to Raphael instead of simply listening. *The plane won't have enough lift! It's already shaking like it's going to fall apart.*

It was also too late for Elena, Aodhan, and Illium to fly out of the plane. The wind would pummel them onto the tarmac before they could gain the sky. The point was moot in any case—not one would abandon Dougal and his copilot.

What's the plan, Archangel? Elena's voice, calm and confident.

Let us test this Cascade power's mettle. He reached for Dougal's mind again. *Cut all power. Release controls.*

One second. Two. Then—*It's done. The plane is now a glider.*

The wind whipping around his face and shards of debris slicing over his bare arms, Raphael flew to under the massive object. It was going fast, but he was an archangel. Matching its barreling pace, he put his hands on the undercarriage. Those hands looked ridiculously small in comparison to the vast metal structure, but this wasn't about physical size. It was about power.

Raphael released his with a tightly focused intent that shaped its expression. Golden lightning kissed with a tendril of Elena's warmth snaked across the undercarriage and along the underside of the wings. He'd never done this with such a large machine, but he'd once helped land a much smaller stricken craft. Then, he'd simply used his strength—a one-seater hopper was hardly a challenge.

But even an archangel couldn't bear the weight of a full-sized jet. Which was why he'd created the network of energy. His muscles strained as he channeled his strength through that network, effectively turning it into a part of his body.

A twister headed right for them, angry and black. There was no way to avoid it. But he heard no cries of panic in his mind, no screams. His people and his consort were trusting him to get this done.

He reached for the Legion. As he did so, he felt a taste inside him that was Elena. Not paying it much mind for she was welcome anytime she wished, he wrenched power from the Legion in a way he'd never before done.

We are the repository, the ancient beings had said when they first emerged from the deep. *We tried to pass it to the Sire, but the Sire is not yet ready.*

Now that power flowed into him and it was different from the Cascade energy. It was painfully old and it tasted of the ocean's cold embrace and time's endless march. A reminder that the Legion had slept eons under the sea, and for much of that time, had been as the dead. But now, they were awake and they whispered in his mind.

Raphael. Aeclari. *We see the mirror. We give.*

The power sighed in his blood, then—under his command—spread outward along the frame he'd already constructed—only this time, it kept going until the entire plane was encased in a web of archangelic energy that repulsed any attempt at destruction.

They flew straight into the twister.

Muscles bunched, Raphael held the plane stable as the winds attempted to tear it from his grasp, even as they sought to collapse his wings. But his wings were rippling white fire and the wind could find no purchase.

Sudden calm, the very center of the angry funnel.

The rage of wind again in a matter of heartbeats, vicious and violent and demanding. His tunic was torn off his body. Something small and sharp slammed into his rib cage. He shrugged off the minor injury, his focus unflinching. Above him, the plane groaned but held together as they emerged out the other side.

Smaller twisters continued to lay waste to the airport around them. The one mercy was that this was a private airport for Tower use and this was the final flight coming in or going out today. All other planes were currently clear of crew and passengers. *Andreja, guide me in.* The swirling debris blinded and confused.

You're right above the runway, sire. Andreja's voice was crystalline; the angel was far more powerful than most people realized. *I see the outline of the plane glowing gold. There's light coming from inside, too. If you continue to come down on the current slope, you'll have plenty of room.*

Andreja kept him updated until Raphael was close enough to the ground to see the tarmac. Dougal had lowered the wheels when he began the landing process, and while the space underneath wasn't enough for Raphael to stand to his full height, it'd be enough if he bent his knees.

Even down and stable, he didn't release the plane. *Stay onboard.* They remained within a howling gray swirl of dust and debris and fury.

Holy shit, Archangel. And I was impressed with Bluebell turning a helicopter upside down. Elena's voice was pure life inside him, a burst of joyous light. *I just said that to him and he's pretending to sulk but his eyes are huge and he keeps staring out the window then rubbing those eyes only to stare again. Aodhan is flat out discombobulated.*

Her words were so normal, so much a part of his life that his cheeks creased despite the winds that surged violently around them. *An archangel must have some tricks up his sleeve,* he said, just as Andreja's voice came into his mind.

Sire. Massive twister building on the tail end of the plane.

46

Raphael glanced in that direction, was just able to see the bottom of the violent rotation of wind and dirt and pieces of plane wreckage. *It's going to get loud,* he warned everyone on the plane as he sent even more power into the energy shield he'd created around the plane.

Light began to spear out above him and at first he thought he'd lost control. But no, the shell he'd erected was holding its pattern. *Elena?*

Yeah, I'm glowing big-time. Happened while we were landing, too. Partial battery kicking in?

I haven't reached for your energy. He'd needed the massive amount held by the Legion. *Do you feel ill or hurt?*

No. I'm just a glowstick. A kiss he felt. *We'll figure it out later. Concentrate on keeping yourself alive so I don't have to kick your ass.*

Again, she worried about him when, of all of them, he was the one most likely to survive. Even if a twister picked him up and smashed him to the earth at terminal velocity, it would not be terminal for him. His body would knit itself back together sooner or later.

Illium would survive, too. His recovery would be far longer, but he was old and strong enough now to make it. Aodhan was the same. Dougal and his copilot, however, would not endure. Their heads would likely be torn from their bodies by the impact and, as vampires, that was it for them.

As for Elena . . . She was far less breakable than she'd been before the Cascade tried to steal her soul, but she remained a young angel. Her body would not last being battered into pieces.

So he'd ensure it didn't come to that.

Staring down at the tarmac, he anchored himself. The tarmac cracked around him as his energy shoved into the earth and clawed itself into stone so far below it was part of the planet's mantle. In concert with the shield, it kept the plane from moving as the twister hit.

Pieces of plane wreckage whacked hard against the sides of the craft, but nothing got through the shell of lightning fire. A bit of debris hit him in the leg, and it was only then that he realized he'd forgotten to create a shield around himself.

It took but a thought.

A roar of noise and dust and nothingness. Then . . . an abrupt silence. *Andreja. Status.*

I'm scanning the skies and the landscape. I don't see any more twisters. All is calm.

Raphael sucked the energy that protected the plane into himself, pouring a vast amount of it back into the Legion, some of whom had fallen where they stood when he grabbed for their power. He had no desire or need to carry that much power in his own body—not when the Cascade lightning was already so violent. *I thank you.*

We are yours, whispered seven hundred and seventy-seven voices. *This power is yours.*

Inside him, the Cascade energy settled back in with a familiar coldness leavened only with a tendril of wildfire and steel. *Deplane,* he said to those inside.

Already out from under the plane, he rose into the air just as the clouds opened up. Pounding rain began to slice in from his right, hitting his skin in hundreds of sharp, cold shards.

The Legion mark on his temple flared.

The door of the plane opened at last, and Elena raced out. He was hovering right outside, hauled her off the top of the stairs and into his arms. She clung to him with a laugh, the lightning storm of her wings brilliant against the gray heaviness of the rain-wet world. A second later, she thrust her hands into his hair, pulled his head down to her own, and kissed him stupid.

Later, they stood with Dmitri and watched the footage from the airport cameras and from a plane spotter who'd been parked at a "secret" location the enthusiasts shared only among themselves. The Tower let them be because they never tried to breach the airport boundaries and policed themselves into good behavior. This spotter had been recording the jet coming in, complete with commentary.

"*Tower 1* is about to land," he said cheerfully. "Like, that's not the actual call sign because the Tower doesn't advertise which of its planes are in the sky, but I can tell this is number 1 from that slight mark on the tail. Means one of the senior people must be onboard. Can't wait—*Fuck*!"

The footage wobbled as he focused in on a tornado that had appeared out of nowhere. He whipped the camera back and forth as another appeared, then another.

"Oh cripes! How's the pilot going to avoid those?" Fear rippled through his words. "That plane is going to go right into that twister. Oh man, oh man . . ." His words mumbled off into a chill terror they could almost feel, until his voice squeaked again. "Raphael! Fuck me! No one is going to *believe* this!"

He'd caught the instant Raphael's energy crawled all over the plane and turned it into a glowing beacon in the heavy gray darkness. The plane was soon obscured by the twisters and the dirt and debris in the air, only to reappear in patches as Raphael brought it in to land.

Through it all was an awed silence that ended with, "That's the fucking Archangel of fucking New York! Suck on that all you cretins who try to attack our city, especially you Zhou Lijuan!"

Elena snorted out a laugh. "I like this guy." She had to laugh or her heart might explode—she couldn't believe Raphael had done that. Seeing the visuals and the size of the jet above his head, viewing the sheer power involved in the landing . . . Her pulse was thunder.

"You would," Dmitri muttered, but his words didn't hold their usual mocking bite. He was too focused on the second recording that had begun to play—this one from the surveillance cameras at the airport. Vivek had stitched together the footage to provide a continuous narrative.

The tornados had sprung up without warning, huge swirls of wind and dirt and flying debris that had become shrapnel. Raphael's wounds had already healed, but Elena was going to be seeing his blood smeared on his skin for a while to come. Andreja at the air traffic control tower had narrowly avoided having her head sliced off when part of a broken-off wing smashed through the glass of her enclosure.

Turned out that had occurred close to the *start* of things; she'd then continued to calmly communicate with Raphael.

"Why is Andreja in that control room?" Elena said to Dmitri. "I'd figure a woman that unflappable would be in the Tower."

"You don't know Andreja." Dmitri folded his arms. "She's seven thousand years old and has decided she's on vacation this century. And she likes planes."

Elena thought it over and realized that when you'd lived so long, taking a century off to relax was no biggie. "Lucky for us she decided to vacation as an air traffic controller."

"Regardless, inform her that all vacation time is cancelled until the Cascade is past." Raphael's eyes were on the screen. "There is no sense to the twisters. It appears to be chance your plane was coming in to land when they appeared."

"Seems to line up with reports coming in from other territories," Dmitri said. "Devastating weather events all over the place. Flash flooding in Chile. Major landslide in Turkey. Whirlpool in a lake in Switzerland—casualties are going to be significant there. Thing swallowed up multiple pleasure craft."

Elena rubbed her hands up and down her arms. "The pace of chaos, it's speeding up." Like a concerto rising to an inevitable crescendo: *war.*

When she and Raphael made it up to their suite at last, it was to find the Primary waiting for them on the night-draped balcony. A patient gargoyle crouched on the very edge, his hair dripping. Sliding open the doorway and spilling light onto the balcony, Elena said, "You know you're welcome to wait inside."

The Primary rose from his crouch.

Elena went motionless when he stepped into the light. "Your second becoming," she whispered, recalling words the Primary had spoken to her what felt like a lifetime ago.

The Primary's eyes remained that pale, pale color with a ring of vivid blue around the irises that echoed the color of Raphael's eyes, but his skin had gained a hue that wasn't gray or pale. It was very much alive. And his hair, it was a vivid black, the shade of midnight skies. The shade of Raphael's hair.

"It happened today." The Primary lifted up his hand to stare at the back of it. "I have not been in full color for . . ." A tilt of his head. "For endless eons. Since the last *aeclari*."

"Are your brethren the same?" If her archangel was disturbed by the strange echo of his coloring, he didn't show it.

The Primary took time to answer. "They are themselves. Only the Primary is of the *aeclari*." His dark pupils suddenly bled outward in waves of silver. Until the silver met the blue and the two merged, with the blue flowing into the silver at the edges. The pupils re-emerged from the silver-blue sea.

Elena put her hands on her hips. *Eerie but pretty.*

Look at his wings.

Elena hadn't paid much attention to the Primary's bat-like wings—the wings of the Legion never seemed to change. Apparently, that rule was now over and done with, because the Primary's formerly gray wings boasted a rim of white-gold that brushed inward into a vivid purple before fading into gray.

"You have pieces of both of us," Raphael said.

"We glimpsed the mirror and the mirror changed us." The Primary went down on one knee. "I come to offer the sire the power that is his. Today, you took only a percentage and returned the overflow to us."

"You told us once that if Raphael took the power, you'd have the choice to stay in the world as separate beings, or return to the deep," Elena said. "Is that still true?"

A small hesitation. "Things have altered. We feel the dark energies rising and rising. We wish to give you not just the power we hold for you, but the power that makes us."

Elena's heart iced.

Raphael's wings brushed hers as he spread them out, her lightning dancing over his feathers before returning to her. "What will that mean for you?"

"We do not know. We may die," the Primary said with no indication of fear or anguish. "We may return to the deep to begin again."

The idea of a city without the Legion's crouching presence, their green home abandoned and empty, was anathema to Elena. Her heart rebelled so hard against the idea of it that she couldn't speak.

"At this moment, I do not need any of the power," Raphael said. "I would rather have my Legion present and at full strength. A battle is brewing and I will need as many experienced fighters as I can gather."

The Primary rose to his feet. "The last *aeclari* were not like you." He seemed to be struggling to untangle memories so old they were beyond time. "You are . . . new. You . . . break patterns."

"Good. It's probably why I'm not a chrysalis battery and Raphael hasn't turned into a cold-hearted villain." She was fucking proud of her archangel for making the choice he'd just made—especially when she felt the chill of the Cascade power continue to roil in his blood. He'd gained considerable control over it, but it took a fierce will not to listen to its sinister promises.

Lijuan had listened. And now Lijuan was a monstrous power that might rule all the world. Being good, being honorable, didn't seem to come with any prizes in this immortal fight to the death.

Arms folded, Elena glared out at the sky. "I don't know what the fuck the Cascade wants."

"To rebalance the world," the Primary said, as if that was self-evident.

When they both stared at him, he stared back for a long moment as whispered voices built in the back of Elena's head. The Legion, talking among themselves.

"We have remembered," the Primary said. "We do not know from when. We do not know from who."

That was a reasonable enough statement given their age and how many memories they carried in their minds.

"Tell us," Raphael ordered.

The Primary took his time to speak, a being so ancient that he had been present at the first end and the second beginning of angelkind. "Power grows. Archangels grow. A balancing is needed to keep the world from breaking."

Elena scowled. "Hold up. This whole power surge thing is part of the Cascade. I don't know about you, but looks to me like it's the Cascade doing the breaking."

Cassandra's owls flew past the balcony on snowy wings, their silent beauty catching all their attention for a moment before they flew out of sight. "It is a paradox," the Primary admitted, then seemed to struggle to find words. "Too many Sleepers. Too much stored power. The earth groans. It must be released."

A susurration of sound, Raphael settling his wings . . . a sound her own wings would never again make. The stab of sadness was unexpected and visceral. Swallowing hard against it, Elena reminded herself that she had fucking *retractable* wings like a comic book superhero. Not only that, her wings were afire with lightning.

Her archangel spoke into the small silence. "The Cascade is triggered when the gathered power of the Sleepers in the world reaches a certain threshold?"

Voices in the back of Elena's head again, the Legion engaging in a furious discussion before the Primary nodded. "Wind, rain, tremors, ice, it is a release."

"Like a volcano letting off a bit of steam." Elena tapped her boot on the ground. "Of course, then the top blows off and everyone dies."

"Yes," the Primary said. "This time, the top will blow. Balance will be found again."

Elena and Raphael asked him more questions, but that was all he had to give them. "Unbelievably, that all made sense," she said to Raphael as they got ready for bed. "I mean, in a race of immortals where some of you continue to grow in power, things are going to get out of control without an inbuilt safety switch."

"Especially when those of us with the most power are all but impossible to kill." Bare chested and barefoot, Raphael walked to stand by the open balcony door, staring out at the night. "Leave us to continue on that trajectory unchecked and we will eventually become world-destroying powers who will annihilate each other."

Admiring him as she walked closer, Elena kissed his spine, right between where his wings grew out of his back. "I don't like where this is going."

"But I think we must confront it. The only way for power to be released back into the system, and for things to come back in balance, is for some of us to die." That was what Raphael hadn't realized for so long—as Elena had said, a race of immortals couldn't keep going forever without consequences. "And the only way for an archangel to die . . ."

". . . is at the hands of another archangel." Elena shifted to face him, her back against the night. "Fucking Cascade's setting up an immortal fight club?" Fury vibrated in her voice. "But what does it get if Lijuan wins and all the rest of you are dead?"

"Think of how much power the deaths of the Cadre and the Ancients will release back into the system." Wave after wave after shocking wave. "It explains why we do not have legends of more archangelic Sleepers. For a race of immortals, we appear to have lost countless prior Cadre without a trace."

"Wait. Wait." Elena rubbed her forehead. "What happens to all the Cascade 'gifts' afterward? Your wildfire, Titus's earthquakes, everything else. Your mother lived through a Cascade and she's not mega-powerful." She paused, squeezed her eyes shut for a second as she fought to get her thoughts in order. "Well, she *is* because she took an entire city with her into Sleep and now protects Amanat with a shield, but she doesn't have a crazy-violent offensive power. Same with Alexander."

"Hers was a 'normal' Cascade." He cupped the side of her neck, stroking his thumb over the delicate skin there. "Yet the question remains. Perhaps the Legion know."

But the Legion had no more answers for them. *We Slept after the Cascade of Terror. Such a deep Sleep that when we woke, none of the old archangels walked the world.*

Elena ran her hands over his chest. "Guess we'll find the answer after we kick Lijuan's butt." But in her eyes was the same dark knowledge that haunted him—that the wildfire hadn't been enough to save Antonicus.

Their only weapon against Lijuan's poison had failed.

47

Raphael was called into a Cadre meeting only three hours later.

Elena woke when he stirred, accompanied him down to the meeting space after pulling on some sweats. Raphael, in contrast, wore his warrior leathers—conversations with the Cadre were never simple things, especially now. The man who'd held her tucked against his bare chest, his wing her blanket, had to give way to an archangel ready for war.

Neha was streaming live from the border with China. Bright sunlight glimmered off the roofs closest to the border . . . on Lijuan's side.

The fog was retreating.

"It's happening all around the territory," Neha said, her voice clipped and precise. "Lady Caliane, Michaela, Alexander, and I have had our squadrons running patrols near the border regions and they all report the same thing. The fog has begun to withdraw toward the center."

The image on the screen changed as the feed switched to a drone flying directly over a section now clear of fog. It showed the edges of a small village.

"A typical border village," Neha told them. "Mostly the

homes of off-duty soldiers. Lijuan and I never displayed enmity toward one another, but it'd be foolish of us not to have soldiers positioned along our borders."

Raphael, do you have soldiers along the border with Elijah?

Yes. As he has his on the other side.

Sometimes, she forgot how many layers there were to the relationships between archangels. Friendship, when it came, was a long and complicated process.

"The homes are empty," Neha continued as the drone scanned the eerily motionless area; not even a tumbleweed blew in the wind. "She must've recalled her soldiers to a central location. Unexpected since she knows I have a strong force of my own, but as I said, Lijuan and I have never gone to war."

Michaela broke in, her voice sharp. "Where are the wives, husbands, lovers, children, servants, pets? This was not a garrison. It was home."

Elena's skin chilled. She stared again at the scene unfolding in front of them. Absolute and utter stillness. A village utterly abandoned. No sense of life at all.

"It's possible she called entire families back to a base command," Titus said, his voice far more somber and quiet than was Titus's normal.

"Possible, but unlikely." Charisemnon curled his lip. "She was my ally, but I do not wear rose-colored glasses when it comes to her. Lijuan wouldn't care about pets and mortal servants. They should be present."

"We need more information." Elijah sounded like the general he'd once been. "An abandoned border village can be explained as a strategic retreat. The animals could've run away disoriented during the fog."

"Eli is right." Raphael's tone was calm, measured . . . but wildfire arced across his fingers out of sight of the screen. "Is it possible to switch views?"

"Yes," Neha confirmed. "However, the border views all show the same thing. We will have to wait until the fog retreats farther inland."

No one spoke in the interim.

The first person to appear in the footage did so on a square rooftop like the ones Elena had seen in India while on a hunt.

She'd slept on a roof like that herself during the heat of summer and for a second, she thought they'd intruded on a poor schmuck who was trying to get some shut-eye under the weird fog night. Though it had to be freezing up there—roof sleeping wasn't a winter activity and the fog must've caused temperatures to drop even further.

Then the drone flew closer.

Her stomach lurched.

The man who lay under the thin sheet was a husk. His skin was dark brown parchment over wide cheekbones and hollow cheeks, his eye sockets sunken black shells, his hair strands of dried-out grass that would blow away in the next wind.

The fog continued to retreat.

The bodies came faster now. Fallen in the streets, more lying on rooftops, several just sitting under a tree. People who had no horror on their faces. People who'd simply been going about their lives when a dark goddess sucked that life out of them.

Elena caught the edge of what looked to be a homemade children's playground created from bamboo stakes and ropes and old tire swings. She wanted to look away, her gorge rising, but forced herself to stand in place. She would bear witness. She would remember.

There were no bodies. *None.*

A cold wind across her skin. *Raphael, where are the children?* They hadn't seen a single living *or* dead child.

I fear the answer, Guild Hunter.

So did Elena, the claw of fear a vicious grip around her heart.

The fog stopped retreating.

They waited for ten minutes, but the barrier had settled at a new point and there it remained. Neha's drone pilots began to explore the exposed areas in more depth: mummified bodies inside the homes, both human and animal, everything desiccated. Plants, food, even a large spider that hung in the corner of one house.

Neha directed one of the drone operators to use the drone to touch the shriveled corpse of what might've been a cat. It collapsed into dust at first contact.

"Abandon that device in Lijuan's territory once we're done," Neha commanded. "In fact, land all the devices on Lijuan's side of the border. We will fly them again from that point. If their energy fails, we will send out new devices. I do not wish anything from that territory to come into mine."

Elena didn't blame the Archangel of India. She had no idea how Neha had managed to stay so cool-eyed and rational. Having that nightmare at your border had to be fucking terrifying. At least Michaela was buffered by a massive expanse of relatively uninhabited territory in Mongolia—in the last balancing of territories, the country had been split between Lijuan and Michaela, and the residents had mostly moved either into China or into Russia.

Alexander also shared a massive border with China, but his people, too, tended to live more inward from the border, for much the same reason. Better to be closer to your archangel and distant from a neighboring one seemed to be the thinking. Neha alone had a border with China that was inhabited—likely as a result of the long-term friendly relationship between the two archangels.

The population there wasn't heavy, but it wasn't miniscule, either.

"She's feeding again." Raphael's voice, cold and remote in a way that raised the tiny hairs on her nape . . . but the wildfire, it continued to dance over his fingers. "And, given the depth of land exposed by the retreating fog, she is already monstrous in her power."

Thousands of people, Elena realized, Lijuan had already fed from *thousands*. Maybe tens of thousands if some of the other border areas had been more heavily populated. Ports, she thought suddenly, China's oceanic borders were home to thriving port cities . . . so much life, so much fuel for Lijuan.

Horror was an acidic taste on her tongue. *Raphael, she only fed on a few people when in New York and she was nearly unbeatable.* It was stating the obvious but she *had* to state it, had to get the horror out of her head.

At least we have warning. He held out his hand, an act he never did when speaking to the Cadre.

Wildfire arced between them as she slid her hand into his, and it was cold, *so* cold. She tightened her grip, set her jaw, and accepted it. Accepted him. Raphael sucked in a small breath at the same time. His skin warmed, his wing brushing across the lightning storm of her own.

On another screen, she saw Elijah turn to drop a kiss on Hannah's black curls as she, too, came to stand next to her archangel. Unlike Elena's hand-combed locks and old Guild sweatshirt, Hannah wore an elegant green-striped blue gown and her hair was braided in a complicated and lovely pattern twined with thick golden threads.

Dismay was a heavy darkness on the face of the only other—living—consort in the Cadre. That was when it struck her: *Is the Hummingbird Aegaeon's consort?*

No. Raphael's grip grew stronger, his voice a whip. *The arrogant fool never understood the treasure he'd been offered.*

"Lady Caliane?"

Caliane nodded at Neha's query. "Tasha's squadron is on the deck of a ship I ordered moved near a port border and their drone machines are about to reach land. Ah, to be young and to quickly comprehend a new world." A turn of her head. "Avi, we wish to see through the eyes of the machines."

The feed cut into static before it switched to an oceanside view. Water lapping against a shore, ships raised up on blocks in a nearby yard, in the process of repair. Nets crumpled on the sand. Baskets piled up on a dock where a small-time fisherman might pick them up to throw back onto a boat.

A view shift to a different drone. Elena clenched her gut. What they'd just seen had been nothing but the tiniest edge of a huge port. Hundreds of containers sat ready to be loaded onto massive ships that sat waiting in the deep water against which the port had been constructed. Large fishing trawlers sat alongside the container ships. Cranes arched overhead, all of them motionless and silent in the sunlight.

No forklifts or other vehicles moved in the container area, industrious ants going about their business. Day or night, no major port was ever this quiet. *Someone* was always coming in or shipping out.

The drone pilot flew deeper into the city.

The only sounds picked up by the drone's systems were the lap of the waves and a dull banging that sounded as if a loose piece of wood was whacking up against the metal side of a ship.

The drone zeroed in on a large warehouse emblazoned with Chinese characters. It had huge openings on either side where roller doors had been pulled up.

It is the fish market such as on our own port, Raphael translated silently for her.

The noisy, busy place where restauranteurs and shopkeepers came early in the day to bid on fish auctions and haggle over the freshest catch. Of course, a few other locals always wandered in, too—you could often get the "leftovers" for trade prices.

The drone flew inside the market.

Bodies lay everywhere. Behind the large display counters full of a mix of rotting and desiccated fish, in the wide aisles, near pallets stacked with boxes ready for the refrigerated trucks that had to be waiting out back, under a massive central scale the market must've used for its showier auctions.

Unlike in the villages, these people had been afraid when they died.

Their corpses lay huddled against walls or curled up in balls on the floor, arms around one another and faces contorted.

Elena didn't realize she was crying until the wet streaked her cheeks. She let the tears fall—some things were beyond politics or games of power. The desiccated body of a small dog lay cradled in the lap of a woman hunched protectively over her pet. A woman's mouth was open in a scream as she reached out a hand in a futile cry for help.

Elena dashed away her tears. "Go back there."

Caliane didn't hesitate to give the drone operator the order despite the abrupt way Elena had made her demand. "What do you see with your hunter's eyes, Consort?"

"That woman"—Elena's face burned hot, then cold—"she's wearing a baby carrier. The ones mortals and young vampires wear in the front so the baby can be up against their heart."

The drone operator zoomed in on Caliane's orders, but there was no dead child in the carrier. The woman's outstretched hand took on a terrible new meaning.

"They stole her child." Michaela's voice, tight with rage.

The drone flew out of the market. Its mechanical eye soon discovered haunting evidence of more lost children: abandoned marbles outside a shop, a rattle lying on the street, balls sitting in gutters, a small and sparkly shoe drowning in a puddle, a schoolbag dropped on the ground.

Then the drones hit what should've been a heavily populated port city.
Silence.
Corpses.
A reign of death.

48

Elena felt as if she'd aged five hundred years by the time Neha and Caliane told the drone operators to stand down.

"We can do nothing at this instant," Caliane said at last, lines of sorrow carved into her features. "Lijuan remains within her borders and we have no way to penetrate the fog."

"We wait," was the consensus.

Elena managed to keep her silence until the Cadre was gone from the room. "How can you all still say she has a right to her territory! Look at what she's done!" Her voice shook, her muscles bunched.

"These are our laws, Elena." Raphael's jaw as hard as stone, his eyes metallic in their remoteness. "Else war would be a constant and the world awash in blood."

Giving a scream, Elena turned and kicked a wall. "Titus and Charisemnon have been fighting forever! And we hunted Uram!"

"A conflict between two archangels is a far different thing from the Cadre interceding in another territory." Lightning cracked his skin, but his eyes were frost. "Uram broke a far more fundamental law prior to the hunt order being decided, you know this. That law stands above all others but it does not apply here. Lijuan's madness is not the kind for which it was written."

She knew he was right. That just made it worse. No matter how ugly and awful an atrocity Lijuan had committed, if the rest of the Cadre breached her borders in a martial strike, they permanently destabilized the world's power structure. Once an archangel was assigned a territory, it was theirs to rule as they saw fit.

No exceptions but for the one that had tripped up Uram.

As long as Lijuan kept her evil confined to her territory, the Cadre couldn't touch her without throwing open a door that could never again be closed. Because what had been done once, *even if* done under exigent circumstances, could be done again and again—no archangel could ever again be sure of their status so all would make war to hold on to their right to rule.

"You know mortals are the losers when archangels battle." Steel edged Raphael's voice. "It would be their annihilation."

She stalked back to him. "Do you think I'm mad at you? Argh!" Gripping his hair in her fists, she rose up to kiss him hard and deep before stalking back to kick the wall again. "I'm mad at Lijuan. If she'd been content with the biggest fucking territory in the world, we wouldn't be looking at mummified bodies and hunting for lost babies."

"I would argue that, if the Primary is correct about the trigger for the Cascade, it may have all ended up this way regardless." Raphael's hair mussed from her fingers, his lips wet from her kiss. "It could've been Uram had he managed to keep his blood treachery hidden."

Elena thought of the naked, violated bodies the dead archangel had discarded like trash, the amputated limbs inserted into the wrong places, the glistening eyeballs held in cupped hands, and shoved a fisted hand against her gut. "Or Charisemnon."

"Disease run rampant." Raphael nodded. "Yes, the Cascade would've found a receptive mind one way or another." Eyes of Prussian blue, violent in their purity, locked with her own. "Before you, it could have been me."

She thought of the cold archangel who'd made her close her hand over a blade, watched her blood drip to the floor, an archangel who'd seen mortals as nothing but pawns to be used and forgotten, and swallowed hard.

"It is a terrifying thing to consider, is it not? We all have a monster inside us Elena, each and every archangel in the world. It is the flip side to such blinding power." He backed her up against the wall, his hands braced on either side of her head. He was big, had always been big, but it was only at times like this that she really became aware of it—became aware that he was deadly strong, *far* stronger than her.

But their relationship wasn't built on such basic lines. "You never broke me even when you could." She wasn't about to allow him to believe such dark lies about himself because toxic seeds took root and dug in. "A pet hunter would've been far more convenient for you, but you didn't steal my mind."

"I played with you as a cat does with a mouse."

"This mouse has claws, in case you've forgotten." She had a blade at his jugular before he realized it—wearing sweats or not, she never went anywhere without a knife or ten. "I'm the one who shot you, hurt you."

A slow blink . . . followed by a smile so devastating that it knocked the air right out of her. "I concede this round, Guild Hunter."

Slipping away the blade, Elena knew the battle was far from over. They'd be dealing with it for eons yet. Both of Raphael's parents had gone mad. It wasn't an easy history to bear. "Smart man."

Raphael pushed off the wall, stripped to the waist, then kicked off his boots; neither of them had bothered to put on socks. "I think it is time we sparred again."

Blood heating, Elena nonetheless raised an eyebrow. "Around all this ridiculously expensive equipment?"

A shrug. "We will make it a rule. Any equipment damage is an automatic forfeit requiring the loss of a piece of clothing."

The man was only wearing pants.

Her breasts swelled; her clitoris damn near did the foxtrot. "You sure know how to talk dirty to me, Archangel." Toeing off her trainers, she got into a ready position opposite him. "Walls, floor, ceiling don't count," she added. "Only equipment."

"Accepted." He followed her subtle movements as she dropped a blade into her hand. They'd worked out the rules long ago—she got whatever weapons she wanted while he

remained bare-handed. It was the only way to fight an archangel.

"A little hesitant today, *hbeebti*?"

"Keep up the trash talk and see how many holes I poke in
you." She threw a blade with pinpoint accuracy but he evaded
it with flawless effort and it slammed home in the opposite
wall, an inch away from a communication screen. Raphael
lunged to grab her arm in the same movement, but she was
already dancing out of the way.

In the process, she knocked over a small thingamajig. She
didn't know what it did but it had lots of blinking lights. Or had
until her unfortunate contact. "Shit." Stripping off her sweatshirt to Raphael's slow smile, she threw it in the corner with her
trainers. Now she was down to her tank top and sweatpants.

Panties hadn't seemed important at the time.

"Go," she said, to restart the bout.

The damn sneaky archangel made a move that meant she
had to throw a blade or get taken down hard. The blade ended
up quivering in a communication screen. The one that had
recently held Charisemnon's face. She felt a momentary
pleasure in that before her archangel lifted his hands, palms
up. "Rules are rules."

Elena narrowed her eyes. "You don't want to win. You just
want me to fight you naked."

A slow, so slow smile that had her going slick between the
thighs. "Off." A nod at her tank top.

Not about to go down easy, Elena smiled and took off her
sweatpants instead. Her loose sleep tank *just* brushed the top
of her thighs. Raphael's abdomen tightened, all rippling
muscle she wanted to lick, his arousal rigid against his pants.
"Go," she murmured while he was still distracted . . . but her
archangel obviously had priorities that involved getting her
bare ass naked.

He spun toward her without warning, coming at a speed no
one could avoid . . . except Elena did. One minute she was
right in his path, the only way to evade him to go low and attempt to sweep out his wings, and the next, she was two feet
to the left.

They both froze. Stared.

Elena blinked. "Did you see that?"

"More to the point, I *didn't* see it." Raphael lunged toward her again, at the same speed.

Elena found herself crouching on the top of an equipment dolly, like a damn *mostly naked* bat. She fell off the instant she realized what she was doing. "Ouch," she said when she landed on the carpet, her wings crackling with lightning on either side of her.

Coming around the dolly to look down at her, Raphael kicked up his lips. "Did you know your favorite tank is so old it's transparent?" He held out a hand.

Taking it, she hauled him down on top of her instead of letting him haul her up. She succeeded because she'd hooked her foot around his ankle at the same time. He caught himself on his hands before he crushed her.

"I could break your bones." A dark scowl, but the heat of him was a kiss all over her aroused body.

"Nah. Your reflexes are too fast." She pressed a wet kiss to his pectoral muscle and that quickly, it wasn't about play anymore—if it had ever been. "I want you. I *need* you." It was a painful ache within, below the momentary amusement of their sparring session. "Everything else can wait."

His wings began to glow. His kiss was pure raw sex, the hand he thrust under her tank possessive and rough on her breast. Elena licked her tongue against his even as she tugged apart the closures on his pants. She wanted his cock inside her, wanted to close herself around him, wanted to reaffirm the beauty of life after all the death, all the evil.

Shoving up one of her thighs the instant she'd freed the thickness of him, he thrust into her while looking into her eyes. Her back arched, her hands gripping at his body, and her eyes never leaving his. Wrapping her other leg around his waist, she held him tight as he pounded her into the carpet, each stroke hard and deep and relentless.

It wasn't gentle. It wasn't distant. It wasn't the least bit cold.

Sweat slicked their bodies. His throat tasted of salt and Raphael. His groan as he drove deep into her before his body stiffened was nothing eerie or strange. It was life stripped to the core. As was the way her inner muscles clenched convulsively around him as he began to orgasm, the muscles of his body beautiful under the shimmer of sweat.

Pleasure wrecked her.

He collapsed on her afterward, his breath hot against her neck and his body heavy. She could barely breathe, but who cared about that when Raphael was stroking the side of her body and moving slightly in her as they both rode out the aftershocks. "I think I have carpet burn on my butt," she said when she could speak again.

His shoulders shook under her hands.

And for a few more stolen seconds, they didn't think about Lijuan or death or the fact Elena had become faster than an archangel.

49

A one-minute shower to hide evidence of their quickie from the smartasses in the Tower, a change into proper sparring clothes, then they went down to the large windowless training ring on a lower floor. "Vivek set up a recording system here for if we want to play back certain moves, figure out weaknesses." She made her way to the control box and started the system. "I want proof."

The two of them began as usual, but every so often, Raphael would rush her at full archangelic speed. Her body reacted to get her out of the way the first five times. The sixth time, he'd have smashed her into a wall if he hadn't pulled himself up.

No matter how many times they tried after that, it didn't work.

"Seven times," Elena said, her hands on her knees and her exercise tank plastered to her body—though the stormfire of her wings never faded. "I can do it seven times in a row before it fails."

"The problem is that you can't control when it happens."

"Yep, I don't feel anything. I just go poof." She put her hands on her hips. "Let's invite the others to watch the footage with us." Their senior people needed to know how she might react if startled in battle. The idea of just disappearing and dropping a fellow fighter in the shit made her grind her teeth, but at this point, all she could do was warn them it might happen.

"First, you need more sleep," Raphael said. "This can wait a few hours."

Illium, Dmitri, Janvier, Ashwini, and Honor proved to be in the Tower when she woke. Raphael met her in the training room and they viewed the footage again before asking the others to join them.

Elena was the one who located Honor—the other woman wasn't far, had just finished up a session with Suyin in a smaller training area. As always when Elena ran into the architect, she felt a visceral punch. The shining hair of ice white, the sharp cheekbones, the striking upward tilt of her eyes, Suyin could've been Lijuan in another life.

Except that Suyin's gaze held a bruised pain Lijuan would never comprehend. "Ellie," she said with a soft smile that didn't banish the sadness that shadowed her.

Elena fought the urge to hug her. Suyin was an intensely private angel, her grief and pain contained and held tight. "You're a lot better than the last time I saw you." The woman responsible for some of the greatest architecture in angelkind had the type of instinctive understanding of movement that made for gifted athletes and dancers.

"You are kind." Suyin's age pressed against Elena's skin with a power that was uncommon; it always made Elena wonder if Lijuan had tortured and imprisoned her niece not only because Suyin knew the secrets of Lijuan's stronghold, but because she'd seen Suyin as a possible rival.

"I know I have a long way to go." Suyin's voice was a haunting melody, her accent that of an old being speaking a new tongue. "As part of that, I must now do flight drills with Jurgen's squadron."

"She's learned to fight and she's good at it," Honor murmured as she followed Elena down the hallway after Suyin had left. "But she'll never be a warrior. It's not in her nature."

Elena thought of Astaad. The Archangel of the Pacific Isles preferred literature over swords, would rather debate a point than start a war, but pushed to the wall, he'd push back as hard.

"For Suyin," Honor continued, "it's about never being helpless again when evil rises."

Then they were at the large training ring, and everyone was soon watching the footage. No one spoke at the first viewing. Illium slowed down the playback for the second viewing and one thing became clear. "You're not disappearing and reappearing, Ellie. Your wings are morphing to white fire and you're moving at a speed invisible to the naked eye."

Thanks for the chunk of your heart, Archangel.

You are most welcome, hbeebti.

"I know you flew at impossible speed once." Dmitri, arms folded, looked to Raphael. "That day Elena collapsed. That wasn't just the white fire wings. It was more."

"I did it another time—again, when Elena was at risk." Raphael frowned, as lightning cracked his arms. "That level of speed, it appears, is also triggered unconsciously."

"So Elena's not doing anything new," Dmitri pointed out. "She's doing exactly what you do, but in microbursts. Seven microbursts to be precise."

Elena didn't like where this was going. "I seem to have stolen a little of your Cascade-given abilities." And he'd need everything he had when Lijuan picked a fight. Because the Queen of the Dead would, of that Elena had zero doubts.

"I am yours, Guild Hunter." No hesitation, nothing but a sense of love so deep it was her bedrock. "I would give you every drop of blood in my body did you have a need."

"It's all right," Ashwini said breezily while looking down at her phone, her hair up in a long ponytail and her lipstick a dark fuchsia "You're mirrors anyway."

Everyone stared at her, but she was involved in tapping out a message.

An amused Janvier gently flicked one of her dangling earrings. *"Cher."*

"Hmm?" She slid away her phone and seemed to notice all the eyes on her for the first time. "Sorry, that was Sara about a hunt. She wanted to know if I could take it—I said I could, since we're pretty much done here?"

"Ash," Elena said very deliberately, "what do you mean about mirrors?"

"Huh?" The other hunter frowned. "Oh, that." A shrug. "No idea. Sometimes words just fall out of my mouth."

Elena knew there was no point pushing her. The last time words had fallen out of Ashwini's mouth, they'd had a geothermal event in upstate New York. "Can you keep your senses trained for any other hints on the whole mirror thing?"

Ashwini nodded, but Elena knew that there would be no quick answers. And they needed those quick answers— because the situation in China was getting worse. That night, they received a dispatch from Neha that said the fog had drawn farther back to reveal even more death—and more signs of missing children.

After that, the report that Cassandra's lava sinkhole had opened up again was almost good news. There'd been no earthquake, no bird murmurations. A passing squadron had stumbled upon the glowing hole in the snow on their way home, the orange-red of the lava a jewel in a bed of white.

"There will be a war," Raphael said to her as they stood inside the fence, beside the heat of the sinkhole, while the snow drifted down in delicate flakes. "This cannot end any other way—Lijuan is not gorging herself for pleasure. Even if we disregard her, there are too many archangels awake and now Cassandra stirs."

His eyes glowed with the reflected heat of the lava. "Our energies will begin to collide. It is a law of nature, cannot be stopped."

"Do you think Lijuan will come here?" The Archangel of China was obsessed with eliminating Raphael. He was the only one who'd ever hurt her, and appeared to remain the only one who had a weapon even slightly effective against her.

"If she does, the Cadre is agreed that all will come here to help defend the city." He looked up at the moonless sky. "They know that if I fall, so do they and Lijuan's dark night will spread across the entire world."

Elena crouched down to stare at the lava moving languorously below. "Same deal if she targets another territory?"

"Yes. It doesn't matter who she attacks, she is a threat to us all."

A golden-eyed owl swept over the lava . . . and in Elena's mind stirred an *old* presence heavy and tired. *Child of mor-*

tals, Cassandra murmured. *Watch the Sea of Atlas. Death comes.*

Cassandra?

But the Ancient was gone.

A stone on her chest, she rose to her feet and told Raphael what the Ancient had said. "I don't know what Sea of Atlas means."

His already grim expression grew lethal. "It is an old name for the Atlantic. I have squadrons patrolling that and every other border and we now have eyes in the sky."

"What if she's figured out a way to make her entire army noncorporeal?" Elena's mouth dried up. "All those dead, all that power she's sucked up . . . What if it's about hiding her assault force?"

"If she can do that, then she has won the war before it begins."

The next day dawned with no sign of a threat on the horizon, but Raphael took Cassandra's warning seriously: he ordered extra watches in the east, on water and in the sky. He'd just finished reviewing their overall border strategy with Dmitri when Neha called another meeting of the Cadre.

Things had changed in China.

"We have begun to see live people beneath the retreating fog," reported the Archangel of India before she switched to the feed from a drone.

Thin people with shocked faces stumbled around the mummified remains that littered the streets. Horror scarred the expressions of many, while others were blank-eyed and lost.

It was Elijah who pointed out that all the survivors were young and—aside from their low weights—healthy. "The women are of childbearing age, the men young enough to help raise those children."

"She has left enough survivors to repopulate her country," Caliane murmured. "If this is madness, it is a cunning one."

And still, they didn't know what had happened to the children.

The fog over China disappeared the next day. Gone without a trace in a matter of seconds. Drone flights over the core of the country discovered several still-living cities . . . but with much smaller populations.

There was just one problem—the warriors, the fighters, were dangerously limited in number. Nothing with which an archangel could hope to defend her territory.

"She knows no one will dare enter," Alexander bit out. "Not with the death she left on the borders and what happened to Favashi and Antonicus—the threat of a contagion is too great."

"Your borders?" Astaad asked the impacted archangels. "Your people are safe?"

Neha was the one who replied. "Yes. If it was airborne, it was confined inside the fog." Her jaw worked. "I have been unable to contact any of mine who were helping to caretake the country."

"I have also lost people." Raphael's anger was a cold, hard thing. "Have any of you managed to initiate communication with your own inside Lijuan's territory?"

Silence.

So many strong angels gone. It was a catastrophic loss if you considered the angelic birth rate and how many of those warriors had been highly experienced.

"She has begun the war then." Alexander, his voice razored. "To kill so many of our own when they were placed in China by the Cadre and would've stepped down at her return, it is a declaration of war."

Raphael's hand fisted as he thought of Gadriel. The angel had taught four-hundred-year-old Raphael how to use a battle axe, his calm, unflappable patience undaunted in the face of the anger Raphael carried within. All that maturity, all that life just gone, destroyed so totally that his parents wouldn't even have a body to bury. "I am in agreement with Alexander. This is war."

No one in angelkind would argue against the Cadre's decision—the terrible loss of mortal and vampiric lives had already begun to make an impact. Immortals weren't without soul, couldn't just shrug off mortal deaths on such a scale. But the angelic lives lost? It would hammer home the final terrible blow.

"We will not get to pick the field of battle." Caliane, her eyes blue fire. "She has poisoned her land to ensure we cannot invade it. Her next act will be to choose where she makes her stand. Prepare for war."

50

Guild Hunter, Raphael said early afternoon the next day, the bite of winter welcome on his bare arms; he'd chosen to pair a sleeveless white tunic with the deep brown of his tough but battle-scarred pants and equally marked black boots. *I am flying out to the lava. Venom's reported unusual movement.*

Wait for me. I just got back from a hand-to-hand combat session with Eve.

Already on the Tower roof, Raphael waited until he saw wings of stormfire take off from one of the balconies before he swept out into the sky. And though he'd said nothing to alert her of his presence, she looked up.

"How is your sister?" he asked once they were at the same altitude.

"Still a little mad at me, but we'll be good I think." Solemn eyes searched his face. "Jason have any luck?"

"No." His spymaster had refused to believe all their people—all *Jason's* people—had been murdered so callously. "Not a word, not even from a minor spy in the kitchens." A vampire so insignificant in the grand scheme of things that it would've cost Lijuan nothing to allow him to live.

"Damn her."

Raphael was silent, his anger a black wave.

They flew on until the lava glowed orange in a sea of white.

Venom watched them land with his gaze shielded against the bright snow-reflected light. Slitted like a viper's and of the same vivid green shade, the vampire's eyes had been known to inspire fear and fascination both—often in the same individual.

"Sire, Elena." He motioned his head toward the lava sink-hole, the fine wool of his olive green sweater hugging his shoulders and his legs clad in black cargo pants, his boots scuffed. "It's begun to bubble. The odd one at first, steady increase over the past hour."

Though he and Elena had seen the bubbles from above, his consort pressed her face to one of the windows in the fence. "I can't hear her but she has to be close to—"

A rush of voices inside Raphael's head. Elena winced at the same time.

Aeclari. We relay for the Blade. He says these words: Inexplicable oceanic disturbance an hour out from Manhattan to the east.

Raphael felt no surprise, only a cold determination. "Head to the city," he ordered Venom. "The enemy may be at our doorstep."

Elena rose into the air with him as Venom ran to his Bugatti—parked in the snow like a crouching tiger.

Go! Elena said. *Do the white fire thing. I'll follow.*

Lijuan may have already managed to steal into our city in her noncorporeal state. Leaving Elena alone under those circumstances was not a thing he would ever countenance. *I will fly us both.* Sweeping below her, he held out his arms.

She retracted her wings and dropped.

He caught her, thought of white fire, and suddenly, his wings were nothing physical, the world a blur. As he flew, he contacted Dmitri and got the exact direction from his second. He and Elena were soon over the water; he slowed as they neared the suspect location.

"There!" His hunter pointed down.

The water surged and flowed in a way that spoke of a large body beneath.

Releasing Elena from his arms with a mental warning, her

wings erupting out of her back to hold her to a hover, Raphael narrowed his eyes and shot a bolt of power in the center of the suspicious area.

The bolt hit something *before* it reached the water. The resulting explosion sent large pieces of metal flying in every direction.

"That was a submarine!" Elena, crossbow out, pointed at a distinctive floating piece. "When did she get a fucking *submarine*?"

"I would assume she's been gathering weapons and tools since the last battle."

No bodies floated up from below. Raphael hadn't held back with that blow; the bodies were apt to have disintegrated into tiny pieces. Neither did he hold back with the balls of wildfire he sent into the sky—one east, one west, one south, one north. Each detonated to cover a massive area.

Screams breached the air before the sky rippled . . . to reveal a winged army. It was shaped into a vee, with the thin point manned by Xi, Lijuan's most trusted general, and the wide end so far distant that Raphael couldn't see the end of it.

That's not an army, it's a fucking continent. Elena's shocked voice, her crossbow cocked and ready.

She does not intend to lose this time. Lijuan had brought a force unseen in angelic history, a force so huge that Raphael couldn't comprehend how it had been built without anyone's knowledge.

We have to retreat. Choppy strands of Elena's hair whipped around her face. *She holds all the advantages here.*

Agreed. Raphael was no longer a boy, to be goaded into fighting without strategy or thought. *Come.*

Elena flew into his arms.

A massive mind smashed into Raphael's as he and Elena left the area on wings of white fire.

BOW DOWN! I AM DEATH. I AM YOUR QUEEN.

Shoving Lijuan out with the coldly vicious Cascade power that knew nothing of mercy, Raphael flew on. *Dmitri, the army should now be visible to the eyes in the sky.* He didn't think Lijuan would waste power keeping them hidden now that they'd been discovered—there was no reason for her to do so, not with so *many* squadrons at her disposal.

We have it. A pregnant pause. *Fucking hell, Raphael. Where did she get that many combatants?*

I have no answers. What he did know was that Manhattan had less than an hour to ready itself to face an enemy so vast no single archangel could've prepared for it. Raphael's entire army, an army spread across the territory, was less than one-tenth of that force.

Launch the battle plans, he ordered his second, for Raphael and his Seven hadn't sat on their laurels since Lijuan's first assault. *Initiate the first line of defense.*

Those defenses were not long-range missiles or bombs. To count, archangel to archangel battles had to be undertaken without large-scale weapons, including any that acquired their targets from afar. It was to protect the world from annihilation—because archangels could survive such violent weapons. It was everyone else who would die.

"At least Lijuan appears to be holding to the rules of war," Raphael said as they hit the edge of the city. "I saw no signs of advanced technology other than the submerged ships." As they'd been used for transport rather than as weapons, the subs were acceptable.

"Too bad," Elena muttered. "I wanted to use a long-range surface-to-air missile and blast off her face." She glanced up. "There they go."

Fire arced over their heads as they flew into the city, the archers who'd taken up position on the rooftops having found the weapons ready and waiting for them in Tower-branded steel boxes that had been positioned at key points throughout the city. The first wave of flaming arrows had no hope of reaching Lijuan's army.

The arrows were a warning . . . and a distraction.

Elena looked over his shoulder. "It's coming up," she murmured. "None of our vessels caught out as far as I can see. Dmitri must've hit the alert as soon as he spotted the disruption."

"Good." He did not want his own people trapped outside with the enemy when the fuel line they'd lain in the ocean went up in flame. That fuel line curved around all the oceanic routes to Manhattan—because it was always to Manhattan that Lijuan would return should she decide to declare war against Raphael.

Manhattan held his Tower. The symbol of his rule.

Destroy it and she struck a savage blow to his people's hearts.

At present, the fuel line was nothing but innocuous buoys of faded blue bobbing on the water. The entire line had been held firmly anchored to the ocean and river floors until Dmitri hit the switches to release them. It was the Legion who'd laid the line—it turned out that creatures who Slept in the deep for thousands of years didn't actually need to breathe.

Strands of Elena's hair kissed the side of his face. "How long do we wait?"

"Until her army is right over the fuel line." Because some of the enemy angels would be flying low—and the fireline was set to ignite in furious vertical blasts. An old technique from wars fought before Raphael was born.

"I hate the idea of crisping angels, but I know these ones want to kill and enslave us." Elena's eyes were resolute when they met his, silver bleeding into gray. "No mercy. Anyone with her has seen her true face, seen her murder and consume thousands, and *still* they choose to follow her."

"Should you falter, *hbeebti*, remember the lost children."

Cheekbones sharp against her skin, she said, "Let's kick her psychopathic ass."

He landed on the deserted Tower roof. Raphael's people would only retreat inward when there was no hope of holding the line—but, regardless, multiple steel boxes sat near the edges of the roof. Each was filled with short-range missiles, bows and arrows, crossbows and such other weapons as could be used with line-of-sight targeting.

The two of them made their way to the redesigned war room from where Dmitri ran battle operations. Where before the war room had been separate from the aerie, the two were now integrated. The entire floor was a single space with toughened mirrored glass on all sides, giving his second a three hundred and sixty degree view of the city.

To ensure Dmitri didn't need to walk around the floor to get that view, in the center of the space hovered a screen that curved fully around *in a single piece*. Dmitri could step below the screen, pull it down so it was at his eyeline, and see everything in a single rotation, zooming in and out as necessary.

Small apertures built into the glass walls could be opened at will to fire weapons directly from the war room. The space also boasted a large flat table to the left, on which Dmitri could run battle tactics as he preferred, as well as a full electronic hub to the right that would switch automatically to generators should the Tower's main power supply be cut.

"I called Lady Caliane," Dmitri said as they entered.

"Good." His mother would've already alerted the rest of the Cadre to head to New York.

But Dmitri shook his head, his expression as black as the tailored shirt he wore with the sleeves folded back. "There's a major problem in India." Walking them to the electronic hub, he pointed to a screen streaming images that had Raphael frowning, for what he saw wasn't a problem but a gift.

"The children." Hope lilted through Elena's voice. "Are they running across the bor—" Her voice broke off with a jagged edge at the same instant Raphael realized the sickening truth.

"Raphael, those children have fangs." Rigid spine, a white face.

51

Raphael knew his hunter could handle her rage. Today, he needed to look after someone else first. *Dmitri, you do not need to watch this.*

I'm dealing with it. A steady voice, though his second's expression was stone. *My Misha is safe from this hell and I like to think he got a second chance at life—as I did. But I would appreciate it if you kill the bitch stone-dead so she doesn't do this to any other child ever again.*

It is a promise, my friend. Raphael squeezed Dmitri's shoulder before looking back at the ugliness on the screen. "These children aren't simply vampires—they've been changed in a way akin to the reborn." Eyes reddened and flesh holding a greenish tinge that spoke of putrefaction, their locomotion a rapid crablike skitter, these innocents were already dead, reanimated only by Lijuan's power.

Elena's hand clenched around a knife blade. "Are they infectious?"

"Looks like it." Dmitri's voice held pure calm; Raphael's second had shut away his violent anger so he could function.

Raphael reached for Honor's mind. *I apologize for the intrusion.* He was not in the habit of making such contact with the wife of his closest friend. *Dmitri needs you. Come to the war room.*

Honor didn't have the ability to respond to him, but Raphael knew she would soon be here. Honor loved Dmitri as intensely as Ingrede once had. Ingrede had known a content mortal husband and father. Honor knew a deadly vampire with scars on his soul. Dmitri loved them both and always would.

"An entire group got through in the first wave," Dmitri was saying to Elena. "The fighters on duty froze."

"Like I did the last time, with the cruise ship passenger." Elena's voice was rough, her neck held stiffly. "Lijuan counted on people's abhorrence of harming children."

Closing his hand over her nape, Raphael massaged it gently. "How bad is it?" Children were *never* to be turned into vampires, much less such abominations as Lijuan had created. Each and every angel in the world would consider it their personal shame that such an atrocity had been committed.

"There are thousands of them—Lijuan must've had them lying silent and unmoving in the forests near the border, or in the basements of houses." Dmitri brought up another set of moving images that showed the children attacking vampiric ground troops and spitting up at angelic fighters who came too close.

None of the adults were doing anything but defending themselves.

"You are right—they spread disease." The spitting, the way the children attempted to claw anyone nearby, it was designed not to kill but to infect.

"That's from the initial invasion." Dmitri's attention shifted to over Raphael's shoulder, the ice of his calm cracking with a flex of his hand.

Not asking any questions, Honor went straight to her husband and wrapped her arms around him with ferocious tightness. Dmitri held her back as hard, his head bent so his cheek pressed to hers for a long, taut second.

Elena glanced up at Raphael, a painful comprehension in her eyes. *Dmitri intimated once that he'd been a father.*

He was beloved by his children. Little Misha had pelted down the pathway anytime he caught sight of his papa.

Swallowing hard, Elena said nothing further, honoring Raphael's loyalty to his friend.

In front of them, Dmitri and Honor separated—but Dmitri kept Honor's hand in his as he brought up another set of images. "This is the current feed."

Yellow and orange licked across the screen.

Neha's angelic squadrons were setting the border aflame. Several of the toughened warriors were crying. To execute a child even when that child had been made monstrous was no easy thing. Neha, too, was in the thick of battle, her face smudged with streaks of soot and sweat plastering her hair to her temples as she used her Cascade-born ability to create fire to speed up their efforts.

No tear tracks marked her face, but the Archangel of India was attempting to drive the children back into Lijuan's territory rather than ending their existence. Even the knowledge that those tiny bodies were rotting flesh held together by infection wasn't enough to stifle the primal rejection of killing a child.

A buzz, Dmitri glancing at his phone. "Rhys just confirmed Lady Caliane is assisting Neha."

Raphael's gut clenched. *My mother's revulsion against harming a child ever again is so strong she'll let them eat her alive before raising a hand to help herself.*

She understands the stakes. Elena shifted so that the side of her body brushed his. *We have to trust her not to surrender to her nightmares.*

Not certain his mother's mental state was strong enough, Raphael said, "Lijuan's eliminated both Neha and my mother from the fight." Neither could leave India lest it be overrun by the infected. Lijuan surely had more reborn hiding close by. The stronger adults would be the second wave, after the children traumatized and weakened the border guard.

"She's taken out Alexander and Michaela, too," said another familiar voice.

Raphael glanced over to the sharp-featured man with a muscular upper body who'd come up beside Dmitri in a manual wheelchair. Vivek Kapur passed across a sheet of paper, the dark brown of his skin shining with health. "Dispatch from the border with Persia. Reborn children pouring out there, too. Lijuan doesn't seem to have targeted the border with Michaela, but she's gone to assist Alexander."

"With their territories connected by land, she has no other choice." Should they fail to stop the scourge in Alexander's land, the infected would crawl unchecked across a vast geographic area. "Elijah?"

"No adverse reports at this point," Dmitri said. "No reports at all from the rest of the Cadre, but it hasn't been long since I fired off my message."

A whisper of black on the edge of Raphael's vision. "Jason," he said. "What have you heard?"

Breath a little jagged—highly unusual for Jason—his spymaster said, "I've just received a report from one of my people in Charisemnon's territory. Nests of reborn are breaking out all over his lands, killing and infecting and rampaging."

Honor spoke for the first time, her forehead wrinkled. "I thought the entire Cadre took precautions?"

"Lijuan's a smart operator." Dmitri stared unseeing at a blank screen. "I bet those reborn were smuggled in during her "Sleep" and someone's been feeding the fuckers in the interim."

"Those things feed on blood and living flesh." Elena's hand was bone white on the handle of her blade, her thigh pressed up against his and the stormfire of her wing tangled with his feathers. "And they can't make other reborn from nothing."

Raphael considered her point. "The keeper or keepers must've hunted locals with stealth over a long period, so the disappearances wouldn't be noticed."

Vivek Kapur had been bent over a tablet in his lap, now shook his head. "Article in not one but three *different* local papers report a rash of disappearances in their areas in the past month."

His fingers flew across the screen with nimble speed. "Looks like each set of disappearances was blamed on a different thing—a bloodlust-ridden vampire, a flash flood, a man-eating pride of lions. Can't find any articles that cross-link the three incidents."

A muscle ticked in Dmitri's jaw. "Someone hasn't been doing their job."

Because Dmitri would've noticed those disappearances and Raphael would've been informed of them. "So Charisemnon is out." The archangel would have to contain the reborn threat to the African continent before he could render any assistance. "And so is Titus." The two archangels were in no way allies, but this wasn't about their differences. It was about a world that would end them all.

Vampires couldn't feed on reborn. They needed mortals.

And the greatest secret of angelkind was that they needed mortals, too.

"She *knows* the danger, knows the reborn are a plague that could spread across the entire world," Elena said, blades in both her hands now, as if she would stab Lijuan in the heart right then and there. "What use is it being goddess of a dying world?"

"She'll have created a protected zone inside her territory," Raphael said, Lijuan's entire genocidal plan suddenly icily clear in his mind. "She intends to win the war, then kill the reborn, and repopulate the world with those loyal to her. It is tempting to call her mad, but she is not mad. She is drunk on her own power."

"The first wave of the enemy are nearly at the fireline." Dmitri zoomed in on the image displayed on another screen. It was being transmitted from a device mounted discreetly on a portside skyscraper. That device was one of a multitude. Devoid of the veil provided by their archangel's powers, Lijuan's people could not move unseen in his city.

Raphael caught a hint of silver blue at the corner of the screen before it disappeared and knew Illium was out there with his squadron, making the call on when the archers would fire again. Neither Dmitri nor Raphael would interfere. Illium was an experienced squadron commander, the decision one that had to be made in the field of battle.

The arrows fired all at once half a minute later. A cascade of fire arced down into the mass of enemy combatants heading for the city, but a single precision set were aimed at the floating buoys of fuel. The impact would contaminate the water, but that couldn't be helped—if Lijuan took New York, millions would die.

If he won, his people would clean the water.

The arrows flew silently to their destinations. The buoy archers had been chosen because they could shoot with near-impossible accuracy. Three of the team were guild hunters, one a mortal who competed in archery as a sport, the rest a mix of angels and vampires. Since no one could predict if all the archers would be in the city at any one time, the shooting team could be put together from double the necessary number.

The arrow points slammed into the buoys while the enemy was focused on the fiery threat from above, the buoy skins designed to puncture under such an impact. Flames shot up with explosive force . . . and angels fell screaming from the skies, their wings destroyed.

Every muscle in Raphael's body clenched.

He had witnessed the Falling, seen the broken bodies and torn wings of their wounded and dead. To see any angel plummet from the sky was a repellant sight, but these winged warriors had come to murder his people.

A strong, slightly callused hand sliding into his. He curled his fingers over hers as she curled hers over his, and together, they watched Lijuan's army come to a halt beyond the flaming wall of fire—an impressive sight, but not enough to be a deterrent once you could see it.

Coming *over* that wall however, was an endless hail of burning arrows.

Illium had taken charge of arrow production and created a stockpile so massive that his archers could keep going for days, with one set resting while the others fired. Those men and women were tough to the bone, would shoot until their hands bled and then they'd wrap them up and shoot again.

Lijuan's fighters hesitated just out of reach of the arrows. Several warriors dropped to the water, going to the rescue of the burned angels. Angels couldn't easily be killed by fire, not unless they were burned down to the bone. Then, without warning, the entire army reversed course to the sky, a massive vee of power and violence.

52

Cowards are abandoning their wounded." Dmitri spat out the words. "It'll tank morale among her troops."

"No," Raphael murmured, "they're too devoted to her. She is their goddess and the burned ones will consider it their sacrifice to sink down to the ocean floor until they can be retrieved. The ones with enough wing surface left to float may survive. Most will die."

Elena sucked in a breath. "I thought angels couldn't drown?"

"That badly wounded? It's possible. Especially if their lungs are scorched and they are young."

The idea of burned and bleeding angels sinking helplessly into the ocean while they drowned over a matter of hours or days made Elena's stomach threaten to revolt. "Can we help them?" She had to ask the question, couldn't abandon her humanity.

The Raphael who looked at her was the deadly archangel with power running cold and hard through his veins. But the Raphael who answered her was the man who loved her. "If we can do so safely, we will float out rafts onto which they can climb."

Shokran, Archangel.

You keep me human, Elena. You stop me from becoming Lijuan. Never stop making such requests. Out loud, he said, "We must prepare for the next wave."

Dmitri pressed a finger to his ear. "Ashwini's got her team in position. Short-range rocket launchers ready."

"Any signs of similar weapons among Lijuan's troops?" Elena asked.

"Unfortunately, yes." Dmitri zoomed in on a particular group of fighters. Rocket launchers on angelic backs, assault guns strapped to the front, that was just the start.

"Satellite's also picking up a ton of movement beneath the water," Vivek added. "She's got more submarines, and I bet you they're overflowing with supplies and people and weapons."

"Her Evilness learned from the last battle."

"No, it would have been Xi," Raphael murmured. "He has always been the most intelligent man in her arsenal—though he is only dangerously powerful when she is nearby."

Elena had nearly forgotten that Lijuan could share power with her troops. "That explains how she pulled off the noncorporeal tactic—she must've temporarily shared that power across her entire army." No one had to tell her it was seriously bad news that Lijuan was now strong enough to spread herself that thin.

"Divers are in position," Dmitri said.

Raphael resettled his wings. "Can they see the underwater craft?"

Dmitri spoke into a button mike pinned to his shirt collar, dark head bent, listened to the reply. "Negative. The water is murky."

"I can use satellites to—" Vivek began.

Raphael swiped out a hand. "No. We stick to the rules of war. I will not violate them and step on the road to becoming Lijuan. If the subs attack, they become fair game at any distance. Prior to that, the divers *must* be able to see them. Line of sight, that is the law."

Pride had Elena lifting their clasped hands to her mouth for a kiss.

In the distance, the hail of arrows continued. "I need to go relieve an archer." That was her assigned task during the initial assault phase; she wasn't expert-level, but she was good enough to take over for short periods so they could rest.

Eyes as blue as a pristine mountain lake slammed into hers, lightning alive in their depths and in the Legion mark at his temple. *Stay safe,* hbeebti.

That goes double for you, Archangel. He was going to be doing something incredibly dangerous very soon.

She made it to her position with two minutes to spare and picked up the shooting where the archer had left off. Her preference was the crossbow, but she'd honed her archery skills after the last battle because at this distance and with the added fire element, the specially designed arrows functioned better at the task.

Heat smoldered against her in every direction, eliminating the chill of winter. In front of each archer was a small flaming pot in which they lit their arrows. Sweat trickled down Elena's face; she was glad she'd taken the time to find a hairtie and pull her hair back into a short tail.

She missed the ease of braiding her hair to keep it out of the way, and was already growing out the strands. Mostly though . . . she couldn't keep seeing Belle in the mirror. Each time she turned and glimpsed the shorter strands without warning, she remembered Belle's delight the day she'd had her own hair trimmed to that length. It hurt too fucking much to have a constant reminder of her dancing, wild, often impatient but always loving big sister.

She reached for another arrow. As with the other archers, she wore a quiver on her back—it was continuously refilled by young vampires or Guild trainees. Elena caught the gaze of the trainee who topped up her quiver without getting in the way and nearly lost her focus. But her body knew what to do and she did it without pause.

Her arrow flew.

She shouldn't have been surprised to see Eve. Her sister was no longer a child. She was heading to sixteen and was one of the top trainees in the Guild despite her diminutive size. But Eve was also the baby of the entire family.

She notched another arrow, dipped it in flame, fired. "When's your shift end?" she called back to this sister of hers who wore a long blade in a thigh sheath. No one would take Eve unawares as Slater Patalis had taken Elena's family unawares. Belle and Ari and Mama, they'd stood no chance. Eve would stand a chance.

As for Jeffrey's first daughter by his second marriage, she stayed out of the way of the immortal world, so perhaps she would remain safe. Elena hoped for a nice staid life for Amy, one cocooned in wealth and privilege. A life of debutante balls, a stockbroker husband, and a magazine-worthy home.

Far better than blood and death and grief.

"Thirty minutes!" Eve called out over the whoosh of the arrows firing. Crossbow bolts were also being prepped for the next phase. The clank of them as they were picked up and set out near where they'd be utilized was a constant.

"Then I'm a spotter with a ground watch team until it's my turn back here again!'

Ground watch would sweep for any land-based fighters or reborn Lijuan managed to bring into the city. If those mockeries of life managed to spread their infection . . .

Elena set her jaw and slid out another arrow. Notched it. Set the tip aflame. Fired.

And waited, her heart a knot.

Raphael rose high above the Tower, taking in the overall battle. He'd changed into faded leathers of a bronzed brown, and wore two swords crisscrossed on his back below his wings, as well as forearm guards. Battle between two archangels never came down to such things, but he might need them to intercede on behalf of his other fighters.

At this moment, the wall of fire kept Lijuan's forces at bay. Any who attempted to fly over it were being picked off with anti-wing guns from shooters positioned close to the waterline for just such a possibility. But the deluge was beginning— Lijuan had such a massive force that he could tell she planned to storm the city with no regard for her own casualties, until his archers couldn't pick off enough of them to hold the line.

Dmitri, how is the evacuation proceeding?

The port and surrounding areas are clear. We can draw back to the first point without leaving anyone behind.

The operation had been completed faster than Raphael had expected, but then, Dmitri, Galen, and Venom had been working on the evacuation plan for months, even while Raphael lay unresponsive by Elena's side. Their people were being moved out of Manhattan with clinical precision. Raphael had used his mental voice to command those who shouldn't be moving yet to stay in place until given the order to go.

Chaos would reign if the entire population attempted to leave at once.

As it turned out, the biggest problem had been making people go. New Yorkers wanted to *fight*. Anyone with a relevant skill was being assigned a job by the teams Venom had on the ground. The recalcitrant were simply being picked up and dumped into people-mover trucks. There was no choice, not this time. Anyone left behind was fodder for the reborn, a way for infection to spread.

Hold the line, Raphael said, able to see that the deluge was not yet critical. *Tell the gunners to prep.* A heavier mass of line-of-sight rocket-launchers and anti-wing guns would be their second line of defense, to be put into operation while the archers and close gunners withdrew to safety. *Get the nets ready to deploy.* Naasir's idea, coming off something he'd done during the last battle.

New York was a city of skyscrapers. Which meant it had plenty of points where you could attach rolled up nets created of translucent wires fused with razor-sharp shards of glass. No mortal or immortal could've woven those nets without slicing their fingers to shreds. It was a machine that had undertaken the dangerous task.

Over the time since the last battle, Raphael's people had quietly attached the nets in ways that made it appear as if the holders were a part of the chosen buildings. An ornamental edging, or an extra air-conditioning pipe, even the odd stone gargoyle replaced by a hollow simulacrum.

All the nets were motorized. One electronic command and they'd engage across a large area of the city, creating a lethal network that'd cut and shred the wings of angels who flew into them. Unless the light hit a net just right, the traps were all but invisible.

All of Raphael's winged troops had been drilled on their

locations. He had absolute faith that none would've betrayed them to the enemy.

Done. Dmitri's clear voice. *I've also activated the booby traps in the projected landing areas.*

Raphael had his eyes on the water, so he saw it explode a second before Dmitri said, *One of our divers managed to get to a sub, plant explosives all over it. He saw through a porthole—thing was full of reborn.*

Raphael hoped the fine nets in place across the mouths of the Hudson and East Rivers would stop the wreckage from floating into his city. The more pieces of infected reborn they could keep out, the better. *Any survivors?*

Unknown, but we have the area under constant surveillance.

Lijuan's squadrons broke fighting formation, scattering in a disorderly manner. They hadn't expected an attack from below. Shortsighted of Xi, but the general wasn't used to fighting at a water border. No one had attacked China in thousands of years.

Another explosion in the water, followed by a third.

Did our divers get away in time?

They're safe, Dmitri confirmed. *We're picking up at least three more subs but they've started firing into the water around them. Short-range guns. No missiles.*

Tell the divers to withdraw. He didn't want to lose experienced people when there was little chance of success. *We'll tangle the craft in the nets below the waterline.* Those nets had been activated when Lijuan and her army were first sighted, would now be rippling silent and invisible in the cold dark.

The nets weren't strong enough to stop the subs, but they'd slow them down. It'd give Dmitri more time to come up with possible solutions.

Raphael. Dmitri's tone was sharp. *Scheduled commercial flights that took off from Charisemnon's territory in this general direction but to different cities are now altering their flight paths to head to New York. Pilots have ignored all attempts at communication.*

Realization was instant. *Charisemnon never gave up their alliance.* The Archangel of Northern Africa and the Archangel of China had played them from the start—there was no way enemy planes, most probably packed with reborn, could take off from another archangel's territory without that archangel being aware of it.

Charisemnon had betrayed them all. *Warn Titus, then alert the rest of the Cadre.*

Titus was an honorable warrior, wouldn't expect a knife in the back during a catastrophic fight to save their people from the scourge of the reborn. Charisemnon, however, wouldn't hesitate to slam in that blade. If they couldn't get a warning to him, Titus would never see the death blow coming.

53

As Dmitri fought to contact a trusted member of Titus's court, Raphael turned his attention to the others of his Seven in the city. *Indications of Lijuan since the previous sighting?* They had to be on constant alert for the possibility that the Archangel of China would go noncorporeal again with part of her army.

His city would never see the ambush coming.

Aodhan and Venom, both positioned a good distance from the port, had caught no sign of her presence in their sectors, but Illium said, *I think she's in the center of her army, three deep behind Xi. Squadron Jason's ID'd as her most elite is flying in a protective pattern around her.*

Jason responded at the same instant to point out the elite squadron.

Raphael rose higher and saw it at once: the pattern being flown wasn't just protective, it was that of an honor guard in old and traditional courts. It could be a double bluff, Xi more than smart enough to orchestrate that, but Raphael decided against it. Lijuan was too aware of her status to be so cunning in this particular way.

He headed toward the water.

Lijuan's forces caught sight of him while he was still on this side of the fireline; arrows whistled toward him, along with lances of energy fired by the more powerful of Lijuan's forces. He avoided the energy strikes, swatted away the arrows. He wasn't about to reveal any more about his own power than necessary. His task was to engage Lijuan, gauge her power.

This was no battle. It was war and this was only the first skirmish.

Wings of brilliant stormfire below him as he passed the skyscraper on which Elena knelt with a bow in hand. He felt her mind touch his, her mental kiss vibrant with the life that ran so defiant and strong in her body.

He crossed the fireline.

A horde of Lijuan's angels streamed at him with swords drawn, battle cries tearing through the air.

Will you hide behind your people? He transmitted the comment widely, so it would hit the mind of every angelic fighter, every individual in the submarines. *Are you so weak?*

I AM A GODDESS! A blast of crackling obsidian twined with pearlescent gray starlight blasted past his shoulder. He barely avoided the obsidian hail and that only by dropping precipitously. So, Xi had managed to get through to her about tactics after all—because that honor guard *had* been a feint.

Rapidly recalculating his options, Raphael nonetheless didn't respond with his own strike despite the volleys coming at him from her fighters. Xi was at the forefront, blasting bolts at Raphael's wings. No starlight shimmer to Xi's blows, but the obsidian of it was a shadow of Lijuan's—a visual confirmation that, unlike with the abilities possessed by Raphael's Seven, Xi's power came from his archangel.

Rather than turning his wings to white fire, Raphael made a point of avoiding the bolts; the less they knew, the better. As he did so, he tried to work out Lijuan's position, but there was no sign of her. She'd faded in and out of her noncorporeal state during the last battle, but it appeared she could now maintain it without pause.

Why wasn't she then right over New York?

Why wasn't she blasting his archers into death?

The air in his lungs turned to ice. This time, she'd done the unpredictable. He broadcast a warning to his entire army. *Mobilize all archers, all gunners, look skyward!* Bloated with power, Lijuan had done exactly what he'd feared and kept part of her assault force hidden even while exposing the rest. The delay in an attack had to mean the broken-off section was getting into prime position—but they had to be deadly close to that by now.

He had to do something to even the odds.

Incinerating the fighters in front of him with a single blow, he drew on the wildfire inside him and released it not in a massive bolt but in a thick spreading blast with him as the center.

Static filled the air.

Lijuan may have gained enormous power, but as he'd seen with Antonicus, her brand of death wasn't fully immune to the wildfire. Even if the effect was only temporary, it'd give his people enough knowledge that they could reposition their forces, defend their home.

The wildfire spread and spread . . . and crackled violent blue and white-gold as it hit the enemy force, stripping them of their noncorporeal cloak. The air filled with fire as all his fighters on nearby rooftops began to shoot up at enemy warriors already wounded by the gleaming scythe of wildfire. His power had been too spread out to kill, but it'd caused major damage.

A number went down screaming, their wings shredded by crossbow bolts or bullets, or in flames.

Fuck, Archangel. Elena's voice, horror in every syllable.

He turned . . . and saw his city surrounded by an army of such magnitude that it had to be every living strong angel in Lijuan's land. Thousands upon thousands of them. So many that his mind struggled to comprehend it.

A shift in viewpoint and he understood why the attack hadn't come yet, why the squadrons had moved so slowly to ambush Manhattan. The majority of them were occupied with hauling huge metal carriers.

Those carriers had to hold Lijuan's vampiric forces . . . and reborn.

Dmitri, call all our people home. This was a fight to the death; they needed everyone. *Nimra, Nazarach, Augustus, all of them.* It was a risk to pull in his people from around the territory, but unlike the last time, he didn't think Lijuan was going to try to eat away at him in small bites. No, she intended to take New York, then crawl out across his land.

Tell Galen and Naasir to send our noncombatants in the Refuge to Eli's Refuge stronghold. They will be protected by Eli's people. It was a decision he and Elijah had made when Lijuan's eventual rise became inevitable—had Lijuan chosen to attack South America instead, Galen and Naasir and their teams would've taken charge of Eli's noncombatants, allowing his warriors to head home.

Today, it was Raphael's warriors who would fly toward battle.

Even as Raphael sent out orders, he was fighting his way through the mass of winged fighters. His sword bled red, but his goal was the archangel with hair of white and wings of a delicate dove gray who soared high above the city, her fingers prickling with an eerily beautiful power that would devastate anything it touched.

He had to strike now, while he could see her. An enemy warrior sliced his sword downward at Raphael's wing . . . and it turned into white fire without Raphael's conscious volition. The sword went straight through without causing any damage—throwing the enemy warrior off-balance.

Slicing off the other angel's head, a spray of warm blood hitting his face, Raphael scalded the remaining enemy fighters around him with archangelic power, then rose high, wildfire building into a lethal sphere in his hand. His initial blast intersected with Lijuan's and the clash reverberated in a massive boom of sound that smashed over the entire city.

He saw some people drop, hands over their ears, but his archers held.

He threw the hidden sphere of wildfire in his other hand in the immediate aftermath, his aim her wing. She wasn't expecting the rapid response and his blow found its mark. Screaming as the wildfire seared away part of her wing before she could go noncorporeal, she retaliated in a fury.

Her obsidian death hit the side of a building, shattering glass and destroying a corner. As if a giant had taken a bite out of the skyscraper. Taking advantage of her anger-fueled lack of strategy, he threw more wildfire in smaller but rapid-fire spheres, only then realizing the wildfire had gained a faint opalescence. Not as strong as he'd seen on the broken pieces of the chrysalis, but present.

A piece of Elena's heart, embedded forever in his power.

The second sphere hit Lijuan's leg. Wildfire burned over her, and in the background of its merciless glow, he saw the skeletal bones of her face fading in and out.

Why wasn't she going noncorporeal? Was it possible the wildfire had evolved to stop her from switching form? Or had she used so much energy to hide her massive army that she'd burned out that particular ability?

Whatever the reason, it didn't stop her from deluging him in a rain of starlight obsidian. But, wounded as she was, her aim was off. Her warriors closed ranks in front of her before he could target her again. Raphael scorched them out of existence, but there were always more ready to lay their lives and bodies on the line to protect their goddess, a flesh and blood wall of mindless fidelity.

The last was a squadron that flew with the precision of a seasoned team. The entire unit snapped around Lijuan in a single heartbeat, then they all dropped as one—right into the thick of the fighting.

Raphael could no longer target her without hitting his own people. She, however, had the same problem—she couldn't attack him without killing a world-class team of her own.

Stalemate.

Utilizing the lull, he scanned the battle zone. The fireline was out and his archers had fallen back. It was no shock to see that Lijuan's people had taken the port—with their numbers so gargantuan, he'd expected this first loss.

Wounded angels lay on rooftops all over the city, their wings crumpled and bodies bloodied. Healers and field medics attended to Raphael's wounded, while hard-eyed warriors watched over Lijuan's wounded to make certain they wouldn't rejoin the attack.

He returned his attention to the enemy squadron that surrounded their goddess. *I am willing to agree to a cease-fire for long enough for us both to collect our wounded.* Some of his people had fallen in what was now enemy territory.

He'd deliberately sent his message so it would hit every mind in the vicinity. So her people would know the choice she made. If he could demoralize her army, he would. As he waited for a response, he told two of his warriors to drop from the air, clearing his line of sight . . . then blasted another one of her squadrons with angelfire. It incinerated them. The massive container they'd carried until their deaths crashed to the unforgiving street far below.

The distance didn't fully muffle the loud shatter of its destruction. From the sky, it was a toybox spilling tiny broken dolls. Most lay unmoving, but the odd one crawled, pitiful and slow.

Ransom's team has it, Dmitri told him, and he knew hundreds of meters below, a group of hunters was bearing down on the crawlers.

Raphael was already moving to destroy a second carrier, but Lijuan's forces had seen what was happening, dropped precipitously to avoid his strike. Lijuan rose up out of the knot of her people at the same time to blast him once again. Her wing was badly damaged but she was no green angel in her first battle. She nearly got him.

He threw wildfire at her in a relentless volley until she dropped back into her protection. Sweat dripped down his back. It might appear as if he was winning, but he wasn't. He'd used up so much wildfire that, Cascade power or not, his body was having trouble generating enough to keep up.

Much longer and he'd be forced to use ordinary angelfire—which didn't have much of an impact on Lijuan. As he'd feared after his failure to heal Antonicus, even his wildfire wasn't working as it had in the last battle.

Then, he'd *truly* hurt her.

Just now, when she'd risen, he'd seen signs that her body had already stopped the progression of the wildfire on her wing, the same for the damage to her leg. If Lijuan decided to wait him out, she'd win by default. He had, at least, given his people a little breathing room by crashing that carrier. Lijuan's troops were being more cautious, and those with the carriers had dropped back behind the fighters and changed direction to head back to the port.

Aodhan, Illium, Jason, can you get to a carrier? They were the only three angels on his team with enough strength to take out the massive metal constructs.

The answer from all three was negative. Jason was fighting an advance on their left flank, Aodhan on their right, while Illium was at the frontline. Any withdrawal and Lijuan's squadrons would fall on the archers and shooters in a bloody massacre.

Izzy is close to the one at your eleven o'clock. It was Elena in his head.

Raphael had included his consort in the communications as a matter of course.

He demolished a swathe of enemy warriors, something about two of them striking him as odd, but he didn't have time to stop and think about it before he obliterated them from existence. *I know he is your favorite,* hbeebti, he said in the aftermath, *but Izzy is a baby angel without the ability to light a candle with his power, much less that to throw bolts of energy.*

That's why he has a missile launcher, his hunter replied patiently. *Ash taught him to shoot one last month and insisted he carry it into battle.*

54

Raphael located Izzy in the chaos of battle. No wonder the young angel was flying slightly crooked. That weapon had to be heavy, even worn across his chest. *Izak, launch your missile at the carrier directly ahead of you. Jurgen and Imani, protect Izak.*

The two senior angels, their leathers already bloody from combat quickly flanked the younger one. Who, to his credit, reacted with smooth precision. Lifting the launcher into the correct position on his shoulder while maintaining a slightly wobbly hover, he ignored the screaming enemy warriors coming at him and launched.

Those flyers smashed into Jurgen's dual swords and Imani's war hammer. A head went flying, a face was smashed in . . . and the carrier was torn out of angelic hands by the power of the blow from the missile. Izak went flying backward from the momentum, was halted by two of the Legion who body-slammed him to a stop.

Archers scrambled out of the way of the carrier as it careened down toward a building, only for one of his people operating a massive crane to whack it out into open air using a huge iron ball hanging on a muscular chain.

Said ball then swung angrily through a heavy knot of enemy fighters. Raphael's portside fighters had clearly already received the order to withdraw when the crane came into operation. Lijuan's people were chasing them, thinking it a true retreat. The crane took them down like bowling pins.

Crushed bones, pulverized faces, red pulp raining from the sky.

Using the cranes across the city as stealth weapons had been Galen's idea. No one really saw cranes. They were a part of the landscape. The surprise would only work once, but it had worked very, very well. Multiple cranes had come online at the same time, and they'd managed to catch Lijuan's forces unprepared, smashing down hundreds in a matter of minutes.

Lijuan's generals rose up high into the air, above the reach of the cranes, their hands ringed with obsidian.

Eject! Raphael ordered the crane operators.

The men and women literally dived out of the control boxes, all of the operators winged for this very reason. Obsidian power hit the cranes on the heels of their dives. Raphael couldn't tell if any of the operators had made it.

Raphael, we're starting to lose people. Dmitri's voice, as steady as he always was in battle. *There're just too fucking many of them.*

I know. His forces had done a massive amount of damage, but no one city could take on an enemy army of this size. It was incomprehensible. *Have you heard from Eli's second?*

They're on their way.

But they wouldn't arrive for at least another day. Elijah would probably come ahead, but even then, it'd take him hours. Raphael's city was going to be dead by then. He had to find a way to delay Lijuan, stop this full-frontal assault. He and his people needed time to reassess their plans. Not even in their worst-case scenario simulations had they imagined an army of this magnitude.

There was no point hoarding power when New York was on the brink of a catastrophic defeat.

Decision made, he ordered all his fighters nearby to collapse their wings and drop. Not all of them could get disentangled fast enough, but enough did that he had an opening. Exhaling, he released all the wildfire in his body and shaped it like a spear, then threw it with tactical calculation at the squadron locked around Lijuan.

The husk of a once-living angel dropped from the core at that very instant . . . right as the wildfire cut through the protective guard like butter.

It punched to the center. And found its target.

Lijuan's scream was a serrated saw in his head. Gritting his teeth as she reappeared at last, burning in wildfire, he lifted his hands as if to throw more at her. She ran, heading to the port area while her fighters collected around her in suicidal loyalty. He followed, smashing them down with archangelic fury, but had to turn back when a large enemy squadron broke through the front line to close in on a rooftop full of archers.

He blew the squadron out of the sky, but Lijuan was out of reach by then, her fighters falling on his people in chaotic hordes to keep him from following her.

I will accept your offer of a cease-fire to gather our wounded. Lijuan's nightmare of a voice, awash with the thready screams and begging cries of the dead.

Both sides will retreat, Raphael replied. *One squadron from each side comes forward to collect the bodies.* His people were lying broken all over the city, too. And he was out of wildfire. Nothing else could really touch Lijuan.

It is agreed. Rage in every word, but he'd done enough damage to her that she was slinking off to lick her wounds.

He waited for her to order her troops to retreat before he gave his own the same order. As expected, Lijuan's army retreated to the neighborhood by the port area. Raphael's people had booby-trapped entire neighborhoods long before and would set off those traps once Lijuan's ground troops began to crawl forward—because his forces hadn't managed to destroy all the carriers.

At least five had landed.

He could hope that the reborn had been in the ones he and Izak had destroyed, knew they wouldn't be that lucky. The Cascade wanted destruction and destruction it would get. But Lijuan wouldn't find any safe harbor in his city. For her, all of New York had teeth.

His archers and shooters stayed in position as the rest of his people withdrew.

Raphael, too, waited until Lijuan's army was far enough away that they couldn't mount a stealth attack while his back was turned. When Elena flew up to join him on his return flight to the Tower, he saw a splash of sticky red on her side. Not her blood. Someone else's.

Enemy angel, she said, having caught sight of his glance. *Someone cut off his head in the sky and he bled all over me as he fell.* Her voice was grim as she continued. *We lost two archers on the roof I was on. Two more are badly wounded.*

Four. It wasn't a huge number . . . unless you considered how long this war would likely rage, and how few people his side had in comparison to Lijuan's. With that in mind, he shifted the oncoming strategy meeting to the infirmary. He might be able to heal enough warriors that his forces could hold the line until Elijah's army arrived.

Ahead of them, the Primary landed on the Legion building. Raphael had seen the gray-winged fighters in the thick of battle. If one fell, another rose in his place. They were Raphael's greatest advantage. Seven hundred and seventy-seven warriors who couldn't be killed. Except . . .

"Something is wrong, Guild Hunter." He dropped into a rapid descent.

The Primary was crouched over one of his people who lay on his back on the ground, one hand clutching at his chest as he coughed black liquid out of his mouth.

"What is this?" As far as Raphael knew, the Legion were invulnerable to disease.

"Death," the Primary said in a voice that held a chorus of hundreds. He slipped out his sword and, looking into the eyes of the other fighter, sliced the cutting edge straight through the other's neck, severing the head from the body.

The body didn't dissolve into dust as the Legion always did when they fell in battle. It began to liquefy into a noxious sludge that had the Primary looking to Raphael. "You must end this, sire," he said as Elena landed beside Raphael.

Raphael torched the dead Legion fighter with angelfire . . . but parts of the corpse yet moved in the aftermath.

"Hell." Elena touched his arm . . . and a lick of wildfire jolted into him even as she gasped. The wildfire tasted of her. Of defiant life.

He used a droplet of what she'd given him to eliminate the last pieces of the corpse before glancing at the Primary. "Do you feel him regenerating?"

The Primary shook his head. "His body was consumed. We are now seven hundred and seventy-six in flesh."

"I'm sorry." Elena placed her hand on the Primary's shoulder, her expression scored with pain. "I know you've been together eons."

Cocking his head to look up at her, the Primary said, "He is not lost. He is part of us. Only his body has been destroyed."

Raphael had never quite understood the level to which the Legion were enmeshed, but he was glad to hear they hadn't permanently lost one of their own. "Was he hit by Lijuan's power?"

"No. He was bitten by one of her angelic fighters."

"Bitten?" Elena shoved a flyaway strand of hair impatiently behind her ear. "Like a vampire?"

"The angel sank his teeth into the arm." The Primary indicated his biceps area. "Others have also been bitten but none of mine."

Raphael took off without warning at the same instant that Elena said, "Raphael! Go!" His flight buffeted Elena and the Primary into flattened positions on the roof, his wings white fire.

He landed on the infirmary balcony in a matter of split seconds, ran inside.

"Sire!" Nisia looked to him with desperate eyes from her position kneeling on a bed. It held brown-haired and blue-eyed Andreja, her wings a slightly darker shade of brown than the rich mahogany of her hair. The tall and muscled angel was twisting and fighting the hands that sought to hold her down for Nisia's attempts at healing.

Her bare leg was bloody from an injury, but that wasn't what caught Raphael's attention. An ugly blackness coughed from Andreja's mouth, stark against the cream of her skin.

Placing his hand on the angel's breastbone, Raphael punched in the tiniest possible droplet of the wildfire Elena had given him.

Wildfire hurt Lijuan, was not meant for even old angels.

The tough canvas of Andreja's fighting tunic disintegrated

in a scorched burst where he'd touched her. She screamed, high and agonized, before collapsing. The visible bite mark on the decaying flesh of her arm crackled with wildfire.

That didn't stop Nisia from putting her hands on the angel. "She's alive. Laric, finish stitching up your patient, then attend to Andreja's leg."

The younger healer nodded, his head bare today. Though he continued to wear a cape over his damaged wings, his hood had fallen off in the chaos of having to deal with so many badly injured patients. It was the first time Raphael had seen the thick, deep auburn of his hair touched by light.

"Watch for the infection and tell me if it returns," Raphael said, catching a glimpse of stormfire wings in his peripheral vision. "Where are the others who came in with bites?"

There were five in all and he was able to drive the black poison from all of them—at a speed that gave him hope that the wildfire *could* cause Lijuan significant damage. Andreja was already conscious and sitting upright by the time he reached the last of the bitten.

"Sire," she rasped after he was done, her voice holding the cadence and rhythm of her long-ago homeland in what was now the far edge of Michaela's territory. "Inside, the blackness, it eats at the soul. It wants to devour and dominate."

Laric moved quietly to assist Andreja, kneeling down in front of her so he could begin to work on the open wound on her leg. She looked down at the top of his head, then moved her hand to put her fingers below his chin, tilt up his head.

Wait, hbeebti, he said when he felt Elena stiffen beside him. *Andreja is not a cruel angel.*

Today, she took in the dark pink scars that ridged the white of Laric's face. They went from just below his hairline all the way through to his throat and farther. Of his face, only a single section around his left eye and cheekbone was smooth and unmarked. His shoulders had gone rigid at Andreja's actions, his hands motionless on her flesh.

"*Hvala,* small one," the female angel said with a slow smile that held not pity but something that had color crawling under Laric's skin before he ducked his head and began to work on her leg again. "You have gentle hands."

Ooooooh. With that, Elena tugged Raphael away and out

of the infirmary. "Did she just hit on Laric?" she asked out-side, a grin curving her features.

"He could do far worse." Of an age that she saw below the skin, Andreja would have a care for the wounded angel's body—and heart. "From what I have seen, she does not mind being the one who initiates a courtship, but she will not coerce or force if Laric indicates he doesn't welcome her attentions."

"I hope she gets a chance to find out." Elena's smile faded, the small moment of happiness dying under the weight of war. "What she said about the effect of the bite . . . Death's not the aim, is it? If it happens, it's as part of a process to a kind of reborn state."

"I fear you are right." He brushed the back of his hand over her cheek. "Elena, my wildfire isn't regenerating fast enough to repel Lijuan should she strike again today."

A tightening at the corners of her eyes.

He kissed her before she could speak. *I have no regrets.* Without his Elena by his side, he wouldn't have wanted to fight for the world, wouldn't have wanted to save it. *I would rather fall as Raphael than win as a puppet of the Cascade.*

Her lips trembled as they parted. "I would still rather die as Elena than live as a shadow."

"So, we are agreed." Pressing his forehead to hers, he wrapped her up in his wings.

An instant of love stolen from the crawling dark whispering at their door.

55

"We have to rethink our plans," he told his senior people only minutes later, all of them gathered around Dmitri's strategy table in the war room. On that table was a full three-dimensional reconstruction of the battle zone.

Joining Aodhan, Illium, Dmitri, Venom, Jason, and Elena were Vivek Kapur, the members of Elena's Guard, as well as Sara Haziz. While not a part of the Tower, Sara represented all the hunters on the ground and needed the knowledge to be discussed here.

Her husband, Deacon, was a brutally qualified hunter but he was an even better weapons-maker. He was working non-stop in a workshop lower down in the Tower, alongside a team he'd hand-selected. Their task was to repair broken weapons as they came in, discard what couldn't be fixed, and make new ones.

The last person at the table was Suyin, here to offer any insight she could on her aunt.

"The size of her army changes everything," Aodhan agreed, the glittering filaments of his wings streaked with rust red and his hair sweat damp. "I've never seen or heard of the like."

"I missed it." Jason rarely showed his emotions, but today,

his shoulders were bunched, his spine rigid. "I can't understand how. I personally confirmed the numbers I gave you. Those were the *only* fighters she had at her various strongholds."

"I might have an answer," Vivek Kapur said. "It's weird as shit." He lifted up the tablet he had on his lap. "I've been watching the battle from every angle I can, trying to feed the computers enough data that we can begin to predict their moves."

Raphael had battle-honed generals for that—and he had Dmitri. His second's brain was a steel trap when it came to battle strategy. But he wasn't about to disparage a man this intelligent. "What did you discover?"

"A lot—and I mean, a *lot*—of the fighters don't look like trained combatants," he said. "Angels are pretty much all in shape, but these ones don't have the look of honed warriors." He brought up a set of images on his tablet.

"Put it up here," Dmitri directed, touching something on the side of the table.

A large screen opened out from the ceiling, directly above the table.

"Give me one sec." Vivek's fingers moved over his tablet. "There."

Raphael saw what the young vampire had meant the instant he set eyes on the images.

"I know him." Jason pointed to an angel with his sword raised and teeth bared, the whites of his eyes showing. "Junior librarian in a minor court. No combat skills." He pointed to another angel, went motionless. "She's combat trained but belongs to Titus."

All of them went silent for long moments.

"It appears we may find ourselves fighting friends," Raphael said at last. "Warn your squadrons—and remember, it is unlikely they are acting of their free will." Titus's people were notoriously devoted to their archangel. "Do to them what we would expect them to do for us were our positions reversed and we were the ones being controlled."

"I'm not sure they're even actually alive," Vivek ventured, his face pale under his brown skin. "I know they look it, but . . . Here." He threw up another image.

It showed an angel with wings of speckled light brown

sinking his teeth into Andreja's arm—who was in the process of smashing the spiked ball of her morning star club into his head. A flail swung from her other hand, that spiked ball on its way to crushing the biter's ribs.

"Talk about psycho eyes." Arms folded across her chest and booted feet set apart, Elena stared at the biter's visage. "There's nothing there."

She was right. The fighter looked dead, the lack of expression eerie.

"His eyes are black." Illium came to stand beside Elena, their wings overlapping slightly—but no energy jumped from Elena's wings to Bluebell's. "Hardly anyone in the world, mortal or immortal, has eyes of pure black, but I came up against a number of other fighters with the same eyes. You can't distinguish pupil from iris."

Raphael recalled his own sense of unease about two of the enemy angels. It had been the eyes, he realized—too black, too flat.

Vivek threw up image after image of blank-eyed warriors, their gazes black. Jason identified half of them as belonging to archangels other than Lijuan. It was a small mercy they hadn't yet come face-to-face with one of their own.

"Vivek," Elena murmured, "can you find more images of the junior librarian Jason pointed out? I want to see him in battle."

"Should be doable. This facial rec software is great, but it needs . . ." His words mumbled off as he worked.

Jason stirred again, his wings rustling as he stepped closer to the screen. "I don't understand how she is even here." He pointed to a female angel whose full breasts bulged from the sides of her improperly fitted armor. "She gave birth to a child two months early—and that was a mere week before China went dark. She was meant to rest and recover, then fly to the Refuge with the babe in the company of a healer."

Sara Haziz spoke for the first time, her tone shards of flint. "Her breasts are engorged with milk."

"A premature angelic infant needs near-constant contact with their mother to have any chance of survival." Raphael had stood watch in the nursery as a youth, watched worried mothers cradle their early-born babes to their bare skin hour after hour.

"Got it." Vivek replaced the photographs on the screen with a recording.

The librarian angel with no combat training sliced and cut through his opponents without pause. His movements were fluid, his reaction time that of a well-trained warrior. His expression, however, never changed. Whether he struck a blow or took one, the dead blankness of his eyes was a constant.

Raphael stared at the images, then he thought of the angels he'd seen in the infirmary and what his consort had said in the aftermath. "I think the reborn are already among us."

"That's impossible." Illium shook his head. "She made reborn with mortals. These are *angels*."

"Charisemnon was able to impact immortals," Dmitri argued. "It's possible."

"Except for the meeting in India," Jason murmured, "Charisemnon has stayed closeted in his palace for months. My spies glimpsed him now and then, but he never appeared outside, even within his own grounds."

Raphael remembered that report, but as Michaela had so cleverly used to her advantage, immortals oftentimes decided to withdraw from the world. Charisemnon had been available to the Cadre and in being so, had fulfilled his obligations. His sociability or lack of it had been no concern of his fellow archangels.

"They did it together." It was a certainty in Raphael's blood. "Whatever created this abomination of death and life, it involves both Charisemnon and Lijuan."

The Archangel of Disease and the Archangel of Death.

"His 'gift' turned on him last time," Elena said. "You think he'd have risked it?"

"He recovered. If it happens again, he no doubt believes he'll recover."

"That might've been a miscalculation," Ashwini said, a throwing star held absently in one hand. "Might be his ability kills him this time—not directly, but by weakening his body in ways that aren't visible on the surface. If I were Cadre, I wouldn't want to battle Titus at less than full strength."

"That just your hope, *cher*," Janvier drawled, "or will our dreams come true and Charisemnon will rot from within?"

Secreting away the throwing star, Ashwini made a face. "I can't tell."

Izak stood silent and awed next to them.

"Even if Charisemnon dies," Raphael said, "the damage is done. He and Lijuan have created a plague upon immortals."

Elena's head snapped up and he knew she'd made the connection to the story the Legion told of the Cascade of Terror. An archangel had created a plague back then as well. As a result, a poisoned angelkind had chosen to Sleep in the hope they could wait out the poison—and woken to find a new people had been born in their absence. A people who held their salvation.

The toxin created back then still lived in the cells of each and every angel and archangel. Only by purging it into humankind at certain intervals could they stop from turning into bloodborn monsters. Vampires were the accidental byproduct of that purging.

"Sire." Jason's quiet but potent tone. "I've just watched a small part of the battle on Vivek's device." He passed the tablet back to the vampire. "It appears that each squadron of reborn fighters is led by a living fighter."

"What happens if you kill that leader?" Illium muttered. "Are they connected to him somehow? Is he—or she—the source of their martial skills?"

"Possible." As possible was the fact they might've all been imprinted from the same source—Xi was a skilled warrior and he'd have no compunction in opening himself up to his goddess. "Regardless, brief all squadrons to try and take out the leader." If nothing else, it'd confuse the group. "Warn your people to avoid being bitten by the other side at all costs, on the ground or in the sky. If that means a broken leg or a gunshot wound, take it."

Everyone nodded.

"I'll warn the healers to use biohazard protocols on any bite victims." Vivek slipped away to make the call.

"We've got ordinary reborn on the ground." This from Dmitri, who'd stepped away for a moment, one finger pressed to his ear. "One of my reconnaissance team's sighted them shuffling around a surviving container."

"City firelines are ready," Janvier said. "Ashwini and I took our teams out, checked them one last time before all hell broke loose. Give the word and the flames go up at the same time the ground opens up."

To destroy his own city was a decision no archangel took lightly, but Raphael had authorized this destruction to save the rest of his territory. They'd lose two skyscrapers, badly damage part of the port area, but the destruction would make it near impossible for the reborn on the ground to get through to their side.

Lijuan's troops would no doubt retaliate by flying the reborn across, but it'd be a far slower invasion than hordes of infected flowing into the streets of Manhattan. "If I'm in battle, Dmitri makes the call."

Dmitri gave a curt nod, but he still had a finger to his ear, his concentration intense. "Lijuan's troops are dumping their wounded in a big pile," he said before breaking off.

Three seconds later: "V, pull up the feeds from quadrant eight."

Having completed his call to the healers, Vivek reacted at once.

Sixteen different live cameras filled the screen. "Full screen on camera seven." Dmitri pointed to the feed on the far left.

Piles of squirming and screaming bodies, one on top of the other.

Angels with their wings half burned, or hacked off.

The broken but live bodies of ground fighters who'd survived the container Izak had sent plummeting to the ground.

The mass of burned and healthy flesh, the squirming, the destroyed wings, it made a dark, angry heat crawl over Raphael's skin. He'd seen many terrible things in battle, but never this kind of callousness from a leader toward their own troops.

"All of them are damaged." Aodhan's quiet voice held nothing but calm, but Illium shifted to stand with his wing brushing the other angel's. "There is no one whole on that pile. No one who will heal quickly."

Dmitri asked a question into the mike on his lapel, received an answer. "Aodhan's right—they're taking the wounded with functional wings and limbs to another area."

Another angel was dropped onto the pile from above, his bloody body sliding down the flesh pile to end at the bottom with his remaining wing smeared dark red . . . and black. Some of those in the pile weren't alive, not as everyone but Lijuan understood life. They were reborn.

A choked-off sound drew his attention to Suyin, so silent till this instant that he'd nearly forgotten her though she stood beside Elena. Her hands clutched the edge of the table, the ice white of her hair a liquid waterfall as she leaned forward.

"Our family line was one of honor." Her voice shook. "Warriors and scholars and an archangel who was the cause of much pride. We are *not* this. *She* is not us." Agony contorted her features. "My memories of the moments after I woke this time are blurred, but I have a vague recollection of a conversation between Xi and my aunt while they stood over me."

A furrow between her eyebrows, those brows black in contrast to the white of her hair. "She said words that made no sense to me: 'Your troops will not die, Xi. Be content, for they will become of me, their goddess.'"

Oh, fuck, Archangel.

Come stand with me, Elena. His rage was a cauldron in his gut, cold and deadly. *I need to remember why I cannot simply fly out right now and attempt to stop this atrocity.*

His hunter slipped to him, coming to stand so that part of her back brushed his chest, wings of stormfire defiant with life against him. *We'll get her.* Steel and wildfire in his mind. *She doesn't get to do this and win.*

A stirring on one side of the camera feed before Lijuan flowed into view, as graceful and regal as ever.

"Her wing's dragging." Suyin's voice steadied, a grim joy in it. "You hurt her."

"Not enough if she's able to walk." He'd expended far more wildfire than he had in the last battle, but done far less damage.

Dressed in a gown of fog gray that darkened to black at the edges and followed the shape of her body until it flared out in waves from the waist, she was an empress in her bearing and in the elegance of her features. No skeletal mask showed through her pearlescent skin, no nightmares danced in her haunting pale eyes. Even her wings, dove gray and soft, were so lovely that the damage to the left one appeared an abomination.

A hush fell on the world.

56

Halting in front of the mountain of wounded, Lijuan smiled with a kind gentleness that Raphael remembered from long ago, when he'd been a boy holding on to his father's hand while they visited Lijuan's court.

She gave me a plate of sweets once, he found himself sharing with Elena. *Then she told me I was free to run around in her maze garden while she and my father spoke—and that I wasn't to cheat by flying to look down at the maze from above.*

Elena shook her head. *What happened to her?*

Greed and ambition. Lijuan had always chafed at not being the oldest and strongest in the Cadre. *I remember my father laughing and telling her not to wish for age; that he knew far too many mad old ones.* The irony of Nadiel's declaration echoed through time.

Onscreen, Lijuan knelt beside the broken body of the last angel to have been dropped into the pile; as they watched, she brushed back his hair with utmost gentleness. The camera had enough definition that when Vivek zoomed in, they saw awe and wonder and joy on the face of the fallen angel. His lips shaped the words, *My Lady.*

Lijuan murmured something that made him attempt to bow

his head even as blood dribbled from a corner of his mouth. Lijuan touched his hair again before rising. Hands dropping to her sides, she threw back her head and—

Darkness.

"Shit." Vivek wheeled to a computer, began to work it with frantic hands. "I don't get it. The cameras say they're transmitting, all functions optimal."

"It's the fog." Jason, his gaze unblinking as he stared at the darkness. "She's created a mini-fog."

"Rouse one of the miniature drones we have in the area," Dmitri ordered. "Get an aerial view."

"I'll pilot," Illium volunteered, and Vivek passed across the controller, but Ashwini said, "Wait," before they could activate the drone. "Fog's fading at the edges."

"I don't see it," Suyin murmured, but that was to be expected. She hadn't experienced Ashwini's third eye.

Five seconds later and shapes began to appear in the blackness, silhouettes that made little sense but for Lijuan's form— she was in the same position she'd held when the darkness first descended. The flesh mountain, however, had become smaller, seemed to keep shrinking as they watched.

The last of the fog whispered out of existence.

In place of a mountain of wounded fighters lay a mound of bodies devoid of any indication of life. Their flesh was akin to paper, their faces twisted into a rictus of gasping mouths and wide eyes. Only . . . there were no eyes. Just hollow sockets that begged for redemption.

The corpses' fingers, stiff and dry, were frozen in curled-up twists, though a few reached out toward Lijuan as if to beg for mercy . . . or to ask for the benediction of their goddess. Feathers divested of color floated in the air, lost from the bodies of angels who'd been stripped of life, of flesh.

An eerie silence hung over the entire scene.

Lijuan lowered her arms and seemed to sigh. Her wings glowed, her face exquisite in profile when she turned to the side. At that moment, she was the loveliest Elena had ever seen her. Her hair was a sheet of glittering ice, silken and healthy. It blew back in a gentle breeze to reveal the flawless lines of her face.

The same breeze also lifted more feathers into the air.

They surrounded Lijuan in a soft halo that glowed with the power reflected off her wings.

Lijuan looked up at the feathers. Smiled.

Hers is not a power I can match, Guild Hunter.

To hear Raphael say that so bluntly, it made the rock on her heart crushingly heavier. *That's because you don't feed on the life of others.* She locked her hand with his, this lethal archangel who would never do to his own what Lijuan had just done. *We'll fight her with honor and with our people by our side, not shriveled into husks.*

"Oh, fuck." Vivek's bitten-out words wrenched her attention back to the screen.

The mummies were crumbling into dust under the glow of the dark orange evening sunlight. All except for a layer of bodies on the bottom edges . . . who were attempting to crawl out and away from the mound.

Elena's brain couldn't make sense of it. No one who looked like that should be able to move. The crawlers' wings were featherless lumps of flesh that curled inward, their bones looking broken or partially disintegrated. As she fought not to bring up her last meal, the fingers of one snapped under him as he attempted to drag the remains of his body forward. His face was all but gone, caved in, his eyes missing.

Striding across the screen, Xi began to behead the "survivors" one by one, with clinical efficiency. It was an act of mercy by a commander, except that you couldn't call it that, not when Xi had stood by Lijuan in all of this. It didn't take him long to behead all the crawlers and step back to his position beside his goddess.

Lijuan sent out power in a languid wave, disintegrating the remains into dust.

That dust rose into the air.

Vivek's fingers went rigid on the wheels of his chair. "We're all going to be breathing that in."

Elena lifted a hand to her mouth and ran from the room.

No one said a word when she returned after emptying her stomach. Raphael put his arm around her while Sara passed her a bottle of water. As she drank, she saw that she wasn't the only one with a white face. Further, Izak and Suyin were also missing.

Both returned to be handed their own bottles of water.

Elena reached out a free hand to take Izzy's. He let her, cuddling in surreptitiously on one side of her. She loved her archangel all the more that he let the young angel be, though Izzy's wings had to be dangerously close to touching his own.

"What did I miss?" It came out husky, her throat raw.

"That commander bowing down on one knee to Lijuan," her best friend told her, while Illium said something to Suyin that made the tight pain of her expression soften. Trust Blue-bell to get through to a woman so wounded she had no faith in anyone.

"The two left together," Ashwini added. "The queen and her knight."

"That's exactly how Xi sees himself," Dmitri said, his cheekbones sharp against his bronzed skin. "Any luck getting us another visual on them, V?"

"Not yet." Vivek had his eyes narrowed, his lips pursed bloodlessly tight as he worked. "Might be time to activate a crawler." A sudden stiffness. "Things look like bugs and are super stealthy, but have a much narrower field of view."

"I suggest a new name," Aodhan murmured. "Bugs."

"Yeah, bugs it is." Vivek took another two seconds. "Bug's on the move."

At first, all they saw from the bug's low position were the windows of the buildings opposite and the odd angel flying low. "Her army isn't all in uniform this time around," Elena said, that fact only now registering.

Raphael stirred. "Are all our people marked?"

"Yes," Dmitri confirmed. "If they aren't in uniform, they're wearing armbands signifying their allegiance." He glanced at Illium. "Bluebell, get your squadron leaders to fly out with extras while we're in the cease-fire. I don't want the bands accessible to Lijuan's troops."

It was only as Illium headed out that she saw he'd had his hand curled over Aodhan's brutally fisted one. What nightmares did Sparkle remember, she thought. What ugliness had this stirred up?

His departure left Aodhan and Suyin side by side, and the picture they made was startling: Aodhan's glittering beauty against the ice white of her skin and hair. A symphony of cold starlight and the heart of the sun.

"No time to make uniforms for such a grand army?" Janvier's molasses of a voice, slow and easy, but the bayou green of his eyes was as hard as jade.

Ashwini ran a hand down his back. All of them attempting to comfort one another.

"Lack of markings could be on purpose, a way to cause confusion in battle," Dmitri pointed out.

Jason opened out his wings, settled them back in. "We could turn that around, use her lack of uniforms against her."

Nodding agreement, Raphael said, "Brief Naasir on the situation so he can utilize it as soon as he arrives. He's going to be heading into enemy territory."

"I heard from him just before the cease-fire," Dmitri said. "He and Galen should be here by morning. They helped Elijah's people move the vulnerable in the Refuge into the most central stronghold. Jessamy and all the babies and kids are in there, along with the majority of the Medica team. Keir's missing, said to be in Michaela's territory."

Elena thought back, realized the most central Refuge stronghold was Favashi's. Her people certainly had no loyalty to Lijuan or Charisemnon. *Keir must be with Michaela's child.*

If I know him, he's already left with the babe, Raphael replied. *He'll be making his way to the Refuge along isolated routes. Michaela would not want her child in her territory when Lijuan's infected present the threat of a plague.*

Will he be safe? He was crossing a massive distance in the midst of a war.

My guess is that he's traveling alone with the child, Raphael said. *He should attract no attention, especially as other noncombatants will be fleeing to the Refuge for safety. And Keir is tougher than he looks—this is not the first child he has carried to safe harbor.*

On the screen, Vivek's bug finally caught sight of Lijuan and Xi. The two stood in a large garden-like square that Elena recognized from her flights over the city. It was a semi-private park created for business workers, a bright green haven in the summer months and a pretty place to catch some fresh air in winter.

Yet today, despite the rich hues painted on the snow by the setting sun, the park was a place of shadows. In the center bustled multiple vampires; they were constructing something out of materials they must've brought with them in one of the submarines. "What is that?" She leaned in closer to the screen.

"I recognize it," Raphael said. "It's the jade throne from a mountain stronghold Lijuan often used as a retreat. I saw it on a visit with my father."

"It went missing hundreds of years ago, is considered a lost relic," Jason murmured.

"Lijuan must've put it in storage." Dmitri scanned the scene in front of them. "It looks like she's busy for the time being. I'm going to set some things in play. Janvier, Ash."

The two slipped away with Dmitri. Together with Naasir, the three led the "sneak attack" section of Raphael's forces. They'd trained multiple small teams in the time since the last battle, and were the reason the city was so well booby-trapped. Venom's Holly was part of their group.

"I can watch the feeds," Vivek said. "I'll send out an alert if I see anything that indicates preparation for an attack."

"You have more of those bugs?" Illium, having returned from the balcony, came to stand next to Vivek's wheelchair.

The hunter-born male nodded. "I seeded them everywhere I could. Bugs are pretty dumb in the brain department and have a tendency to fall off buildings and get squashed, but no one much notices them. Where do you need eyes?"

"I want to get a real count of her forces."

Sara and Venom walked over to join them. "It'd be good if we could separate out ground and air support numbers," Sara said, to Venom's nod.

While the four of them worked on that, Suyin and Aodhan decided to rejoin their squadrons. Both those squadrons were in the air, maintaining the watch. Raphael stayed in the war room to speak to Suyin while she put on her battle armor, while Elena walked out onto the balcony with Aodhan.

With the twin swords that he wore in a dual sheath down the center of his spine, his well-worn leathers, and muscular build, he was a battle-honed warrior whose beauty was brilliant in the last of the sun's light. But beyond all that, he was her friend. So she held out her hand.

He closed his own over it without hesitation, his palm warm. "Illium's not as stable as he appears. His father's waking threw him badly."

No surprise that Sparkle was more concerned about Bluebell than himself. "He talking to you about it?"

A clenched jaw, Aodhan's bare biceps bunching. "He's the most stubborn person I know." Releasing her hand, he prepared to take off. "But as the Hummingbird pointed out, I am no pushover."

His takeoff was flawless, the glittering filaments in his wings ablaze. Suyin took off with a quieter whisper not long afterward. In this light, the dull silver of her armor appeared nearly the same bronze as the primaries that edged the snow-white of her wings.

Not all angels wore armor, but it was a smart move for Suyin, given her level of training. Designed for the angel, it featured a breastplate that fit exactly right, a neck guard, thigh guards, leg guards integrated into her boots, and forearm guards.

Elena's own "armor" was integrated into her leathers, everything triple reinforced. She liked the freedom of movement it offered. "Suyin doing okay?" she asked Raphael as he came to stand behind her.

"She is haunted by the knowledge that she is of a bloodline with Lijuan. What hidden capacity for evil, she asks, does she carry within?"

Retracting her wings, Elena leaned back against his chest and drew in the masculine heat of his scent. "That they share nearly the same face must make it even worse." It'd be like watching a horror version of yourself.

"I have told her it comes down to choices. Such as the one Lijuan made to murder the mortal who awoke in her what you do in me." Arms already around her, he kissed her temple.

In front of them, their city was eerily calm. Sentries stood on rooftops around the entire perimeter, with archers and shooters on standby. Elena spotted a medic lift off from one rooftop, head to another. Bandaging wounds that didn't necessitate a trip to the infirmary. "Do you know how many we lost?" It was a hard question to ask; the one question she couldn't ask was if someone she knew was already gone.

"Six percent of our overall force." Raphael's wings became limned with a deadly glow. "It does not seem a large number against such a massive enemy, but for our first battle we projected a one percent loss as the maximum." Though he was talking in cold percentages, his hand fisted against her abdomen.

These weren't just numbers to Raphael.

Throat thick and eyes hot, Elena slid her hand over his fisted one and held on. They stood in silence as night fell on the first day of a war that had just begun.

57

Lijuan launched her next assault under cover of night.

Thanks to its watchers, living and electronic, Manhattan was ready.

Squads of black-clad angels had taken to the skies in absolute silence only ten minutes after Vivek's bugs picked up the first signs of preparation in her camp. All the flyers for this op had been chosen because their wings were naturally dark. Each angel took off on their own, as if heading home to the Tower . . . but used the moonless night to disappear into the clouds.

Jason led the team.

Once in the sky, the squadrons did silent sweeps in a holding pattern above Dmitri's predicted attack zone. When an angel needed a break, he flew back a short distance and dropped down on a rooftop.

No one from Lijuan's side seemed to notice—lone angels all over the city, enemy and friendly, were dropping down or taking off. Aside from those taking a break, Jason's team stayed high.

Now, Jason! Raphael sent the command as Lijuan's forces rose en masse from their base by the water; he'd waited until they were high enough that no soft landing was possible.

The nets were fine and black and invisible in the darkness as they fell from the sky. He knew the instant they made contact with Lijuan's winged fighters because the fighting formations collapsed into chaos, angels tumbling uncontrolled from the sky as their wings became tangled in nets that cut and made them bleed.

Their nets successfully deployed, Jason's team emerged from the skies behind enemy lines, and the sky crackled with black lightning. Jason's power was enormous in comparison to most angels' and he sent his energy directly into the heart of Lijuan's disoriented forces, while other angels in his team used line-of-sight grenade launchers to blow up enemy supplies and ground teams.

Aodhan supplied violent backup from this side.

Raphael, meanwhile, was facing off against Lijuan. Jason's team had made no effort to tangle her in nets—given her power, it'd have been a waste. She was his to neutralize. But while his wildfire had regenerated to a certain point, he had nowhere near enough to take on an archangel who'd so recently fed on the lifeforce of at least a hundred people.

Turning his wings to white fire, he moved so quickly in and out of position that her shots went wild, smashing into buildings devoid of residents or workers. Step by step he managed to draw her past her collapsing night assault force and out over water. Now past enemy lines, he took her high, where none of her angels could interfere.

Her next attempt at hitting him smashed into the water. It caused that water to foam and spout, but the ocean was vast enough to absorb the energy without damage. Her fury at his avoidance of her strikes made her face turn skeletal for a haunting instant . . . before she turned without warning and headed straight to Manhattan.

Raphael fired, aiming at her wings.

She went noncorporeal right before the wildfire reached her. Raphael swore under his breath . . . except it appeared Lijuan hadn't shifted location when she went noncorporeal. Wildfire fractured inside the hauntingly translucent form of an archangel, her mouth falling open in screaming pain.

Her body reappeared.

Rage a cold mask on her features, she shifted position to

rain her own power at him in a wide spread he couldn't fully
evade. One bolt hit him hard on the shoulder, spinning him
around. But he'd already thrown the ball of wildfire in his
hand and it smashed into the tip of her right wing.

He had only droplets left inside him—and Lijuan was healing in front of his eyes.

He flew straight at her, sliding out his swords as he did so.
When she responded with a barrage of poisonous blows, he
made no attempt to dodge them. He was already hit. He'd deal
with the damage in the aftermath.

He had to stop her before she took his city.

Blades of starlight obsidian slammed into him with brutal-
izing force, the poison spreading below his skin in an oily
slide. Lijuan laughed at the sight of his swords, the two of
them close enough now that she spoke aloud. "You should've
killed her when I told you." In her voice whispered thousands
of ghosts, their pleas piteous in the maw of their terrible goddess. "Now you are a little bit mortal and weak with—"

Raphael sliced one razor-sharp blade across her neck, the
other across her thighs. Blood splurted and her hands flew up
to hold her head to her neck.

One leg fell into the ocean, while the other hung half severed.

Managing to get his hand on her stump, he sent the last of
his wildfire directly into her bloodstream.

She shrieked in true pain, the sound agony along his nerve
endings.

Eyes red and blood overrunning the hand she had around
her throat, she sent out a blast that caught him at point-blank
range. His vision wavered, but he saw her turn and fly toward
her base of operations. Already, her fighters were coming toward Raphael, ready to intercept him.

His wings grew heavy with the blackness spreading over
them. He couldn't make them turn into white fire. Even his
ability to create angelfire had flatlined. The ocean awaited
below—if he fell, it was over. Lijuan's forces would take him.
And she would feed on an archangel.

Sire. Jason dropped out of the sky, Jurgen with him. Falling
on either side of Raphael, the two dark-winged angels literally

dragged him into the air, while Andreja covered their retreat with a machine gun.

Run, Raphael commanded her and she followed them up, firing at the enemy the entire way.

The rest of Jason's stealth squad appeared around them.

All of them made it to safety, with the majority of the squad splitting off to return to the front line. *Leave me on the roof of the Legion building and go,* Raphael ordered, even as blackness began to creep across his vision. *This is when Xi will launch a secondary attack, while he believes we are at our weakest.*

Sire, Jason argued, *why the Legion building and not the infirmary?*

Because Elena is waiting for me there. Alongside their Legion. *Go.*

Jason and Jurgen eased him to the rooftop, then took off. That they weren't happy about it was obvious even through his increasingly narrow field of vision.

Eyes of liquid silver above him, the near-white of Elena's hair windswept around her head—and her expression ferociously set. "Shit, Archangel, you look like crap." Cutting away his leathers to expose his chest, she pressed both hands to his skin. "If this doesn't work, I'm going to kill you."

Nothing happened. The world hung in balance.

"Black stuff's trying to crawl onto my skin."

"Break contact." He lifted his hand, caught her wrist.

"No, wait." She dug her nails into his skin when he would've moved her. "Hah! Stupid stuff can't get a grip."

Before he could ask what she meant, the opalescent wildfire contained in Elena's body jolted into his in a savage blast that had his back arching as he clenched his jaw and attempted not to scream. The wildfire was unrelenting torture through his veins, along his wings, on his eyes as it ate away at Lijuan's poison.

Elena never broke contact with his skin. He could hear her voice in his head and though he couldn't divine the words through the howl of the battle taking place in his body, it was a reminder that he was not just the Archangel of New York.

He was Elena's lover . . . and her beloved.

It was only when his body slammed back down onto the hard surface of the roof that he realized he'd lifted partially off. Breath heaving as wildfire continued to shoot through his veins in sharp stabs, he opened his eyes. "How does it look?" His senses remained dazed from the dual punch he'd taken—first from Lijuan, then from Elena.

Such a vicious punch for so small an amount.

Yet Lijuan had survived blow after blow after blow with little effect.

"Eyes clear." Breaking contact, she watched with intense care as he got to his feet.

Upright, he flexed his hands and saw that his veins were wildfire, a glowing network of midnight and dawn that flowed to living green. Shifting to go behind him, Elena ran her hands over his wings.

"Clean," she pronounced, just as the lovely, strange wild-fire under his skin faded and settled. "No sign of the poison." Exhaling on a shudder, she pressed her head to his back. "Fuck. I can't believe that worked. Not after what you told me about Antonicus."

"Neither can I." It had been a desperate gamble put in play when it became clear Lijuan was planning to strike.

"Could be you have a level of immunity because of the dregs of wildfire always inside your cells."

"Perhaps." He looked out at where battle had broken out once more, the dazzling light of Aodhan's power coming up against the obsidian of one of Lijuan's generals. "I've bought us a little time before Lijuan rises again. It may be enough for my wildfire to fully regenerate."

Dmitri, report.

Lijuan's soldiers are building another mound of bodies for her to feed from, but other than that they look to be hunkering down in a defensive formation. Aodhan and Jason are dealing with a small air attack, and Venom's cleaning up one on the ground. No loss of territory.

The Legion, who had stood watch around the rooftop during the transfer, began to whisper in his mind. *Raphael.* Ae-clari. *We give.*

Raphael found the Primary, shook his head. "Not yet. I can recover without it this time." He didn't know if his body had developed enough to hold both the Cascade power and the Legion energies. "Give me the power only when there is no other choice, when I am dry of power, and we are on the verge of losing the war."

We understand. A rain of whispers. *We hold. We wait.*

"We believed the Cascade of Terror was the worst that could befall the world." The blue in the Primary's eyes appeared to glow. "We were wrong. This is the Cascade of Death and it could end immortals and mortals alike."

58

It turned out that the small air and ground strikes had been nothing but a feint.

An hour into the tense quiet that followed, scuttling reborn appeared in the darkness, all jerking their way toward Raphael's side of the border. Alerted by their surveillance team, Venom was in position with a team of vampires and guild hunters—a team that included Dmitri's wife, Honor. They were armed with flamethrowers, ready to offer a scorching welcome to any reborn that got through their booby traps.

A junior squadron trained and helmed by Miuxu provided air support to ensure the reborn couldn't scrabble through gaps in the defensive line.

A single infected individual could lead to a death toll in the hundreds or thousands.

"She's figured out a way to protect her own people," Illium said at one point when he and Raphael were both awake and on watch in the war room.

Of the main Tower team, Vivek and Elena needed the most sleep. Vivek had gritted his teeth and gone when the time came, as had Elena—frustrated or not, she accepted it as the cost of being functional in battle. He'd kissed her bare shoulder when he left her in bed earlier; ten seconds after her head hit the pillow and she'd already been half asleep.

Now, he saw what Illium had noticed on the surveillance feed: Lijuan's reborn were skirting her own troops, their eyes fixated on Raphael's side of the line. "I wonder . . ." He asked Illium to zoom in on a section of the footage. "Do you see?"

A hiss of breath. "All the enemy soldiers in the reborn's path have the blackness in their eyes. They're already infected."

"Sire." One of the mortal surveillance techs raised her hand just as Dmitri walked back into the room after taking a short break to shower and drink a glass of blood. "We have movement at the new flesh mountain."

It proved to be Xi, carrying his mistress's bloody body in his arms. Firelight flickered over them and over the faces of the healthy who'd joined the wounded on the flesh pile, their faces shining with worship. Raphael's people had cut off the enemy from the city's electrical grid, but the other side had not only the torches, but lights run off the power generated by the submarines.

Lijuan offered no gentleness or theatrics this time, just fed.

Were you able to get in touch with Honor? Raphael asked when the black fog descended.

Arms folded across his stone gray T-shirt, Dmitri gave a curt nod. *Quick one-minute call. She says not to worry, that the reborn aren't getting through them—and oh, she'd like a personal firethrower for her next birthday.* A hard shake of his head. *Why do we love such fucking courageous women?*

They shared a look of understanding. Before Elena, Raphael hadn't known the cold grip of fear, and before Honor, Dmitri had been quite content to exist inside an impenetrable emotional shell.

On the screen, the fog began to lift. Lijuan was back on her feet . . . but she was being supported by Xi, her face twisted with pain and one side of her body dragging.

Dmitri viewed the footage with no mercy or forgiveness in his expression. "Get enough wildfire directly into her bloodstream and the bitch might actually die."

"It won't work so long as she can feed." Already, fresh wounded were being dropped onto the crumbling remains of the last mound. Dust puffed into the air, the dead nothing but dried out cells.

Sire.

Report, Venom.

Ashwini got through enemy lines and she's reporting a massive swarm of reborn inside a warehouse, ready to be unleashed.

Raphael considered the best use of their resources. *Tell her to warn us when the swarm is about to be released. We'll burn them up from the sky before they ever get close to the ground troops. You can pick off any stragglers.*

He turned to Illium, explained the situation. "You have the oil prepared?" Sometimes, the old ways worked just fine.

"Ready and waiting." Illium thrust a hand through the blue-tipped black of his hair. "I'll prepare my squadron. I don't think Lijuan's going to wait much longer to release that swarm. You enraged her by winning the last skirmish."

"It wasn't a win, Bluebell," he said grimly. "At most, I bought us a day."

There was no way to win against an enemy who could shrug off all wounds. The Archangel of China could claim victory simply by exhausting them into weakness and despair.

Elena was putting knives into her forearm sheaths when the world went up in flame in the distance. Stepping out onto the snow-dusted balcony devoid of owls, she watched the heat brush the predawn sky, the dark yellow curls brilliant. Above the inferno flew angels dropping what she knew to be large "bombs" of oil.

Galen had designed the skins so they'd hold their shape until dropped from a certain height. All you needed after that was a source of fire—which the archers were happy to provide.

And the enemy would burn.

The idea of anyone—reborn included—burning alive was not a thing that sat easy in her gut, but they were fighting for the survival of every man, woman, and child who called this territory home.

A huge winged bird flew across her vision. Her heart jumped.

Raphael, I just saw a condor. Another winged across the front of the balcony, then another.

Elijah has arrived.

Instinct made her look up—just in time to see her archangel take off from the Tower roof. The golden rays of the rising sun hit the white-gold filaments in his feathers, no sign apparent of the white fire.

Too much energy used.

Too little time to recover.

Come, Elena-mine. Hannah is with him.

Elena swept off the balcony. The two of them joined up in the air just as she made out a smudge on the horizon. Elijah's army. Hope was a candle flame inside her. Surely this would even the odds a little.

Is it safe for you to head out this way? She rode a helpful wind. *Lijuan won't take advantage?*

She remains incapacitated. Your hunter friend Demarco was able to put eyes on her—the stump I filled with wildfire isn't healing as quickly as the rest of her body.

Elena's gut iced; she'd known Demarco would be going into enemy territory, but it was still a shock to hear he was in the heart of danger. *Who else is behind enemy lines?*

Janvier, Holly, Ashwini, and the rest of Demarco's sniper team. They entered via the tunnel system.

Those tunnels were on no maps except those kept in a secure Tower locker—and in the minds of every member of the senior Tower team. *They're all insane.* Worry pounded a drumbeat in her blood. *Naasir?* The sneakiest of them all and the acknowledged leader of the stealth team.

He is in the city, doing what he does best.

The smudge in the sky began to take shape. Dawnlight glinted off the gold of Elijah's hair and shimmered over the black of Hannah's. As they got closer, Elena felt her eyes widen. She'd always before seen Hannah in elegant gowns, her hair in styles as elegant. Today, Elijah's consort wore a simple brown tunic and pants, an outfit similar to fighting leathers.

A sword was sheathed and strapped down the side of one thigh. Tightly braided to her skull, her hair had then been wrapped in a knot at the back of her head. "I didn't know Hannah could fight."

"Do not forget, Elena-mine, Hannah has lived many mortal lifetimes and she's long been consort to an archangel who was once a general." He angled his wings in a signal to Elijah, who angled his own in return.

"But you are right in that she has never been a warrior at heart—however, Hannah has always stepped into battle as one who will assist fallen warriors. She has carried countless wounded to safety, bandaged injuries enough to hold them together for survival, worked alongside medics trying to save the fallen."

Well able to see Hannah doing all of that, Elena raised a hand in a wave to her fellow consort. The other woman waved back. Condors and other winged birds of prey danced in front of the archangelic couple, several coming forward to sweep around Elena and Raphael.

When the four of them met, it was several beats ahead of Elijah's army. That army spread out behind him on a wave of wings and below him in a sweep of heavy-duty vehicles. Raphael had told her that Elijah was later than expected because he'd chosen to bring everyone in together rather than flying ahead with his aerial troops. Splitting the two had risked leaving the ground forces without aerial support should Lijuan decide to aim her eyes in that direction.

"Eli." Raphael clasped the other archangel's forearm as Elijah did the same to him.

Elena exchanged a hug with Hannah.

"Your wings, Ellie," whispered the other woman. "I am astonished." Despite the wondering words, lines of strain marred the normally smooth darkness of her skin.

"I have only been able to bring half my army, my friend." The Archangel of South America glanced behind then below him to take in that army. "All those who were close enough to your border to get here in good time."

"That you have come, it is an act of friendship I will never forget."

"My intention was to bring all of them," Elijah continued, "but Lijuan was clever in a way I did not predict." He exchanged a tight smile with Hannah. "My people were successful in halting the majority of attempts to bring in a single reborn to begin a nest."

"We never expected to catch every one," Raphael said. "I believe the only reason I have not had news of any infestations in my territory is because Lijuan didn't bother with such a stratagem here. Her plan was always to take Manhattan, then loose her creatures."

Elijah nodded. "The few nests that got through are not the problem—my teams are well able to eliminate them. Charisemnon, however . . ." Elijah's eyes grew cold enough to cause goose bumps on Elena's skin, his wings limned with light. The hilts of the swords he wore crisscrossed on his back glinted with jewels.

Hannah had once told Elena those jewels were part of a large horde Caliane had gifted Elijah prior to his ascension, in thanks for Elijah's loyal and courageous service.

"While I have never fully trusted Charisemnon," he said now, "our territories have done trade with each other for centuries. I was complacent, for never has an archangel used trade as a back door for an attack. It is not an action of integrity or valor."

That sounds ominous, Archangel. Do we do any trade with Charisemnon?

I have asked Dmitri to check. Out loud, Raphael said, "The fault is not yours. You are right to say such things are beneath the Cadre. What did he do?"

"Use his access as a trade partner to spread disease." Elijah's cheekbones sliced against the sun-brushed warmth of his skin. "Well-hidden within his recent shipments were insects infected with the same disease that killed a vampire in your territory and caused angels to fall from the sky."

Wings of lush cream with a blush of peach on the primaries holding an effortless hover, Hannah picked up the thread. "Our people in the ports are trained to treat all shipments with tinctures against insects."

Elena figured by "tinctures," Hannah must mean fumigation.

"Many of the shipments were also personally checked." Elijah pressed his lips together. "But to find such miniscule and cleverly hidden things . . ." A shake of his head. "We believe he had operatives in my territory who retrieved the insects from their hiding places and held them safe until Lijuan's assault against Manhattan. They are spreading like a plague—and the disease is far more virulent than the last time."

"We've lost a hundred vampires already." Hannah's eyes shone. "A vampire must be bitten many times to die, but their poison incapacitates with only three or four bites, leaving the victim helpless to crush or otherwise annihilate the creatures."

"I have ordered the other half of my army to evacuate a large infested area, and to then scorch the earth with fire." Elijah glanced back as his aerial army came to a hovering halt a respectful distance away; the ground troops followed. "If you've any containers from Charisemnon's territory and they are mercifully unopened, destroy them at once."

"I will, my friend." Raphael began to turn. "Come, I will lead you to where your army may settle."

They angled their wings toward Manhattan.

Dmitri says we have had ten recent shipments from Charisemnon.

59

Raphael's statement froze Elena's veins. Their city couldn't handle an infestation, not with Lijuan at their doorstep.

Then her archangel's lips curved in a smile that was deadly. *All those shipments are sitting on a cargo ship anchored far off the coast—and crewed by Tower personnel. Your friend with the third eye told Dmitri that she didn't think they had good "feng shui."*

Feng shui? Ash said that? Elena laughed, the relief a sweet rush. *And he listened to her?*

We have all learned to listen to what comes out of Ashwini's mouth. Dmitri quarantined the containers at such a distance offshore that there is no chance the insects could make it to land even if released.

You going to order that ship blown up?

It can wait until we can burn it to ash, eliminating any risk of insectoid survivors. He led Elijah's forces to a skyscraper beside Central Park. A team overseen by Elena and Raphael's architect, Maeve, had turned the plush building into barracks within an incredibly short period. It helped that the entire operation had been preplanned as part of their war strategy— Central Park had always been in the frame. At the moment, it was being used to muster Raphael's forces, but there was plenty of room for Elijah's people, too.

Supply lines with enough capacity to sustain both armies were running smoothly, with multiple fail-safes in place. A number of strong angels loyal to Raphael were in charge of feeding and protecting those lines. It wasn't only a matter of food and water, but of replacement weapons and gear.

"A war," Galen had said at one point, "can be won or lost on supply."

Elijah's squadrons began to land, while his ground troops filled up the streets leading to Central Park. New York's forces had just swelled in size by a considerable margin . . . but even combined, their numbers were a fraction of Lijuan's.

That they still held the city was a miracle.

A fact made even clearer when she, Elijah, Hannah, and Raphael walked out onto a balcony below the war room. Dmitri had come out here to discuss a strategy with Andreas's elite squadron. A feather of delicate topaz drifted down as that squadron took off before they reached Dmitri.

"Sire." Dmitri bowed his head.

Elena almost misstepped at the unexpected formality. Then she got it. It was because of Elijah, a show of respect from a second to his archangel. When he wasn't being a dick, Dmitri was scarily likable.

Truth to tell, Elena *wanted* him to pull a scent trick or shoot off a sarcastic remark—it'd mean things were back to normal and they could snipe at each other without worrying about the zombie-creating Goddess of Death camped on their doorstep.

Today, Dmitri turned to indicate the current battle zone. Fires continued to burn in the distance, while in the sky raged a winged battle as Lijuan's forces attempted to stop the oil drops.

"At this stage, we've lost no more winged fighters," he told Raphael, "though a few are wounded. Several of the ground crew were burned when they went too close to the flames to finish off a reborn, but all are vampires."

Elena started breathing again. A lot of her Guild friends were down there. Others were on teams of archers or shooters positioned on rooftops. A small and select number would, by now, be sitting still and silent in sniper nests right in the thick of enemy territory.

Demarco was one of them.

Elena's stomach hurt. They'd planned this, she reminded herself. During the rebuild after the last battle, they'd created secret hidey-holes accessible via concealed "service shafts" inside buildings. Those shafts linked directly with the tunnel system, so their people could get safely into enemy territory—then wreak havoc from the inside.

Each of the nests had clear visibility of the landscape outside.

As if he'd heard her, Dmitri said, "One of our snipers was able to take out a powerful vampire general in the chaos after the last skirmish. No one noticed. He was dumped on the flesh pile."

That comment necessitated an explanation of Lijuan's horrific feeding habits. It made Hannah raise a trembling hand to her mouth and turn into Elijah's embrace. The Archangel of South America was rigid as he held her close, streaks of angry red on his cheekbones.

"We received a fresh report from India," Dmitri said while the couple tried to digest the ugly information. "The stream of infected children isn't stopping. It's as if Lijuan turned the entire child population of her territory into . . . whatever these children have become." His neck was stiff and a tic pulsed in his jaw. "Not vampire or reborn but an amalgam."

Light sparked off a pair of wings in the distance, right before a bolt that glittered like shattered gemstones slammed into a squadron of Lijuan's fighters. *Aodhan,* Elena thought, just as one of the angels in their squadron took a direct hit and began to spiral down from a catastrophic height. If his head separated from his body . . .

Wings of shattered light in her vision.

Aodhan had caught the falling angel. Elena exhaled . . . right as another bolt, the color shining copper, came from the other direction. It was going to slam into Aodhan. There was no way it could miss—he couldn't move fast enough with the weight of the other angel in his arms.

Elena wasn't aware of running or flying, but she was suddenly in the air beside him. She slammed herself into him, her body acting out of old knowledge learned from hundreds of hunts.

The bolt of power singed the tips of her hair as it went past to slam into the side of a high-rise. It blew out the windows in a cascade of glass, some of the small square pieces hitting Elena. Tiny jewels that were designed not to cut but they hurt all the same at that velocity.

Aodhan had already passed the wounded angel to another fighter, was turning to fire back at the enemy. Elena dropped out of the battle zone. Sparkle needed to fight, not worry about protecting her. She landed behind a row of shooters on a rooftop.

Glancing back toward the Tower, she said, *Sorry, Archangel.* Terror would've gripped him when he realized what she'd done, where she was. *I'm fine, no damage.*

The sea crashed into her mind, the salt spray of it a familiar kiss. *I'm certain you just saved Aodhan's life—bone-chilling fear is a price I'll pay with no complaints. That bolt came from Philomena, one of the few of Lijuan's generals who doesn't depend on her mistress's power. She's strong enough to have ended him with that hard a hit.*

Her hands shook as she brushed back her hair. That they could've lost Aodhan so quickly . . . *Since I'm here anyway,* she said, forcing calm because anything else could be deadly in battle, *I'll give someone a break.*

Scanning the shooters, she noticed one who was moving a little slower than the others and tapped him on the shoulder. "Hiraz. You want a break?"

"Yes, Consort." Sweat dripping down his temples, he turned away and let her take his position. He was wearing a camo green T-shirt and cargo pants in black. It was the first time she'd seen the senior vampire in anything but a button-down shirt and suit pants. The T-shirt had gone dark, was stuck to his skin.

The two things that hadn't changed were the wedding ring on his right hand and the expert cut of his hair—currently black with streaks of bronze. She'd woken from the chrysalis to the news that his lover, Jenessa, had proposed.

He'd accepted on the condition they wait to marry until ten years after her transition to vampirism. In the interim, he'd wear the wedding ring she'd chosen on his right ring finger instead of his left. Elena didn't think Jenessa would change her mind, but she liked Hiraz for thinking first of the woman he'd saved from a life on the streets, and not just his own need.

After catching his breath, he said, "My relief was badly wounded soon after taking her position."

So he'd effectively done a double shift. It put the continued speed and accuracy of his shooting in a whole different light. "Get some rest," she said to him. "I can spot you for a while."

"I'll be back soon. I just need a blood boost." Shifting into a low crouch, he headed out of the live fire area.

Elena had already begun to pick off enemy fighters with precision shots of the surface-to-air weapon that could fire both single shots and a burst. It wasn't her favorite, but she'd trained on it because she knew it'd be used during battle. She'd made sure to update that training the instant she recovered enough after the chrysalis.

Given that she was a—limited—backup power source for Raphael, Dmitri had fought hard to have her stay safe in the Tower and out of the fighting. Elena had pushed back as hard. That was not who she was—and having the consort and "hunter angel" MIA from the field of battle would demoralize their people.

Raphael had agreed with her.

Her archangel understood what drove her, she thought as she targeted an enemy angel aiming his crossbow at the wings of their fighters. He'd already badly wounded one; the angel was only alive because Aodhan had managed another air rescue. Before today, she hadn't known how fast Sparkle could fly—his speed tended to be eclipsed by Bluebell's.

"Fuck you, you asshole." She fired. Her shot hit the enemy angel in the eye, exactly as she'd planned. Screaming, he spun in the air as red bled down his face. She struck him twice more, shredding his own wings.

He fell.

Part of her would always mourn an angel's fall, but she couldn't be sorry. Not when he'd come to this city as part of an attacking force—and not when his eyes had been an ordinary blue instead of the ugly black that marked Lijuan's puppets. It wasn't like Raphael had gone to China and picked a fight. Lijuan had come here and all these clear-eyed fighters had followed out of *choice*.

A massive shattering sound, shards of concrete flying up into the air. Something struck Elena's cheek hard enough that blood dripped down her skin. She glanced back to see a smoking hole in the center of the roof. "What the fuck was that?"

"Look out!

Her head jerked up at the warning . . . to see a bolt of shining copper power heading directly for her. She rolled up to her feet . . . and found herself on the Tower roof, her breath gasps and her heart thundering from the speed of her flight. Raphael was already above her previous position, his wings white fire.

I'm safe! she yelled to him mind-to-mind, as angry frustration gnawed at her. She wasn't the kind of woman who abandoned her fellow soldiers and ran from danger. She stayed and she fought! Fuck this ability that wouldn't let her choose!

Elena. A single word that held Raphael's heart.

Philomena directed her blows toward Raphael, but Raphael was an archangel, Philomena a mere angel even if she was experienced and old. The piercing blue of his angelfire hit Lijuan's general on one side of her body and that was it.

She disintegrated from the inside out.

Angelfire was designed to kill archangels; ordinary angels stood no chance.

Raphael then blasted angelfire across a heavy line of enemy squadrons coming at theirs and the sky glowed for a long moment before things quieted down. Lijuan's forces didn't withdraw but they became warier, more careful.

Come back, Archangel. You're our only hope when Lijuan rises. You can't afford to get injured. If the enemy managed to shoot off part of his wing while it was in its physical form, he'd be grounded until it grew back. It might grow back faster than before the Cascade filled him with power, but it wouldn't be immediate.

There are so many of them, he replied. *Our people are exhausted.*

I know. But if you fall, we all fall.

A silver-green power cracked the sky at that moment, and Elena stiffened . . . until she realized it was coming from their side. *I forgot about Elijah.* Her grin was surely manic.

Raphael didn't reply until he landed beside her on the Tower roof. "Eli is of the same opinion as you." He folded back his wings, his skin glimmering with perspiration. "He will help our forces while I hoard my energy to take on Lijuan."

He stared out at the battle zone. "He is a good man. Not many generals, far less archangels, would put themselves in the position of being the assistant."

"Yeah, he is." Leaning her head against his biceps, she let her wing overlap his, the energy that danced between them a familiar caress by now. "I have to be more careful where I put myself if they've begun to target me."

It had happened in the last battle, too, but this time around Lijuan had appeared so obsessed with Raphael that the entire army had forgotten Elena. Too bad the memory lapse hadn't lasted. "I don't want to put our troops in danger. I could—"

A door banged behind them, Dmitri running out. "Titus is wounded," he said, a phone held to his ear.

Elena's entire body tensed.

"How bad?" Raphael asked at the same time.

A pause while Dmitri listened to the person on the other end of the line. "He's not incapacitated but he's down for at least a day." Another pause. "Charisemnon is also down. Titus wounded him at the same time he was wounded."

Exhaling on a shudder, Elena leaned forward with her hands on her knees.

"Good," Dmitri said curtly, putting away the phone. "Tzadiq says Titus caused massive quakes through Charisemnon's territory, including one that collapsed land under a significant percentage of Charisemnon's ground troops. Injured as he is, Charisemnon won't be able to make much headway while Titus is down."

Tzadiq, Elena remembered as she rose back to her full height, was Titus's second—and Galen's father.

Dmitri's T-shirt pulled against his pectorals as he put his hands on his hips. "I finally managed to get an update on Astaad and Aegaeon. Charisemnon got his insects into Astaad's territory. He's evacuating those who haven't been bitten to clean islands, putting the infected on a single quarantine island, and burning the rest down to soil and rock. Aegaeon is assisting."

Elena had seen pictures of Astaad's lands, many of them

lush and tropical. How it must hurt the archangel to deliberately destroy all that beauty, all that life. As it must've hurt Elijah to give the order to scorch his lands. "What about Australia?" It was the biggest swath of Astaad's territory.

"Infected." Dmitri's jaw worked. "But it's also where he bases a good percentage of his army—they're burning out the areas closest to the ports and shepherding the uninfected inward. Infected are being quarantined in various small towns."

"The enemy has poisoned our world to win this war," Raphael said and in his voice was the cold of the Cascade. "If we do not stop them here and now, their plague of death will cover the planet."

60

The smoke over the city finally began to dissipate after sunset—when Lijuan's reborn stopped attempting to cross the border. A few of the macabre walking corpses apparently had a semblance of primitive brainpower, because they caught a clue and began to hunker down on the other side of the line of blackened remains that marked where their brethren had burned up.

Lijuan's squadrons drew back at the same time.

Now, the moon a spotlight in the sky, Elena sat on the edge of the balcony with her legs hanging over the side, Illium beside her. Raphael was up in the sky with Elijah, giving the other archangel the lay of the land.

"Naasir's behind enemy lines," she told Illium. "No one saw him enter the city but Raphael's spoken to him."

"I figured as much when I saw Galen in the sky."

"Did you know Galen brought in a freaking catapult in pieces? It's being set up on a rooftop, ready to pelt Lijuan's people."

"Makes sense," Illium said. "Lijuan's got a ton of old vampires and angels in her forces. Catapults are intimidating and something they fear." He took a drink from the bottle of vodka in his hand, then passed across the bottle. Elena took a hit, the warmth of it spreading like fire through her system. "We fought together in the last major battle of the day."

"How long do you think this pause will last?"

"I'm more worried about *why* they've pulled back." He took the bottle back from her but didn't drink, the aged gold of his eyes focused on the distance, where Lijuan's troops were doing something they couldn't quite figure out.

The enemy had finally begun to stomp on Vivek's bugs. Most of the drones were also down. Lijuan's people hadn't found the cameras hidden in the facades of buildings, atop roofs or on streetlights, but many of those buildings—and cameras—had been damaged during battles. As a result, there were blind spots.

"Elijah hurt them pretty bad," she pointed out. "He was throwing angelfire around like it was candy."

"It's a question of resources," Illium murmured. "Lijuan has an overwhelming number of fighters who will follow her commands without hesitation. She—or her generals—could've simply kept sending through wave after wave of people. And Philomena wasn't her only naturally powerful fighter.

"Even Elijah and Raphael couldn't hold off that entire mass of fighters, not if they swarmed. No one but Lijuan could kill either of them, but the army could do damage and take over the city, lay siege to the Tower."

"Yeah, I see your point." The moon's silver light shimmered on the ocean in the distance. "Have we kept an eye on the other waterways around New York? She isn't sending people into the water so they can sneak up on us?"

"We've got dive teams double-checking on the sensors. Nothing. They're not in the water. And they're not in the sky—not unless . . ."

Horror curdled Elena's stomach. "Oh, shit."

Illium jumped to his feet, hauling her up at the same time. Vodka abandoned, they raced into the war room.

"Vivek!" Illium said. "How much has she fed?"

Vivek's head snapped up from his focus on a computer screen. "Two mountains of flesh," he said, "and they're building another one it looks like. I don't know how many bodies.

Lot of wings in the last lot." A frown. "But she was still limp-
ing badly afterward."

"Bring up the images."

A woman in a lovely gown made up of myriad shades of
gray . . . the skirts of which shaped against her legs in a passing breeze. Two *complete* legs. And she wasn't dragging either
leg, the limp only a thing of motion.

Elena ran out of the room, her mind reaching for Raphael's.
*Raphael! We think there's a chance Lijuan's fed enough to go
noncorporeal with a bunch of her troops!*

The sea crashed into her mind, the taste of salt sharp
against her tongue. *Elena, if you are in the sky, drop! ALL
FIGHTERS, DROP!*

She heard the troop-wide command just as she burst out
onto the nearest balcony. The sky above her head crackled an
incandescent white-gold shot with scorching blue. Precious
wildfire going into the void to try to unmask Lijuan. If they
were wrong . . .

*Illium, Andreas, Nimra, Nazarach move your squadrons to
the East River! Lijuan is halfway to the Tower! Elijah has
activated his resting squadrons and they'll join you! Galen,
Aodhan—take the port! Ground teams on break—return to
your positions. Venom, get ready for a renewed reborn assault.*

The sky filled with wings on the heels of Raphael's orders.

Elena rose into the air just enough that she could see what
was going on. The battle was close, far closer than on the first
front. Lijuan—legs definitely fully regrown and fuck it was
freaky how quickly she'd done it—was spraying the sky with
shards of starlight obsidian that were ruthless in their beauty.

Raphael was blocking the spray with wildfire, while Elijah
attempted to hit her with angelfire. Around them, their troops
were badly outnumbered; most had not been anywhere near
the site when the order came. Even the vast majority of the
Legion wouldn't make it in time. Which meant Raphael and
Elijah were under attack from not only Lijuan but a massive
chunk of her army.

It was shaping up as a massacre.

Meanwhile the troops that had gone quiet near the port had
risen again with bloody fury. At the front were three generals

whose power was Lijuan's obsidian. Galen and a tired Aodhan were in the air, but the numbers coming at them were catastrophic. They needed Raphael or Elijah, but neither archangel could break off from the fight against Lijuan.

Elena flew up to the Tower roof. Lifting open a specific weapons locker, she picked up a grenade launcher. The shot wouldn't go far, but she didn't need it to go far. Not if she could make this fucking work.

Hauling the thing up to her shoulder, she rose back into the air.

Focusing on Raphael and the lethal threat of Lijuan, she let her rage and her worry rise to fill her throat, her *need* to be next to him a pulse in her mouth.

Nothing happened.

Raphael barely dodged being skewered by Lijuan's poisonous energy. She was releasing huge sprays of bolts rather than one at a time—because the Archangel of China didn't have to conserve her energy. She could waste as much as she wanted.

And Elena was still too far away to help.

Think Elena! Why had it worked with Aodhan but not Raphael?

Because he is an archangel, child. The voice was old and tired and heavy with Sleep. *You cannot interfere in the wars of archangels.*

That's bullshit, Elena said, not having the time or the inclination to be startled by Cassandra's reappearance. *If I'd been a fucking battery, I'd have interfered wouldn't I? But thanks for the tip.*

Willing to believe that the Cascade could be so arbitrary, she focused on Illium instead. Fast as he was, he'd outpaced his squadron and was about to fly directly into the line of fire, had nearly a hundred percent chance of being badly wounded before the rest of the warriors caught up with him.

Not my Bluebell, she thought, letting all her fear and anger coalesce into a hard knot in her gut.

Her breath came in pants when she appeared beside him.

"Ellie!"

"Cover me!" She dove in front of him while he shattered the sky around her with his power, driving off would-be assailants. It wasn't as good as if she'd come out next to Raphael, but it was good enough.

Ignoring the death bolts the fucking Queen of the Dead was throwing her way, she fired the grenade launcher. Lijuan ignored it. Of course she did. She didn't pay attention to mortal things. Or a baby angel.

Elena dropped at the same moment, screaming at Bluebell to do the same.

Lijuan's poisonous spray flew over them to smash into the buildings at their backs. And the grenade went straight into Lijuan's chest . . . or it would have if she hadn't smashed her hand across it at the last moment. But all was not lost. Because the thing blew up as her hand connected with it. It took her hand and a section of her ribs with it, while peeling back part of her face to reveal the skeletal understructure.

Elena fired again while the bitch was distracted, and this time, she aimed for the lower half of Lijuan's body. The grenade punched out the side of her hip and amputated her thigh. Raphael slammed Lijuan with wildfire at the same time, aiming for an open wound.

The Archangel of China went noncorporeal.

Elena had a moment of hope, thinking she'd turned tail and run. But the sky erupted with shards of starlight obsidian a moment later . . . right on top of the incoming squadrons. Angel after angel went down, even as Raphael and Elijah attacked a rematerialized Lijuan. She was bleeding and listing badly to one side, and her face was straight out of a horror film, but she had enough power to make a return volley before she flew toward her troops.

Half wrapped protectively around her as an escort, while the other half continued to fight. But with Illium, Andreas, Nimra, and Nazarach all here with their highly trained squadrons, along with two archangels, the advantage was now on their side.

Archangel, Galen and Aodhan need backup!

Eli is going to them. I need to clear up the mess on the ground. Venom's ground teams are already overwhelmed on the port side and Jason is taking care of a skirmish to the west.

That was when Elena saw the scuttling movements below.

Landing on the nearest roof, she flipped open weapons lockers until she found a flamethrower. Raphael beat her down and used his power to burn the things up before they could scramble any deeper into Manhattan, but there were a fucking lot of them.

While he took care of larger groups as battle raged over-head in a clash of swords, she flew in and out through gaps and alleys, burning up the loners sneaking through. She saw fallen angels as she flew, sent their coordinates to Dmitri to organize rescue—while she crisped the reborn trying to get to those angels.

"Hurry!" she yelled into the mike on her collar. "There're too many wounded angels. The reborn are heading straight for them!" To Elena it seemed they were acting with resolve and planning.

They're being guided. Raphael's voice in her mind. *Look for a vampire at the head of each group.*

Elena switched focus. *There.* She flew right over the bas-tard and turned him to flame. She took no pleasure in his scream, but he had to die. As he did, she saw things crawling out of him and scuttling quickly away. Her blood ran cold. *Raphael, they're bringing in the insects!*

A breath of cold in her mind she could almost feel. *This part of the city is now infected. A moment while I take care of the aerial assault—there is no point in accumulating power to fight Lijuan if she takes the city by stealth.*

Elena had to turn away from the furious blaze of his power as he raked angelfire across Lijuan's troops. Ash fell like rain from the sky. She tried not to think about what she was breath-ing in—but Raphael's deadly assault achieved its intended outcome. Lijuan's people retreated en masse.

Elijah had achieved the same outcome by the port.

Raphael's next order to the ground and aerial troops was to evacuate their wounded and create a fireline that would en-compass a large chunk of the city. As soon as that was done, the area clear of their people, Raphael began to rain down hell on the infected area. Standing watch on top of a skyscraper just behind the blaze of the fireline, Elena watched and felt tears burn her throat, her eyes.

New York was going up in flame and that bitch Lijuan was responsible. Her and her disease-ridden friend. The only

mercy was that the entire city had been evacuated of noncombatants. "We'll rise again," she promised herself and all their
people.

Another woman stood not far from her, her moonlight hair
dancing in the hot winds and her armor glowing in the firelight. "It is a horrible truth to accept that the person I most
hate in this world, the person who is my worst nightmare, is
so far beyond me in power that I can never do her harm."

"But you'll try anyway, won't you?" Sometimes, you had to
fight the monsters even if you knew you'd fail—as a frightened and traumatized ten-year-old Elena had fought Slater
Patalis while Ari and Belle's blood was an iron-rich scent that
clogged her throat.

"Yes." Suyin's murmur was a soft vow, the weight of her
presence a portentous heaviness. "To the death."

It took pathetically little time to erase so much of Elena's
beloved city. The angelfire not only razed buildings, leaving a
smoking red ruin of earth, it ate up the reborn and any insects
they'd brought with them. *Do we have to worry about the side
Venom's ground team is handling?* she asked her archangel as
she swallowed her tears for her city.

No. He landed next to her, his wings aglow and his eyes
chips of Antarctic glaciers. *There have been no reports of insects there—I don't think they can be controlled. Even Lijuan
wouldn't risk releasing them so close to her own people.*

Below them, the lost part of their city smoldered.

61

Once the casualties from the engagement were tallied up, Raphael discovered that, together, he and Elijah had lost an entire squadron of strong, powerful warriors. Rage burned in him, but it was a cold hard thing. He couldn't afford to be hot, to give in to the sorrow that bit at his throat. To lose warriors in battle was a thing that could not be fought. But he had never lost so many so rapidly.

Elijah's face showed the same strain and anger.

The sheet-wrapped bodies of their dead lay in the cold embrace of a morgue set up in a warehouse. It was a necessity Nisia had quietly taken care of when battle first began. Each and every fighter here, Raphael promised himself, as he carried in one of the fallen himself, would have a burial with full honors. They would go home to the Refuge.

The meeting he next held, with all his senior people and Elijah's who weren't out on watch or fighting in small skirmishes, was brutal in its grimness. Now that they knew Lijuan could turn part of her army noncorporeal again if she had enough fuel, they had to be ready for an attack from any quarter.

"My entire city is seeded with machines that watch." Raphael waved Vivek Kapur forward. "But we can't watch for what we can't see. And even if we could, the feeds would be far too many for even a team to monitor constantly."

The angels and vampires gathered around Dmitri's battle strategy table parted for Vivek's wheelchair. A few of Elijah's warriors gave him a curious look, but that was to be expected. It was rare that a vampire was Made when he had such terrible injuries.

"Tell us of your machines," Raphael said.

The vampire—ridiculously young in immortal terms—did not flinch at being the focus of so much powerful attention. "The surveillance grid covers nearly the entire city—the only gaps are where Archangel Lijuan's forces have destroyed cameras, drones, or bugs."

Taking a small "bug" from his pocket, he put it on the table for reference. "I've been able to set the sky-focused system to sound a warning for any movement big enough to be an angel but I still need bodies to look at every alert and verify if it's a friendly or an enemy."

"The wounded," one of Elijah's female warriors suggested. "They are distraught at falling at the dawn of battle—to watch for the enemy, it will give them life."

Elijah, new lines carved around his mouth, glanced at Vivek. "Can wounded warriors do this task?"

"As long as they have their sight," Vivek said. "I also have another job that only needs hearing, no sight—I was able to reprogram our electronic spies to listen for dialects you'd usually only hear among older residents of Archangel Lijuan's territory. I don't know if noise escapes that invisible thing she does, but it can't hurt to listen—and I figured since a lot of her generals and commanders aren't exactly young . . ."

The looks shot Vivek's way by Eli's people were not curious this time—they were assessing.

I see why you Made this man, Raphael, Elijah said. *He is an asset.*

You cannot steal him yet, Eli. He is under Contract.

"I also thought of trying to program a system to alert us of areas of dead air without birds," Vivek continued, unaware of the judgments being made around him, "but with all the fighting, the only birds still in the city are yours, Archangel Elijah."

Even Elena's owls had disappeared, perhaps because their lady was stirring.

Discussion ensued, but no matter how they looked at it, they had no way to moderate Lijuan's one major advantage. "The only reason we managed to hold her off in the latest attack," Raphael said, "was that we were both close enough to respond quickly."

"And because your consort can do something I have never seen anyone do." Elijah smiled at Elena, who stood silently beside her onetime nemesis, Galen.

Her responding smile was enigmatic. "A woman must have her secrets."

Shifting their discussion to what they *could* control, they used the battle layout on Dmitri's table to plan troop movements, but the harsh fact was that they did not have enough people—not when faced with the size of Lijuan's army.

"How is she feeding them?"

Everyone turned to Vivek. He flushed under the deep brown of his skin, realizing he'd interrupted two archangels and their most senior people, but to his credit, he held his ground. "Archangel Lijuan has far too many people for there to have been enough food on the submarines. So how is she feeding them?"

"Angels do not need to eat as much as mortals," Raphael said, but he was frowning. "Wounded angels, however, do need food to have enough energy to recover."

"Well, that explains it," his consort muttered. "She just eats her wounded."

Everyone stared at Elena this time.

"What?" She threw up her hands. "It's the truth."

"It is indeed," Elijah said. "That leaves blood for the unwounded vampires. So she must have a store of mortals who've been kept away from the fighting."

"One second." Dmitri grabbed Vivek's ever-present tablet and brought up something. "This came in just before all hell broke loose—one of the snipers reported seeing a small group of 'scared mortals' being ushered into a building. They were dressed like farmers. Healthy, but only about fifty in number."

Cristiano, a powerful vampire in Elijah's team, shook his head. "That's nowhere near enough for the number of vampires she has in her ground forces. Also, she still has to feed the mortals and Venom tells me you left no food behind when you evacuated that area."

"Her plan was to take this city in a violent surge—plenty of food and blood then." The courage of Raphael's people had stopped her advance, but they were exhausted and they had lost too many of their own.

He locked eyes with those of liquid silver, his hunter with whom he had no shields. *If we do not stop her,* hbeebti, *Lijuan will feed on our own.*

The fighting over the next two days was brutal. Lijuan was still down, possibly as a result of having been badly injured twice in quick succession, but her generals and commanders were determined not to let that stop them. Even more of them were now shooting Lijuan's obsidian power from their hands.

When Elijah got hit in the chest with a bolt, they all panicked—but it became clear in a matter of seconds that while the energy was deadly to an ordinary angel, it did not incapacitate an archangel. Neither were their strikes infectious. Elijah was soon able to shake off the effects.

The law that only an archangel could kill another archangel remained an immutable one. However, that so many of Lijuan's senior people could now end members of New York's troops in a single strike meant both Elijah and Raphael had to be out there—being worn down by constant battle while Lijuan rested.

Elijah's birds of prey were vicious fighters who'd torn holes in angelic wings and gouged out eyes, but neither they nor the Legion could even the odds when Lijuan was feeding neararchangel level power to the top echelon of her army. Take Raphael and Elijah out of the field of battle and it'd be a bloodbath.

"I will not sacrifice people," Raphael said to Elena in the short lull between one battle and the next. "I will not allow them to be mowed down like dispensable pieces on a chessboard."

"You know I'm on your side." If he won the war by walking on the bodies of his people, he would lose the greater battle—to remain Raphael.

She was bone-tired, too, but she stayed on the front line beside their people, sometimes with the ground teams fighting the reborn, others with those on rooftops. With her wings retracted and her hair hidden under a knit cap, the enemy couldn't find her. Permanent dye would've been better, but they'd discovered it didn't stick. The energy that arced through her wings occasionally zapped her hair, too, and poof, no more dye.

Yesterday, she'd been back-to-back with Venom as they cut down a swarm of reborn. Today, she was firing a ground-to-air gun. When three of Lijuan's squadrons managed to overwhelm them with sheer numbers, swarming the rooftop, she fired the weapon at point-blank range until it ran out of projectiles, then threw it aside and went for her knives.

Blades were close combat weapons, no room for squeamishness.

Blood sprayed her face, but she continued on with relentless focus, images of Zoe and Maggie held close to her heart. If the city fell, the little girls would become prey for Lijuan and her forces. A momentary gap between two sets of wings and she saw that Hiraz was trapped behind the enemy soldiers, his sword moving with blurring speed. But even a skilled swordsman couldn't hold off that many of the enemy.

If he didn't get some backup soon, he was dead.

She stabbed one of her assailants in the eye, threw a blade that slammed home in the eyeball of the second attacker. One thing she'd learned during all of this—didn't matter if it was a vampire or an angel, they hated to get a blade in the eye. Both of the two that she'd attacked had the dead black eyes, but even they screamed and pulled out the knives, putrid greenish-black fluid leaking down their cheeks.

Elena had seen enough of these reborn angels now that she didn't flinch. As the loss of an eye led to a loss of coordination, she was able to slice open the throat of one, while an archer who'd been fighting beside her used a small scythe to slice off the head of the other.

Archers were elite specialists. But turned out that when you had hundreds of years to become a specialist, you picked up a few other skills along the way.

Dropping and rolling as an enemy combatant swung for her own throat, she slid her blades across the back of his ankles, severing the Achilles tendon on each foot. He dropped to the ground with a scream, but she was already moving, confident the archer would finish him off. Hiraz was fighting three angels at once now, and he was losing. Blood dripped from his arm and his cheek had been sliced open.

Elena wrenched a knife through the wing of the nearest angel while kicking out the knee of another, giving Hiraz enough room to thrust his sword into the stomach of the third angel and twist. But the one whose wing she'd injured wasn't down; he spun around with blank-eyed determination . . . and she faltered. "Gadriel."

The haunting gray-green eyes were gone, his pink-tinged skin holding a greenish cast, but it was the solid senior angel she and Raphael had last seen in China. Her entire being rebelled against seeing him turned into this abomination.

Teeth bared, he swung his sword toward her neck.

Instinct took over. Ducking, she slammed a blade into his gut, then ran straight through to slam into Hiraz, taking them both off the roof.

It had been a purposeful action and she managed to slow their descent, though the vampire's weight was more than she could handle. When they made a bruising but survivable landing on the balcony a couple of stories down, Hiraz ran back inside the building without a word. She knew what he was planning—to go up a set of internal fire escape stairs and come up behind the attackers.

Elena had the same idea. Rising up into the air, she went to rejoin the fight, coming at Lijuan's troops from the back—but it was too late. Another swarm of troops was heading their way. *Fuck!* She didn't have the mental ability to tell their people to withdraw and they *had* to withdraw. They couldn't win this one, not with so many fighters coming at them. It would be a slaughter.

Raphael was involved in heavy combat against multiple

squadrons and at least five of Lijuan's generals. Elijah was
down with a wounded wing that would take a couple of hours
minimum to heal.

Wiping the sweat and blood off her face with her forearm,
she looked desperately around—and spotted Galen. Raphael's
weapons-master was on the leading edge of the fighters on the
roof. He moved like lightning, his red hair sweat damp and
two swords dancing in his hands as if they weighed nothing
when she knew they were heavy as hell.

Dropping down beside him, she took on an assailant and
yelled, "Massive incoming force! We have to retreat!"

Galen was a warrior, and the light of battle glinted in his
pale—almost translucent—green eyes, but he was also a
highly intelligent angel. Slicing off the heads of the two angels
he'd been fighting, then finishing off the one she'd taken on,
he followed her gaze to where the new squadrons were heading their way.

Opening his mouth, he issued a command in a voice that
carried across the entire rooftop—she'd known he could do
that, had heard him do the same in the Refuge. Then, he'd
been yelling at a group of recalcitrant children to fall in line.
Though the kids had obeyed at once, they hadn't looked the
least scared; most had been grinning while trying hard to
maintain correct wing posture.

The sight had gone a long way toward making Elena understand how kind, soft-hearted Jessamy could've fallen in love
with this barbarian angel.

"Fall back!" he ordered. "Begin defensive maneuver alpha!"

Elena continued to fight beside Galen as the rest of their
people fell back behind them; she swapped out her knife blades
for a long blade another retreating fighter slapped into her
hand. Her own had been lost in another skirmish earlier
that day.

Everyone had their assigned tasks in this maneuver and
hers was to hold the line and buy their people time. The vampires and two other guild hunters on the roof would be flown
to the next nearest safe position by the angels who were strong
enough, but before the guild hunters went, they'd lay a little
trap for Lijuan's troops.

Gadriel, wing damaged and stomach bleeding, was suddenly in front of her again. Her eyes burned as she swung the deadly sharp blade of her weapon across his neck, separating head from body. Gadriel had died in China. This was nothing but Lijuan abusing an honorable warrior's corpse. She would remember him as he'd once been, not as this monstrosity.

"Run! You will all run in the end!" yelled one of Lijuan's squadron leaders as he landed on the roof, his face bloody and his eyes hot with battle fury—he had normal hazel eyes, which meant he'd chosen this, chosen to walk with Lijuan. "We will own you!"

Elena lodged a knife in the back of his throat the next time he opened his big mouth. She and Galen were falling off the edge of the roof even as he gurgled and struggled to remove the weapon. The two of them made a hasty retreat, following the rest of their people. A number of Lijuan's warriors flew after them, but Jason dropped out of the sky to score black lightning across the space, cutting them in half and driving back others who would've followed.

As with all of Raphael's Seven, he was tired and worn, but he would fight to the very end.

The boom came seconds later, the explosives planted on the roof by Rose, one of the Guild's demolition experts, going off with such violence that the resulting collapse sucked in a number of angels who'd been attempting to fly off. Dust and stone flew into the air, tiny pieces of shrapnel hitting the back of Elena's neck and getting caught in the energy of her wings before being spit out.

She made a hard landing, the vibration going through her entire body. The first thing she did was look around to see if Hiraz had made it out from inside the building. *There.* The vampire sat slumped against a wall, his eyes on the collapsing building across from them. His expression was bleak, the look shared by many of the others around him.

Elena understood why. They were losing.

This wasn't the first of their buildings that had fallen to Lijuan's people. Elijah was wounded. Raphael was exhausted. The Seven were reaching the edge of their endurance. Dmitri had taken to the battlefield with his sword a deadly menace in an effort to give the others a break, but the enemy was just too big in number.

And Lijuan was yet to rise again.

Another enemy squadron rose into the air behind the dust of the collapse, heading right for them, and the battle was on again.

62

Raphael felt the explosive force ripple through the air, and knew his people had detonated another building. They weren't destroying every building as they retreated. Some had been left whole but stuffed with explosives—in the hope that Lijuan's people would settle in and the delayed detonation would take out hundreds of them at once.

But with every boom of sound, every call to retreat, Lijuan's grip around the city tightened. All his people were fighting to their limit—he could ask nothing more from them. Elijah's predatory cats were stalking the enemy throughout the city and his birds of prey fought in unnatural squadrons formed by Eli's knowledge of tactics.

Deacon and his repair team had left their workshop to wipe out a surge of reborn in an unexpected corner of the city. Janvier and Ashwini had flooded an enemy weapons cache with seawater and made it appear an accident, while Holly had managed to taunt and lead a couple of reborn right into an uninfected section of Lijuan's army. Demarco and the other snipers had stealthily blown off the heads of more than one senior member of Lijuan's forces, timing their assassinations to get lost in the mass of battle injuries.

Dmitri had mowed down an entire squadron that'd had the misfortune to land on the rooftop where he was fighting, his weapons a blur. Naasir was deep in enemy territory and had successfully fouled the enemy's main water supply by rerouting sewerage into it. Venom had beheaded reborn after reborn, his clothing stained with blood. Galen hadn't stopped fighting since his arrival. Aodhan, Jason, and Illium had forgotten sleep.

His Legion had fallen again and again only to rise back and fight with unflinching courage, but even they couldn't make up for the massive disparity in numbers.

Lijuan's forces had begun to pincer the city in their grip, the battle now being fought on two major fronts.

He deflected a hail of obsidian from one of her generals, struck back with angelfire. The general collapsed his wings and dropped out from under the electric blue ball. It smashed into two other fighters beyond him; they died without having a chance to scream.

Another bolt arrowed toward him, but Raphael didn't duck. If he did, that bolt would hit a mass of his own people. Instead, he went to deflect the power with angelfire . . . when something about the energy coming toward him had him responding with wildfire instead. His instincts had understood what his mind took a moment to process: this obsidian had a piercingly lovely starlight shimmer.

The two powers collided in a crash of light and sound that echoed through his head. *Lijuan is awake! Drop drop drop!*

He sent out a pulse of wildfire in a three hundred and sixty degree circle only seconds later. Enemy fighters died in a single breath, and the air rippled bare meters from him. He pulsed more wildfire in that direction. Lijuan shimmered and came into focus, and despite the amount of wildfire he'd expended, she didn't appear wounded.

The hail of return fire she sent toward him was vicious.

Elijah had rejoined the battle only minutes earlier, was fresher than Raphael, but the other archangel stayed back. Raphael knew the action went against every bone in Elijah's body, but they had agreed to this. Raphael and his city couldn't afford to lose their only archangelic backup. Elijah had to keep his distance from Lijuan—as with Antonicus, he had no defenses against her particular brand of death.

Elijah's voice in his mind. *I will take care of her generals.*
Silver-green fire erupted around Raphael.

Your city is falling. The cold words held a taste he could only describe as death, the screams of the lost Lijuan's terrible symphony. *Surrender now and I will cause you only a modicum of pain when I absorb you.*

Raphael took no pleasure in being proven right in his supposition that Lijuan didn't intend to kill him and Elijah outright. As powerful as she was now, how much more powerful would she become once she fed on two archangels?

He warned Eli of her intent even as he directed a pinpoint strike of wildfire to her heart.

Deflecting it with a wave of her hand that shot the shards of starlight obsidian in every direction, she smiled. *So, you choose pain. So be it.*

One of the shards hit him on the shoulder and spun him around. Using the motion instead of fighting it, he shot back a wide arc of wildlfire. Lijuan couldn't avoid it, as he hadn't been able to avoid her strike. The wildfire hit her around the solar plexus, causing her body to bow inward and her skin to glow from within.

But she held her ground, as he held his.

He could feel her poison working its way through the bones of his shoulder, but the wildfire in his body was fighting against the virulence. That wouldn't last much longer, not if they kept battling at this level. If he ran out of wildfire, that was it.

Crossbow bolts thumped into Lijuan's shoulder. She turned and swiped out a hand. "Know your place!" Suyin flew back to slam into the side of a building, her wings crumpling and red streaking the moonlight of her hair, but she'd bought Raphael precious time.

He sent out two more arcs, one horizontal, one vertical. Lijuan moved just in time that the cross point of the arcs didn't hit her face. Instead, she took the vertical line on one side of the body and the horizontal one on the heart. Raphael didn't see what happened next because he was drowning in a rain of starlight obsidian.

He threw up a shield of wildfire. It began to buckle nearly at once.

His body, worn out from the constant fight against her proxies over the past two days, struggled to produce more wildfire and failed. Lijuan rammed herself toward him at the same instant, her hands spread out even as his wildfire crackled under her skin in an effort to take hold. If she touched him with those hands, she'd punch her poison into him at point-blank range.

Sweeping sharply to the left, he released the shield and that wildfire returned to him. Lijuan twisted to a halt, then turned to come after him again. Gathering the last of the wildfire in his hand, he held it up in a glowing ball. *Come close by all means,* he said. *We will meet and see who survives.*

A slight hesitation, her wings braking. Then she smiled and lifted her hands and he knew he'd soon be buried under a rain of death. He threw the wildfire, manipulating the energy so it would spread and encase her. It was the thinnest of barriers, but it blocked her energy for a moment or two.

He drew both his swords. There remained a limited amount of wildfire in his system, but he had to husband that on the off-chance he could get close enough to Lijuan to do what he'd done once before—send the energy directly into the bloodstream.

Tearing herself out of the thin skin of wildfire, she looked at him with irises so pale she appeared blind, her face hauntingly lovely and the ice white of her hair a silken fall. *You will come to me,* she said in that voice filled with ghosts. *In the end, they all come to me.*

Starlight obsidian rimmed her hands, her malevolent energy powerful beyond comprehension. Raphael's left arm was already going numb, his body losing the battle with the poison she'd managed to get inside him. But he faced her with no fear—he would fight to the end to save his people. His Elena.

Archangel.

His consort in his peripheral vision, the stormfire of her hidden in the shadow of the nearest building. Then she flew forward and into the light.

Across from him, Lijuan smiled. *How lovely of your consort to present herself. I will take care of her after you. A pity I will not be able to pin her up in my wing museum.*

She was toying with him now. Taking her time before the kill. But she'd given something away—she didn't realize Elena stored power for him. He and his consort had pulled off a similar action in the last battle, but Lijuan must've assumed all the power came from him.

To her, his consort was a former mortal and baby angel. No threat at all.

Wildfire licked across her eyeballs, danced in her hair. She shuddered and seemed to set her jaw. Blood dripped from the corner of her mouth. His power was having an impact, but not fast enough.

Already, she was lifting her hands, in readiness for a strike.

A sudden smile before she lowered her hands. *You are no threat,* she said in a laughing tone. *I will absorb you in the way most pleasurable to me, then I will feed on your consort.* She dove toward him, as if diving into a lover's arms.

Archangel, here I come.

He thrust out his swords at the same instant that Lijuan stopped on the other end and laughed. *What can sword wounds do to me now?* Holding his gaze, her smile taunting in a face covered with moonlight skin, she pushed herself deliberately onto the blades, allowing them to sink into her flesh. *I am a goddess. I will rise and rise and rise into my reign of death.*

His consort touched her hand to his ankle. And the wildfire that had grown inside her over the past two days jolted into him in a direct line. It wanted to go toward the poison in his shoulder, but he shoved it all down the swords and into Lijuan.

His blades danced with white-gold and blue edged with an opalescence of midnight and dawn that shifted into an unexpected wild green, then back again.

Lijuan's scream threatened to pierce his eardrums, a million deaths hidden within it. In her face, he saw the ghosts of the countless people she'd killed, her flesh morphing too fast to hold in the mind. Her facial bones turned skeletal right then, the flesh receding, before she was the lovely Archangel of China once more.

A woman he had once respected and looked to for advice.

But that wise archangel was gone, lost in the Cascade madness that had created this monster. One day, Raphael might

mourn her, the Lijuan she had once been, but it would not be
today. Today, he fought for the life of not just his and Elijah's
people, but for the survival of the world.

Lijuan's hands turned into blood as she tried to wrench
herself off the swords. He kept on pushing them into her even
as she tried to pull away, until at last she shot a river of starlight obsidian down the swords, using them as a conduit as
he had.

He broke contact with the hilts, and she wrenched.

He got out a warning to the angels directly in the path of
the falling swords and the blades hit the street below without
harming any of his people. In front of him, Lijuan was coming
apart at the seams, the wildfire literally pulling her to pieces,
the edge of defiant green causing searing burns along the
ruptures. But even as he felt a flicker of hope, her obsidian
starlight wrapped around her, as if sealing the cracks.

When Elena threw him another blade, he moved to cut
Lijuan's throat. The more they could hurt her, the more time
they'd gain for the wildfire to regenerate. That deadly living
green wasn't his or Elena's but formed of an amalgamation. If
their combined wildfire could do so much damage now when
he'd only had dregs to contribute to the strike, what might they
be able to do if they combined their wildfire at full strength?

He sliced out . . . but Lijuan was no longer there. Once
again, she'd gone noncorporeal to escape a killing blow,
must've had a store of power in reserve for just such a possibility. Throwing back his head, Raphael roared out his rage.

She would be back.

And they had nothing left, no more aces up their sleeve.

63

Exhaustion hung over the Tower's as well as Elijah's forces. Elena could see both groups of troops as she walked through a snowy Central Park at Hannah's side. Some members of their combined forces were sitting and resting with tired but open eyes, while others had their heads tilted back and their eyes closed. Another lull had fallen, except for brief skirmishes here and there.

The cause of the lull seemed to be a similar exhaustion on Lijuan's side. Unexpected given their numbers, but Xi had sent all their forces into battle as one, instead of resting groups and sending them one after the other. Losing Lijuan this time had fizzled out the proxies, too. Even Xi was no longer shooting the obsidian bolts.

Elijah and Raphael had considered pushing forward, forcing Lijuan's tired army to engage, but the numbers worked against them. Their forces were even more exhausted than Lijuan's, and both Raphael and Elijah were on the edge of endurance.

Elijah had actually had to pull power from the city's electrical grid, shorting out connections all over the city. It had been a desperate reach for power as he attempted to keep Lijuan's most dangerous surviving generals at bay. Having barely recovered from his injury, he'd taken on at least ten of them while Raphael fought Lijuan.

As a result of Elijah's stand, they still had at least five squadrons of fighters who would've otherwise fallen under the assault. But even if Raphael and Eli stripped the city's entire grid, they didn't have enough remaining power between them to demolish Lijuan's forces. They'd do severe damage . . . but they'd flatline afterward.

Manhattan would then be helpless prey for a rejuvenated Lijuan.

Better for everyone to recover in readiness for her return—this time, they had a better idea of her vulnerabilities. Especially when it came to the bright new-leaf green that resulted from the amalgamation of Raphael and Elena's wildfire. That stuff had *hurt* Lijuan.

Now, in this tenuous instant where they could catch a breath, Hannah was doing the rounds. Her people expected this from her, and their faces lit up when they saw her. They seemed to gain a fresh energy when she touched her hand to theirs or spoke to them for a moment or two.

Elena didn't have the same relationship with her and Raphael's people, but she had a relationship of her own, warrior to warrior. They told her about their injuries and asked her questions about the overall losses of the war. She didn't lie to them—she and Raphael had agreed they'd tell their troops the truth.

Their courage deserved nothing less.

The only thing they wouldn't share was Raphael's depleted state. Angels, vampires, mortals, everyone needed to believe that their archangel was a power. Raphael had never before been so worn out. Even when he'd fallen with Elena in his arms that first time, he'd done so as a being of power who'd taken out a murderous enemy.

"We are holding up against impossible odds," one of the senior soldiers said after her update. "No one could've expected Lijuan to bring her entire country into battle with her."

It was about to get even worse, though they'd wait to share the news until after they were certain. Raphael's forces had been able to neutralize the planes that had taken off from Charisemnon's territory what felt like a lifetime ago, but their surveillance system had now picked up signs of ships heading toward New

York. Those "trade" ships bore Charisemnon's mark, and had been prowling in international waters prior to the war.

Lijuan was either about to get even more reinforcements, or the ships were filled with insects who'd become a plague. Raphael was currently holed up in the Tower with Dmitri and Galen, as well as Elijah and his top people, in an effort to come up with a way to take those ships out of the equation. Because if they landed . . .

Her phone buzzed. "If you'll excuse me," she said after a quick glance. "It's my sister, Eve."

A vampire so old that his face was ethereal in its beauty, said, "The little warrior? She is a brave one."

"Yes, she is." Stepping away, she took the call. "You're okay." She'd lost track of Eve in the chaos of battle, had had a fist clenched around her heart since her attempt to touch base with her sister got kicked to voicemail.

"I've been helping out in the Guild infirmary." A slight tremor in the words.

"Tough gig," Elena said softly, because underneath the bravery, Eve remained a child in the midst of the worst war the world had ever seen. "Your friends all right?" She couldn't ask about her own, wasn't ready to handle it if the news was bad. Ransom, Demarco, Rose, Kenji, and so many more of her Guild friends were on the battlefield. No one would've begrudged Ransom for going to safety with his wife and newborn baby, but he'd said, "I'm fighting for our kid's future. Nyree understands."

Eve inhaled on the other end of the line, the sound a touch shaky. "A friend of mine has a broken arm, another's got bruises, but nothing worse than that. Sorry I missed your call—it got crazy in here after the reborn swarmed again. I have a bunch of messages from you and Amy, and Mom and Father."

Father. Jeffrey had never been Daddy to Eve. Not as he'd once been to four little girls who'd laughed in delight as he pushed them on a swing.

Higher, Daddy! Higher!

Echoes of yesterday, poignant and beautiful.

That same man had danced one of his daughters across the living room floor, while another daughter took photographs with her beloved camera, and the baby of their family played in the corner.

Marguerite had often sat in a sunny spot in the living room, making this or that on the sewing machine Jeffrey would push out of her small sewing room and into the sunshine. Elena's favorite spot had been on the bench of the sewing machine. Her mother had teased her that one day, she'd get too big to sit there and they'd have to reinforce it, but Marguerite had been long gone by the time Elena reached that size.

Today, her daddy was Eve's father, and she didn't think he'd ever laughed with his two youngest girls. Elena's half sisters had grown up with a very different man than the one who'd loved Elena, Beth, Ari, and Belle. "How are they?"

"Good. Amy and Mom are volunteering in a warehouse that's packing supplies for us, and Father's involved with transporting them into Manhattan."

Elena hadn't known that, but it made sense. Jeffrey Deveraux had tentacles in every area of business in the city. If anyone knew supply logistics, it was Elena's father. "But he's outside Manhattan?" Their father was a brilliant businessman, hard as nails in the boardroom, but his kind of battle didn't involve blades and guns and flamethrowers.

"Yes, he's with Mom and Amy in New Jersey." Eve exhaled slowly. "I said they should go farther away. Things are bad here."

"I know. But the thing is, Eve, if we fall, it doesn't matter how far they go." Lijuan would spread like a virus across the land. "I think they'll probably feel better if they stay and help in the fight how they can."

She almost heard Eve swallow. "Yeah, that's what Amy said. She said she might be crap at holding a sword and would probably vomit if she had to chop off a vampire's head, but she's *really* good at making sure supplies are packed exactly as they need to be packed so that all the space is used up. They put her in charge of one whole area of supplies."

"Your sister is tough in her own way." Had become so after realizing that Jeffrey would never love her own mother as much as he'd loved Marguerite. It had grown a hard angry core inside Amy that Elena wasn't sure would ever melt—but that clarity of vision came from a tough, pragmatic nature.

"Amy always protected me when we were little. She never backs down from bullies and she says Lijuan is just a very powerful bully."

"Your sister's right." Not for the first time, Elena wished she had a relationship with Amy, but she wasn't about to push where she wasn't wanted.

A noise in the background before Eve said, "I better go. There're so many wounded—the healers and doctors need all of us who can run and grab necessary stuff and do errands, so they can focus on their work." A pause. "Ellie, don't get hurt okay?" The tremor was back. "I can't lose my biggest big sister."

Elena pressed her palm to her abdomen, blinked away the heat in her eyes. "I have plans to kick Lijuan's butt," she said . . . but she made no promises that she'd end this alive. She couldn't.

After Eve hung up, she took a couple of seconds to find her feet again, then called Beth. It turned out that she was with Gwendolyn and Amy at the supply warehouse. Also with them was Majda.

Elena knew Beth's husband Harrison was acting as a gofer in the Tower. That was harder than it sounded. He'd been running nonstop for days and, to his credit, hadn't complained once. As for Jean-Baptiste, she'd spoken to him only a couple of hours earlier.

"Grandfather's fine," she told her grandmother when Majda came on the line. "Just tired." As a highly experienced vampire, he was in charge of one of the ground teams under Venom's overall command.

"And you, heart of my heart?" Soft words, infinite care. "How are you?"

"I currently have on new boots because some asshole angel stabbed a hole through my favorite ones and I'm annoyed." It was such a petty thing to be irritated over that she clung to it. She needed petty right now, needed something that felt normal and not a matter of life or death. "I'll probably get a blister."

Majda's tone held a smile when she replied. "May that be your biggest worry today, *azeeztee*."

Elena clenched her stomach against the slamming wave of memory. Soft hands on her face. A laughing woman in the sunlight. The scent of gardenias. Lips pressed to her brow. "Maggie?" she managed to get out.

Last Elena had heard, Beth had decided to keep her daughter with her rather than send her away deeper into the territory.

"You know Sara's parents are still happy to take her until this is over." They already had charge of Zoe; with both Sara and Deacon in combat and little Zoe familiar with her flighty, kooky, but loving grandparents, it had been the best choice.

"Our little Maggie is with us," Majda confirmed. "I think for us, for Beth, it's the right choice. Whatever happens, this child will always know what it is to be loved by her mother." In her voice lived a thickness of memory, cherished pieces of the little girl she'd left behind in order to keep her safe.

"*Maman* lived a joyous life for many years," Elena reminded her grandmother. "And she remembered you with love all her life." Never once had Marguerite said anything negative about the mother who'd left her to wake alone in an old Parisian church. "I think she always knew you would've come back if you could have."

"Take care of yourself, Elena," Majda whispered. "I could not bear it if I were to survive you as I have survived my daughter and two granddaughters."

Elena hung up the conversation with a heavy lump in her chest that she had to quickly breathe past when she saw a young warrior heading toward her. The female angel had a bandaged-up arm, which meant she'd sustained a fairly significant injury. Young by Tower standards, she was still two hundred and fifty years old.

"Deep sword wound?" Elena nodded at the injury.

"No, Consort. Even worse. One of the dead-eyes got me with a knife." A flare of her nostrils, her lips pressed flat. "I can't believe I allowed him to get that close. But I did manage to slice off a piece of his wing, so I salvaged my honor that much at least."

"We take the ones we can get, Ahayl. Personally, I'm most proud of taking out an eye with a grenade launcher." She'd actually taken out the entire side of an angel's face, but the fucker had been so strong he'd survived it and flown off toward Lijuan's territory.

Not that it would do him much good—Lijuan seemed to have only one solution for her injured: she ate them. Then again, that particular angel had been old and experienced. Could be Lijuan would shove him full of power to accelerate his healing. She was certainly doing *something* to keep her generals in the game even after they took grievous injuries, and they'd all seen that she could share power.

Elena wondered that the generals weren't sickened by knowing the source of that power. Did the dead scream in their heads as they screamed in Lijuan's voice?

Ahayl nodded. "That is a good win." Then she was gone, their conversation having fulfilled its purpose—contact with the consort. The troops knew Raphael couldn't be on the ground much, but that was all right because Elena was his heart and she was with them.

Pushing aside the pain of the past, Elena carried on. She fixed a vampire's scabbard so it'd hang properly on his back. She helped sharpen the knives of an older angel who didn't speak much. And she told warrior after warrior that they were doing well, that their archangel was proud of their spirit and courage.

Andreas was also in the park, dirtier and more rough-edged than she'd ever seen him. Twin swords curved like scythes crisscrossed his back under the amber gray of his wings—she could just see the hilts over his shoulders, but she'd seen him working those gleaming blades in battle.

As she'd seen him use the hunting knives he wore in thigh sheaths. As with most of the angels in the park, his leather tunic was sleeveless regardless of the snow and cold. "We will battle to the death for Raphael," he said to her when their paths crossed, the pale greenish hazel of his eyes unflinching. "Better to die with honor in his service than be a slave in Lijuan's."

It was a feeling she heard articulated a hundred different ways that day. The same song sang in her soul. She would die in freedom beside her archangel a thousand times over than trade it for even an extra day on Lijuan's leash.

If death is our destiny, Archangel, she thought, then I'll see you on the other side.

64

Raphael managed to bring all of his Seven into the discussion after Elijah and his people left to go prepare for their part in what was to come. Only Galen and Dmitri stood with him in the war room, the others all voices on the speakers.

"I did not want you all back in the city in such a way," he said to them after they'd talked through tactics and strategy, conscious that it wasn't only his Seven in the line of fire but their women. Holly—liquid fast and with significant training under her belt—was behind enemy lines, while Honor—a honed hunter under her preference for scholarly pursuits—fought beside Venom.

Naasir's Andromeda had stayed in the Refuge with Galen's Jessamy. Both women would die before allowing harm to come to their charges—the precious children of all the warriors who'd flown to fight in the various battles going on around the world. Should the enemy turn their eyes toward the Refuge, Naasir and Galen would be far from the women they so fiercely loved.

As for Jason, his princess was tougher than she looked. Mahiya was working in the infirmary. It turned out that she'd quietly studied with Tower healers in the years since it became clear Lijuan would rise again, was skilled enough now that she could take care of minor injuries, leaving the healers free to concentrate on the more critical ones.

Then there was his consort.

He'd last seen her with a streak of dried blood on her face and a tear in the reinforced leather of her jacket where a sword had come dangerously close to her neck. He knew she was in Central Park right now, among the troops. He wondered if she'd realized how very regal she was in her own way—not in the distant mode of an empress, but in the calm, capable way of a warrior queen.

She would ride with him into battle until the end.

Archangel. As if he'd conjured her up by thinking of her, the warm steel of Elena's voice filled his mind and all at once, the power in his veins felt a touch less cold, a little more human. *Do you have some time? I think it'd do our troops good to see you.*

I will be there soon.

He returned his attention to his Seven. "You have your tasks. Rest if you're able, put in place that which you can, and ready your fighters for what is to come." It would be the most terrible battle of them all, of that he was certain.

Vivek had managed to sneak more of his bugs into Lijuan's area, and the images that had come back to them—scattershot though they'd been—showed a flesh mound of impossible size. Many of the angels and vampires on it were barely injured, and yet sat in place, ready to be consumed by their goddess. Not all had the dead eyes that spoke of a lack of freedom.

"I can't understand why they follow her even after they've seen what she's become." Aodhan's quiet voice, the angel calling in from a sentry position near the port. "It is no longer a question of loyalty. It is a question of honor."

The most beautiful of the Seven, his skin a thing of light, his hair strands of shattered diamonds, said, "Sire, had you become as she is now, I would not have stayed loyal. I would've understood that the archangel I loved, the archangel to whom I had sworn fealty, was gone. I would've mourned your passing, and then I would've battled to end the horror that you had become."

"It's why you are in my Seven." His men were not automatons, did not follow him without thinking. "Lijuan has never liked too much strength around her." There was one exception to that rule—Xi.

Xi's ability to think for himself as well as his previous track record in looking after his troops was why the general's current slavish devotion surprised Raphael. He didn't know if Lijuan had done something to Xi that led him to follow her even when she fed on fighters he'd promised to lead with integrity and care, or if he'd always had that weakness inside him, but the question was moot in any case.

They were facing an army that had swallowed the poison pill and passionately believed that Raphael and the rest of the Cadre were a threat to Lijuan because they did not accept her as their goddess. And, after all that they'd already done, they had no choice but to follow Lijuan to the end.

For it was the victors who would write history.

"I'm going to meet Elena in Central Park," he said. "Dmitri, take a break." His second had either been in battle or in the war room nonstop. "Trace can cover for you while you rest." The vampire had been in India when hostilities began. Flights had been grounded in the aftermath of what was happening in Neha's land, sea crossings a slow and treacherous risk. Yet Trace had made it home in time to join the previous battle.

"He's one of the few men I'd trust in the position." Dmitri pinched up the shoulder of his T-shirt, lowered his head to sniff at it. "I need a shower at least. Those dead eyes release putrid decaying blood when decapitated."

"I'll hold the watch here until Trace arrives," Galen offered, his red hair a shaggy mess around his head and streaks of soot on his arms. "Go bathe. You stink."

"You're not exactly a fragrant rose yourself, Barbarian," Dmitri muttered.

A snort from the speakers. "Don't speak to me about bad smells until you've been covered with half-fried reborn flesh." Venom's languid voice. "Your wife threw a grenade into a knot of them that scuttled toward us like crabs even while on fire."

Dmitri grinned in a way that would've shocked those who had never seen the man under the deadly thousand-year-old vampire. "That's my Honor."

As his Seven began to speak among themselves, taking a minute or two to feed their souls, Raphael walked to the balcony and took in his abused city. Smoke snaked into the sky from areas where groups of reborn had been spotted and eliminated. To the left was a huge scar in the landscape, barren and black.

It was a small mercy that the insect incident hadn't been repeated.

In all likelihood, Charisemnon could only make so many at a time before his ability flatlined. As far as Raphael was aware, the only one of them whose Cascade power was limitless was Lijuan—and that because she fed off others. Raphael's healing and Charisemnon's disease creation both had a limit.

Not that any of them were taking the latter fact for granted. A group of wounded soldiers did nothing all day but zoom in on any suspected enemy movement in the streets no matter how small. They'd discovered multiple reborn and three vampiric stealth operatives, but no insects.

Spreading his wings, he took off into the dusty, smoky sky.

It took him time to reach his destination. His troops were scattered all over the city; whenever he saw a group on a rooftop, or gathered in the street, he landed and spoke to them. He couldn't speak to each and every member of his army, but he knew word would travel through the ranks. It would matter that he cared enough to check in with junior vampire soldiers and senior squadron leaders both.

Rising into the air after a short stop to speak to a young ground unit, he sent a message to his army. *You have courage, and you have heart. This is our city and we will never surrender it. But for now, if you can, rest. We must be ready to strike when the battle begins again.*

He saw movement on several rooftops, noticed a number of gunners lay down their weapons and begin to stretch out their shoulders. The Tower had already sent out the same instruction, but it was different coming from their archangel. He knew the watch would remain constant, that no one would fall into a deep rest, but any break was a good thing.

He made it to Central Park five minutes later.

The ensuing conversations were much the same as those he'd had on the journey here. All knew that their status was dire, but again, there was no talk of defeat. They spoke only of skirmishes won, or ideas they had for future operations.

He listened to all of them.

He found young Izak seated on the snowy ground with a number of his squadron. The angel was fast asleep with his head against a tree, his wings folded around his body like a blanket. A tumble of yellow curls fell across his forehead, making him look like a lost child, but Izak was not a boy. Not any longer.

Even in his rest, he had his sword by his side. Blood, dried an iron red, coated the soles of his boots and was sprayed across his feathers. Those feathers were a rich cream for the most part, except for the lower third of each wing—there, his coloring was cream speckled with dark blue, akin to the egg of some small bird.

Today, flecks of rust red joined the blue and cream.

"I want to find a blanket and snuggle it over him." Elena's whisper was followed by the brush of her wing against his, her stormfire arcing through his own feathers in an electric caress. "I know I need to treat him as a warrior, but he'll always be Izzy to me."

The entire world stilled. Snow began to fall, soft and delicate.

Raphael turned, cupped her cheek, and did what he'd been aching to do for the entire past day.

Dipping his head, he kissed her. He had never loved before her and he would never love after her—there *was* no after Elena for him. *My love for you is the deepest truth of my existence. Spring and summer, fall and winter, I would spend all the seasons of my life with you.*

Raphael. Her hand flat against his heart, his hunter kissed him back with a love that was fierce and defiant and forever. *When our winter comes, I'll go to sleep in your arms with a smile.*

A glow surrounded them as they kissed in the falling snow, his golden lightning dancing over her skin and her stormfire possessive over his wings.

"Hello, Archangel." Spoken against his lips.

He rubbed the pad of his thumb over the snow-cool skin of her cheek. "Hello, Hunter-mine."

Around them, their people smiled and carried on in their tasks.

"Just so we are clear, *hbeebti*, I am not over the fact that you flew directly into an archangelic battle."

A grin broke out across her face. "But I did it with a *grenade launcher*," she said proudly. "Admit it, that was some major badassery on my part." Her eyes flicked past his shoulder. "Speaking of which, damn but Imani is good with the war hammer. She's got no manners at all when she goes to whack off an enemy fighter's head."

Raphael felt his lips twitch. "The rules of war are different from the rules of the household or polite society. If you recall, her etiquette guide had a full chapter on such 'acceptable deviations from the norm.'"

"I was probably going la-la-la and trying to drown out your voice then," she admitted, unrepentant. "After this war is over, you can read it to me again."

Falling into step with one another, they carried on speaking to their people—including an Imani who had her curly hair tightly braided to her skull and was clad in armor of weathered black that featured layered arm plates as well as neck protection. "The young and foolish"—a pointed look at Raphael—"can expose their arms." Lush lips pursed in a tawny-skinned face of arresting beauty. "I prefer to keep my limbs."

Is Imani scared of anyone?

How did you describe her to me once? Ah yes. A grande dame who has no time for anyone's bullshit. That is Imani. Raphael wanted to smile. *I have always liked her for that.*

I should've guessed. A laughing glance. *You do have a thing for a certain kind of woman.*

It is a weakness. Raphael sometimes thought he must've fallen for Elena the first time she stood toe to toe with him, though she'd been a mere mortal and he an archangel.

Later, after they'd moved on from Imani, she said, "Why *don't* most of you wear arm and neck protection?"

"Such armor has little impact on one who fights with a heavy weapon such as a war hammer, but the added weight and stiffness causes a minor reduction in speed for those who use a lighter weapon." And in a battle among immortals even that miniscule reduction could mean life or death.

"Got it," Elena said at once. "Either you all wear it or none of you do."

They reached a gathered squadron a moment later, and their attention shifted

When they finally took off from Central Park, it was to heavy darkness. Flames flickered against the night sky, as both his people and Lijuan's lit them for light, for heat. Elijah's pulling energy from the city's grid had blown out critical circuits in many areas. The Tower itself had large generators, but they'd decided to prioritize use by the infirmary and by the Tower's technical team.

Raphael's side also had flashlights and high-power lanterns at the ready, batteries stored all over the place. They would show none of that right now, however. Let the enemy believe that Raphael's army was blind in the dark, too. All the while, Naasir and his team crept about in enemy territory, their task to cause as much destruction as possible.

It was time they took the war to the enemy's door.

65

The explosions came at three o'clock in the morning.

Warned by Naasir, Raphael was high in the sky near the main front, while Elijah had taken the other half of the city. Their troops were hunkered down and ready to move using the cloudy and moonless night as a shield. Ten senior squadrons had made their way to rooftops close to enemy territory.

Others watched to ensure Lijuan's people weren't doing the same.

Elena had joined one of the archer and shooter teams. She'd given him all the wildfire she'd regenerated, but it had little to work with in him—the constant battles against Lijuan's proxies had taken a toll, his body struggling to produce wildfire at a fast enough speed to keep up with his expenditure.

So be it.

He remained an archangel, one more skilled in strategy and tactics than Lijuan. Lost in her delusions of godhood, she could be pushed into unwise decisions. If she rose today, it wouldn't be at full strength—he'd husband his and Elena's combined wildfire, use it in a strike that turned Lijuan into a mindless creature of screaming pain.

Regardless of the threat posed by Lijuan, they couldn't *not* launch the assault today—they had to find a way to cripple her army or his and Elijah's troops wouldn't have a fighting chance of survival. Another major battle and their people would be massacred, the streets awash with their blood.

A fireball punched the night sky as the windows of the first building blew out with a massive smash of sound. Many of Lijuan's troops had bedded down in that building. They died in a hail of heat and crumbling foundations. Another building blew at the same moment, then a third.

Raphael scraped the sky with angelfire in the aftermath, cutting down the disoriented mass of fighters attempting to escape the shrapnel from the buildings.

More explosions lit up the night in enemy territory, these finely targeted. Naasir's team was blowing up the remaining pipes that brought in clean water, and they were disrupting sewage lines so that the filth would flow into the enemy camp. A small demolition team had been tasked with destroying roads that led out of the port area.

Their aim was to trap Lijuan's ground troops and annihilate her winged fighters.

Raphael's archers slammed fiery death down on anyone who escaped the angelfire that burned in the sky. His troops began to move forward, squadrons landing on rooftops in a wave of silent death, while ground teams pushed their way through the rubble, eliminating the enemy on every side as they went.

Obsidian rain began to slam at them minutes later, but it was too late. They'd reclaimed much of what they'd lost. Raphael didn't hold back his angelfire, his aim to wipe out as many of Lijuan's generals as he could. But the senior leaders suddenly all dropped out of the way at precipitous speed.

KNEEL TO YOUR GODDESS!!

He saw her then, higher in the sky than him.

Her face was skeletal, and she appeared to be missing one side of her body. Her gown flapped against empty air where her thigh should've filled it out, and above, the fabric was being sucked in against her side—her rib cage was partially or fully missing. None of that stopped her from raining death down from the sky across a vast, vast area.

Lovely shimmering starlight obsidian shards of pain and horror.

He'd intended to save his wildfire until he could get it into her body, but hundreds of people would die if he didn't stop her.

He spread out his wildfire in a shield across the sky. The deadly rain hit and dissipated. But Lijuan wasn't done. She threw down another barrage. His shield held. Just. Wounded she might be, but her power was a terrible thing.

Whatever Lijuan had become, she was growing *stronger* with each passing day. Even at full power, he couldn't hope to defeat her, not in a direct fight as this had become. Not when she could spread her attack across such a devastatingly large area.

He could carry on, infuriate her into a mistake so he could get close enough to inject her with wildfire, but the price of his choice would be grave upon grave upon grave.

He had no choice. *Retreat!* he ordered. *Fall back!*

Even as he gave that order, he shaped the last drops of wildfire in his body into small pellets, then shot them through his shield. He'd taken a precious extra second to time it just right, so the pellets—so small they were near invisible against her rain of starlight obsidian—would pass through in the gap between one blast of the rain and the next.

Lijuan hadn't moved since this began; he hoped that held true for another second.

Two of the pellets were smashed out of existence by falling shards, but the other five punched into Lijuan's heart.

Lightning lit her up from within. Blood trickled out of her mouth.

Raphael didn't take that for an advantage of any kind. The only reason he'd achieved so much with so little was because she was already wounded. But wounded or not, she had plenty of firepower in her. She targeted him alone with the next volley.

His shield collapsed, the wildfire dissipating under the rain of black.

Raphael had nowhere to go that wouldn't put his troops in the line of fire. An angelic squadron was retreating below him.

He used angelfire to disrupt the starlight obsidian. It couldn't eliminate or cancel out Lijuan's poison, but it was strong enough to send it off course.

The shards smashed into the buildings on either side of the squadron; they flew out of danger moments later. It was the ground troops he had to worry about now—they were too deep in enemy territory. It'd take them time to retreat to safe ground. Even had the subterranean network of tunnels survived the aboveground detonations, they'd been designed for lone operatives, not large numbers of troops.

Lijuan laughed and the sound was incongruously lovely. *Why do you fight so?* A chiding tone to her mental voice, almost of the archangel she'd once been. *You have only the power in your flesh. I am a goddess. I have the power from my people.* Another hail of pain and death clothed in beauty.

He had nothing left. No wildfire. No angelfire. Nothing but his swords, with which he'd attempt to deflect some of the shards, so his ground troops would have a slightly higher chance of a safe retreat.

Gray bodies suddenly filled the sky in front of him.

His Legion took hit after hit, each body falling limply to the earth as the black poison ate them up from the inside out.

Bronze lightning fell from the sky at the same instant, aimed directly at Lijuan. One got her in a direct strike, burning great swathes of flesh from the healthy side of her wildfire-riddled body. She screamed and aimed her firepower up above, but the person there was invisible against the smoke-hazed sky.

Raphael recognized that lightning but he couldn't spot Michaela, either. Infuriated, Lijuan shot another hail of black at the Legion, poisonous shards that they blocked with their bodies. Michaela hit Lijuan with another direct strike—this one succeeding in destroying a wing. Lijuan's face faded and then her body rippled and she was gone, no doubt to feed again.

Raphael had survived the skirmish but the damage done was catastrophic. For the first time, he saw despair in the faces of his people. It had cost them so much ingenuity and skill and blood to gain that ground. Only for Lijuan to claw it back in a matter of minutes.

Elena. Fly with me. He needed his consort in a way that

had nothing to do with war or power—and his people had hurt Lijuan's forces enough that they weren't pursuing the retreating soldiers, just holding their side of the line.

Stormfire wings rising from one of the rooftops. "We'll get that land back," she said when she reached him. "We did it once, we'll do it again."

"No, Guild Hunter. You know as well as I do that the explosions gave away one of our only advantages—Lijuan's people will even now be scouring any buildings within sight for booby traps." He just hoped Naasir, Janvier, Ashwini, Demarco, Holly, and the others would make it out. "It is not the loss of territory that worries me, it is what that loss is doing to our people."

Faces looked up at him from rooftops and even in those who had managed to hold on to hope, the hope held a ragged edge. "They just saw their archangel consummately defeated. Had the Legion not stepped in and taken the blows meant for me, I would not be here speaking to you now."

"You're in pain." Elena's tone was sharp. "She got you."

"Twice," he told her. "Once on the shoulder very close to my neck, and the second at the side of my rib cage. It's eating away at me."

"The wildfire," Elena began.

Raphael cut her off with a shake of his head. "There is nothing left. I am out of power and I know you gave me the last droplets in you." He deliberately brushed his wing across Elena's even as Lijuan's starlight obsidian dug scalding channels of agony in his ribs and shoulder.

He'd be in the same shape as Antonicus if not for the fact the two hits had been glancing and his ability to generate wildfire seemed to come with a limited immunity. But that would only slow the process, not stop it. Already, the black poison was attempting to get to his heart, the channels all aimed in that direction.

A couple of minutes later, her stomach a nauseous knot, Elena stood on a high Tower balcony and looked up at the sky to see a meeting akin to one that had taken place during her first meeting with Raphael. Two archangels in the sky, one with wings of gold and white, the other with feathers of shimmering bronze.

Michaela was even dressed in a long-sleeved bodysuit as she'd been that long-ago day. When the Archangel of Budapest landed on the balcony with Raphael, the bodysuit proved to be a dark green with a slight shimmer to it. Her hair was the same silken tumble down her back, her face startlingly beautiful. The milk chocolate hue of her skin was rich despite the night darkness, holding a warmth that Elena had always thought at odds with the biting edge of her personality.

Today however, there was no sarcasm, no curl of the lip. Michaela just nodded at Elena—her gaze narrowing slightly at the sight of Elena's stormfire wings—before turning to Raphael. "I saw reports from this city, knew I had to come."

"What about your territory?" Raphael asked with no indication of pain in his voice, though Elena knew it had to be torturous. "The reborn infection? The children."

"If she wins this war, it will not matter that my territory is clean of infection." A gravity to Michaela's presence that Elena had never before felt, the sudden sense that this woman was an archangel. "If we beat Lijuan here, then we have a chance to salvage my territory."

"You have made a difficult choice." Raphael inclined his head in an acknowledgment between equals. "Your babe?"

A tightening of her features. "The Cascade gave me the ability to create power constructs that survive outside my body. I built Keir a shield that protected him and my babe—he says it held until he was nearly to the Refuge. They are safe."

Elena found herself exhaling a breath she hadn't been aware of holding. The idea of Keir and a newborn dodging the death stalking the world had been a horrific one.

"My power did damage to Lijuan," Michaela said. "Is it possible I can assist you to victory?"

To Elena's surprise, Raphael nodded. "My wildfire in her likely increased the impact, but you read slightly differently to my healing senses—there remains an imprint inside you of the life you so recently birthed. It is fading but not yet gone."

And Lijuan was a creature of death.

"Good. I will assist you in ending her, then I will return home."

"What is the situation on your side?"

Elena knew Raphael had to have that critical information, but panic clawed at her—the poison was eating at him from the inside out. Already, she could see the creeping edge of blackness on one wing.

"Bad," Michaela said shortly, her face grimmer than Elena had ever seen it. "When I left, Alexander and Zanaya were attempting to drive the reborn into a single valley so that we could scorch them with fire." The vivid green of her eyes took in the smoldering city around them, smoke yet rising to the sky from the earlier detonations. "I have told Alexander that *this* is more important. It is where we win or lose the world. But he sees coming here as abandoning his people. He is a fool."

Elena wouldn't describe the Archangel of Persia as any kind of a fool, but she had to agree with Michaela that the long-term picture had to take priority.

"The children . . . It is difficult." Michaela blinked rapidly, her throat moving. "All our troops are severely demoralized from having to cut down those we are programmed to protect. I kept seeing my own babe, kept thinking that each child was another woman's heart."

Elena couldn't imagine the horror of facing infected child after infected child. She'd frozen when faced with a *single* infected child during the last battle, a sundress-wearing girl who'd come off an infected cruise ship. The idea of having that nightmare moment repeated in a continuous loop . . . Bile coated the back of her throat.

The sky boomed with a massive burst of sound without warning, a huge overwhelming force that was a roundhouse punch to the side of the head. Elena's ears popped, her head ringing. *Archangel, what the hell was that?*

Eyes the most violent shade of blue in this world held hers. *An archangel has died.*

66

As Elena's skin chilled at Raphael's words, the sky began to fill with clouds pregnant with snow. *That didn't happen with Uram.* He had died in a blast of pure white light that lit up the entire city before it faded out of existence, no trace left of the Archangel of Blood.

The impact is never the same, Raphael said. *I am told that, only an hour after Uram's death, while we were both unconscious, it began to rain across the entire world. It did not stop for three days.*

Elena realized they'd never spoken about this. That time had been well past when she woke from her long sleep. The whole "I'm an angel" thing had taken up her attention, Uram a bad memory better left to the annals of history.

"Which one of us was it?" Michaela's cheekbones were like knives against her skin, her wings held with vicious tightness. "Other than you and Lijuan, Titus and Charisemnon are the only two currently in battle with one another."

Elena's chest hardened to granite. Titus was one of her favorite archangels. She couldn't countenance the idea of him being gone from this world.

"We will not know until the news filters out of the territory." Raphael shifted so that his wing touched Elena's. "Until then, we must believe that Titus has taken an enemy from the world."

Elena caught another glimpse of the spreading black on Raphael's wing and all at once nothing else was important; she had to get Raphael somewhere private. "You must be tired," she said to Michaela, deliberately switching to a slight formality to hold with angelic etiquette in this kind of a situation.

She didn't give a flying monkey's ass about etiquette, her heart a staccato beat, but it got things done when it came to powerful angels used to certain modes of behavior. "Please," she said, "make use of one of the suites in the Tower. It appears Lijuan's troops are content to hold their territory and wait for her to rise. We'll have a little time at least."

"Thank you, Consort," Michaela said with a sincerity that was *almost* real. "But if you do not mind, Raphael, I would speak to your second and gain a greater understanding of how this battle is being fought, and the enemy we face."

"Elijah, too, will meet you in the war room," Raphael said after a moment.

The three of them parted ways after showing Michaela to the war room. Elena caught Dmitri's eye, then used Laric's "silent tongue" behind Michaela's back to quickly sign out a message. The corners of his eyes tightened at the news that Raphael was wounded, but he moved smoothly to intercept Michaela so she and Raphael could get away.

Dmitri had a dark sensuality to him even when he wasn't trying, and Elena saw Michaela react with a slight softening. Her opening comment held a husky laugh to it. "You do get better with age, Dmitri."

"And you get more ravishing," he replied with a slow smile you'd take as real if you hadn't seen him smile at Honor.

Elena took the chance and dragged Raphael away.

She all but tore his top off his body the instant they were in their quarters. The leather was cracked and smudged and dented, scorched in places, torn in others. When it stuck to his shoulders for a frustrating moment, she used a knife to just cut it off.

"Fuck, fuck, fuck." His left shoulder was nearly all black and trickles of that blackness had begun to streak down his side toward his heart. The rib cage one was larger than the span of her hand—and it was sending lethal tendrils to his heart, too.

"I'm afraid I am not in the mood, *hbeebti*."

"I'm going to kill you in a second." But her hand was gentle as she checked the area around his rib cage, then higher.

He gripped her wrist when she would've touched the blackened flesh. "No, Elena. We can't take the risk it will jump to you. You are currently devoid of wildfire and Lijuan is becoming more powerful—we do not know the properties of this poison."

Jaw set, she nonetheless nodded. "It hasn't reached your eyes." The blue was painfully clear, the color intense. "Your body's holding it at bay."

"No. It *is* growing, simply slower than before because of the depth of the initial hit. She didn't get as much of the poison in me this time."

Elena wanted to argue with him that he was wrong, that the poison wasn't creeping over his body in a toxic wave, but she couldn't. The stuff was determined to claw around his heart, eat him up.

"Amputation," he said, "may be the best option."

Elena's entire self rebelled at the idea of Raphael being brutalized in such a way, but she nodded. As an archangel, he could heal an amputation—and this deadly poison would be out of him. "You'll be crippled on the battlefield."

"Yes." A warrior's acknowledgment. "We leave the rib cage infection, and remove the shoulder one. I can still fight with one arm and shoulder gone."

Heart ice, she stared into his eyes; he was signing his death warrant. That patch on his rib cage would continue to eat away at him. And battling Lijuan as desperately as they were, meant he'd have no time or resources to fight back, heal. "Together," she reminded him on a harsh whisper. "You take what you need." Her body was a paltry battery at best, but she was still generating droplets of wildfire.

When she pressed her hand against a clear part of his chest, a pitifully thin crackle of wildfire tinged with an opalescence of midnight and dawn spread from her into him. Maybe she'd bought her archangel another thirty minutes.

He closed his hand over hers. "Together."

Elena wanted to wrap her arms around him, hold on tight

forever, but with the infection rampant in his body, she knew he wouldn't permit it. So they simply stood there, exhausted, in love, and determined, until a voice entered their mind.

Aeclari.

Both she and Raphael turned toward the balcony doors. It was no surprise to see the Primary standing outside, framed by a Manhattan that had gone painfully dark against the night. Snow fell in soft flakes to lie against his hair, his shoulders, this being from the deep who now walked the world.

She and Raphael walked over together to open those doors, but when they gestured the Primary inside out of the cold, he shook his head. "It is time." In his voice lived hundreds of others, all his brethren, including those whose bodies had been poisoned.

Elena's spine stiffened.

Raphael went motionless. "I would not lose my Legion."

"You need all of what we can give—what we carry for you, and the energy that makes us." The Primary's eyes, dark pupils against a rare silver-blue, held Raphael's. "The power is needed—and it can do more than this Legion." He shifted his gaze to the black patch on Raphael's shoulder. "We are not meant to outlive our *aeclari.*"

Heat burned Elena's eyes. When the Legion had first arrived, they'd been an eerie mass of gray. Beings so *other* that she couldn't comprehend them. Now, they were her friends. Strange and old and childlike at once. They gave her potted plants, and flew with her sometimes for no reason but that they wanted to. They'd built a lush green home in the center of Manhattan, a home filled with life.

"Is the energy that makes you only of the body?" she whispered. "Once you . . . unravel, will your minds and memories be lost, too? Can you ever come back?"

The Primary angled his head to the side. "We do not know. We have never given that which makes us. We are of the earth, so perhaps we will grow again from the seeds of our energy left in the world. Or perhaps we will die a true death."

Tears fell from her eyes. The Primary looked at her with a strange quietness. "We have never had tears shed for us." His voice was hundreds at once in her mind, and she was okay with that today.

Stepping forward, she hugged him tight. His body was cool, and she felt no heartbeat, no breath. Yet the Legion were deeply alive in a way Lijuan would never be. "I promise to watch over your home until your return."

His arms were hesitant but they came around her. "We may never return." Not a cold denunciation but a quiet warning.

"I don't believe that." She couldn't; her heart was already breaking. To think the Legion, unique and different and seven hundred and seventy-seven, would disappear forever from this world . . . She couldn't bear it.

The Primary held her gaze when she drew back. "This is our purpose. We were created to be the right hand of the *aeclari*, to rise when darkness rises, and to fall when it is needed. We are content with our destiny. It is . . . honor."

Raphael held out an arm in the way of warriors, and the Primary clasped it after another small pause. "You are my Legion and you will always be my Legion. As long as I exist, you are welcome in my territory, in whatever form you choose to take."

"Sire." The Primary inclined his head. "Consort, you must make contact with the sire."

Wiping off her tears with one hand even though her nose was already stuffed up and more tears burned in her eyes, Elena curled her hand around Raphael's uninfected upper arm.

The Primary placed his free hand over Raphael's heart. *Raphael. Elena.* Aeclari. *We give you what is yours.* It was his voice and it was the Legion's voice, so many differing notes in the words, so many differing personalities, until it was a wild song.

A single organism with many parts.

She heard the one who'd been so fascinated by the velvety *stachys byzantina* she'd had in her greenhouse that he'd lit up at being offered a seedling she'd grown for him. She heard the one who'd been trying out different hues of skin on the back of his hand, to see if he liked one better than being gray. She heard the one who always turned up on this balcony at night, to say good night. And others, so many others, each a specific memory in her mind.

Elena.
Aeclari.
Raphael.

Aeclari.

It is time.

They hovered beyond the balcony in endless rows of silent wings. *You are in our memory. The* aeclari *of the Death Cascade. The* aeclari *who . . . loved us.*

This isn't good-bye, Elena said in reply. *It's only until the next time.*

You will always be our Legion. Raphael's voice came on the heels of hers, each word potent. *Remember this place. Remember your home.*

Elena. Aeclari. *Raphael.* Aeclari.

Thousands of whispers, building in a crescendo until Raphael gasped as a jolt passed from the Primary to him—and down into Elena. Her back bowed, her veins lit from within and the stormfire in her wings turned into an inferno, though she'd received only a tiny percentage of the power that had punched into Raphael. She recognized this power.

It was of blood and of darkness, a red storm.

The first time, she'd taken it to be a thing that wanted to control Raphael, but now she understood. Blood was life as much as the earth was life. It was power rooted in the basest elements, to be shaped by the bearer.

Above them, the snow-heavy sky began to turn blood red in an echo of the bloodstorm that had terrified her what felt like a lifetime ago. Golden lightning cracked that bloodstorm, and in the midst of it, she suddenly *understood.* Knowledge poured into her, the knowledge of millennia kept by the Legion.

Her brain wasn't vast enough to comprehend even a single mortal lifetime's worth, but it didn't need to; it only needed to comprehend small fragments. Somehow, the Primary had made sure those fragments were at the forefront of what he gave to her and Raphael.

We show, the Legion whispered. *We show. We show. Mirrors.* Aeclari *are mirrors.* Aeclari *are life.* Aeclari *are the channel.* Aeclari *. . . we love you.*

The last was said in a tone of surprise, as if they had never loved in all their millennia of existence. Then the Legion were gone, their bodies collapsing into dust, as they did when they died in battle, only to rise again. But this time, though both she and Raphael waited, they didn't rise.

Elena's hand trembled against her mouth, a sob catching in her throat.

The Legion were gone.

So was the black poison on Raphael's shoulder, his wing, and on his rib cage. His eyes glowed from within when he turned to her, his wings limned with light. Closing his arms and wings around her as she cried for the ancient beings who might've just erased themselves from existence, he said, "Your eyes are liquid silver and fire dances under your skin. Your wings are full of so much lightning, you burn."

His voice was rough and she knew he, too, mourned. *It's suddenly too quiet in my head.* The Legion had become a part of them, a murmur that was there without being intrusive.

Mine, too.

They held on to each other as the pain settled into their hearts and bones, a memory that would never fade.

When they parted at last, Elena glanced down at her arm, saw the golden lightning. It broke her skin in a river of molten gold, only for the wound to seal up again and a different one to open. "It's like what happened to Illium." Too much power thrusting into his body, power that had been meant for Raphael.

Raphael ran the fingers of one hand over her forearm. "Yet he would've died had I not taken it, while you hold it with ease." He pulsed with the intensity of what was inside him.

"You don't feel as you did in the bloodstorm. A little like it, but not the same." Not as distant, as devoid of emotion.

Yet above them, the sky swirled a dark red that bathed Manhattan in a macabre light.

"It is a power that is cold and dark and deep."

"Like the ocean where the Legion sleep."

"Yes." He shot a bolt of light into the bloodstorm clouds. The sky erupted with gold, drowning Manhattan in brilliance for a long moment. "A small exertion given the power inside me—and the display may cause Lijuan to hesitate."

Since he was still glowing like a lightbulb, she saw his point. "Energy's already started to turn into wildfire." It was the only way his body could've fought the poison.

Raphael nodded. "But even were I glutted with wildfire, I fear it would not be enough." His face was lines of pure beauty, an archangel at the apex of his power. "She has risen again and again after feeding."

"What the Legion showed us . . ." Her mind struggled to grasp the concept; she could suddenly appreciate the difficulty the Legion'd had in describing the phenomenon.

"It was a moment of blinding clarity," Raphael said, "but now it slips in and out of my grasp like a half-remembered dream."

Elena tilted back her head and took a deep breath of the cold air, on the theory that *not* thinking about it would bring the concept to the surface. "I feel so powerful." Her skin continued to break open but nothing hurt; she felt better than she had in her whole life. "I think I'm drunk."

"Would you like to send a fireball to the sky?" She heard the smile in his tone.

Dropping her gaze from the sky to him, this creature of power and beauty, she grinned past the anguish. "You're still a little bit mortal."

"I have pieces of your heart inside me, *hbeebti*. I will always be a little bit mortal." He looked again at the bloody sky. "Blood is not evil. Blood runs in our veins. Blood is life."

"They gave theirs so we could fight for ours." She couldn't look toward where the Primary had stood, the pain too raw and fresh.

"The Legion were warriors, Elena-mine, and they laid down their existence for their *aeclari*. We will honor that."

Elena flexed her hands, focusing on the energy that lit up her veins and not on the loss that would hurt for a long time to come. "We better go see Dmitri, see if he knows anything more about that boom we heard."

They stepped off the balcony together. As they did, she wondered how they looked against the night sky. Shirtless and beautiful, Raphael was glowing almost too bright to look at, and she was painted with rivers of liquid gold. *I hope someone snaps a photo,* she thought to Raphael. *We are never going to look this badass again.*

He laughed and he was her Raphael, even if there was a heavier darkness to him now, the darkness of an ancient power that had found home in his veins. This, she thought, was permanent.

He would carry the imprint of their Legion through eternity.

67

Dmitri took one look at the two of them and found a pair of sunglasses from somewhere. Elena had to laugh. The vampire had a sense of humor at times that very closely resembled hers. Not that they'd ever be friends. It was an unspoken law of nature.

Her laughter fled with Raphael's next word. "Titus?"

"No news." Taking off the sunglasses, Dmitri put them on a computer table. "Whatever he and Charisemnon did, it succeeded in blowing out all communications from those territories to the outside world. No one from another territory's flown there and back yet to pass on the information."

Dark eyes hard, Dmitri added, "Our own communications are sketchy at best. I think Lijuan or her people did a bit of deliberate damage at some point."

"Have we lost our eyes on that side?"

"Vivek's still got a few. It's about what you'd expect. She's getting ready to feed again, though we can't see the flesh mountain—those bugs were crunched." Dmitri brought up a feed on a nearby screen. "I sent Vivek to sleep after Michaela left with Elijah. He's not meant to be awake and in the chair for such long stretches yet."

Tell your friend to stop acting so human. It's annoying.

I would not dare get in the middle of your and Dmitri's special relationship, hbeebti. Light words, but he made sure his wing continued to touch hers, the glow coming off their bodies a silent testament to the sacrifice of seven hundred and seventy-seven exceptional beings.

Dmitri pointed to movement on the screen. "Wounded are being carried in that direction. Could be being taken to an infirmary, but my cold, dead heart has other thoughts."

"What about the ships?" Raphael asked. "The possible troop or reborn transports?"

"Definitely coming this way." Dmitri indicated a map on another screen; it had various lines dotted on it. "We're updating this as we get any data—it's become fragmented as communications continue to go out around the world."

"I don't suppose we can fly a jet out there and punch a few holes in the ship using grenade launchers?" Elena folded her arms, her booted feet set wide. "I mean, there're no rules about how you *get* to a battle, right? Lijuan used submarines."

"I thought about that," Dmitri said, "but she's ahead of us." Minimizing the feed from enemy territory, he flicked up another image.

It was of the ruins of a jet, its wings broken off and its fuselage cracked in half as it lay on the tarmac. Elena recognized the paint job. "Dougal, the others?" she whispered.

"As far as I know, the planes were empty." A glance at Raphael. "Images were hand-delivered by one of Jason's people. I didn't want to interrupt whatever was going on that had you turning the sky the color of a nice blood wine."

"Xi must've sent out a stealth team under cover of darkness." Raphael sounded cool, clearheaded. "Did she hit all our planes?"

"I don't have a report from the secondary airport, but chances are high. I had to pull protection from both airports when we saw the size of Lijuan's army—it's why I told all pilots and airfield crews to evacuate to housing a short distance away."

"You made the right call. We had no way of knowing the ships were en route."

"Did they attack nearby civilians?" Elena was deeply conscious of the vulnerability of her friends and family.

"No, it was a targeted strike."

"Lijuan might be mad, but she remains a goddess in her mind," Raphael murmured. "Goddesses do not win battles by attacking the weak."

"She did and is doing horrible things to her people."

"But they *are* her people, Elena. To her, that means they belong to her, to do with as she wishes." Raphael looked once more at the images of the broken planes. "What are the chances Xi will launch a major assault during the hours of darkness that remain?"

"Naasir's been skulking around out there and managed to pick up some high-level chatter. Together with what we're getting from Vivek's technological spies, I'd say it's low to negligible. My feeling is they're waiting for the reinforcements to arrive. With that and Lijuan at full power, that's it. Game over in a single strike."

"That is exactly what I would do were I running Lijuan's war room." Raphael looked out beyond the glass, to the fires on the various rooftops. "We must make the assault before they are ready, but when our people are not so exhausted. In the interim, I must think on how we can kill an archangel who appears to have become truly immortal."

First, however, the two of them flew over their side of the city and landed on those rooftops and streets nearest where they'd lost ground. They met with the troops who'd been so badly demoralized by that loss, and whose faces now lit up at seeing the power burning off both of them.

Izzy's eyes nearly popped out of his head. Coming closer, he reached out a finger to Elena's arm, hovered.

"Go on," she said. "I should warn you I have no idea what will happen."

The warriors around him looked even more intrigued. Izzy was undeterred. "I'm part of your Guard, Ellie. Your power won't hurt me." He touched his finger to a section of her skin that held tributaries of liquid gold. The gold twined around his finger for a second before returning to her and continuing on in its business.

He dropped his hand, his smile a thing of beauty. "See? Your power knows me."

Patting his cheek because seriously, he was the most adorable adult angel she knew, she said, "Long as you don't steal the last slice of pizza like you did last time. Then all bets are off."

As his friends laughed and slapped him on the back, the sky continued to swirl blood red, and Elena knew the power in Raphael's veins was bedding in, becoming a permanent part of his cells.

Later, back in the suite, their first goal was to be clean.

"I have dirt on top of my dirt," she muttered, but it wasn't a true complaint. No soldier cared about being clean when those few minutes might mean the fall of their city. This time was a luxury.

Soon as they'd stripped, Raphael scooped her up in his arms, her wings lightning and fire around them, and took her straight to the bath. Steam rose from the top of it.

"I swear, Montgomery has better spies than Jason." She sighed as Raphael lowered her into the bath before following her in. It was a place where they often played, but not today. Today, it was about scrubbing off the dirt while their wings brushed against each other and their legs touched.

Afterward, they jumped in the shower for a final rinse. That was when Raphael lifted her up by the hips and pinned her to the wall. They came together in a hot, hard fury, a moment stolen on the eve of a battle where all could be won . . . or lost.

No foreplay, no teasing, just the raw need to be one.

Limp against him in the aftermath, she sighed when he pressed a kiss to her shoulder. They took a long second more to be together, to find strength in one another before they drew apart and began to dry off.

They didn't dress in full combat gear, but put on enough that they could be on the battlefield in a matter of seconds should it be necessary. Clean, ready, they lay down in bed, Elena's head on Raphael's chest and her wings sprawled over him in a dance of lightning, while he cupped her nape with his hand, his thumb stroking absently.

They talked about Lijuan and about the knowledge the Legion had tried to give them, attempting to make sense of a shattered kaleidoscope of memories. Elena fell asleep at some point; her exhausted body still felt very mortal at times. When she woke, it was to a reddish light falling through the balcony doors they'd left uncurtained all night.

Raphael remained in bed with her and awake, his free arm bent behind his head as he stared at the ceiling. His other arm was yet wrapped around her. He was warm and strong and smelled like home—and the glow of power burned from his skin.

"Mirrors and channels," he said, picking up their conversation as if she hadn't conked out in the middle of it. "Let us recap our thoughts, *hbeebti*: mirrors reflect objects and light, but a certain kind of mirror can make light stronger, too, focus it."

Elena yawned, her brain fuzzy. "Gimme a minute to throw some water on my face." It took more like five, but she was refreshed by the time she returned to the room. "What time is it?" It had been long enough for her own glow to disappear, though her veins did turn to liquid gold now and then without warning.

"Seven in the morning."

She poked her head out the balcony doors. In the distance was a gray sky that might mean it was raining out there, but directly above . . . "Raphael, the bloodstorm sky is still swirling away above the Tower." A slow-moving cyclone with a heart of red so dark it was black.

"I know." Raphael's voice was a little absent. "I decided to let the enemy wonder what exactly is happening to me."

"Excellent evil plan." Going back to the bed, she took a cross-legged position facing him. "How about an experiment? Throw a little power at me."

When he did, the energy sank into her, only to release back into him the instant she made contact. "I guess that's a mirroring effect in a way, but I don't think that's what the Legion meant."

She pressed her fingers to her temples, squeezed her eyes shut. "I have fragmented images of massive explosions, of power narrowing to a single point . . . and a sense of things being made . . . bigger. Does that make sense?"

"The Legion want us to do something that magnifies power." Raphael sat up, the sheet pooling at his waist and his bare chest a seduction.

But no matter how they approached it, they couldn't find the truth hidden in the Legion's enigmatic words—or in the memories the Primary had tried to pass on. The only thing that was indisputable was that even wildfire could only injure Lijuan now. If they did what they'd done before, they'd waste the Legion's sacrifice for no final outcome. Yet doing nothing wasn't an option.

When they rose not long afterward, Elena ate, then flew across to the front line to relieve a gunner who'd stayed up overnight. "I'll take the day," she told him. "Get some rest, and you need blood, too." The male was too pale, his face thinner than was his normal.

When he protested that he was fine, she pointed out that he'd be useless as a gunner if he fainted mid-shot.

"I do not *faint*." Arms folded, eyes narrowed, affront in every breath.

Jeez, four-hundred-year-old vamps could be so tetchy. "Then do it for me," she said. "I need to feel useful."

"Consort, no one could ask more from you." Arms unfolding, his expression earnest. "You fight by our side every day."

Despite his response, her words did convince him to take the break. That done, she turned her attention to another vampire. "You, too." She pointed a finger. "Take the time while things are quiet. It's all going to go to hell sooner rather than later."

Setting down her weapon, the experienced vampire with whom Elena regularly played poker, sniffed at her. "Ellie, did you have a shower?" A gasp.

Elena waved her hand from her body toward the other woman. "Smell my lemony freshness. You, too, can have this scent if you leave before Her Evilness wakes."

"I'm gone."

Seeing that others who'd taken a rest break were arriving to relieve the remainder of the night watch, she settled in to her spot. It *was* raining on this side of the city, but the thin drizzle didn't penetrate her jacket or pants. She'd walked up to this roof after landing lower down on a balcony invisible to

Lijuan's forces. At which point, she'd retracted her wings and covered her hair under a black knit cap.

The energy fissures didn't often happen on her face, so if she kept the knit cap snugged down and her hands in her gloves, no one from Lijuan's side should make her. Should that change, she'd return to the Tower.

She was here to help, not draw danger down on their troops.

Raphael, meanwhile, was in a meeting with Elijah and Michaela. The three archangels needed to make strategic plans about how best to utilize their energies in battle. For one, while it was clear Michaela could hurt Lijuan a little, her strikes would have more impact if she waited until Raphael had softened up the goddess of fricking zombies with wildfire.

They couldn't afford to waste any advantage.

A strange calm hung over the city. A shooter would fire a potshot from Lijuan's side every so often, and Raphael's side would retaliate, but for the most part, things were eerie in their stillness.

Everyone was waiting for the last battle.

68

Raphael was standing on the Tower roof under the moonless night sky, watching his consort fly home after a long day spent as a gunner, when he received an unexpected message from Aodhan. *Sire. Unless my eyes deceive me, Titus is heading your way.*

Given Aodhan's current position, that was the wrong direction for the Archangel of Southern Africa to have flown to New York, but then, he must have known or guessed that Lijuan controlled the other approach. Communications hadn't become problematic until well after Lijuan's initial assault.

Continue to watch, Raphael ordered. *Report if anything appears untoward.* He swept off the Tower roof, his wings slicing through the chill night air. *Eli, it's possible Titus may be closing in on the city. Will you stand sentry while I head that way?*

Consider it done.

He angled his wings so his flight path would intersect with Elena's. *Come, hbeebti. We may be about to welcome an old friend.*

Her face lit up when he shared the news.

The night air was cold over their bodies as they flew on, but only Elena's wings glowed against the black. The energy fissures in her skin had stopped around midday, the same time that the glow began to fade from his body.

Their cells had absorbed the energies, made it their own. They would be the strongest they'd ever been when the war drums beat again.

A shadowy presence in the distance that resolved into large wings, an angel in flight.

"Well met, stripling!" boomed a familiar voice not long afterward.

"My old teacher, it is good to see you." They clasped forearms in the way of warriors.

"Titus, you're hurt." Elena's eyes were on the splint on Titus's other arm, the bandage wrapped around it dusty from his travels. Raphael knew it must've been a *very* bad break for Titus to have allowed it to be splinted.

"That dog's excrement of an archangel was rotting from the inside at the end—his breath was foul and putrid—but he got in a lucky blow," Titus muttered—at Titus volume, which was a low boom. "He broke it to pebbles. It's healing, but I will be one-armed for some days."

That wasn't the only damage. The usually smooth near-black of Titus's skin was baby pink on one side of his face when he angled his head, though his eye had escaped injury. *It will all heal,* Raphael reassured his hunter, aware of her feelings for the archangel. *His body has focused on the worst wound first. The facial damage is superficial.*

It's just hard to see Titus of all people hurt.

Yes.

"You fly strongly," Raphael said aloud, conscious that was what would matter to this generous and honest archangel in whose army he'd once been a green recruit.

"I shoot well, too." Titus's smile was a slash of white in his face. "I saw a ship on my flight here. It was crawling with that infectious filth my once wise friend Lijuan calls the reborn. It is now at the bottom of the ocean."

"Titus, I think I want to kiss you."

Elena's declaration had Titus throwing open his arms. Laughing, Raphael's consort went into them and planted a kiss on the other archangel's uninjured cheek. "Your wings . . ."

Titus stared at the brilliant stormfire. "New things are not always good, but this I like."

"Come on," Elena said. "You need to rest, eat. You flew a long way."

"I would've been here earlier, but I had to wipe that bearer of disease, that betrayer of honor, that putrid pustule, off the face of this earth."

"Charisemnon is dead?" Raphael asked, for they couldn't afford mistakes on this point. "There is no doubt?"

"Not a one, young pup. I eliminated his sorry being from existence with angelfire." He settled in to fly beside Raphael. "I could not bring my army—they would have been too slow and it would have left my people with no assistance in fighting the reborn plague."

"I would not expect it, Titus." That the other archangel had come, injured and straight off the field of battle, it was more than enough.

"So, who else has made it?"

"Elijah and Michaela."

"She's a beautiful dagger, but she knows her duty. And Elijah has always been a good man. What excuse do the others offer?" He didn't wait for an answer before booming, "If I am here, they should be here! I had to fight another archangel to do it!"

Sire, I may be hallucinating this time, Aodhan said, *but Astaad just dropped out of the clouds. He has another angel with him*—A jagged pause. *It is Aegaeon.*

Raphael stopped. "We may have more company." He turned, watching the skies until he glimpsed the wings of the Archangel of the Pacific Isles. A deep black where they grew out of his back, Astaad's wings faded in a gradient to pale gray at the tips—it made him very difficult to see against the night sky. Only the paleness of his skin gave him away.

The angel who flew beside him had far flashier coloring.

"Astaad! You took your time!" Titus called out when the two were close enough. "Did you bathe in dirt on your way here?"

Astaad, his goatee not as neat as usual and his tunic and pants a dark brown instead of his preferred white, smiled with the ease of a man long used to Titus's ways and well able to hold his own. "I see Charisemnon got in a few licks."

"Hah! You should've seen the mongrel dog by the time I got through with him." Titus clasped forearms with Astaad, while Raphael welcomed Aegaeon out of political necessity. At this point in time, he had to be one of the Cadre, not the young archangel who'd once held a small blue-winged boy's heartbroken body in his arms.

Astaad then turned to say a personal hello to Elena. "Mele sends her best. She is at home, safe on an island free of noxious contamination."

The rest of the journey passed quickly, but they landed at the Tower to find Neha and Caliane waiting for them. Neha's face was smudged with dirt and tired in a way Raphael had never seen it, her dark green leathers dusty. Caliane wore old white leathers, the color now closer to a pale yellow where it wasn't smudged with dirt and soot.

Both his mother and Neha had their hair in braids at the back of their heads, swords at the hip. Neha took in the landing party. "So, it was Charisemnon who died. Good. Those who betray the Cadre are better off as forgotten fragments of dust." Right then, Neha was a warrior queen, one who had old blood splattered on her leathers.

"We heard of the situation in your lands," Astaad said to Neha in his quiet, elegant voice. "It is a horror your people have faced."

Neha's mouth firmed into a hard line. "My troops will survive this, and afterward, we will find a way forward. For now, I have left them to come here so we can end this forever. *Never again* will an archangel dare to use children as battle fodder."

"It is a breach that will not be forgiven or forgotten," Caliane added, the echo of nightmares in her eyes. "But my son, do not tell me that Alex has let us down?"

"He fights to save his people," Raphael said, because he could understand Alexander's choice even if he didn't agree with it; it would've torn out his heart had he had to leave New York in the same situation.

"It will not matter if he wins the battle there if he is left to fight Lijuan alone." Caliane pursed her lips. "I spoke to him personally before these new ways of communication stopped working and made it clear the war must be won before we can begin to fight lesser battles."

Elena spoke into the small silence that followed Caliane's words. "I don't suppose any of you sank a ship full of reborn?"

Everyone but Titus shook their heads.

Ah well, Archangel. One out of three isn't bad.

69

The war room burned with so much power that the tiny hairs on Elena's arms stood straight up. Vivek wouldn't even go near the knot of angry archangels. "Cadre's fucking terrifying as a group," he muttered to Elena when she came to get some information for the discussion. "You get my balls of iron award for this century."

It was as she was walking back to the Cadre that the salt-laced sea crashed into her mind. *Alexander has just been spotted entering the territory, together with Zanaya.*

Every single archangel in the world would soon be in Manhattan.

When it was time, the two of them excused themselves to go welcome the Archangel of Persia and the newly awakened Ancient. Zanaya, stunning in a way that slapped you in the face then wrapped around you with sensual grace, gave Elena the once-over.

"A mortal turned angel," she said, her lips soft and full, and her body clad in a simple black wrap that barely brushed her thighs. "How extraordinary. And such wings."

A statement like that could be made or lost on tone, and Zanaya's lyrically accented one held only wondering astonishment. Elena felt a bit like an interesting bug, but not one the Ancient wanted to squash. She went to compliment Zanaya on her sword—it was serious metal, not a pretty toy—when her gaze was caught by a rippling light beyond. "The sea aurora's back."

Zanaya's lips tilted up. "Qin's legend, that is what we called it in child tales. An old one. Will he rise, do you think?"

"He does or he doesn't," Alexander snapped. "We must prepare for battle."

Leaving the lovely beauty of the sea aurora to play out on the water, they walked into the war room. *Do you think Lijuan will try to attack this Qin?* Elena asked Raphael.

It will be madness on her part. His aurora may play there, but it does not mean he Sleeps directly beneath.

"I left my territory overrun by reborn to come here." Alexander met the violent blue of Caliane's gaze across Dmitri's strategy table. "We must end this here and quickly."

Dude has no idea, Elena muttered to Raphael a half hour later, while Aegaeon spoke about how they could take Lijuan if they all worked together.

He is used to fighting ordinary foes, and even the experience in India cannot change the imprint laid by millennia. Raphael nodded at Dmitri and the drop-down screen opened up. "Before we go any further, you should all watch this."

It was a replay of their last two encounters with Lijuan. The replay was choppy, the footage cobbled together from various surveillance and spy cameras, but it told a chilling tale.

"That is the fire with which you made her retreat in the past?" Astaad asked, dark eyes intent and hands braced on the edge of the table; his biceps were bunched, the sleek muscle of him evident for the first time since Elena had met him.

"Yes," Raphael confirmed. "And this"—another glance at Dmitri—"is how she refuels herself and rises again, glutted with power."

The flesh mountain came into view, squirming with life. Dmitri had chosen the footage from the very first feeding, as it was the clearest. It showed Lijuan going from wounded to a healthy glow while her people shriveled into desiccated mummies. The other archangels said nothing for a long time after the last frame blinked out.

It was Zanaya who broke the silence, her stunning face solemn within the frame of silver hair washed with purple. "Can this being she has become be killed?"

"All we can do is try." Caliane's quiet statement held resolve. "The only other option is to swear allegiance to the goddess she believes herself to be and watch the world drown in death."

Her appetite will never be satisfied, child of mortals. She will feed . . . feed . . . feed into her reign of death.

Elena staggered at the old voice that had entered her head without warning. Vestiges of Sleep lingered in Cassandra's tone, but they were only remnants. The Ancient was awake or very close to it.

Elena. The sea crashing into her mind, the salt-laced waves powerful. *What is it?*

Cassandra's newly awake. She took a discreet step back from the table, then another. *Let me see if I can talk to her.*

Raphael's eyes flicked over her head. *Her owls await you on the balcony. Go. I will ensure no one in the Cadre notices.*

Elena slipped away to join the lovely snowy birds with golden eyes, while Raphael stayed with the other archangels. Hannah, the only one who probably would've noticed her retreat, was with the injured members of Elijah's army.

Prophecy of mine. A brush of thought against her that felt like a smile. *You altered destiny. You are whole.*

Elena's heart clenched at the open joy in the Ancient's voice. *Thanks for the assist along the way.* Cassandra had come through in the end. Elena didn't hold her delay in doing so against her—to change the mind of a being so old required a tectonic shift.

I don't suppose you can give us a heads-up on the final battle? One way or another, it would end the next time Lijuan rose. After that, they had no more aces in the hole, no more Legion, no more power.

The threads are too tangled. A sigh. *In the center is a mirror that distorts the images on the other side. I cannot see what will be. I see only a chaos of possibilities. I see death. I see life. I see a mockery of both.*

Elena stilled. *The mirror. Is there anything special about it?*

A long pause but she didn't think Cassandra was gone—

not when the white owls preened their feathers on the edge of the balcony.

The mirror changes that which it is given, Cassandra said at last. *It does not reflect the truth but it does not lie. It is . . . a channel.*

Elena asked the question different ways, brought Raphael into the discussion, too, but that was all the Ancient could tell them. Cassandra sighed before her mind faded once more.

Elena met Raphael's eyes as she walked back into the war room, the endless blue a familiar shock. *You think she'll join us for the battle?* Cassandra had already altered her pattern of behavior once by acting to help change the future.

Ancients are difficult to predict. Even if she does, it may not be enough to balance the scales of power.

Elena nodded, her jaw tight. Because this time, the Cascade might've outplayed itself by giving one player a seemingly unbeatable ability.

How could you win against an enemy who could regenerate at rapid speed?

". . . happened to Antonicus," Neha was saying when Elena quietly rejoined the group. "Simply being an Ancient, with powerful energies, will not protect you." Her eyes were trained on Aegaeon. "Don't be an arrogant fool."

The Ancient's nostrils flared, the blue-green of his hair liquid silk around his harshly handsome face. "Remember to whom you speak, girl. I was a ruler before you were ever a thought."

Illium's father is an asshole. She couldn't see how their bright, beautiful, beloved Bluebell had come from this man. Yeah, fine, the wild blue feathers had definitely had their genesis in Aegaeon—the streaks of blue in the predominantly sea green hue of the Ancient's wings were identical to Bluebell's, but that appeared to be his sole contribution. *What the hell did the Hummingbird see in him?*

Aegaeon was well known for his ability to seduce women. I am told that, in the beginning, he was often a different man with the Hummingbird, as you say Dmitri is with Honor.

I'll deny it until I'm blue in the face if you tell Dmitri this, but there's no comparison. He's a prince in contrast to this pompous ass.

Despite all their powerful clashing personalities, the Cadre managed to come up with a battle plan by the time dawn's light touched the sky. Elena had made herself do the sensible thing and gone to bed to catch some rest so she could be at her best when morning broke. As it was, she returned in time to hear their decision.

The first was one Raphael had already made: to begin the battle on their terms, not Lijuan's. "The tiredness of our troops is no longer a handicap. Not when we have all of you." He looked around the table, his hands braced on the side and his wings held neatly to his back. "Even the sheer numbers at her disposal can't outweigh the power of ten archangels, four of them Ancients."

His next words were cold with power, demanding attention. "If there is a risk that you will be taken by the enemy and rescue is unlikely, do what must be done. We cannot know how strong she'll become if she feeds on an archangel."

Aegaeon banged his fist on the table, scattering the markers they'd just laid out as they discussed the battle plan. "You truly believe she would dare cross that line?"

"She turned children into infected vampires," Neha spit out. "There is no line she will not cross."

No one had anything to say to that.

"Two hours until we strike." Raphael pushed off the table, rose to his full height. "Prepare for battle."

70

Titus was glorious to watch. The Archangel of Southern Africa had planted his booted feet on the ground on this side of the front, his wings spread wide and his golden breastplate gleaming even in the dull morning light that got through the snow-heavy clouds. The equally gold "tattoo" that had formed on his skin was visible only in glimpses on his thickly muscled shoulders and equally impressive biceps.

His roughly hewn and square-jawed face was set in a glower that dared the other side to shoot anything at him.

The man was beautiful—and also a little arrogant, Elena thought with a grin. She was on a nearby rooftop, her crossbow pointed at one of those on the other side who might try to take out Titus's wings. She fired just as she saw a hand go to press the trigger. More crossbows and guns fired all around her.

A roar of sound, Titus's growl rising to the skies as he lifted up both his uninjured arm and his splinted one. And rained down hell.

The road lifted up under the feet of the enemy, cracking and rippling as if it was a river. Buildings shook hard. Glass that had survived the earlier detonations shattered. The quake seemed to go on forever, sending angels into the sky—butterflies disturbed from a tree. Dust blurred the landscape, floating up to further dull the turgid gray skies.

Ice, hard and biting, sleeted from the clouds at that very instant, pounding at the angels who'd taken off. Neha couldn't totally control the area hit, so their side also got a dose of frigid cold, but they were prepared for it. Clothing, gloves, cap, Elena was dressed for the heart of winter.

Howling mini-tornados whacked into the angels on the other side on the heels of the ice, taking them down like dominos. Zanaya was not playing.

Neither was Alexander: every bit of metal on the ground on the enemy side began to liquefy even as the angels fell. Alexander couldn't affect things that weren't touching the ground—so the weapons held by fighters would survive, as would any that were stored in buildings or crates that protected them from direct contact with the earth.

But Alexander wasn't targeting the weapons anyway.

At first, all Elena saw was a fire hydrant that melted, spraying water everywhere . . . but then the buildings that were still standing began to shake, as the metal rods within started to quiver and fail.

Ground fighters looked up at those precariously swaying buildings, their eyes huge.

Waves rose from the water on the other side, smashing into the shore and washing away vampires and reborn and fallen angels before the waves sucked back out with unbeatable force, taking anyone on the ground out to sea. Astaad and Aegaeon had to be careful how far they pushed things, because too much water and it'd wash away their own side, but the two seemed to have calculated it just right.

They'd had Caliane standing by to create a shield to protect their own, but it wasn't needed. Michaela had been told to stay back, keep her power in reserve for a direct strike against Lijuan, while Elijah hung to the far back, his job to protect their flank until Lijuan was sighted—in case the Archangel of China decided to pull another noncorporeal ambush.

Raphael waited for Lijuan.

As with all archangelic powers, the Cadre couldn't keep this up endlessly, but when the ground stopped shaking and the rain and ice stopped, and the tornados halted, the seas retreating, Lijuan's forces were in disarray. Buildings had collapsed into melted shapes straight out of a Salvador Dali painting. Roads no longer existed.

A massive chunk of the ground troops had disappeared into the ocean, as had large numbers of angels who'd been battered to the ground. Yet their sheer numbers meant a vast army remained.

They fought back with devoted fury.

Lijuan's surviving generals shot waves of obsidian fire, each one aiming themselves at an archangel. After having injured Elijah, they knew they could disable the Cadre; take out enough archangels and New York lost any advantage it had in launching the attack now, before Lijuan was ready.

Raphael had planned to seed the sky with wildfire to try to unmask her, but live battle had a way of interfering with strategic plans; too many of their own fighters fought at too many different elevations in the sky. Elena sent up a prayer to any *actual* gods that Lijuan hadn't fed enough to go noncorporeal.

Her prayers went unheard.

Elena had just shot out the wings of an enemy angel who was trying to hack at Aodhan's wings when Lijuan appeared without warning behind Zanaya. It also put the Archangel of China at the farthest point from Raphael. *Archangel!*

Even as he reacted to make it to that location, Lijuan grabbed Zanaya by the upper arms and bit down on her neck. Zanaya twisted with a snarl, attempting to reach for her sword and kicking back with her feet as mini-tornados appeared around Lijuan . . . but then her body seemed to slow down, her reactions stiffen.

The tornados faded.

Lijuan was sucking the life out of an *Ancient* and doing it at vicious speed.

Elena willed her body to go there, help Zanaya, but the speed still didn't work with archangels.

Though Raphael arrived at the location of the attack in a matter of seconds, his wings pure white fire, Lijuan turned noncorporeal again before he could hit her with wildfire . . . and Zanaya fell from the sky, her wings crumpled and her body far smaller than it should've been. Alexander caught her partway, cradling her close as he flew her toward the Tower.

Elena's heart pounded. *Archangel, how do we find her?* She could be at any elevation, at any location. Always before, she'd had a single target. Now she had many. Raphael couldn't spread his wildfire that wide without wasting the one weapon that might halt the Queen of Death.

Wildfire ringed his hands. *I must remain within equal distance of as many of the Cadre as I can.*

Lijuan appeared beside Alexander.

Raphael threw wildfire in her direction without a single hesitation. It hit, crackling energy through her system, but she went noncorporeal a heartbeat later. And Raphael realized that feeding on Zanaya had done what they feared; it had supercharged her.

Thank you for bringing me so much POWER! Laughter in Lijuan's mental voice, a kind of girlish delight that was disturbing in its facsimile of innocence.

She appeared behind Neha this time, but Galen—nearby—bought the Archangel of India a moment to react by slicing his broadsword down toward Lijuan's neck. She flicked him away and the heavily built weapons-master smashed into a building, but that minor delay gave Neha a critical second to turn. She struck out with the curved edge of one *kukri* blade, managed a deep slice across Lijuan's cheek.

A flap of skin and flesh slapped against her jaw, a wet red hole where her cheek should be. Blood splurted out . . . then vanished. The wound had closed by the time Raphael threw wildfire in her direction. She laughed and was gone before the wildfire hit her, and the bolt exploded into a knot of fighters, taking out several from both sides.

Raphael's rage was a cold thing with a heart of fire. *This was always her endgame.*

Perhaps she'd intended to "absorb" the Cadre one by one, but they'd served themselves to her on a platter. She didn't have to consider anything else beyond her urge to feed. She certainly didn't care that her troops were dying under waves of archangelic power. She would have more people once she owned the world. Mortals, vampires, angels, all were disposable to her. *Galen? Are you down?*

Few broken bones but not enough to take me out of the battle. Go toward Astaad. He's the most vulnerable right now.

Astaad was fighting alone against three of Lijuan's generals. It looked like he'd taken a hit of obsidian rain on his right forearm. The arm dragged, numbed and possibly eaten away with infection, but he continued to do battle, taking out one general as Raphael flew toward him. This time when Lijuan reappeared, Raphael was close enough to hit her, but though her face contorted at the wildfire strike, the skeletal understructure glowing into focus, she was still able to go noncorporeal.

She didn't appear again for five long minutes, giving neither him nor Galen any way to predict her actions. When she did, it was behind Astaad once more. He had Michaela by him, but though she reacted rapidly, her bronze lightning smashing into Lijuan's shoulder, Lijuan dragged Astaad close . . . and both disappeared.

Raphael, fuck.

Yes, Guild Hunter. We are in trouble.

Both archangels reappeared in the sky moments later, not far from where she'd first taken Astaad.

The Archangel of the Pacific Isles was fighting, but she had her face buried in his neck and already, Astaad looked emaciated, his wings limp. *You are all NOTHING but fodder for a goddess. Watch me feed. Know me as your superior!*

Raphael released a ball of wildfire. *My apologies, my friend,* he said to Astaad, who was in the direct line of fire.

The other archangel's face eased, as if in gratitude.

The wildfire hit them both. Screaming, Lijuan released Astaad. She went noncorporeal again as Astaad's body fell, riven with wildfire. No one was close enough to catch him. The Archangel of the Pacific Isles crashed to lie broken on a rooftop. Jason landed beside him a second later. *He's alive,* Raphael's spymaster reported. *His body has lost nearly all its flesh, but his eyes are lucid.*

Rather than killing him, the wildfire appeared to have ameliorated a little of the damage Lijuan had done. *Get him to safety.* As helpless as Astaad was now, Lijuan might come back to finish him off. *Eli, protect Astaad and Jason.*

The Archangel of South America took up an escort position—and the former general did something clever. He began to fire his power erratically around them, where it would either hit enemy troops or go into clear air. It made it nearly impossible for Lijuan to appear nearby—she'd have to risk being hit by one of Elijah's bolts. It wouldn't badly hurt her, not the way she was now, but the delay while she dealt with the shock would give Raphael time to drown her in wildfire.

Shooters and soldiers armed with flamethrowers had already begun laying down fire around the Tower. Again, Lijuan could survive that, but it might leave her vulnerable for a moment. The Tower guard paused only long enough for Jason to get through with Astaad, and Elijah to clear the area, before starting up again. Elijah continued to fire around him as he returned to battle, but no archangel could keep that up nonstop, especially when fighting against Lijuan's army.

Obsidian fire was now erupting not only from the hands of the generals, but others. Lijuan had to be bloated indeed to be fueling so many subordinates.

Titus was Lijuan's next target—but he reacted with warrior speed to smash his splinted arm into her face. Blood splurted and she was gone. Only to suddenly be behind Aegaeon. Raphael shouted out a warning. Illium's father ignored the obsidian rain coming at him from her forces and sliced both blades backward into her stomach, wrenching up.

Lijuan turned noncorporeal as her gown became drenched in red, even as Aegaeon took a massive number of blows from the generals. He began to fall, his wings shredded. Aodhan slammed into him, slowing his descent enough to bring him to a softer landing on a rooftop. It had been a risk on Aodhan's part that he'd become infected but it looked like the subordinates' fire wasn't infectious. Only Lijuan's.

He left Aegaeon on the rooftop, where the Ancient managed to get himself to a position near the archers. Though the generals had done significant damage, he continued to fight, while his body dealt with the obsidian. Courage had never been Aegaeon's problem. Not far in the distance, Neha destroyed three of Lijuan's generals in a single precision strike with the vivid green of her poison whip.

Raphael! Look out!

He blocked the shards of starlight obsidian dropping at him from the sky, only for Lijuan to repeat the attack again and again. He couldn't allow even one of the shards to burrow into him, not now she'd fed on two archangels, had to waste precious power maintaining the shield.

She was trying to wear him out. And hugely bloated with power, she was going to succeed. Then Michaela shifted position without warning—and ended up face-to-face with Lijuan. The Archangel of China had obviously meant to appear behind Michaela. No hesitation, no thought, Michaela blasted Lijuan with her power point-blank.

Raphael targeted the Archangel of China with a massive jolt of wildfire at the same time.

It punched through her entire system, turning her skin into a pattern of broken light but she was nowhere near down. She directed a hail of starlight obsidian shards directly at Michaela before going noncorporeal again. Michaela dropped and Lijuan's poison smashed into a skyscraper that was already half destroyed.

"Why won't the fucking bitch die?" Michaela's scream of frustration rent the air.

But they had no time for discussion, for frustration, because Lijuan had reappeared behind Alexander. She had her mouth on his neck before anyone could react, but she'd made a miscalculation. Illium was right beside Alexander and sliced off one of Lijuan's arms before she had any warning of what was to come.

As the severed limb fell to the ground, she disengaged from Alexander with a sound that was ten thousand screams in their minds. And went noncorporeal again.

Alexander?

I'm a little weaker, but she didn't get much, barely a sip.

Sweaty and bloody, they fought on. Raphael wasn't the least surprised when Lijuan reappeared with a whole arm only five minutes later. This time, she didn't attempt to feed—she aimed a bolt directly at Illium, her face wreathed in malevolence.

Illium twisted with speed, but even Bluebell's agility wasn't enough to fully avoid the blow. It went through the tip of one wing and began to spread blackness over his wing in a rapid surge. Illium wasn't an archangel. His body had no defenses. Raphael was too far from him and Lijuan was now raining her power down at his troops in a merciless hail that would murder and destroy if he didn't stop her.

He put up a wildfire shield.

Despite taking a catastrophic hit, Illium did the impossible. He went straight at Lijuan and slammed his favorite sword, Lightning, through her heart. She and the sword disappeared even as his wing blackened—but there was a flicker in her disappearance this time. He'd got the heart itself, damage bad enough that most archangels would've gone into *anshara* while it healed.

Go to Elena! Raphael told the angel, aware he couldn't lower his shield and go to Illium when Lijuan was apt to return at any moment. He didn't know if Elena could release wildfire on her own into anyone but Raphael, but it was Illium's only chance. *Elena, Illium's been hit.*

Lijuan returned in a viciousness of starlight obsidian.

71

Pulse in her mouth, Elena was ready for Illium.

Bloody from the spray when he'd cut off Lijuan's arm, his blue-tipped black hair matted with sweat, he came down hard. One of his wings was almost fully black at this point, the infection gaining ground with every second that passed. Elena touched her hand to it even before he'd caught his balance. Wildfire sparked over her skin in a protective glove but none passed from her to him.

"Cut it off." Illium handed her his other sword, the edge a deadly gleam. "Stop the spread. Now Ellie."

Elena set her jaw and took the blade. There was no point in arguing. His wing would grow back. He wouldn't survive if the poison reached his bloodstream. Using one wildfire-gloved hand to hold the blackened wing away from his back, she sliced. The blade was razor-sharp, went through the feathers and bone and tendon like they were butter.

Illium's spine went rigid, but he didn't cry out. Elena didn't cry, either, even as she excised off half of one of the most beautiful pair of wings in the world. She made sure to cut as close to the inner edge as possible, removing a clear two inches of healthy wing to ensure none of the poison would get into his bloodstream.

The blackened and dead wing fell to the rooftop.

He incinerated it with his power.

"You're bleeding," Elena said as she returned his sword.

"It'll stop soon." His face was pale but marked by lines of determination. "Slice off the healthy wing. I can't fight with it pulling me off-center."

It was harder this time, because there was nothing wrong with that wing, his feathers a vivid blue edged with filaments of silver, but she knew why he was making the choice. Illium was lethal with a sword in the air or on the ground but a messed-up center of gravity would make him clumsy, easier to kill.

"Done." Her voice came out a rasp.

Shifting to face her, his eyes dilated but his resolve unshaken, he touched his fingers to her cheek. "Wing loss is a foreseeable battle injury, Ellie. They'll grow back. I'll just have fluffy duck feathers and be grounded for a while—I'm very strong. It won't take long."

He incinerated his remaining wing, as if able to tell how much it hurt her to see it lying there, severed from his body. "Not sure if this'll make you feel better, but the first time this happened, my feathers grew back even prettier." A wicked grin.

"No." She poked him in the chest. "That does not make me feel better." But weirdly, it did. He'd been so much younger then, and he'd come through fine.

His back was a mask of blood when she checked again, but the first wound had already stopped bleeding and there was no sign of any further infection. For a second, she thought she saw a faint glow, similar to what happened with Raphael's wings when he was feeling lethal—or when he was overflowing with power.

Then an entire squadron of Lijuan's fighters landed on the rooftop and they had no more time. Elena brought up her crossbow, Illium sliced out with his sword, and they exchanged grins before diving into battle.

Elena was on the edge of the building, having just brought down an enemy angel when she saw one of Lijuan's poisonous bolts drop down directly at Galen, who was in the air on the far side of her roof. She was beside him before she realized it, shoving him out of the way. The bolt hit her instead, punching all the air out of her lungs.

Her entire body erupted with wildfire, encasing her in light. Lijuan's bolt dissipated.

Handy, but it used power. She flew back to her rooftop just as Illium finished off the last assailant. Grabbing a crossbow from a fallen enemy fighter, he took up a shooting stance beside her, and they aimed up. Not far from them, she saw Michaela deliberately put her body in the path of a bolt that would've otherwise hit and disabled Jason.

The Archangel of Budapest shrugged it off and kept going, flying to take on a general who'd pinned down a squadron. Turned out some people's true colors were hella surprising. She'd never again look at Michaela the same way.

Elena saw Raphael hit Lijuan in the fucking center of the chest, the wildfire turning her veins electric, but not only had the damn immortal monster healed devastatingly fast from Illium's heart blow, she remained able to turn noncorporeal. When she appeared by Michaela this time, neither the archangel nor anyone around her was able to interfere before Lijuan disappeared—taking Michaela with her.

She reappeared less than a second later only a meter from the edge of Elena's rooftop, hovering over clear air with Michaela in her grip.

"Fire! Fire! Fire!" Illium yelled and all the shooters unleashed their arrows or bolts or guns at the Archangel of China.

Several hit Michaela, but Elena knew an archangel could survive those. If they didn't disengage Lijuan from her neck however, she'd be dead or close to it very soon. Not that Michaela was taking this lying down—she'd created a collar of bronze energy around her neck that appeared to be repelling Lijuan's attempts, and she was trying to swamp Lijuan in her bronze fire.

Face icy in fury, Lijuan went to put her hand directly over Michaela's heart.

Taking a breath, Elena paused for a split second, exhaled . . . and shot. Her bolt went through Lijuan's eye, causing her to rear back, both her hands flying up to her face.

Raphael hit the injured eye with wildfire at the same time, getting it directly into Lijuan's blood. Lijuan shimmered then reappeared and Elena thought they'd got her. But she disappeared fully the next second . . . even as Michaela fell, fell, *fell*. There was no one in her path who could catch her, nothing to stop her catastrophic impact with the city street far below.

Trusting Illium and the others to hold off enemy troops, Elena retracted her wings and jumped off the rooftop, only reengaging her wings when she was nearly at the ground. She was beside the fallen archangel mere seconds after the impact. Michaela looked stunningly beautiful even now, with her legs broken under her, bones piercing her bodysuit to gleam wetly in the light, and her neck at a sickening angle, her arms like matchsticks someone had snapped into tiny pieces.

Blood spread from beneath the fan of her hair, a scarlet carpet on the asphalt.

But even worse was the creep of black that was a growing sun around her heart. "Lijuan got her poison into you." At point-blank range.

Cat green eyes held Elena's. Flickers of fire lit the archangel's irises.

Elena looked up.

The sky was aflame above them, as Neha unleashed the flip side of her ability to create ice. Even from so far, it felt as if the heat kissed Elena's skin through her clothes.

"My son," Michaela whispered and it was barely comprehensible. "The healer . . . he will be kind."

"Keir? You want Keir to be the foster dad?"

"Yes." Rattling sounds in her throat. "Tell him . . . tell him . . . I did not mean . . . to leave him. My . . . son. Protect . . ."

"We will." Elena wanted to close her hand over Michaela's, but the archangel's bones were shattered. When she looked up again, to see if Raphael could help, she found him in a pitched battle against Lijuan.

Fires continued to burn in Michaela's eyes when Elena turned back to the archangel. A sudden fierceness lit them. Her voice came into Elena's mind now, the feel of her a sensual perfume. But the words she spoke were hard with resolve— though her voice, it was faded there, too.

I need you to lift my hand and bring it to my chest, above the infection. A cough that bubbled blood. *Once I do what needs to be done, take me to a safe place.*

Elena had no idea what the hell Michaela was talking about, but she lifted one shattered hand, not flinching when the bones rattled, and placed it in the correct spot. "You're about two inches from the top of the infection."

Bronze fire erupted from Michaela's fingers.

Elena closed her eyes reflexively against the sudden brightness. When she opened them again, Michaela's eyes were closed, her body limp . . . and most of her chest gone, cut out by her own power. Elena could see the gleam of bone, the spongy texture of one lung.

And blood, so much blood.

Stomach roiling, Elena nonetheless looked carefully at the massive open wound. No sign of infection, all the black cut away. Along with most of Michaela's ribs and internal organs, part of one hip, a section of pelvis.

"Ellie." Dusty black boots slamming down beside her, Jason's wings in her vision. "I'll carry her to the infirmary."

Elena nodded jerkily. "I think her neck's broken."

"No," Jason said after crouching down to examine Michaela more closely. "It's not broken. It's almost severed from her body."

Swallowing hard, Elena said, "She was *talking.*"

"She is an archangel." He gathered Michaela into his arms.

Elena didn't ask him if Michaela would survive; as long as none of Lijuan's infection remained, the Archangel of Budapest would come back. Given her massive injuries, however—injuries that had come on top of having given birth not long ago—it might take a long time.

She flew escort for Jason until they were in friendly territory, then he went onward and she flew back to the battle zone. The sky remained full of fire. Neha was attempting to burn Lijuan's troops out of the sky.

She thought suddenly of Laric, scarred by his time caught in a fire sky. She hoped he was deep in the infirmary far from any windows. And she hoped the flames didn't bring nightmares to Caliane and Raphael.

As she got closer, she saw Aegaeon was right next to Neha, appeared to be protecting her so she could focus on her fire. In the orange-red glow, his wings appeared as pure blue as Illium's. As she watched, he razed an entire squadron with a scythe of sea green power.

"At least the bastard is useful," she muttered before firing a crossbow bolt through the wing of an angelic fighter who was about to thrust his sword into Andreas's gut.

The squadron leader raised a hand in thanks before slicing out with his blades to remove the head of another winged fighter. Surrounded by battle, she couldn't take even a second to search for Raphael in the sky, but she could feel him high above, exchanging blow after blow with Lijuan.

Lijuan, who could heal from any injury.

Fear tried to clamp its claws around her heart.

Gritting her teeth, she shoved it off, and fought on.

Sweat dripped down Raphael's back, and dampened his hair. His wildfire was being rapidly depleted. He was going to need to draw from Elena again soon, but the second he did that, they were in the endgame. There was no more power after that and Lijuan appeared unstoppable.

He'd deliberately drawn from Elena before battle began—not the totality of what she held, but enough so their energies would combine to create the green-tinged wildfire. However, since feeding from two archangels, Lijuan seemed all but impervious to even that.

Not far in front of him, Caliane took a massive wave of poisonous strikes from Lijuan's troops. His mother fell to a rooftop held by Raphael's people, her wings badly mangled and her bones shattered.

Mother?

I will survive this, my son. But I am out of the battle. Her mind cut off on the heels of that statement.

Just as Lijuan went noncorporeal again. He'd done enough damage that she couldn't seem to hold it for long, but even a second was too long. This time, she appeared close enough to Elijah to target him with her starlight obsidian.

The Archangel of South America couldn't avoid it, but Raphael was close enough to slam wildfire into both him and Lijuan. Eli's body jerked as the wildfire punched through to the poison in his system and began to fight it, while Lijuan's eyes lit up with wildfire before she screamed and fired back at Raphael.

Galen caught Elijah as he fell, lowered him to a rooftop. A flash far below caught Raphael's eye, Venom's face outlined in heat as he blasted a flamethrower at a horde of reborn right on top of him.

Raphael had no time to check on Eli or help Venom—Lijuan hadn't gone noncorporeal after wounding Elijah, and he blasted bolt after bolt at her. Her entire body burned the white-gold and blue of wildfire kissed with green, but she didn't break apart. Instead, she ran from Raphael and directly toward Neha. The Archangel of India avoided her bolts, but her avoidance strategy put her under a massive hail of obsidian rain shot by Xi and another general.

Neha went down.

Aegaeon attempted to cut Lijuan with his sea-green scythe, but it only seemed to irritate her. He did manage to avoid being hit, which meant Raphael still had three other friendly archangels in the sky with him. Then a mind with a weight as heavy as Caliane's touched his.

I am running out of power. Alexander, his words spoken in the instant between one attack and the next. *I have never in all my existence come this close to the edge. Aegaeon will not admit it, but he must be the same.*

Raphael got Lijuan once again, just as she readied herself to hit Alexander. Spinning around, she sent her power at Raphael instead. "You cannot kill me!" she roared as wildfire arced through her veins . . . and didn't end her.

The hail of starlight obsidian she sent at him was a wall.

He threw up a wildfire shield but it threatened to buckle under the pressure almost immediately.

Archangel. Elena's hand on his calf, the wildfire from her body entering his.

Using some of that power to dissipate Lijuan's as Elena broke away to take position by his side, he saw the reason why he wasn't under a secondary attack. A burst of violet energy had broken the sky to slam into Lijuan. A woman with hair of lilac, her gown pale green and her eyes impossible to see from here, was pounding Lijuan with blow after blow.

Another thinner figure joined her, and her eyes were visible to Raphael. What had once been brown was now liquid fire. As if the flame that had cleansed Favashi of infection had become part of her. Her Cascade-born power was rumored to be control over the winds, but it was liquid fire that she wrapped around Lijuan, trying to burn her down to the bone.

From the other side of the battlefield came another massive bolt of energy, this one holding the poignant beauty of the sea aurora.

Alexander fired at Lijuan at the same time, the silver of his wings brilliant in the blasts of energy lighting up the sky.

Raphael shot more wildfire at Lijuan, even as beside him, Elena used her crossbow to take down a flyer who'd come at them. He wanted to tell her to go back to a rooftop where it was safer, but no place was safe in war. And if this was the end, then they'd go into it side by side.

Then Lijuan managed the impossible and broke away from the combined attack.

Alexander fired after her.

Lijuan made an unpredictable move to the left.

Elena moved at the same instant to shoot out the wings of one of Lijuan's generals who was raising his hand to fire at them.

The bolt of Alexander's silver energy came straight at Elena.

72

Elena!" Raphael smashed into her, and the bolt hit him while the two of them were connected . . . but there was no pain. It bounced off him and as it did so, it changed form to become wildfire. White-gold and blue. Midnight and dawn.

Lijuan avoided that blow to rain down her own violence at him.

Even as he blocked it, Raphael's mind was racing. But it was his consort who yelled, "A mirror that's a channel! Tell everyone to throw their power at us!"

Raphael reached for his consort's hand. "Hover," he told her, knowing it would make them targets. But he also knew their people would protect them to the end. "Ready?"

"Always," she said, as if they weren't about to put their lives on the line.

Fire at me, Raphael told the surviving archangels. *Do not hesitate! Fire at me!*

It was Alexander who obeyed first, the metallic brightness of his wings flashing in the distance as he fired directly at Raphael. Then came Favashi, Titus, and Aegaeon. Cassandra and the sea aurora angel fired at the same time. Their combined power was a huge and old thing, and it stunned with its force. But Raphael and Elena stood firm under the barrage, and the mirror they became together bounced all the energy toward Lijuan.

It became wildfire that engulfed her. So much wildfire that it filled her mouth, lit her eyes, became her skin, burned in her hair. But still she didn't die. They hit her with more and more, as around them, her troops slammed obsidian rain at the archangels to try to take them down, and Raphael's people fought back with blood and fury.

He saw Jason eliminate a proxy, Aodhan another, Galen a third before he took a sword blow to the chest that made him stagger and fall. Jason came to his aid and a bloody Andreas took up Galen's fight.

Battle raged.

In the center of the vortex of power, Lijuan was an eerie mass of wildfire. Throwing back her head, she screamed, and wildfire erupted from her mouth to scar the sky. That was when two of Lijuan's troops managed to slam into Aegaeon. Illium's father had been in the process of firing more energy at Raphael. It went wide.

The vicious power of an Ancient punched into Elena before Raphael could shove her out of the way.

ELENA!

He would never have a clear memory of the moments that followed. There was too much power in the air, too much fear in his heart. He just felt energy flow violently into his body from hers. He threw the power at Lijuan almost instinctively, though his eyes were searching for Elena through the blaze of light around her.

I'm right here, Archangel. A little breathless but that was definitely his hunter's voice. Her fingers tightened on his.

Heart thundering as the other archangels stopped firing, the sudden change in pressure causing his ears to pop, he turned to see the new ball of wildfire he'd thrown crash over Lijuan. It spread over her as with the others . . . but this wildfire was different. It had a verdant green heart so brilliant it was the kiss of spring, the lush grass under your feet, the rustle of a tree in full bloom.

That green speared into Lijuan's mouth, her eyes, leached through to her cells. Leaves erupted over her skin, only to curl up and die. Her hair turned into vines that blackened and fell away. More leaves erupted on her face before being destroyed.

But underneath it all, her skin was steadily going green.

"Um, Archangel. Remember when I grew that tree in the lobby?"

He looked for his consort again . . . and saw her. The blaze of energy had faded to reveal an Elena whose clothing was scorched—*badly*. The black leather had gone a strange greenish silver at the solar plexus, where she'd taken Aegaeon's rogue blow.

It spread out from that point in lighter shades all the way to scorched brown edges at her shoulders and her thighs, curled around her waist. But no skin showed through and what he could see of her body was undamaged.

Her eyes were locked on Lijuan.

He followed her gaze.

Lijuan was screaming soundlessly as leaves poured out of her mouth.

"Life," Raphael murmured. "Despite all the efforts of the Cascade, all the efforts of immortality, you are raw, defiant life, *hbeebti*. And she is death." The two could not exist together in the same being.

Roots erupted out from Lijuan's body and though they shriveled away, they left holes in her. The wildfire infiltrated even more of her until Lijuan was a being of pure wildfire become an explosion of searing white light.

Raphael's arm flew up to shield his eyes, even as he pulled Elena close.

The wildfire explosion seemed to go on forever, and when it ended, he could only see white spots in front of his eyes. But he could feel Elena in his arms, her hair soft against him and her hold strong.

"Can you see?" Her voice, dulled and distant, as if his ears had taken a pounding.

"Barely." A minute later, the spots began to clear at last.

There was no Lijuan in the air.

Thousands of bright green leaves fell to earth in a gentle rain.

"Jeez, don't tell me I turned her into leaves and she's going to get together and become a zombie tree."

Unfamiliar laughter in their minds, an old voice saying, *Child, she is dead. There is no future line for her. It ends here.*

You're certain? he asked Cassandra.

Her line in time has been permanently severed. She stops forever.

"It's over." Elena exhaled on a shudder. "It's really over."

Before he could answer, he saw golden fire arc up from a rooftop to hit Xi. Lijuan's most trusted general had been a bare meter away from Elena, his sword raised and his eyes red with battle lust, but he died there, in a single blow from Illium.

No longer able to create the obsidian fire, more and more of Lijuan's generals fell to Raphael's people and to the other archangels. Their dead-eyed brethren *literally* fell, crashing to the earth or onto rooftops without control.

Hundreds, thousands, of broken dolls over his city.

He and Elena flew toward the closest fallen fighter in silence.

The putrid smell was a noxious wave in the air before they landed. Body already partially decayed, the fallen angel's arm rotted off in front of them.

Elena pulled out her crossbow. "Incoming."

Raphael rose into the sky to help finish off those who continued to fight. It didn't take long. Without their archangel, even thousands of warriors couldn't beat seven archangels, the majority of whom were Ancients. Those who tried, died. Those who laid down their arms and showed no signs of infection were given safe passage out of New York. In the wars of archangels, the victor always showed mercy.

"They're foot soldiers," he said to Elena a day later as they watched the last of the troops depart—it had taken this long because each was checked for infection. But all those with the black poison in them were dead—and a cause of the ugly smell that hung over the city. He and the other archangels had worked overtime to incinerate the bodies, but the smell would take time to dissipate, even with the sea winds Aegaeon had stirred.

"Whether those foot soldiers followed Lijuan out of fear or out of loyalty, they must live with their choice through eternity—it will not be forgotten. Wherever they tread, they will be known as those who chose to swear fealty to the Archangel of Death."

"Where will they go?"

"With Lijuan dead and as evidenced by the way the black-eyed ones fell, China is most probably no longer infected with the darkness that impacts immortals and near-immortals—but even if it is, these people have no other safe harbor. They will go there. And they will wait for their new archangel. What that archangel does with them is that archangel's choice."

The two of them didn't move until the last fighter was nothing but a far-off blur. Multiple squadrons were following those troops out, and those squadrons would stay on alert until they received word that the remnants of the defeated army had landed in China.

Their next task was to go to a special private area of the infirmary with the rest of the Cadre, and consider the catastrophic damage to so many archangels.

Zanaya appeared dead, her body mummified and her eyes shriveled in their sockets. Astaad was in a better condition, with more flesh on his bones, but still unresponsive.

Caliane was down but would recover, as would Neha.

Elijah was worse off. Though Raphael's wildfire had stopped the spread of the infection on the battlefield, it hadn't dispelled it. So Eli had made much the same choice as Michaela, though in his case, he'd amputated an arm and shoulder, as well as part of his heart.

He was in *anshara*, the deep healing sleep where his body could make repairs. So was Caliane. *Anshara* couldn't always be held back. Michaela, too, was in a state conducive to healing, but in her case, it was deeper than *anshara*; she appeared as the dead, but her body didn't decay.

Raphael had his mother moved to a Tower suite where she'd be protected as she healed. Hannah asked to take Elijah back with her.

"We have a safe place for such times," she said, her face stark with worry and tight with determination at the same time. "And I think no archangel will be making war anytime soon."

No, they were all too battered, their lands in chaos. Lijuan's dead-eyed angels might've fallen from the sky, but her reborn seemed to have become a permanent species on the planet. It would take a coordinated effort to wipe them out—and to eradicate the disease-bearing insects Charisemnon had created. The two ships full of reborn still in the ocean were an easier matter—Raphael would eliminate them after this meeting ended.

Eli's troops left with his wounded body two hours after Lijuan's army departed the city.

"It comes down to us," Raphael said to Titus, Alexander, Favashi, Aegaeon, Cassandra, and Qin.

His consort had called Qin the most beautiful man she'd ever seen, and Raphael had to agree with the assessment. The Ancient was tall and slender, with silky black hair that ran to his shoulders in an onyx rain, his sharply slanted eyes the same shade but striated with a hue that echoed his sea aurora.

His wings were white where they grew out of his back but by the time his feathers reached his primaries, they were a delicate deep pink. Before that came myriad watercolor shades, Qin's wings a "soft focus photograph" according to Elena. By contrast, his cheekbones were razors, creating hollows in his cheeks, but he was not a hard archangel. His face held a sorrowful softness, especially the eyes that were always on Cassandra.

"Eli will recover, as will Caliane and Neha," Raphael said. "If you will stay, Lady Cassandra, we will have a full Cadre of Ten until we know whether Astaad or Michaela will survive and rise again." Michaela should've been facing the same recovery time as Elijah, but whether it was because she'd given birth so recently or because of where Lijuan had injured her, she'd shown no signs of even minor healing as yet, while Elijah's body *had* begun to knit itself back together.

As for Astaad and Zanaya, no one had any idea of the recovery process—or if recovery was even possible—for those archangels from whom Lijuan had fed; that no ordinary angel had survived was a bad sign, but archangels were archangels because they had magnitudes more power. The worst possibility was that Astaad and Zanaya's power meant they wouldn't die . . . but wouldn't wake either, caught forever in a horrific limbo.

By that same token, was it possible Antonicus wasn't dead and would lie in his half-decayed state for eternity?

Shaking off that ugly prospect because it did no good to dance in the unknown, he caught Cassandra's gaze. "Will you stay?"

73

Cassandra, whose eyes were a haunting seafoam green melded with indigo and blue when she wasn't clawing them out, smiled sadly at him. "The knot of chaos has untangled. I see clear paths again." A tear rolled down her face. "I will be a mad archangel should I stay."

Moving forward, she touched her hands to Elena's cheeks. "Such glory you are, prophecy of mine. I will wake again when you next change the world."

A kiss pressed to Elena's cheek before Cassandra came to Raphael. "Child of flames, how strong you have become. And yet . . ." She pressed a hand to his heart. "Your heart is a little mortal." She smiled, as if that pleased her, but the smile held a terrible sadness. "It is time for me to Sleep. Do not disturb me, children, for at least a thousand years. Perhaps then, I will be ready."

She turned to walk to Qin, wiped the tears that ran down his cheeks. "My Qin."

Raphael and the others all looked away as she laid her head down on the silent archangel's chest and he put his arms around her. Beside Raphael, his hunter's eyes shone wet.

Cassandra's skirts stirred the air and when they looked up,

she was no longer in Qin's arms. "I will take with me the broken ones," she said. "They cannot find a safe place to Sleep. I will find it for them."

"Will they wake?" Alexander asked, grooves marking the sides of his mouth. "Zanaya, Michaela, and Astaad?"

Cassandra's lilac hair blew back in the breeze coming through the balcony doors. "This, I do not know," she said. "Some futures are not yet written."

Raphael met her haunted eyes, wondered if they would be bloody holes when he next saw her. "I will ask my people to prepare to escort Michaela, Zanaya, and Astaad." He sent the instruction even as he spoke.

Not long afterward, they watched Cassandra walk to the edge of the balcony. Her white owls took off in a symphony of silence. A single look back, the brush of an old, *old* mind, then Cassandra followed. Behind her came Jason, with Astaad in his arms, Aodhan, with Michaela, and Andreas, with Zanaya. An honor guard flew behind them.

Alexander ran to the balcony edge without warning, wings of silver spread for flight. He took Zanaya from Andreas before they'd reached the city limits. The squadron commander dropped out to return to his other duties.

I need to take her to her resting place, Alexander said to Raphael, *but do not consider me gone from the table.*

I will ensure your voice is heard.

"Nine then," Raphael said afterward. "Three of whom are incapacitated." With Eli, it might be for months, while Caliane would rise again within days or weeks, depending on how much damage she'd taken. Neha would be up even sooner.

"I do not know who I am." Favashi held up her hands and on her skin played the slow, sinuous glow of lava. "I do not know what I have become."

"You're an archangel," Aegaeon said flatly. "You do not get to rest while the world burns."

Raphael didn't agree with how the message had been delivered, but Aegaeon was right. The Cadre needed Favashi to step up.

Her face pulled taut over bones that were too prominent, but she inclined her head. "I will not go back to China."

"I will visit China," Raphael said. "No other of the Cadre

will be expected to go there until Elena and I confirm it is uninfected."

Curt nods all around.

"I will hold my territory, and Eli will hold his," Raphael continued. "I will maintain a watch over Eli's territory in the interim, so that bloodlust does not rise among the vampires."

No one argued with that, either. They had bigger problems.

"I have just asked Alexander and he will continue to hold his, and he is willing to assist whoever takes over Michaela's until her return. There is also Astaad's territory. Neha's and Caliane's generals will manage theirs for the short duration the two will be in *anshara,* though Neha's people will need our assistance to wipe out the reborn scourge."

"I will take Michaela's lands," Aegaeon said. "I do not wish to be awake, but to leave the world with only eight archangels at this time is unacceptable—and I am honorable enough not to steal Astaad's lands when he has fallen in battle."

Raphael looked to Qin, this Ancient who had not said a word to any of them since his arrival. "Will you accept a watch over Astaad's lands?"

Qin's face twisted. He looked out to where Cassandra had disappeared. "I do not wish to live in a world without her," he said in a mellifluous voice that was like music. "But this is a duty of archangels. I will stay only until another rises to take my place."

Raphael inclined his head. "Titus, Favashi, can you work together in Africa?"

"I would be honored to work with an archangel who cares for her people," Titus said with a nod aimed at Favashi. "Africa is a large land and that boil on humanity left things a putrid mess. Your city is in ruins, Raphael, but you are luckier than I."

"I will assist you and anyone else who needs it." They had come to his aid at the critical time, and he would never forget that. "Favashi?"

Favashi, her eyes a flow of lava, smiled. "Yes, I would be pleased to have Titus for a neighbor." Then she collapsed, her bones liquid.

Cassandra's voice filled their minds even as Elena caught the former Archangel of China. *I am sorry, children. She was too weak to rise but this was her battle and her time. She must return to her Sleep.*

Raphael could see Favashi's bones through skin gone translucent, fire under her skin. The others saw the same. Aegaeon's face grew tight but even he knew there was no fighting this. Scooping her up in his arms, Raphael called Andreas and told him to head in the same direction as Cassandra and the others. "Cassandra is waiting for you."

"She's too light," was all the warrior angel said before he took off with Favashi.

"Eight in the Cadre?" Aegaeon growled. "At *this* time? *Five* until the three who are in healing sleep return? The vampires will run amok across the lands."

Raphael knew that was a valid concern. "We don't have to worry about China," he told them. "Most of the vampiric population is dead." Very few of Lijuan's ground troops had survived the war. "We'll have to roster archangelic flights over India and Japan. Titus, you'll have to handle Africa on your own for now, but we will assist as required."

"I will need it," Titus said bluntly. "It is a large land and it is riddled with reborn."

"It is decided," Raphael said two minutes later, after receiving Alexander's agreement to their decisions. "The Cadre has spoken."

The sky broke with a sparkling black rain only a quarter of an hour later. It washed away the smell of death, made destroyed buildings beautiful for long moments and collected in glittering puddles on city streets.

And it destroyed one wall of the Tower infirmary as an injured Suyin smashed through it to rise into the sky. Raphael caught her bewildered eyes as she rose upward but there was nothing he could do.

Suyin, too gentle, too untried, was ascending.

Energy danced over her skin, in the gleaming ice of her hair, flowed into her body.

"The Cadre will eat her alive."

"Not just yet, Guild Hunter. The world is in too much chaos. She will have time."

Ascension was unpredictable. It could take hours or days.

Suyin landed in front of the rest of the Cadre that night. Her rain yet fell across the world.

"You have Northern Africa," Aegaeon said with no moment for Suyin to breathe in her new reality.

But Suyin showed her spine. "No. I will take China." Unflinching determination in her eyes. "My bloodline broke it. My bloodline will heal it. I will not discuss this."

"It seems a fitting choice," Titus said. "I have no disagreement with it."

No one did, though Raphael warned Suyin about the possibility of lingering poison. Her lips twisted. "If poison remains, it will not harm me. I am her blood."

Titus and Qin left soon afterward, flying off into Suyin's rain. Alexander had already stated that he'd depart straight from Cassandra's lava sinkhole. Aegaeon turned to Raphael and Elena when only he and Suyin were left. "I wish for my son to come with me. I believe he is in your service."

Elena's back stiffened, but she kept her mouth shut because she'd seen the dangerous gleam in Raphael's eyes.

"Your son is his own man," he said with utmost politeness. "Should he wish to go with you, I will not hold him to his sworn vows."

Aegaeon inclined his head with a smile. "I thank you. I see him on that rooftop—I will speak now with him."

"Why did you say that?" Elena hissed at Raphael the instant the other archangel took off—Suyin was far from them, on the very edge of the balcony. "Illium doesn't want that!"

"I have warned your Bluebell, Elena. And I have told him that if he chooses to leave, we will hunt him down." His lips curved. "He was most mollified by the latter. He also understands that if I say no to Aegaeon, I make an enemy of him. If his son says the same . . ."

"It's just a family matter." Sighing, Elena leaned up against him. "When am I going to get this angelic politics thing right?"

He stroked the line of her spine, the stormfire of her wings faded and weak. "You are young, child of mortals." Even her wings needed to recover after that battle.

She elbowed him, but this wasn't done.

In the distance, Aegaeon took off with a hard beat of his wings. They couldn't see his face from this far, but Illium turned and shot a salute their way.

Grinning, Elena waved back at him.

They walked to Suyin. Bruised eyes held theirs, the hand she lifted crackling with a black-hued power that sparkled diamond bright. "Is she *in* me?" A rough whisper. "Am I her legacy?"

"No." Elena held Suyin's gaze, certain deep in her gut that she had to stop that line of thought here and now or it would eat Suyin up alive. "This is yours and yours alone."

"I am an architect." She stared uncomprehendingly at her hands. "I am no battle-honed warrior. I should not be Cadre."

"The world needs rebuilding. Who better than an architect to begin that rebuild?"

Raphael's words settled against Elena's skin, felt right. Yes, the world needed builders now, creators.

"I have no guard, no one loyal to me. An archangel cannot rule without a second."

"I will send a guard with you," Raphael said. "To be by your side until you find your own people."

Suyin, still disoriented, decided to stay in New York for three extra days to settle into her skin, before she headed to China.

She'd just left to go to her room and spend some time alone, think over the cataclysmic change in her life, when golden light began to emanate from the direction of the Catskills. "Cassandra is saying good-bye," Raphael murmured.

The two of them watched the strange sunset until the last flicker disappeared from the sky. Elena's wings went with them, disappearing with an audible pop that made her ears hurt. Raphael gasped at the same instant and went down on one knee. His wings shimmered for a second, then settled, solid and strong.

The Legion mark on his temple blazed before going quiet.

Elena dropped down beside him, her hand on his wing and her lungs struggling to gasp in air. "Archangel."

"The golden lightning of the Cascade is gone," he said, his breathing unsteady, "as is part of what the Legion gave us."

Her heart squeezed. "Maybe the part that makes them?"

"That is my hope, *hbeebti*." He flexed his hand. "The bloodstorm power remains."

"Can you make your wings turn to white fire?"

A pause before his wings morphed into pure flame. "Yes, and . . ." Blue wreathed his hand. "I can still heal."

"So now we know what happens to superhero powers after a Cascade." Her voice shook. "My wings came from the golden lightning. And now my back feels weird."

Raphael rose, his jaw set. If the world had taken her wings again, he would savage it. What he found was that the slits in her jacket where her wings had emerged were glowing . . . the same hue he did when he was angry, or filled with power.

"You have a piece of my heart, Elena," he murmured. "That heart is full of archangelic cells. Those cells can heal nearly any injury, any damage, any mutation *if* no other strange power is getting in the way. And the golden Cascade power is gone."

Elena sucked in a breath. "What're you saying, Raphael?"

"I need to see your back." Wrapping her up in his arms, he flew her up to the privacy of their suite and the two of them tore off her arm sheaths, then her clothing. Her naked back was flawless but for two glowing lines where wings grew out of an angel's back.

Raphael touched his finger to one.

Elena shivered so hard it was a shudder.

"Pain?" he asked.

"No." She moved restlessly on her feet. "Just . . . sensitive. *Very.*"

"Do you have the urge to scratch as you have never scratched before?"

"Dear lord, yes! Argh!"

Hope exploded into certainty. "You are in the first stage of wing regrowth."

Elena was silent for a long time. "You're sure," she said at last.

"Yes, but let us go to Nisia."

The healer took a minute from her heavy workload to confirm Raphael's diagnosis. "I can see the faint ridge of two developing stubs," she said after examining Elena's back closely. "I'll give you an oil for the itching."

Before they left, she took blood so Lucius could rerun DNA tests.

"Am I going to have fluffy duck feathers soon?" Elena asked Raphael after they were in their suite again and he'd rubbed in the heavenly oil. The relief was so great it was orgasmic; right then, she was glad she'd slept through her first time growing wings.

"I'm afraid so. Will you miss the energy wings?"

Elena's eyes were wet when she turned to him. "They were amazing and they took me to the sky . . . but Raphael, I'll have proper wings again, feathers you can stroke, feathers I can give Zoe and Maggie." She cried then, in joy rather than sorrow.

Later, they looked out over their ruined city. At least seventy percent of the buildings had been badly damaged or fully destroyed. Even the Tower hadn't escaped unscathed, but the Legion building hadn't suffered a scratch.

It hurt Elena's heart to look at it, but she would keep her promise. She would keep it safe for when the Legion returned. Beings that ancient couldn't simply cease to exist.

Raphael's hand closed over hers, warm and strong.

"What happens now, Archangel?"

"We walk into the future."

"Together."

"Always."

Aftermath

Elena took to wearing capes to protect her sensitive stubs. Illium—still so angry underneath his joie de vivre—thought it a grand idea and bought a rhinestone-covered silver one that threatened to turn them all blind. He just laughed and swirled it around like a B-movie villain.

Elena stuck with hunter black.

Capes were suddenly all the rage in their battered city.

The itching made her want to crawl the walls, but there was too much to do. Raphael rubbed in the oil and they carried on. Life carried on. They'd been lucky, so fucking lucky. All of their closest friends and family had made it out alive. In honor of their victory and because it was a name from Nyree's family, Ransom and Nyree finally settled on a middle name for their son: Viktor.

Hudson Viktor Winterwolf.

Big name for a little dude, but Elena had a feeling the kid would grow into it. As for the other newborn in their world, Riker told them Michaela had named her son Gavriel, after her father. Little Gavriel was safe with Keir, loved and protected, his parentage hidden. So many angels had died in battle that no one questioned it when Keir said he was raising a war orphan.

In other news, Galen and Naasir had returned to the Refuge, while Aodhan was with Suyin as her temporary second.

"I must give him this chance to spread his wings," Raphael had said.

Every so often, as time passed, a kind of dawn-colored lightning would arc through Elena's growing wings, far weaker than the Cascade power, but lightning all the same.

No one had any idea what that meant, though Keir had a theory. "You are the only living angel whose heart is formed of archangelic cells. A piece of you is an archangel. And when it ended, the Cascade left behind gifts in all of the archangels who were not already Ancients."

Elena truly didn't care as long as her wings kept growing. Illium outpaced her, but she'd expected that. Bluebell might not have ascended at the end of the Cascade, but his power was growing so strong that it frightened her for what it augured for his future.

When it came to her, Lucius told her that her cells were "almost" back to angel-normal. "Except for the odd glowing one. But Raphael has a few, too, so you're still compatible."

The meaning of his words didn't really penetrate until Nisia called them into her office a month later, after Raphael had returned from helping Titus deal with the reborn problem in his massive territory. It wasn't an issue that would be solved quickly, but all of the Cadre who were up and functional were helping each other out.

"Do you remember what I said about the super-parasite?" the healer asked.

Elena's hand flew to her abdomen, all thoughts of wings momentarily forgotten. "Don't even mention that."

"Super-parasite? What horrors have you been amusing yourself with this time, Nisia?"

Poker-faced, the healer said, "Fetuses, sire."

"I see." Her archangel's lips twitched. "You have such maternal ways."

"Don't encourage her," Elena muttered. "She told me that the child of an archangel would be a super-parasite. But we don't have to worry about any of that for a loooong time. I'm too young."

Nisia coughed into her hand. "Yes, about that . . ."

Elena swallowed. Hard. "No more parasite fetus jokes."

"The chrysalis changed you." Nisia's gaze was steady. "You heal faster, are more resilient, with stronger bones. No longer a newborn." She smiled an evil smile. "I tested compatibility. It's perfect. You could conceivably fall pregnant to Raphael."

A strangled eek of sound escaped Elena's throat. Raphael, the fiend, gave her a sad look. "Are you so terrified of our adorable little parasite?"

"Don't make me stab you." Folding her arms across her chest, she stared at Nisia. "Do I need to, you know, take birth control?"

It turned out most angels didn't bother because their birth rate was so miniscule, but as it had been proven that angelic fertility rose in the aftermath of a catastrophic loss of life— such as had occurred in the war—Nisia hooked her up with a small pot of dried leaves of a vivid green striped with blue that came from a plant that only grew in the Refuge.

A leaf a day would keep the baby away.

It was only once the two of them were alone in the humid warmth of the Legion building, Elena's hands in the soil as she tidied up, that she looked at Raphael and said, "You don't mind? That I'm not ready for a child?"

A browned bloom unfurled to new life in Raphael's hand. "I never expected you, Elena." Crouching down beside her, his wings spread on the grass and flowers, he tucked the bloom behind her ear. "A child of my own was such a distant matter that it never crossed my mind. We have eternity, *hbeebti*. There is no rush."

Sitting back, she hooked her dirt-covered hands over her knees and admitted the dark truth that was a knot in her chest. "I don't know if I'll ever be ready. Every time I even imagine a baby, I think of Belle, of Ari." Her eyes burned, a brush fire that scalded her from the inside out. "Our parents loved them *so* much, but they couldn't protect them."

Seated opposite her, his booted feet on either side of her

hips, Raphael placed one hand on her calf. "I understood terror when I loved you." His grip tightened. "I cannot imagine the depth of that terror should I have a child."

Elena shuddered out a breath, changed the topic of conversation because this one was too scary, hit too deep. "It looks like the dawn lightning in my wings isn't going away."

"Wings of midnight and dawn with lightning arcing through them. Your Bluebell will be jealous."

Laughing softly, she shifted position so that she was kneeling beside the garden plot again. "Pass me that seedling." She'd found a stock of them ready for planting. The Legion had grown them for her greenhouse, but she would plant them here.

The construction of her and Raphael's Enclave home was no longer a priority, not when so much of the city had been destroyed. For now, they'd live in the Tower and this place full of memories of the Legion would be her greenhouse. "I miss them hanging about just watching," she said as she gently removed the seedling from the pot.

"Do you think we have solved their riddle? Do we know the full meaning of *aeclari*?"

Seedling freed from the pot, Elena held it cupped in her hands as she thought. Of the Legion's age. Of their innocence. Of their knowledge. Of how they were of life, of growing green things and—

Her mouth dropped open.

Tilting back her head, she stared . . . at the seedling that was shooting up and up. Raphael had to remove it from her hands and put it in the ground. The two of them sat there in silence, as the seedling turned into a tall rose bush filled with glorious blooms the color of fresh blood.

Petals floated down from above, heavy with scent and soft as velvet.

And in Elena's nascent wings arced the dawnlight lightning.

Closing her eyes, she fell back on the grass and let the petals fall over her. When they stopped, it was because an archangel with eyes as blue as Arctic ice was leaning over her, his wing spread in a magnificence of white gold, and there, around the gunshot scar on the underside, a burst of midnight and dawn. The rest of his feathers had returned to their usual shade, but the kiss of mortality remained around that one spot.

She brushed her fingers over it.

Hair darker than the heart of night fell over his forehead as he lowered his lips to her own. They kissed under a soft rain of petals that was a thing of life, of growth, of beauty in terrible darkness. The world was badly wounded, bleeding in many places, vampires had begun to stir in bloodlust, and the Cadre had two Ancients who didn't wish to be awake, as well as a new archangel wholly untrained for her duties.

It was one hell of a mess.

And yet . . . "Architects, builders, growers," she whispered against Raphael's lips. "We can snatch life out of the horror."

His mouth curved into a sinful, youthful smile he gave no one else. "Careful, Elena-mine. You do not wish to tempt the super-parasite."

Slapping her hands on his chest, she glared. "I'm going to wash your mouth out with soap."

He laughed, her archangel strong and beautiful and deadly . . . and a little bit mortal, the laughter yet in his taste when he kissed her again. The last thing she saw before she fell into him, into love, were petals the color of fresh blood lying on his wing . . . and the glitter of life in the Legion mark on his temple.

Aeclari.